OTHER BOOKS BY WAYNE M. MILLER

Nonfiction

BURN BOSTON BURN
The Largest Arson Case in the History of the Country

BANG BOOM BURN
*Explosive True Crime Gun, Bombing and
Arson Cases from a Federal Agent's Career*

In *FLAMES OF SECRECY*, Wayne is at the top of his game, blending science, forensics, intrigue, romance and procedure in a thrilling ride of fire investigation and humanity. Mark Miller is a cocky, smart, funny and troubled federal agent who you will be rooting for until the very end.

The author is a superb storyteller who has crafted an amazing novel. He shows off his writing skills with the ability to create characters who come alive on the pages. He puts the reader in the middle of every twist and turn. This book is filled with evil, harm, human struggles and angst. It has a perfect plot and a brilliant and complicated hero. It is a read that once you start you will not be able to put down until you are finished.

Robert M. Luckett, Author,
Solving For X: Tracking the DC Serial Arsonist

FLAMES OF SECRECY is an exhilarating read from start to finish. Wayne Miller takes his decades of work in the ATF to ground his story in a propulsive investigation that keeps the pages turning and an exploration of the criminal mind that leaves you unsettled long after it's over. Crime fiction fans will not want to miss this!

Rob Bell – Vice President,
Production and Development,
Dark Castle Entertainment

***Flames of Secrecy** is a well-written book that delivers a well-developed, intelligent and creative plot. His complex characters bring a unique dimension to his work, grabbing your attention from the start.* Wayne M. Miller's new book offers fascinating details about the challenges of arson investigation and the work that the dedicated professionals in this story (and in real life) have to do to unravel the truth and bring closure to a case. As the story evolves you are not disappointed.

This new book introduces Mr. Miller as a novelist, following his previous award-winning non-fiction books, and showcases his skills and creativity as a writer. **Flames of Secrecy** is a page-turner that delivers first-class entertainment. If you are looking for an interesting and intelligent book that combines the knowledge of an expert fire and arson professional and a first-rate thriller, you have found it.

Tiza Pyle, Author
Possibilities

Two-time award-winning author Wayne Miller has made it a trio with his new novel, **Flames of Secrecy**. After writing a pair of captivating fire-related accounts based on true events in his stellar career as an ATF agent, Miller has successfully delved into the world of fiction with **Flames**, spinning a macabre tale of murder and mayhem at the hands of a deranged culprit. Although a fictionalized story, the accuracy of the many Boston locations will make the readers question how much of the story is actually fabricated. His descriptions and character-building are impressive.

Daniel Zimmerman, Author,
Shots In The Dark: The Saga Of Rocco Balliro

Intense, raw, and relentless…*FLAMES OF SECRECY* is a story just itching to be adapted for the big screen, especially given the author's firsthand experience with the subject matter, which helps elevate this tale to the very top of the genre.

Michael McGrale, Writer, Producer, Editorial Department,
The Following, CSI Miami,
Rizzoli & Isles, Witnessville,
RIP (in pre-production)

FLAMES OF SECRECY

A Psychological Thriller

WAYNE M. MILLER

FLAMES OF SECRECY-A Psychological Thriller

This is a work of fiction. All of the characters and events portrayed in this novel are either products of the author's imagination or are used fictionally.

To the extent that the image on the cover of this book depicts a person, such person is merely a model not intended to portray any character in this book.

Cover Design: Pro_eBookcovers at Fiverr.com
Editor: C. Susan Nunn, csusannunn.com
Book Interior and E-book formatting: Amit Dey, amitdey2528@gmail.com

ISBN: 978-1-7333403-7-3 Hardcover
ISBN: 978-1-7333403-8-0 Paperback
ISBN: 978-1-7333403-9-7 E-book

This book, as well as other books by Wayne M. Miller may be purchased in bulk for promotional, educational, or business use. Please contact your local bookseller or go directly to Wayne's website, www.AuthorWayneMiller.com

*To my wife, Joyce,
my family, and my friends who have all had my back,
supporting me as I continue to write.*

TABLE OF CONTENTS

The mind is its own place,
And in itself can make a heav'n of hell,
a hell of heav'n.

John Milton, *Paradise Lost*

CHAPTER ONE

What the hell is with all this traffic, Brantley wondered. Stepping warily between parked cars, he paused before crossing the bustling intersection of Hereford and Marlborough Streets in Boston's posh Back Bay. The early morning sun shone brightly onto the stately four-story brownstone at the corner. With a bunch of colorful flowers in one hand, he sprinted across, a cacophony of horns following him. One elderly driver in a late 70s sedan continued to lay on his horn, showing his dissatisfaction with his morning drive interrupted by a jaywalker. After Brantley glared at him, angry that his focus had been broken as well, he let his gaze drift up to the charred windows on the third floor of the structure.

The odor of burned wood drifted on the light spring breeze, tingling his nostrils. With a sinister smile, he deeply sniffed the air. Walking up to the wrought-iron fence separating the building from the sidewalk, he bent down to lay his flowers among a vibrant array of bouquets. Despite the swelling, fragrant makeshift memorial, the death of the young woman who died in that apartment fire left a pall over the normally vibrant neighborhood. Standing upright, lost in reflection, only Brantley knew exactly what had occurred in that apartment hours earlier. *She got what she deserved. She never would have changed.* His placing of the flowers concealed the truth beneath his façade of mourning.

* * * * *

The night before, Brantley's spirits soared with lofty aspirations, as was his routine of hoping for a meaningful connection with a young woman, one that could blossom into something deeper. He hungered for a true relationship, envisioning a captivating beauty with eyes that sparkled with life and lips he yearned to both listen to and taste as their conversations turned intimate. Yet, he knew these fantasies never seemed to materialize for him.

The fraternity party was in one of those elegant brownstones lining Commonwealth Avenue, often divided up to accommodate students from one of Boston's numerous schools of higher education. Scores of noisy college kids packed this first-floor party. The clamor from their voices in varying levels of inebriation reached beyond the elaborate, rich brown wood and glass front door atop the granite steps. As Brantley walked through that door, he spotted his reflection in a glass sidelight window of an interior open doorway.

I've been told I'm really not a bad-looking guy, he mused. Seeing the room full of frat boys though, he knew he was out of his league. I might not be as polished as these guys, but I can hold my own. He ran his hand through his thick light brown hair, and it fell neatly into place. With his crystal blue eyes, a rugged once-broken nose, and a full, but trimmed mustache that curled around his upper lip, Brantley appeared masculine, yet sensitive unlike so many other men. At least that is what he thought.

A solid body filled out his nearly six-foot frame. That night Brantley took great pains dressing, wearing well-fitting jeans with a relaxed blue-striped, button-down shirt. He was quite satisfied with his appearance, but not in an overly cocky way.

Once inside, as Brantley perused the oversized dimly lit room, checking out the feminine talent, his heart raced with hope. There were plenty of young women in the party room, most of them enjoying the free booze, the pulsing music and the company of so many eligible men. Everyone stood elbow to elbow, standing room only.

✳   ✳   ✳   ✳   ✳

Over the years, Brantley had attended countless frat parties, always searching for a girl who understood him, someone who could connect with him on a deeper level. But despite his best efforts, he usually felt alone in the crowd. His journey to this party, as all the previous ones, had been a long and grueling one.

Brantley drove himself nuts, convinced he was a misfit, struggling to find his place in the world. Dwelling on his torturous upbringing by his single mother, he wallowed in his misery, often making it difficult for him to move forward.

Why can't I just let go of the past? No, somehow I must enjoy living it over and over again. One of my many therapists had told me more than once that I needed to learn to forgive and forget my past miseries, but, no, it plays in my head on a continuous loop that I can't escape. Forgiveness is great for those people to say, but for me, it is not an option. I choose to live on a darker side than other people.

Little did Brantley know, despite his counseling, forgiveness was the way to rid his soul of all his internal torture. He always expected to find peace through others, never realizing he could only find true peace from within himself. But facing the deepest, darkest truths within oneself was the most painful and elusive undertaking for him to accomplish. He avoided introspection at all costs.

After high school, he had worked at various jobs over the years, but he was always dissatisfied and unfulfilled. He tried fast food restaurants, retail shops, and even toiled as a manual laborer for contractors, but always ended up quitting or getting fired because he argued with his bosses over his failure to follow directions.

Desperate to turn his life around, Brantley finally took a chance on college in his early twenties. One Boston community college gave him a shot, where he had enrolled in business courses. It was college that finally provided him with some sense of direction in his life. Despite his constant struggles with concentration and motivation, he managed to score respectable grades through sheer determination and full use of his intelligence.

But, no matter how hard I've tried to right my ship and worked my ass off to climb the ladder toward a better future for myself, I continually manage to only hang onto the bottom rung. Since I've always been an outsider, I now have resigned myself to being a loner by choice by living in a boarding house.

I don't even like most people, avoiding contact with others whenever possible. I certainly notice how people give me odd looks and how they keep their distance as well. I guess those who have crossed my path have come to know my legendary temper. When aggravated I tend to stare down anyone who dares challenge me with a look that could kill.

Tonight, Brantley had taken another chance at going out in public. With considerable effort, he mustered all his courage to attend the frat party. Hoping to find that perfect someone to talk to, and eventually share his dreams and fears, he yearned for a woman who would accept him for himself, plus make him feel less alone. It was always a struggle for him to put himself out there, but he knew he had to try. *Okay, here I go, but, God, how I hate these things.*

As he walked through the crowded darkened room, a sense of dread washed over him. Already he didn't feel right. Not knowing any people there, he wasn't even sure how to approach anyone. The pounding bass of the music rattled him, making it hard for him to think, but Brantley pushed forward, scanning the crowd for someone who piqued his interest. For a moment, he thought he found that someone looking in his direction. His heart leaped with optimism, but then the figure turned away, leaving him alone once again. The familiar ache of loneliness settled in his chest, and he wondered if any of this was worth his time or the mental anguish it caused him.

As he made his way around the room, Brantley felt more and more out of place. The groups of people were laughing and having fun, but he couldn't bring himself to join in. His isolation overwhelmed him, like he was invisible, just didn't even exist. Eventually, he worked his way to a corner, dejected, watching the partygoers as they danced and chatted.

Damn, will I ever find that special someone? Or will I be lonely forever?

✳   ✳   ✳   ✳   ✳

But within minutes, a ray of sunshine pierced his loneliness. His gaze fastened on one brunette with long hair and soft curls. Definitely cute, animated, spunky. *I like that.* What a smile! Eyes that light up when she laughs. Cocking her head as she flicks her thick locks back from her gorgeous face. *I like that.* A compact, tight body with some sexy curves. *I like that, too.* Just imagining what it would be like to hold her, Brantley's breathing quickened with a quivering sensation throughout his body.

While keeping his eyes on his newly attained target, with a mixture of nervousness and anticipation, he slowly approached like a lion stalking his prey. Sidling up next to her, above the din, he loudly introduced himself, "Hi, I'm Brantley." A slightly sweet, flowery aroma wafted from her. He sucked in his breath to get the full effect of her fragrance. "You smell terrific!"

That smile, tantalizing sky-blue eyes! "Hi, Brantley. I'm Wendy." *A nice start.* She reached out a delicate hand to shake his as she held a drink in her other hand. *Soft, but with a surprisingly firm grip.* "Are you a frat member?"

"Nah, I enjoy being independent. I don't like being part of a regimented group. It's not my thing."

"Ohhh…" Wendy's gaze shifted as he felt a chill spread from her body to his. Her sudden disinterest in Brantley had her scanning the room for someone who better suited her long-term life goals.

Instantly, Brantley's spirit was deflated. That void instead flooded with anger. Her rejection stung. His face reddened as he seethed with embarrassment at the instant dismissal. "Really! You're gonna blow me off just because I'm not in a frat?" His stare at her was menacing.

"Leave me alone." As Wendy spun away from him, she teetered slightly, almost losing her balance. Brantley flicked a hand out to grab her, partly to steady her, partly to prevent her from leaving. His hand caught the back of her loose fitting gauzy blouse, ripping it up the backside. Her drink, in a red plastic cup, splashed beer to the floor, splattering several nearby party goers.

Now glaring with her own rage, "Look what you've done now! You're a fucking asshole." She then unsteadily staggered away as inquisitive onlookers stared at the exchange.

Brantley retreated in the opposite direction, like a whipped puppy. He grabbed a beer as he fumed, simmered, and sulked in his corner of the room, no longer up for meeting anyone. His thoughts turned inward, spiraling into darkness.

He stared at Wendy as she flirted with a couple guys wearing fraternity shirts. She was smoking a cigarette, lifting her face upward, blowing the inhaled smoke from her red pursed lips. Now, cocking her head while flipping her hair behind an ear no longer excited him. Instead, her actions infuriated him.

Brantley's breathing quickened with deep breaths, his nose flaring, his face scrunching with his brooding fury. For another hour, he scrutinized her every move, internally ridiculing each aspect of her demeanor. He watched as she drank herself into oblivion, a stark contrast to the image of grace he had admired earlier. *She's nothing but an uppity friggin' party girl.*

Still, with a single train of thought, his resentment festering, Brantley rode the wrong track down a rabbit hole. Heading outside, he didn't know what he was going to do, but he was determined to wait for Wendy to come out. And he did wait. And he waited some more in the chilly night air, but yet the steamy internal heat from his emotions rendered him unaware of the chill. From a bench on the grassy tree lined mall that separates the east and west bound lanes, he stared at the front door where the party continued.

A strange feeling welled up within Brantley. Intense burning consumed the surface of his butt and the rear of his upper thighs. This fiery pain was a chronic affliction whenever he sensed life treating him poorly.

Just then Wendy stumbled down the front stairs of the building across from where he watched. She stood for a moment and struck a match to light another cigarette. Unsteady on her feet, Wendy turned right as cars whizzed past. Brantley followed within the shadows provided by the mature oak and maple trees that obscured the streetlamp's illumination.

As Wendy weaved left onto Hereford Street, he waited momentarily before crossing the street to narrow the gap to his quarry. From thirty feet behind her, Brantley saw how wasted Wendy was. She wobbled perilously over the uneven Boston sidewalks. His stride quickened at the corner of Marlborough Street as Wendy stumbled off the curb. He caught her before she crashed to the tarred road surface.

"Thank you." She slurred without looking up at her rescuer.

"Here, let me help you. Where do you live?" She pointed across the street to an upper level of a late 1800s brownstone. Brantley cradled an arm around Wendy's back, extending under her right arm, to walk her across the street. He felt the allure of intimacy holding her close, but now instead of smelling delightful, he found her repulsive, tainted with the gross combination of sweat, stale booze and cigarettes.

Up the front steps, he guided her inside the foyer. She never could have made it up to the third floor on her own. He noisily dragged her up the stairs. At the door to her apartment, Wendy pulled a set of keys from the pocket of her jeans, but her hands shook unsteadily and the keys fell to the floor.

Brantley reached down, picked them up and unlocked the door. He flicked the light switch. A dim ceiling light illuminated the living room. He then walked Wendy over to a stuffed wingback chair. The beige-patterned upholstery material was thread-bare, exposing the foam padding. Wendy plopped sloppily into the chair. She lit another cigarette and placed the pack with the matches on her small side table. Pointing toward a bottle of whiskey, "Get me a drink, will ya'." She ordered, rather than asked.

Wendy still did not recognize Brantley as he handed her a glass with a couple fingers of oaky golden brown booze from the bottle next to her chair. She irked him. How could she not know him?

He tossed aside a section of The Boston Globe as he sat on a lumpy worn sofa, facing the drunk Wendy. "Look at me for a minute," he commanded with his voice raised.

She lifted her eyes, her vision seriously blurred by alcohol. "Yeah?"

"Do you remember your top getting ripped at that frat party?"

Suddenly, her eyes brightened with awareness. "Oh, you're that shit who did that. What the hell are you doing here?"

Brantley's patience wore thin as Wendy's insults cut deep, re-igniting old wounds. "Listen, bitch. I just saved you from doing a face-plant on the street and helped your drunken ass up to this shithole." He scanned the filthy room with a view to the kitchen counter piled high with dirty dishes. Brantley despised anything unclean and soiled.

"I don't care what you did. I told you to leave me alone. You're nothing but a fuckin' pathetic loser, and that's what you'll always be, a useless, fuckin' loser." Her chin sunk to her chest, as she drifted into a drunken stupor. The cigarette dangled loosely between her lips, hanging precariously. The glass of whiskey fell to the floor onto an ancient, dirty area rug, spilling the remains of the drink.

As Wendy's words registered, Brantley's ass and thighs felt as if they were on fire, burning more intensely than when he was a kid trying to grow up under the thumb of a ruthless mother. Even his ears blistered with pain as his mother's disturbing voice reverberated within his head. 'You're lazy, no good for nothing. You think you're special. You're not, you're pathetic. And you'll end up being a useless loser. Worthless, just like your father!'

He could hear his mother's piercing words, her anger spewing as she whipped him with a man's belt. 'You good-for-nothing son-of-a-bitch! See what you made me do to you.' Repeatedly, she whipped me on my bare backside, stinging me with the buckle end of the belt. The ugly burning welts stood out from my skin in neat straight lines as wide as the leather strap, marred only by irregular patterns caused by the stinging smack of the metal buckle. It hurt so bad.

But as bad as the physical pain of the beating was, it paled in comparison to the agony inside my head, my heart. Never daring to speak the words aloud, I silently wondered, why are you doing this to me, how could you hurt me so much? The misery of not understanding why I was the object of such cruelty crushed me. I never knew what I did wrong to deserve such a whipping. But I would never outwardly cry when she hit me, always remaining defiant, angry, stubborn. I wouldn't give in to her or let her see me weak. No way! Never! But my inner turmoil ate me up. I hated her so much when she beat me.

When Wendy uttered those words to him, the searing pain he felt fueled a rage he no longer could contain. The same burning pain now festered from within as it did back then when he laid face down, naked on his twin sized bed in the small bedroom within the 1950s single floor ranch-style house. *Well, I'll just have to turn that burning pain into something equally hot.*

Brantley grabbed the cigarette from Wendy's mouth, setting in motion a chain of events that would seal both their fates. Picking up several sheets of the newspaper, he packed them loosely between the sleeping woman's slumped body and the chair. He even stuffed a few sheets under her thighs. She didn't even move, but she did begin to snore, her lips fluttering as her breath escaped. Not a pretty sight.

Brantley flicked the cigarette ash off the end of the butt and blew on the end to brighten the brand as he touched the glowing end to several areas of the paper. His igniter burned small circular holes in the pages, slowly spreading outward with charring and flickering tiny flames. Then, he struck a match and lit the inside corner of the chair cushion with newspaper draped in a vertical position next to Wendy's body. By now, she had completely blacked out. *Probably a common occurrence for her.* She barely reacted, then went limp.

Smoke and flames edged upward on the chair igniting Wendy's ripped top, plus yellow orange flames spread rapidly within the newspapers. The heat from the growing blaze instantly warmed and illuminated Brantley's face while he calmly watched the display. The woman who looked so good to him hours earlier hardly flinched as flames impinged onto her clothing. As Brantley spun away from her toward the door, he didn't care what happened to her. *She can burn in hell for all I care. This was a fitting end to an unworthy life.*

Taking the stairs two at a time, he hastily made his way outside. At the bottom of the stairs, he stopped, took a deep breath, then he cooly crossed the street and continued a block away so not to draw unnecessary attention to his escape. When he heard fire sirens approaching up Hereford Street, he strode back toward the burning apartment building.

Brantley joined an enormous mass of onlookers standing across the opposite sides of Hereford and Marlborough Streets, all gawking at billowing flames and smoke pouring from the third-floor windows of her apartment. The Boston firefighters attacked the fire both from within and from the exterior, knocking the blaze down after a valiant effort. Only clean-up and an investigation of the fire's origin and cause needed to be completed.

He smiled and went home to get some sleep. It was a long, interesting night unlike any previous night in his insecure life. A tired Brantley fell into a deep sleep. His last and only thought was that he would check the doings at the scene when he woke up.

CHAPTER TWO

Boston fire fighters are a proud bunch, having been formed in the colonial days of 1631.

Among the stalwart guardians of the city, Lieutenants Dick Scherner and Mike O'Brien, two veteran Jakes assigned to the Boston Arson Squad, caught this fatal job in the Back Bay. They both were awakened from their bunks in the middle of the night at the BFD Massachusetts Avenue office. Fires with loss of life most often came at night. Scherner, now in his late forties, was still in good shape, but his body needed a few minutes of stretching on this chilly night to prepare for working a fresh fire scene.

O'Brien, a couple years older, injured on a ladder company the previous year, could no longer work on a truck due to continued back spasms, but he relished working investigations that allowed him to keep active at fires. The difference between these two tasks was an investigator rarely performed under the urgency of life or death conditions like a firefighter attacking a fire who had to be ready for everything and anything at all times. O'Brien's back still revolted with the rude awakening, but he knew someone else had gone through something far more horrific. His mission was to find out where and how this fire started and why this person died rather than making it out to live another day.

As the pair jogged down the stairs to their BFD car parked outside, Mike asked, "What do you think about giving Miller from ATF a call for this one? We can wake him up in the middle of the night, too."

"Screw him and ATF. This is our fire. Besides, it's in a residence, not a commercial building. And we don't even know anything about the fire yet. Miller, like the rest of ATF, shows up 'After The Fact' hardly ever getting dirty."

"Yeah, but he needs to see all types of fires so he can keep his fire investigation certification. He would be an extra set of eyes and pair of hands. Plus, with his training, he always passes along some lessons he learned. He just needs to get more experience by getting to more fire scenes and he asked me to include him whenever I could."

Scherner argued back, "If you give that hotshot too much experience, he'll take your job away. This is our city. He's already too cocky. I'm not too keen about him working my fires. You can call him when I'm not around. He'll get plenty of work from other departments."

"Yeah, okay. Let's get going." Somewhat dejected, O'Brien liked to be helpful to other guys whenever he could. The extra help on the scene wouldn't have hurt either. Something else Miller would have brought to the scene, as he frequently did, was hot coffee and doughnuts.

Steering the worn red BFD Ford up Southampton Street toward the Back Bay neighborhood, Scherner added one final thought, "It would have been fun waking him up though."

It only took five minutes to drive to one of the few areas where Boston streets were laid out in rectangular grids. Most of the upper floors of the four-story brownstones along this narrow one-way tree-lined street held residential apartments, with the first floors often occupied with restaurants or boutiques. Normally, a fairly quiet city street this time of night, it was oddly busy as the two fire investigators pulled to the curb around the corner from the fire building. BFD engines, ladder trucks, and a rescue unit blocked the intersection of Hereford and Marlborough Streets. The flashing red lights from the mixture of apparatus competed with the alternating glare of numerous Boston PD cruiser blue lights.

From the trunk of their car, Scherner and O'Brien donned their turnout gear, boots and helmets. They also grabbed a camera, flashlights, rakes and shovels, all necessary tools when working a fire scene. Their first order of business was to locate the Incident Commander, the person in charge of the scene, check in with him and get background information on the incident.

Looking up, the investigators could see four broken windows wrapped around two elevations of the third floor. Smoke and steam from the freshly quenched fire were drifting from the darkened windows. O'Brien pointed to the two front windows with charred frames. "Well, not to jump to conclusions, but it looks obvious the fire started right there where it vented through the windows after it developed within that room."

A Deputy Fire Chief met them on the water and debris soaked front sidewalk. "Hi, boys. Welcome to another nasty nighttime fire. There's a charred young lady up there inside those third-floor windows. Nobody noticed anything unusual, but one neighbor said the girl's a student at BU and he heard her get home about 2:30 A.M., probably been drinking because she made a lot of noise in the hallway. She lived alone. A passerby noticed fire in the front living room window about 3:00 A.M. We knocked the fire down before it spread beyond her apartment," he said, pointing toward those same windows.

"Thanks, Chief," Scherner replied, then adding, "For keeping us busy. Do you know if anybody moved the body? The Medical Examiner on her way yet? And anybody from the D.A.'s office or detectives here? We'll take it from here and let you know what we find."

"Nobody touched her. It was obvious to the first-in crew she was already gone. You guys do your usual bang-up job."

After taking exterior photos and making additional observations, Scherner and O'Brien made their way through the first and second floors documenting the rooms, but there was only water damage on these floors. The entire building had been evacuated during the fire.

Briefly skipping the fire floor, they also checked the fourth floor where there was little damage. Back on the third floor, from the fire patterns they noted her apartment door had been closed during the fire, and secured, but the deadbolt had not been locked.

There were no pry marks indicating possible forced entry, but the door had been busted in by the firefighters so they could access the seat of the blaze. The scene patterns were relatively easy to follow. Stepping inside Wendy's apartment, Lieutenants Scherner and O'Brien worked their way through the charred remains, their purpose clear but weighed down by the loss of life. Their task was to piece together the puzzle by unraveling the threads of this tragedy.

Except for the open living room, dining area and kitchen, the bathroom and bedroom only had smoke and heat damage to the upper portions of the rooms. In the main area, the sofa had much of the material evenly burned off, with some directional burning toward the upholstered chair where the woman took her last breath. The chair and the victim were heavily charred.

Neither Scherner nor O'Brien noticed the damp odor of the recent fire, or the stench of death. The men had experienced enough of both to desensitize their sense of smell. Most ordinary people retched at such repugnant stench.

The investigators made several key observations. Wendy had been facing the sofa when she died. The clothing on her lap, stomach, chest and upper legs had been consumed. Her skin in these areas was a blackened, charred mass. Her lower arms had folded up toward her shoulders in a common pugilistic pose caused by the heat contracting the arm muscles. "No open casket for this girl," Scherner whispered, almost no more than a thought escaping from his lips. Wendy's face showed extreme thermal damage, full depth burning, a very unpleasant visage.

"Here, Mike, look inside her nose nostrils." Scherner focused his light up Wendy's nose. "Black soot. Looks like she was alive and breathing when the fire started. It looks like she never moved, probably so drunk at the time."

They saw a partially charred pack of cigarettes on a small side table, and on the floor they found a glass lying on its side next to an overturned nearly empty liquor bottle that smelled like cheap whiskey.

O'Brien, down on his knees, cleared away some ceiling debris that had fallen during fire extinguishment and overhaul, the process of searching for any hot spots above the ceiling and elsewhere. On the floor, he found the remains of another cigarette pack and matches.

The sun shining through the two east facing living room windows cast an eerie glow through the steam and smoke. The light illuminated a small rectangular pattern on the side table. "Hey, Mike, looks like this cigarette pack could have been here on the table. I think she had a little too much to drink, and she was smoking. Never a good combination. And look, a section of the Globe is still tucked under her butt, a good first fuel that could easily ignite from a cigarette or match."

The duo used their flashlights to check out the rest of the apartment. Nothing appeared amiss or askew. A photo on her bedroom bureau showed a group of young ladies with their names. The picture of Wendy confirmed what she looked like before fire forever disfigured her. Also, a check of her purse found her driver's license. Mike O'Brien sadly confirmed, "That's her all right."

"So what are we going to call it, Dick? Improper disposal of smoking materials? With the area of origin being on the chair, there is nothing else that could have caused the fire. And there is no evidence to suggest someone set it on purpose."

"Yeah, we'll end up going with that, but we'll call it under investigation until the ME tox results come back, possibly confirming she was intoxicated. What a shame, another young life gone too soon."

✳   ✳   ✳   ✳   ✳

ATF Special Agent Mark Miller had a horrible night's sleep. Something was eating at him, but he just couldn't figure out what it was. Since he couldn't sleep, he got up early. He had a cup of coffee while watching the morning news. A breaking news story about a woman killed in a Back Bay fire aroused his attention.

He wished the Boston Fire guys had called him. His thoughts turned to his professional career desires.

This is exactly the kind of fire I should be working. It's so hard to convince these guys that I could be an asset to their team. With all of my training, I could share some expertise with them while they show me the fire scenes. But that God-damned Dick Scherner is so friggin' jealous, he'll always be a pain in my ass. I'll have to work on them, especially Lt. O'Brien. He and I get along well. We just need to convince his partner.

✳   ✳   ✳   ✳   ✳

Shortly after Brantley placed his flowers within the memorial, word filtered through the gathered crowd on the street that the Boston Arson Squad had concluded the fire started accidentally on a chair where a woman had been drinking and most likely fell asleep while smoking a cigarette. So the official cause for this fire was careless or improper handling of smoking materials that ignited readily combustible materials.

Oh, well. She got what she deserved. She never would have changed. And, to think, I thought she might have been the one.

Brantley suddenly noticed the burning pain that had plagued his backside the night before had completely dissipated. His anger and resentment had fueled his burning actions. But, for the moment, he was cool and satisfied.

Brantley turned, then slowly walked away from the scene. His heart held no remorse for the victim. But in the solitude within his mind, the echoes of his past and the specter of his own darkness would continue to haunt him.

CHAPTER THREE

As ATF Agent Mark Miller stepped away from the podium basking in the glow of the successful press conference, a whirlwind of emotions churned within him.

The United States Attorney's words echoed in his mind, praising the efforts of Miller's team in what was hailed as 'the largest arson case in the history of the country.' As the case agent for this monumental investigation, Mark felt a surge of pride mixed with exhaustion after pouring every ounce of his being into unraveling the intricate web of nine arsonists plaguing Boston.

He was on a high, a rising star in the Boston office of the Bureau of Alcohol, Tobacco and Firearms, the agency delegated with investigating arson fires and illegal firearms cases on behalf of the Federal government. Less than four years earlier, Miller was the case agent in the largest seizure of stolen M16s in New England.

As part of the Boston Arson Task Force, he and his fellow investigators from ATF and the Boston Fire Investigation Unit (FIU) are tasked with solving the many arson cases in and around Boston. Miller was relieved now that he and his colleagues arrested the nine arsonists in this high-profile case. But now, the Task Force members had a lot of leg work to prepare for any trials that were sure to proceed since not all of the defendants would plead guilty. There was still a lot on the line to secure successful convictions.

But, for the remainder of this day, Miller, although dead tired, was going to revel in the success of the arrests with no incidents. Or so he thought.

"Hey, Miller, what's the big idea?" It was the booming voice of Boston Fire Lieutenant Dick Scherner whose red face and searing look indicated he was more than a little upset. "We were supposed to be on that podium with you instead of you hogging the limelight. You couldn't have put this fuckin' case together without our help!" he raged.

"Whoa, whoa, Dick, I was looking for you and Mike when the U.S. Attorney was speaking. Did you guys get tied up at another fire or what?"

"No, you ATF guys screwed us when you moved up the press conference to noon time instead of the scheduled one o'clock. Look, that's what time it is now. We were supposed to get some credit for this case, but you typical Feds came in and grabbed all the credit. You guys suck! Hell will freeze over before we ever work with you again."

"Oh, man, I'm really sorry about that. I thought my supervisor, Jack, or the U.S. Attorney's Office called you to update you on the time change. I really did. I was so busy with the arrests today and the court appearances, I didn't have time myself to do anything else. I'm as surprised as you are that this got fouled up.

You should know I would never do that to you guys. I realize how much you all meant to me and the success of this investigation. Check the news story tonight because I made sure I gave the Fire Investigation Unit kudos for all the time and effort you guys put into the case. I'm so sorry this happened. I hope you believe me."

Mark had spent years of arduous effort building relationships with members of other police and fire agencies. To his way of thinking, it was the best approach to successfully prosecute difficult arson cases. Today's roundup was a prime example of this teamwork. Too bad a screw-up by his bosses caused so much hardship among the working grunts.

He always had a strong desire to be liked by everyone, and this kind of crap didn't sit well with him. It brought up memories of trying to please his overbearing mother, but ultimately failing.

"Yeah, sure, sure. It's actions I believe, not words. You can stuff those," Lt. Scherner concluded as he turned, walking away still pissed.

"Dick, don't be a prick. And don't call me a liar. I like Boston Fire. So let's work as a team. It's the best way it seems."

"What the hell is that?" sneered Dick.

"Sometimes I find rhyme time can be so sublime. It takes down the tension."

"Oh, God. Miller, you're such a goofball."

✳   ✳   ✳   ✳   ✳

Walking into the seventh floor ATF office an hour later, Miller immediately heard a familiar Boston accent, "Hey, Bon. Great job today! Congratulations. You looked good in front of the cameras."

"Thanks, Wojo! Much appreciated. You know the case couldn't have been made without your help, along with Carlo and the guys from Boston Fire." Wojo was the nickname for one of Mark's best friends, Tom, going back to their days in the ATF academy years earlier.

The TV cop show, Barney Miller, was a highly popular comedy when Mark and his buddies went through the academy together and were all stationed in the Boston office. Mark was given the moniker, Barney, Barn, or as a Bostonian who drops his 'r' would say, Bon, after Captain Barney Miller. Mark even had thick wavy dark hair and a full mustache like the Captain.

Wojo, a tall kid from the Polish enclave in Chelsea, just outside of Boston, got his name from the character, Detective 3rd Grade (later Sergeant) Stanley Thaddeus "Wojo" Wojciehowicz. The other agents in the office often chuckled at how perfect Tom's character and personality fit with his new nickname.

"Hey, Wojo, where's Carlo? Let's all head out for a couple drinks after I take care of a few things here in the office."

"Sounds good. I'll let him know. We can celebrate at Doyle's. Six okay for you?"

"See you there. Try to round up a few others. I'll buy the first round."

"In that case, I'll be there early with the entire Task Force group!" They both laughed and headed their separate ways.

The paperwork on Federal cases always took precedence; it had to be done immediately. And it always took longer than anticipated, causing Miller to run late. Rushing out of the Federal Building, the Boston late spring heat and humidity smacked him in the face as he hurried down the crowded noisy street to Doyle's on Canal Street.

Doyle's was a Boston tradition. Everything inside the joint was old. The dark, worn L-shaped bar was original, dating to the early 1900s. The yellowed walls were still stained with cigarette and cigar smoke from days past before smoking was recently prohibited in restaurants. Although the light fixtures had been updated, the dim lighting they provided hid the scars on the ancient tables and round-back chairs scattered around the equally dark-stained wood floor. It was this ambiance that law enforcement types enjoyed as their predecessors had for generations. The crowds kept coming back for the cold beer, a generous pour of hard liquors, decent food at modest prices and the camaraderie of friends.

Several ATF Agents often made up a raucous part of that crowd, letting off steam from a hard day in their chosen field of fighting crime and paperwork. Tonight, a large section of the bar was packed with members of the ATF Arson Task Force. They had a lot to celebrate following the arrests of those involved in setting fires all over the Boston area for the past two years. It was a long-term, complex and demanding investigation that finally panned out.

When a sweat-soaked Miller entered through the double set of doors, the ATF and Boston Fire crowd spotted him. They erupted in a cheer, probably waiting for that round of drinks he promised. The cool AC also greeted him. Everyone was in a jovial mood – they were ready to celebrate. This was sometimes the best part of the job. Mark relished the friendships, something he would never forget.

"Hey, Barney, we saved you a seat," Wojo pointed to an empty oak barstool at the bar where they were congregated. Wojo then exclaimed, "Barn, this case was phenomenal! You'll get a promotion out of this. Cheers!"

Carlo patted Mark on the back, "Congratulations on bringing the case home, buddy. I knew you could do it." Since they met, Carlo has been one of Mark's biggest supporters. Mark appreciated the genuine warmth from his two best friends. They always had his back and he had theirs.

As soon as he sidled up to the bar, Frank, the lifetime bartender, placed a Boston Lager pint in front of him. "My best pour just for you. Very deserving. I saw your press conference on TV. You looked great!"

Mark nodded with a wink, "Thanks, buddy, I couldn't have done it without quite a few of your perfect pours." Hoisting the glass above eye level to his crowd of friends and associates, "Cheers, and congratulations to us all for getting these guys off the streets. It was one hell of a slog, and it could not have happened without the hard work put in by so many of you. We hit a home run, now the torches are done, so let's have some fun. Thanks, one and all!" That first swig always tasted so good.

Wojo yelled above the din, "Oh, no he's rhyming again!" It was one of Mark's quirky habits.

Mark added, "Some lucky breaks helped a lot. I'm certainly glad I was friends with the TV cameraman, Nat. Without him catching these guys on video, we may never have had the names of these guys, front and center."

Carlo added, "Yeah, but then you got that lieutenant from Boston Housing to feed you some info that helped nail these guys. Did you ever find out why he was telling you all this stuff, but never confessed to you that he helped set over fifty fires himself?"

"As Winston Churchill once said, 'That is a riddle, wrapped in a mystery, inside an enigma.' I can't figure that out. He had a chance to avoid prison time and stop these fires just by letting me know the truth about the fires his crew was setting." Mark abruptly became quiet.

He was eyeing a young strawberry blonde agent sitting across the table smiling in his direction. Her presence ignited a spark within him. Lowering his glass, he caught the gaze of the rookie agent, Michelle Monihan. There was a certain twinkle of admiration in her eyes as she stared directly at him. Mark knew she was on the job for only a few months, but because he was so busy with putting the arson case together, he really hadn't had a chance to talk to her beyond an initial meet and greet.

He was no stranger to fooling around with the young ladies in the office and in other law enforcement agencies since his divorce. The job taketh away, then giveth back. That's what he believed.

Just thinking about his divorce brought back unpleasant, painful memories that rolled in on him like waves into Boston Harbor from the open ocean. Initially, as his marriage of six years fell apart, Miller was beyond devastated.

I tried everything in my power to keep it together. But Ellen had enough of the long hours and me. She called me an emotionally distant husband, who acted like he didn't give a damn and was often angry with her for no apparent reason. She was just plain tired of everything and fell out of love with me. How does anyone just 'fall out of love?' Does it happen as easy as it does to 'fall in love,' or does it happen over years?

I thought love was unconditional and you worked 'through thick and thin.' If we only knew how to communicate better, maybe we could have made it through. But that is all ancient history now.

He remembered how bad things had gotten, and Wojo coming to his house one evening asking for his gun. "I can see you're suffering, buddy. Let me take this for safekeeping until you can get your head on straight. It's for the best. You'll be back on your game soon."

Mark shook his head, I had never considered eating my gun or worse, using it on my wife, but it was obvious I wasn't myself. That talk with Wojo that night may well have been what pulled me out of my funk. It wasn't long after that when I began to right my ship, mostly by plunging into my work again. All those damn memories, somehow, I have to replace them with pleasant ones. Somehow.

The conversations in the bar drew him back to the present. Words flowed freely, like the booze, covering the gamut, from the struggles of the Red Sox to investigations to family outings. After mixing with the others for over an hour, Mark found himself elbow-to-elbow with Michelle.

Again, as he stared at her face, he saw how soft and smooth her young lady skin was with no extra make-up to hide her appealing natural features. Forgiving hazel eyes, dimpled lower cheeks when she smiled, a perfectly formed nose that fit her face to a T, and natural full, kissable, even suckable lips. Her shoulder length, highlighted hair was so smooth and glossy, perfectly framing her face. She was adorable, cute, even sexy in her form-fitting A-line skirt with a matching powder blue sleeveless top glued over her small, yet shapely breasts.

Wow, I had better watch out! She is six years my junior, and a rookie agent, although she's not under my command. Thinking like that could only lead to trouble.

Now she cocked her head upward toward his gaze. That twinkle divulged her respect for this agent who had perfected two of the biggest cases in local history. Was she infatuated by his celebrity status, or was she interested more in him as a person?

Mark opened with, "So, how is the job going for you so far?"

Michelle was poised and not terribly shy for a young woman in a job still dominated by men. "It's going even better than I could have hoped." A giggle escaped her lips, as she pushed her hair behind one pierced ear.

"I have Billy MacDonald as my training officer. As you know, because he talks about you two working and hanging out together, he's one of the best agents. And he knows how to impart his experience to a newbie without coming on too strong, unless he needs to hit some point really hard. It's been great! I certainly get a lot of hours working with him chasing cases with Boston PD, doing surveillances. The gun investigations are good and working with him on organized crime guys is absolutely exciting, but I think I eventually would like to work on arsons and explosions like you. For me, in the long run, it would be a better, more interesting fit."

"You sound like me a couple years ago. Even after that big machine gun case, I felt investigating fires was a nice niche. There's always a puzzle that needs to be pieced together. It's challenging, and fun, too."

Michelle added, "After I go through this gun squad stint, I would love to work with you in the Arson Group."

"It seems like you have a lot on the ball. I think you could be an asset to the group." Mark couldn't help fantasizing about Michelle's assets. He couldn't deny the attraction between them. As they exchanged pleasantries, Mark was drawn to her warmth and enthusiasm, a stark contrast to the complexities of his own emotions.

He knew himself—he was a male whore. This was one reason Mark was divorced. Long hours working and more hours playing where he shouldn't have. At least now, he was free to do as he pleased when it came to consensual relationships with the opposite sex, unless it was a subordinate of his on the job. That could derail his long-term plans to be the best agent he could be.

For a moment, standing within the celebratory crowd, he was alone amidst his thoughts. How can I be two different guys at the same time? I know I come off as a little cocky and self-assured, but then, I second guess myself, so unsure, even insecure. Like, why would Michelle have any genuine interest in me? What makes me so special? What if I'm not enough? Will I ever be able to earn the respect she's showing me?

I'm still a kid in a man's body. Will that ever change? As I look around me I see so many grown men who act like adults, not a boy like I feel. I don't know, maybe I'm just not mature like they are. Sometimes I still don't think like an adult. Is it a lack of confidence? Is it because I never had a father to emulate? I don't even know how to describe what I feel. But I believe I have to be more. No, I know I need to be the best.

After an awkward pause, Mark said, "Well, Michelle, I'll see what I can do about getting you into the Arson Group when the time comes. Just keep learning every day. Listen as much as you can. Don't speak until you have a question. There is a lot to grasp along the way. And make sure you stay safe. I wouldn't want to see a smart, sweet kid like you getting hurt. I'd better mingle more before someone gets the wrong idea."

Did his smile and comments betray any stirring he felt inside as he spoke to her? Michelle looked a little disappointed, her radiant smile dimmed to a more neutral face. She found Mark to be a completely charming man. "Sure, we'll catch up soon. It's your night to celebrate."

Busting chops was what Mark's friends did best. "Hey, hotshot," called out Carlo. "If I didn't know better, you have a fan there who would be happy to head home with you! And the look in your eyes say you would like that, too."

Dennis "Carlo" Caggiano, a wiry Italian kid from the South Shore was a mover and a shaker. His pick-up style was to walk up to the prettiest girls on the beach or in a bar and ask, 'Would you like to get married for a day?' He approached them in such a way that the women never seemed offended, merely amused by his dramatic flair. One in ten women usually ended up with Carlo for a day or night. His over-the-top productions on the job and in his personal life earned him his nickname from the highly successful Italian producer, Carlo Ponti.

"Screw you, Carlo. It's a good thing you finally got married. Otherwise, you would be hitting on her, asking her if she wanted to marry you for a day." They both laughed, but then Mark added, "She's cute as hell but fooling around with a rookie in the office can also lead nowhere but to trouble." Pausing momentarily, "But on the other hand, I wouldn't mind hooking up with her someday."

Lt. Mike O'Brien from the Boston Fire Department walked up to Mark, handing him a glass of bourbon. "Well, Mark. With your tenacity and guidance, we did a great job! Thanks for taking us along for this ride. How are you feeling?"

"Mike, really fantastic! I'm just sorry about the screwup at the press conference. That really pissed Dick off. I tried to apologize to him, but it didn't seem to sway him.

"Shit happens, Mark. I think I know you well enough to know you wouldn't do anything intentionally to hurt us. But Dick has always had that competitive nature and lack of trust in other outfits. He thinks you Feds take, take, take, giving us nothing, never sharing information with us. I'll work on him to soften him up."

"You, your crew and our task force put such a great effort into this case. I was only the case agent. You wouldn't believe what appreciation and gratitude I have for all your work on this investigation. And we ended up getting an unbelievable arson ring off the street, possibly the biggest ever! Thanks, buddy."

After a couple more drinks and additional banter with his friends and associates, Miller excused himself. All of the excitement and adrenalin from the day's arrests started to wear on him. Before leaving, he needed a quick pit stop in the men's room. When he exited into the narrow back hallway, he physically bumped into Michelle as she exited the ladies' room.

"Oh, sorry, kid, excuse me. I was just leaving."

Michelle put her hand on his arm. She liked what she saw; a good looking, physically fit, and an apparently confident young man. His blue eyes made her melt. He took great care of himself, from his perfect brown hair to his sexy trimmed mustache, to his clothing and down to his shined shoes. "I'm not really a kid, you know. You're not leaving already, are you? I wanted to talk with you more, and I usually get what I want."

Mark blushed. He was not used to this more aggressive, forward attitude of today's younger women. "Well, we'll get together soon and talk. I have a lot to do tomorrow, and I need to get some sleep."

He saw the disappointment showing in Michelle's eyes and her pouting lips. Oh, don't do that to me! I could just suck on those lips all night long. Just not tonight.

As Mark made his way to the parking garage below the Federal building, he sucked in a deep breath and slowly exhaled. He aimed his Government car southbound, a forty minute journey to his empty house. It gave him time to reflect upon his life with its most recent accomplishment and the ups and downs that brought him to this day.

Quietly proud of himself for being good, even great at his job, he never bragged, but he wanted to be known by everyone else as the best. He always had to prove himself, just like he always tried with his mother.

She may have cared, but she never outwardly showed it, quite the opposite. "I don't care if you ever do your homework or how well you do in school. If you want to become anything in life, that's entirely up to you." That woman knew how to motivate me by never showing she cared. And I always wanted to please her by being the best I could be, or maybe just the best overall. This drove me to consistently be near the top of my class all the way through college. But she never said, "Good job." or "I'm proud of you."

I laughed when she gave me a suitcase as a graduation gift. The message was obvious. I may have been a self-made man, but I carried plenty of baggage and insecurities.

Would she be proud of me now? He wondered what it would have taken, how much more would I have had to accomplish before I ever won her approval. But I'll never know. Her health failed rapidly two years earlier from colon cancer. It took her way too young, partially because she would never go to the doctor when she began to notice unusual symptoms. She died within ten days of moving into a nursing home.

Mark thought back to that rare moment, just before her downward spiral, when she asked him to visit her that day in the nursing home.

I remember walking into her room. Her condition was dire, much worse than just days earlier. I was so uncomfortable seeing her that way. I also wonder if my part of uneasiness was because I knew she was going to unload something that would change my life forever.

Something was really bothering her. I could see her agitation. As she started talking, there seemed to be bitterness in her weakened voice. "I just think it's time before I'm gone to let you know these things," she began. I fidgeted in my chair, as I felt like I was about to crawl out of my skin.

She started talking about her background and upbringing. "Growing up during Hitler's war in Europe was pure hell. I was a member of Hitler's League of German Girls, the female unit of the Hitler Youth that indoctrinated girls into Nazi ideals while preparing them for motherhood. My schooling was frequently interrupted due to the war raging at our doorstep. My parents, your grandparents – you would have called them Omama and Opapa – divorced, but both of them brought me up in a strict, Germanic style. I survived the war, but my life was not pleasant. Despite the war being over, there was little joy, and less money, for an Austrian woman barely twenty years old."

Her voice dropped and became shaky. I could tell she was looking inside her mind's eye, reflecting on the grit of her life story, her reality, but she wasn't about to divulge all of the details. She was tougher than that. Showing emotion was never her thing. She had more to say.

"I had one bit of luck, like a door opened for me to get a job with the post-war American rebuilding machine, putting me in close contact with American G.I.'s." She began squirming in her bed, as if all of this was getting a bit too close for comfort. I felt her growing anxiety.

"I met a soldier," she said, "Bill Miller, and I got pregnant shortly thereafter." Then came her rage again. "Imagine the stigma," she cried real tears, "a young pregnant, unmarried Catholic girl in late 1940s Europe. I was shamed and ashamed." Her body shook, heaved and shivered as she cried. This wracked her physically and mentally. I had never seen my mother cry. All those years of pent-up emotions drained what life she had left within her. She collapsed, never completing the story. Death came shortly after this episode.

Mark felt his own eyes moisten as he drove. That was the day he could finally answer some questions about her coldness towards him and at least understand a bit about his mother and what drove her. Yes, she certainly was a driven woman. And he remembered how her tears that day must have seeped through the ironclad shell she had built around herself. And, when it did, there was nothing left to keep her here. But after all of that, and the ensuing time since her passing, her spirit still haunts him, never allowing him to show weakness. His eyes blurred for a moment as he thought of her, which he rarely did. But only for a moment. Even now Mark wouldn't, couldn't show vulnerability.

He just made his second massive case in four years, his second in his first eight years on the job. Now, he already felt obligated to make his life's quest to find and make his next big case. It has to be pretty impressive to match or beat the last two.

As trains of thought went, Mark's reflections flowed from the good to the bad and back again. From self-doubt to self-confidence and back again. His demons spooked him, but amidst the chaos and uncertainty in his head, a glimmer of hope flickered.

His optimism rose to the surface as he thought of Michelle, with her sweetness, her enthusiasm and her cute sexiness all bringing a smile to his face. Man, it would be real nice if that young lass would be coming home with me. But, hell, it is not a home. It's nothing but a damn cold, empty house.

Mark had been divorced for three years. He knew he always worked too hard, never paying enough attention to his wife when he was home. She had a valid complaint when she said he never talked about anything important with her. From his viewpoint, she would never understand. They just had nothing much in common.

Another issue that caused his divorce was Mark's struggle with his passive-aggressive nature. With his wife, he held everything in, never talking to her, or anyone else, about things that bothered him. He let everything build up within him until the slightest infraction would cause him to explode. Often, his wife took the brunt of his eruption even though she didn't deserve it or wasn't even the appropriate object of his wrath.

This is how it went. They both allowed walls to be built, brick by brick, course by course, layer by layer until the divide between them was too high for either of them to see over the wall.

A brief stint in counseling while he went through the divorce at least helped him recognize weaknesses in himself, even if he sometimes still lets them get the best of him.

Since that time, Mark bounced in and out of relationships, some lasting a night, if you call that a relationship. Others lasted three or four months. Mark was not an aggressive guy when meeting women, which may have been just the aspect of his modest mannerism that made him attractive to women. It also helped that he had an actual job, a house, and decent manly looks. Looking upon the revolving door of ladies who passed in and out of his life, Mark sometimes felt like a male whore. There's that word again. At least I acknowledge it, he thought.

But he felt something click with Michelle, mentally, emotionally and sexually. He also knew what a bad idea it would be getting mixed up with her. Besides being a rookie in the office, even though she was in another group, office affairs can get messy.

Arriving in his driveway, Mark tucked all thoughts away. He needed to get some sleep for a busy upcoming schedule. But he could never imagine the tribulations that would soon challenge every aspect of his upcoming life.

CHAPTER FOUR

Although he thought of many women as vile creatures, Brantley had no interest in raping women. Whenever he thought about sex, the same recording played in his head. At twelve or thirteen years old, he had his first dreams of sex or wet dreams. His mother always found out. Her responses stuck with him to this day. "You're a filthy pig, making a mess in your pajamas and bed. Can't you control yourself? What the hell kind of dirty thoughts do you have, anyway?" She belittled him in so many ways.

Because of this, he never even masturbated as he grew older since he had trouble getting and maintaining an erection. His mother's nagging voice made it nearly impossible for him to have normal male urges. She pounded into his head that sexual self-gratification was such an unclean, immoral act.

It also carried over to his attempts at relationships with teen girls, and later with women. In those rare circumstances when Brantley had a chance to score with a female, he failed to get hard. Just thinking about the nasty act of sex produced severe angst within Brantley's head and stomach. Women, in turn, reacted with such disdain or frustration when they couldn't satisfy him or be satisfied themselves. Feeling exasperated and embarrassed, Brantley never had another date with any of these women again.

Eventually, by his mid-20s, even though he fantasized about making love to a woman, he gave up on pursuit of sexual encounters. His feelings of inadequacy were just too great for him to overcome. He didn't have a clue how to pull himself out of his agonizing mental abyss. His only reaction was to strike out and strike back, but never at his mother.

And his mother still continued to add to his struggle. She virtually demanded he call her several times a week. If he failed to call for a few days, the next time they spoke, she would always make him feel guilty by playing the poor martyr. "I guess you don't care about me. I'm just here all by myself. What if something happened to me? Nobody would know for days if you don't call regularly. Why don't you move in here with me anyway? I'm not going to live forever, you know. You have always been an ungrateful, selfish bastard. You don't care about anyone but yourself, especially me. Maybe I should just kill myself!" She was a master manipulator.

On and on she would drone. Always so loud. Screaming, screaming, screaming incessantly! *Please stop. I hate that noise, that voice so much!*

It was true she was all alone. Brantley knew nothing about his father, absolutely nothing. He always felt a little lost, maybe because of not having his father, but there was something else missing. *You know when you're about to complete a puzzle, but a couple pieces are missing, that's what I feel like, incomplete.* Whenever he inquired of his father's whereabouts or identity, his mother replied he didn't need to know anything about him because he was a useless drunk who left when Brantley was a baby.

Of course, Brantley sometimes wondered what his father was like, but then he would push the thoughts from his mind. What difference does it make anyway, but the thoughts always managed to creep in uninvited.

After all, he left me and never even checked on me to see if I was dead or alive. I guess he never cared about me. Just a burden who resulted from a woman, sex and a baby.

The guilt trip his mother thrust upon him ultimately worked its demonic magic. Brantley finally yielded to her unrelenting assault, reluctantly moving into his childhood bedroom to live with her outside Providence, the capital of Rhode Island. It was a small ranch-style house, the kind that was mass-produced in the decade after World War II. The layout consisted of an eat-in kitchen, a living room and a hallway with two bedrooms on the right, the only bathroom on the left and a third bedroom at the end of the hall. Everything in the house was shabby, drab, and outdated. Kitchen cabinets were nearly thirty years old, as were the worn carpets, the paint and peeling wallpaper.

Cigarette smoke had stained all surfaces with a sickly yellow-brownish stain. His mother had chain-smoked cigarettes throughout Brantley's childhood. That was another thing he despised about his childhood. The stink and haze of smoke was always pervasive on the furniture, on his clothes that he wore to school, in his nostrils and in his head. Whenever he complained about the smoke while they drove in their car on a rainy day, she answered, "Oh, suck it up, you weak pathetic wimp. It's my car and I'll do what I want."

Despite the smoky film on the older interior surfaces, his mother always made sure the house was clean, no matter how sick and frail she was. That was the way she was throughout his adolescent and teen years. Much of the cleaning was accomplished through the labor of her sole child. How many other kids had to dust every piece of furniture several times a week? And Brantley detested the vacuum cleaner! One summer, he had to vacuum someplace within the house daily. The noise, noise, noise! Just like her voice, it was loud, appallingly loathsome.

This is the house Brantley grew up in after moving from the Albany, New York apartment where he had his earliest memories. This was the house he despised. It had been his living hell, but it was the woman who lived there who was the devil.

She always acted like she was the damn Gestapo, ordering me to do this, then ordering me to do that. And most of her mannerisms were not child-friendly.

Besides the whippings, verbal abuse, yelling and screaming all the time, nothing she commanded Brantley to do was ever done correctly, prompting further cruel mistreatment. He could never bring friends home because she would loudly scream and swear plus demand Brantley clean the house right then and there. The word "love" was never spoken from her lips. A life of tough love was more than Brantley could handle. He was about to go down a deep, dark rabbit hole.

Trying to sleep that first night in his childhood bed, all he could do was toss and turn, stare into the blackness toward the ceiling. His mother had just told him she has stomach cancer and there was nothing that could be done to prolong her life. For the first time in her life, she had opened up to him.

"Brantley, it hurts so bad most of the time. I can't eat. It may not be long before I'm gone. Or maybe you can help me with that."

"What are you talking about?"

"Put me out of my misery."

"That would be murder, you know. Even though we haven't gotten along for a long time, hell, we have even hated each other most of the time, I'm not so sure about this."

"Of course you can do this. It's my time. But first I have to tell you something."

"I don't know if I want to hear it."

"Here goes. I'm not your real mother," she announced, wincing as she confessed her long-held secrets.

"What the fuck are you talking about?"

"Now, don't you swear at me. Hear me out, then you can do whatever the hell you want."

"Your mother is my sister. Nothing was ever easy for either of us. We grew up in a broken home and, even worse, under Hitler's rule in Nazi-occupied Austria in the late 1930s and early 1940s. We had no desire to join his army of girls indoctrinated into their beliefs and values, but we had no choice. That lifestyle, and a general Germanic upbringing, left indelible personality traits for the remainder of our lives. Your mother died a couple years ago." Brantley's mouth hung open in utter shock. "She couldn't handle you shortly after you were born, because," she stumbled, "because, you have a twin brother that she kept."

Brantley leaned forward on his chair, with a twisted look he shouted at the top of his voice. "No, no, no! Why didn't you ever tell me? Secrets, friggin' family secrets! I'm freakin' nearly thirty years old, and I never knew I had a brother. And you're not even my mother! And now I'll never get to meet her. Was she a witch, like you? You're a she-devil. I hate you!" He was stewing. He could only scowl at her. His words were lost as a jumble of thoughts churned within his brain.

"Listen! You've been a little bastard your entire life. I've never felt motherly love for you. You needed every whack I ever gave you because you never learned discipline. You've been nothing but an albatross around my neck since I took you in."

"So why did you? You've been a miserable bitch for as long as I can remember. And you have never told me anything about my father. More secrets I presume?"

"But before we get so off track with our mutual hatred, there's still more I need to tell you."

"Oh, more, what more can you spring on me in one day?"

"It's nothing really big, just some details. You're right about me. Growing up during the war was so hard. And our parents were unloving to say the least. I never learned how to love. My heart never felt love. Forget about ever having a man in my life. I didn't really want to raise you. I did it for my sister. She needed help even though we weren't close, so I agreed. And I took all of my life failings out on you, an easy target for my frustrations."

"So, do you know anything about my father?"

"That louse left your mother when you were only six months old. He drank all the time and he apparently wasn't up to being a father for you and your brother, whose name, by the way, is Mark Miller. Your father was Bill Miller. My last name, and yours, Mueller, was our family name in Austria. It translates from German to Miller."

"Do you know anything else about them?"

"Well, your Dad…"

Brantley snapped, "Don't call him my Dad! He's only my father because of his sperm. A Dad is altogether a different person."

"Okay. Fair enough. Late in Bill's Army career, he became an air traffic controller and when he retired, he did the same at a small airport in Alabama. I heard from your mother a couple years ago she found out he never wanted anything to do with you."

"Well, screw him too!" Brantley's eyes bulged as he seethed, his emotions boiling. "I'll never have anything to do with him either, if he's even alive. Who does that bastard think he is?"

"I think he's still alive, but in failing health. Probably drinking himself to death."

"Good riddance to an asshole, apparently. What about my brother?"

"Mark has been a success story, I guess. From what your mother told me, he became a federal agent of some sort. He specializes in fire investigations, somewhat of a local celebrity in Boston because of some massive arson case he cracked. He's apparently done a lot more with his life than you've ever done, or probably will ever do."

Brantley stayed silent upon hearing this. His brain began working overtime. I'll show her. I won't be a nobody forever. My whole life was a lie, a joke. I lived this despicable existence while he lived the good life. My brother's a hotshot fire investigator, very interesting. Maybe I'll see just how good he is at his job.

✻   ✻   ✻   ✻   ✻

Lying awake in bed for over an hour, Brantley tried to make sense of what his "step-mother" revealed. His mind ran in continuous circles, just too much to take in.

She's not my mother. I can't believe she's not my mother. Good grief! Why didn't she just give me to an orphanage. I would have been better off. At least that answers why she treated me so badly. She used me as an excuse to exercise her own demons. She has always been the same, a damn demon.

My "real" mother has never been a mother to me, either. And now I'm burdened with a golden boy brother. It would have been nice to have grown up with a brother, but now I get to have my nose rubbed in the fact that he is some big shot and I'm a nobody.

The sudden weight on Brantley was nearly unbearable. What the hell am I going to do? It took only a few more minutes of contemplation. I think I'll start tonight. Take care of two problems in one swift act. After all, I murdered someone already in my life. I can do it again. Let me put my fake mom out of her misery. And mine, too. That's right, I'll be a man of action.

Slipping silently out of bed, Brantley formulated his plan. He made his bed and gathered all of his belongings, making sure there was no obvious trace of a second person staying at the house. He didn't need to worry about making too much noise. His "mother" had taken some sleeping pills on top of pain pills so she could sleep through some of the agony.

One other trait his "mother" exhibited was that of a hoarder. She always saved everything, saying she did so because as a child she grew up in depressed, hard times during the war when goods were so scarce. Most of this stuff was hidden in boxes, dozens upon dozens of boxes. They were neatly stacked in the corners of every room, plus a three-foot high regiment of boxes orderly lined against one wall of the hallway.

Brantley slowly, silently opened the door to his surrogate mother's bedroom to look in on her. For a reason he could not explain, he walked over to gaze down upon her sleeping body. He leaned down and planted a soft kiss on her cheek. Then, after, at the door, he turned back toward her once more, giving her the finger before quickly exiting the room, closing the door to that living part of his life forever.

In the bathroom, Brantley took his mother's ashtray off the counter. He dumped the few cigarette butts into the small plastic trash can next to the bathroom vanity. A towel hook was attached to the side of the cabinet right above the waste basket. He strategically draped a bath towel so it hung onto the top of the container. Adding more tissues to the container, he then used his mother's own matches to set a fire. Moving with urgency, he also set fire to several of the cardboard boxes lining the hall to ensure the fire grew swiftly, trapping his mother behind her closed bedroom door.

Brantley grabbed his stuff. From the kitchen, he turned to watch the fire rapidly develop in the hallway. That should work he surmised. He turned his back on the fire, but his former life wouldn't die in the inferno. Stepping through the side door, he passed into the darkness and the unknown. *Good riddance, bitch.* That woman had never changed.

As his 'mother' perished in the fire, a deep hurt welled up within Brantley. *She left me without ever saying, "I love you."*

CHAPTER FIVE

Mark hung up the phone in the office. He had just been requested to assist at a fatal fire scene in Rhode Island. The local Fire Chief explained that he and the State Fire Marshal had done a preliminary fire scene examination. It wasn't the toughest of fires to figure out he said, but they wanted another pair of eyes to examine the scene prior to removing the body.

Before leaving the office, Mark checked with Michelle's supervisor to ask if she was available to go with him to conduct a fire investigation in Rhode Island. She got the green light to go as there was nothing much going on in her group that day.

While traveling the fifty miles to the scene, Mark considered the possibilities based on what the Chief had already informed him. He shared his thoughts with Michelle, "As my normal routine, I approach each fire the same way. I listen to the information provided about the fire response, the victim and the early investigation, but I invariably conduct my independent scene analysis. A trained investigator will usually conduct the scene inspection in a consistent manner. Starting with the exterior, I make my observations and take photos before doing the same on each side of the building in a clockwise direction. Inside, I generally photograph and make observations in each room usually from the least damaged room or area with the most damage."

His conversation covered the seriousness of the task before them contrasting with the playful tension that crackled between them. This was typical for people across the police and fire professions, including Mark, to rid themselves of the tensions created by the work. He couldn't deny the magnetic pull between them. Up to this point, Mark managed to keep their relationship at arm's length. But he could tell from her looks, body language and her remarks, Michelle wanted to take their connection to the next level.

"I hope you don't get offended, but I have never seen anybody look as good as you do in BDUs!" Mark, his words laced with a hint of mischief, hoped he wasn't out of line. Those matching navy blue tops and bottoms with multiple large pockets were form fitting on her young curves. "I can't wait to see how you'll look dirty with black soot covering that outfit, and your face, too."

Michelle playfully responded with an impish, blushing smile. "You never said anything about getting dirty! It's a good thing I have another regular set of clothes under this less than flattering uniform. But, as I've told you before, I would get down and dirty with you anytime." Their flirtatious banter betrayed unspoken desires.

Quickly changing the subject, "So, seriously, a woman died in this fire? Any information that this was an arson or she was murdered? If you don't mind, could you share all your thoughts with me at the scene?"

"I sure will. We'll have to do a thorough job to make sure this woman gets the justice she deserves."

✳   ✳   ✳   ✳   ✳

After parking his vehicle directly in front of the ranch-style house, Mark wasted no time in making his initial observations. The Chief's car and a SFM van were parked in the two-car driveway, which had concrete walls on both sides as the single-car garage was located under the main house. There was also a man-door next to the garage that led into the basement level. There was no evidence of fire damage in the basement or garage. On the front of the main floor, there were two sets of side-by-side windows spaced about twenty feet apart. All four windows were broken with signs of heavy soot and blackened char damage extending from the openings.

At the rear of the house, the only window with fire damage around it appeared to be the center bathroom window. It was higher and smaller than all the other windows. Chief Kelsey and David Smith of the Fire Marshal's Office greeted Mark at the side door. As he shook Mark's hand, the Chief welcomed him and expressed gratitude for coming down so quickly.

"Well, thank you, Chief, for the heads up. I'm always happy to help and it gives me a chance to examine more fires. I learn something new each time out. Hey, Dave, how have you been?"

"Exhausted at the moment. This is my fourth fire this week, all in the middle of the night, but this is the first fatal."

"This is my new colleague, Michelle. She's got a keen interest in learning more about fire investigation. What can you tell me about this one?" Mark asked as they entered the kitchen, which still reeked of the night's smoke and charred material.

"Hi, there, Michelle. I'm glad to see young, fresh blood getting into this business. The house was secure upon arrival. We have one middle-aged woman deceased in her bed, smoke and thermal damage evident."

As they walked into the hall, Dave continued, "It appears the fire started here in the bathroom trash can. Look at the melted plastic container with the remains of cigarette butt filters." Mark nodded. "And the fire grew because her towels hung right above the trash. Then, check out these charred boxes with combustibles lining the hallway. The fire burned through the upper half of the hollow-core door into her bedroom. As the smoke, heat, and by-products continued to spread, the windows eventually failed."

Mark gazed at the victim still lying in the full-size bed. The sight of the deceased sent a shiver down his spine. He noted she had slept on her right side, as her night gown was entirely consumed on the top side from being exposed to temperatures of several hundred degrees. The heat also charred and blistered her skin on that corresponding side of her body. The upper portions of the bedroom suffered the most damage, typical in many rooms where the fire didn't originate.

Michelle retched a few times at the sight of the crispy semi-nude body. The other investigators snickered as they watched her struggle to maintain her composure. Dave asked, "Is this your first burn victim?"

Still gagging and turning away from the sight, Michelle weakly responded, "My first dead body of any kind. She looks disgusting." Unfortunately, the stench of charred skin doesn't help either. She had a green tinge to her cheeks.

Her mentor asked, chuckling, but showing concern, "Do you need to step outside to get some fresh air?"

"I'd better go before I embarrass myself and you." She headed down the hallway toward the side door.

The Chief called out, reassuringly, "Kid, don't worry about that, we all had our first body. Everybody reacts differently. I've seen many men with projectile vomiting." Just the visual from his words caused Michelle to heave again.

Returning to the investigation, "What is your theory on why she didn't move or attempt to escape?" Mark asked.

Chief Kelsey opined, "First, there were no smoke detectors in this older home. Records show she owned the home since it was built nearly three decades ago. A neighbor told us that she had some sort of terminal cancer. Then, there's these. We found this on the floor."

He handed Mark a prescription pill bottle. It was for combination pain/sleeping pills made out for a Brigette Mueller. "Yeah, it all sounds right. She never felt a thing, a rather peaceful way to go instead of waiting for the cancer to eat away at her."

Mark passed the pill bottle to Michelle, who had just returned to the room looking pale. She wanted to tough it out, but she had been quiet while taking in everything the others said and pointed out. He guided Michelle through the complexities of the grim scene. Then she interjected, "Have you located any family?"

"A neighbor thought she was never married, but she may have had a grown son. But we couldn't find any record of a son," Dave said. "The neighbor is the same guy who discovered the fire. When he got up to take a leak, he saw flames coming out from the front bedroom windows. Also, we didn't find anything to indicate a second person lived here."

Mark looked at the pill container again, flipping it around in his hand, mulling over something that began to gnaw at him. "You know, guys, Miller is the anglicized version of the Germanic name, Mueller. The name is so common. She was probably a cousin of mine," he quipped.

Dave added, "We had your Massachusetts accelerant-detection canine run through the hallway, the bathroom and the bedrooms, but he made no alerts. His handler was needed at another fire, so he took off right away."

Mark explained to Michelle. "I know I briefly mentioned using the canines at fire scenes before. It's too bad you didn't get to see him work. It's really pretty cool. They are extensively trained to smell numerous ignitable liquids that may be used to cause more rapid spread of a fire. The dogs alert to the slightest trace of a substance. Then, we take a sample where the alert is, as well as some other places, and send the samples to the lab to see whether the alert is confirmed."

"Yeah, we were supposed to watch one of the canines work at the academy, but he was busy since there are only a few dogs trained so far," Michelle stated. Didn't the first canine come online only a couple years ago? 1986, right?"

"You're right. Connecticut was first, then the Mass State Police got one," Mark replied. They are so invaluable. Before we essentially guessed as to where we took samples based on fire patterns. Now, our sample taking is far more accurate."

Mark continued, "So, Chief, Dave, I totally agree with your assessment of the scene. There's no evidence to suggest anything but an accidental fire. You guys still waiting for the ME's people to come out? Thanks for giving me a call. If anything unusual pops up, please give me a shout. I'll see you at the next one. Maybe I'll be more help then."

Michelle and Mark headed north toward the Bay State. It was now late afternoon. Too late for the office, but just right for an early Italian dinner in the famous Federal Hill section of Providence. Some of the best food in the Northeast.

As they sat down with some fresh Italian bread and olive oil dip, Mark asked, "How're you feeling now? You were a little touch and go for a while there."

"I know, I know. I'm perfectly fine now, but I was so embarrassed until everyone said nice things to ease my shame."

"So tell me some of your thoughts about today's fire and fire investigation in general."

Michelle had a lot on her mind. She couldn't shake her feeling of sorrow for the woman, a reminder of the fragile nature of life itself. "First, what an awful, absolutely disgusting business this is sometimes. I mean with charred, burned bodies. It's bad enough to think about the horrible way some of these people die if they're awake and conscious, but it's also dreadful for the investigators to see and deal with such a sight. How do you deal with it, especially when you've seen nearly a hundred bodies at some of your scenes? Don't they haunt you in your nightmares?"

"Well, that's a good question. Yes, I think about these people in their last moments of life. Also, just imagining the psyche of the perpetrator can take an emotional toll. At least now, there are support groups and counseling when someone needs it. A few years ago, that was nonexistent. Sometimes a fire becomes a funeral pyre. Sometimes you have to joke to clear up the smoke.

Seriously, though, the one fire that hits me the most was when several firefighters died in a warehouse fire. Like this one time when I was speaking to a large group in Wisconsin, I was walking down the center aisle surrounded by the class of police and fire investigators. As I got to one point in my talk about the aftermath of that fire, I choked up with tears filling my eyes. I had to stop talking as I turned back toward the podium at the front of the room so I could compose myself. I don't recall any dreams about fatal fires, but sometimes I'll have a dream where I'm working on a fire.

It can be a dreadful business, but if somebody has to investigate the cause of the fire, whether to seek justice, or to prevent a future accidental fire, then I am confident that I can carry out the investigation correctly, considering my education, experience, and training. I will do the investigation right. Every person deserves the best investigation possible. I will always give it my best, even though I may not always be right about what happened."

After contemplating what her mentor just said, Michelle replied, "You sound very noble. I like the way you think." She was beginning to admire and appreciate this guy even more. "So, do you believe that woman suffered today?"

"No, because when you examine her and the bed, the totality of the evidence suggests she remained motionless throughout the fire. The sheet and mattress, as well as what remains of her nightgown were all intact directly under her body. There also appeared to be no movement of her arms or legs except what constriction of the muscles normally occurs because of the extreme heat. She most likely slept through it because of the pills she was taking for the pain from her cancer. And the smoke and toxic gases probably got to her even before the heat and fire."

Michelle said, "Are there always useful evidence patterns like the points you just made?"

"No, no, not at every fire because of the heavier destruction in certain fires where there is collapse of the ceilings, multiple floors and the roof. And there are total burns where nearly everything consists of charcoal pieces lying in the basement."

"So, what's your opinion on trying to locate the son she might have had?"

"That's a good point," answered Mark. "It's possible someone will come to claim her body, or maybe he'll show up at her funeral. But, if we're calling it an accidental fire, then essentially the case is closed."

When a heaping platter of house-made pasta in red sauce with a side of meatballs and sausages arrived at the table, their talk turned away from the gruesome to banter about them becoming a twosome. "Well, Miss Michelle, would you still like to work with me?"

"Seriously, are you joking? I love working with you. Besides explaining every detail to me, it's obvious how much passion you have for what you do. And considering the tough job, you still have great compassion for people, whether dead or alive. I would be proud to be your partner someday."

"And do you still want to work fires? I want you to realize that we only work a fatal fire a couple times a year where the body is still there. Another thing to keep in mind, today's weather was near perfect in which to work. My coldest fire so far was in Vermont where it stayed about 18° all day. And my hottest and most uncomfortable fire was a humid 95° when I had to collect neon lighting components from the attic of a building. The soot and ash stuck to my sweaty arms making me as black as coal. Let me tell you, the stuff that came out of my nose was pretty gross. I had to ask myself why I was doing this work. But I'm still here today. So, what do you think?"

"It sounds pretty nasty but I'll toughen up. I think I'll grow used to working the fatal fires. And from the little experience I have plus listening to all you veteran agents, I realize there are going to be plenty of long, hard and dirty days.

Since I was a kid, I have been fascinated by mysteries. I used to read every book I could get my hands on trying to solve the case before the ending was revealed. It's similar to your liking to solve the puzzle that investigations present to you. I feel that fire investigations will be great mysteries for me to solve. But I could tell today that I'll have to read everything I can about fires and take as many courses as possible to become a respected fire investigator."

"You have the right attitude. But there's another super important thing I want you to always keep in mind when you're at a fire scene, especially a fatal one, that you'll never learn from a book. You should not be standing outside the building while laughing and joking with other investigators. If they want to do it, let them. You just turn around, walk away, separate yourself from any antics. You need to have respect for people's loss. You never know when the press is recording you or when an owner or family member is watching what you do."

"I'm looking forward to facing adversity, overcoming it and succeeding. There will be plenty of rewards along the way. You're one of those rewards."

Michelle's smile validated her statement. Her hazel eyes glistened with adoration as her fingers gently pushed her hair behind one ear. With her other hand she nervously fidgeted with a charm at the base point of a silver chain necklace nestled just above the slight cleavage now showing above her tight knit turquoise top she had worn under her BDUs.

"Oh, really? I'm glad you think so. Not only do I think you're cute, and even gorgeous, I know how intelligent and inquisitive you are, which really attracts me. Oh, wow, look at the time, it's getting dark out already. Let's get going."

Outside, they walked around the corner to the darkened parking lot with their hips, arms and hands playfully rubbing. Mark opened the passenger front door to the government Chevy sedan. As Michelle moved toward the door, she pulled Mark into her. The two leaned into each other, kissing lips, ears, necks fervently. They couldn't get enough of each other. Breathless, they fell across the front bench seat, Mark on top, their clothed bodies intertwined.

It was nearly midnight when Mark dropped Michelle at her place. The two had stepped over an invisible line. Their entanglement was to be tested at every turn.

✳   ✳   ✳   ✳   ✳

As Brantley laid in his hotel bed the night after he murdered his step-mother, he tossed and turned, but not because of any remorse over burning her. Something else was tormenting him. Why do I feel this noose around my neck, tightening? I don't like this feeling. Maybe once I get an apartment and get myself squared away, this unusual pain will disappear. When I start this new phase of my life, I'll be fine. It's the women who I toast and my rising star brother, Mark, who will be in pain from now on.

CHAPTER SIX

After setting the second deadly, murderous fire of his life, Brantley now knew what path his life had to take. Determined and resolute, he went to the South Boston branch of the Boston Public Library on East Broadway. Approaching the librarian, he asked her to research what was available in the way of fire investigation books, concealing his dark intentions.

The woman at the desk was extremely helpful. "Wow," she said, "It looks like you're going to learn a lot from these. Are you a firefighter? You look familiar. Have I seen you on TV?"

"No, and no, I don't think so, but I would like to become the best at investigations someday." She unearthed a trove of fire investigation literature that Brantley ordered including one that apparently was quite popular, *Kirk's Fire Investigation*. There was another called the *Physical and Technical Aspects of Fire and Arson Investigation* plus a few others dealing with the science of fire, arson detection, fire-related deaths and even information on serial arsonists. Brantley was excited. He even felt a little giddy as he thought how this woman blindly, but eagerly assisted his plan. Beneath his façade of interest in a noble pursuit lay a twisted desire to master the art of avoiding detection while setting fires. These books were more than guides, they were the stepping stones by which he would sculpt his legacy of burning retribution.

"You know, while I'm at it, can you recommend any more books specifically dealing with serial arsonists and murderers? The two crimes often go together," Brantley stated.

"As a matter of fact, I absolutely love the macabre myself. There's something about the gruesome stories that give me a chill up my spine. The sinister for the spinster, I guess," she laughed.

"Yeah, I know what you mean. Maybe I'll be able to tell you one of those stories someday," replied Brantley. In his warped view, he sensed a kinship with the librarian as they shared an appreciation for grim human depravity. For sure, he thought, there was a huge difference in their point of view. She read about it, he lived it.

"Here's a good list of serial murder books, but most of them are fiction. But as is often said, 'Life imitates art, while others believe art imitates life.' Good luck with your endeavors."

He wondered why everyone wasn't as nice and helpful as the librarian was. After walking through the stacks, finding several of the books on his list, he took a seat to scan through them. Reading about serial murders jolted an old remembrance, one he hadn't thought about since one night years ago.

In his late teens, one summer, Brantley had a janitorial job in an old factory building converted to offices. He worked from five in the evening until nine. After leaving work one night, while waiting at a red light right outside of the building's parking lot, he looked toward the four-story building. The lights were on in several offices where he saw workers huddled over their desks near the windows.

I could take a couple of those worker ants out with a rifle from right over there by those bushes. They would never know what hit them. Just random killings. There would be no way for anyone to connect me to the murders. Kind of cool, but what fun would that be with innocent victims? I will be targeting my quarries because they must be punished for their ugly deeds. I guess I've been a psychopath for a while now, but I'm not so bad because I only kill for a reason.

With that thought behind him, he packed up his stash of books and checked them out, then headed for the main door to leave the library. He was feeling good about his plan.

He pushed open the first door to the vestibule, holding it open for a woman he noticed following behind him. She didn't say a word as she walked past him. He then stepped forward to push the exterior door open for the woman.

Instead of saying thank you, the woman assailed Brantley, "What the hell, buddy, don't you think I can open my own doors?"

"I hold doors for all people, whoever they are. What the…?" She cut him off at the knees. Brantley's good mood instantly evaporated.

"You're just a chauvinistic pig, like most men!" The volume of her voice rose with each sentence. "Do you think you would score points by getting the door for me? I'm quite capable of doing anything you can do loser. Now, get out of my sight before I kick you in the balls, if you have any! You're just a pitiful bastard."

Brantley was baffled. Why can't everybody be nicer? But not her. Just looking at her, he could have judged she was a tough bitch. Her exterior persona portrayed a heavy Goth person, wearing a black t-shirt, with both a black jacket and jeans, and heavy black boots. She also had super black hair, lipstick, and fingernails. Her eyebrows, nose and lower lip had piercings that repulsed him. He barely had a chance to judge her by her looks when she confirmed she was one ugly person inside as well as outside.

Her venomous assault on his character ignited a primal fury within him. The heat began welling up his backside again. That burning feeling told Brantley what he must do to relieve the pain. She would pay for her insolence by experiencing that same scorching burn he was feeling.

He jumped into his 1971 fiery red Dodge Challenger and tore out of the parking lot to catch up to his target. After I find out where she lives, I'll take my time setting up for her. I'll read through these books so I can do her right without getting caught in the process. She'll regret the day she yelled at me for no good reason. The stinging to his backside grew more intense as he thought about her nasty, screaming voice spewing through those foul black lips. *She'll give my dear brother something to ponder. I'll make sure of it!*

Brantley discreetly followed the woman to East Fourth Street in Southie where she parked her beat-up, filthy, never-washed black compact in the one open spot. She got out of her car and plodded to the front door of a small gray two-story single-family home. Even though it was dark gray outside with heavy threatening clouds, there were no lights on inside the place until after she unlocked the door and went inside. One light flicked on immediately after she entered, possibly the living room. Then, he saw a second floor light illuminate, probably her bedroom. Her silhouette was visible through gauzy curtains. Her arms lifted as she took off her top. Brantley drove away, not wanting to see more of her, nauseated by the thought.

I'll check her place out again after I prepare for her demise. She is useless to society. Does she bring happiness to anybody's life or does she just suck the life from everybody? Nobody will miss this piece of crap.

✳   ✳   ✳   ✳   ✳

In the quiet solitude during his research, Brantley delved into his stash of fire investigation books, absorbing the nuances of what investigators look for at fire scenes and how they determine whether the fires ignited accidentally or were intentionally set. He also learned that gasoline was probably the liquid most often used to rapidly spread or accelerate a fire, but it was also the easiest accelerant to detect by investigators. Not that Brantley cared whether investigators determined that his future fires were intentionally set. He just wanted them to be bewildered by the puzzle he presented to them; who set the fire and what was the motive for the fire.

After he read about the different motives, including setting fires to get the insurance money, fires to conceal other crimes like murder or theft, he self-analyzed where his fire setting fit in. Brantley quickly realized the motivation for setting his fires was revenge for the culmination of years of neglect and abuse, more specifically, for the hurt and misery his mother and "stepmother" inflicted on him his entire life. Then an epiphany hit him. His upcoming actions were also a twisted version of sibling rivalry taken to its darkest extreme, maybe even on the order of the Cain and Abel saga played out in the flickering flames.

Brantley was smart enough to realize he was jealous of his brother, even hated him, because his new found brother had the chance to grow up with his mother, plus Mark appeared to be successful in his life whereas he wallowed in his self-pity. But that was okay with him, because instead of pulling himself up to be an upstanding citizen, he was not only going to become an arsonist to challenge his fire investigator brother, he was also going to rid the world of some nasty women, some who were child abusers.

Wow, they will have one hell of a time figuring out my motive for setting these fires. And, good luck, Mark, trying to pin them on me!

✳   ✳   ✳   ✳   ✳

Through his dedicated investigative work over the next couple weeks, Brantley confirmed the library bitch did live alone, making her an easy target. This was going to differ vastly from his two previous fires. He knew he would have to subdue her.

When the evening came for Brantley to strike, he parked down the street from his target's house. After exiting his car, he secreted himself between two dense fir trees next to the road directly across from her front door, mostly obscured in the waning daylight from anyone's prying eyes. There, he only waited for an hour before she pulled into her parking spot.

With his baseball cap pulled down tight and his hoodie pulled up, Brantley readied his "go" bag. It was filled with a variety of goodies—a pair of Playtex rubber gloves, a soda bottle filled with isopropyl alcohol, a cigarette lighter and matches, rope and cloth strips cut into 3-foot lengths, and plastic zip ties.

From Connecticut, he had purchased a container of pepper spray to make it difficult to trace the sale. Lastly, he picked up the latest copies of The Boston Globe and the Boston Herald. Brantley wanted to be fair to both of the city's two major newspapers. He knew from his first fire experience of that college girl a couple years ago how well crumpled newspaper helped to start and spread a fire, and both papers would burn equally well.

As the woman stepped from her car, Brantley made his initial approach, silently crossing the otherwise deserted street in his soft-soled shoes. She reached her front door but struggled to put her key into the door lock because her thick body cast a shadow, blocking the only light from a nearby dim streetlamp. Brantley was now next to her car.

"Excuse me, lady, this slipped out of your car," he called out as he lifted an envelope that he had placed on the ground. She instantly jerked and whirled around in fright. "Oh, I didn't mean to scare you. Here you go," he said as he raised his left hand to give the envelope to her.

Suddenly, Brantley, with his right hand pulled the pepper spray out of his hoodie pocket. Before the woman could comprehend and react, he pulled up a navy blue and white kerchief to cover much of his face while giving her a shot of the irritant directly into her face. Now, her response was predictably instantaneous. Her eyes closed in pain while her hands went to her face. She gasped and as she opened her mouth to scream, Brantley covered her mouth with a small towel from his pocket, stifling any shriek that could alert neighbors. He then used his body to push her through the open doorway.

"Get up the stairs," he commanded, as he shut the door, struggling to haul her up the straight stairway across from the doorway as she continued to writhe in pain.

The woman began to snivel, whimpering to him, "What do you want? Please don't rape me. You can take anything you want."

Now Brantley tossed her face-up across her unmade bed on the second floor. His only goal was to manipulate, dominate and exterminate her to his satisfaction. "I wouldn't rape you if you were the last woman alive. You're a nasty skank. And your attitude toward people is even nastier. You're not even worthy to breathe the air. So, with your last breaths, maybe you'll think about where you went wrong in life."

The bed had solid wood posts in all four corners. As Brantley grabbed her right wrist to zip-tie it to the post, the woman finally tried to fight him, kicking and thrashing. Another squirt of pepper spray put a quick end to her feeble efforts. Quickly and efficiently, Brantley secured her right leg, then he moved to the opposite side of the bed to complete her ensnarement. He then tied a double thickness of cloth strips around her mouth to stifle any of her attempts to scream.

Brantley looked down at the woman. His scrunched-up scowl expressed nothing but vile contempt for her. Remorse for this piece of crap of a woman was not in his vocabulary. He considered her only as a contemptible object.

She managed to finally open her eyes for a moment. They only revealed terror as she looked into her tormentor's eyes.

"You really should have been nicer to people. But that's one life lesson that you'll never get to practice, bitch." She thrashed against her restraints to no avail.

He wasted no time assembling his fire set, crumpling newspapers from his bag all over, on and around the bed as his quarry continued to squirm and cry. She really couldn't see what was going on as her eyes were still burning and painful. Next, he sprinkled the alcohol around the papers, her bed, and even some on her black clothing.

Upon smelling the alcohol, multiple muffled cries escaped her mouth, "No, no, no." Perhaps she realized what was about to happen.

Finally, Brantley wrapped several pages of the newspaper into a 12-foot length trailer that he learned from the literature could lead the fire from one point to another. It tracked from the bedroom door to a pile of crumpled papers against the bed skirt and sheets hanging off the foot of the bed. He flicked his lighter, touching the flame to the end of the trailer. A controlled fire with flames only inches high crept along yesterday's news. Satisfied that this would work, he fled down the stairs and out the door.

"*Adios, bitch. May you continue to burn in hell! Another one who would never have changed.*"

As he drove slowly past the building, Brantley saw the second floor room alight. Dancing flames became readily visible as they bobbed and weaved with the abundance of air being devoured by the vigorously growing blaze. He drove away with a smug satisfaction, vowing to continue with his burning quest of vengeance.

Brantley glanced at his rear view mirror. *Is somebody following me? Is somebody after me? It can't be. I was so careful.* His nervousness intensified into paranoia. *Who's after me?*

CHAPTER SEVEN

Boston Fire Lieutenant Mike O'Brien from the Fire Investigation Unit headed to the South Boston fire scene. He was alone for the time being as his partner, Lt. Dick Scherner, and others from the unit were scattered across Boston, tackling the onslaught of fires that plagued the city. O'Brien knew this was going to be a tough fire because he had been told there was a female fatality.

Upon arrival, Lt. O'Brien spoke with the Chief in charge of the incident. "Good morning, Chief. What can you tell me?"

"Hi, Mike. Oh, it's morning already?" responded the weary Chief. Checking his watch, he noted it was well after midnight. "This fire came in about 10 P.M. As you can see from the charring around those second floor bedroom windows, the fire was concentrated there." He pointed toward the front left corner where there were two vacant window openings and a third, windowless opening on the side elevation. Each opening showed a similar burn pattern of heavy charring of the wood clapboard siding. The pattern extended from the base of the opening fanning upward and outward, roughly in a V-pattern to the roofline. O'Brien noticed the blaze had not vented from any other window on either the first or second floor.

"It looks like the body of a woman on the bed in that room. She and the bed are burned badly. The room went to flashover and full involvement before we got there. My team took a hose line through the front door up the stairs. The front door was unlocked, by the way. We also hit the fire through those window openings. Everything else in the house looked normal, but the bedroom and the body position seem fishy to me."

"How so, Chief?"

"I'll let you see for yourself, Lieutenant, rather than taint your opinion."

O'Brien made his way around the building, making observations and taking photos along the way. Once inside the building, he readily saw minimal damage on the first floor. But as he walked up the stairs to the second floor the heat, smoke and burn patterns increased. The patterns led him to the bedroom where the deceased was still on the bed.

Lt. O'Brien felt uncomfortable when he saw the heavily charred remains of a woman, contorted by the flames, spread out on the bed, which was now not much more than springs with a little material under her body. It was grim, a stark reminder of the unforgiving nature of fire. He instantly decided to call for another pair of eyes to examine this scene.

He radioed Fire Alarm to call ATF Special Agent Mark Miller, giving them the phone number from his personal notebook. The Lieutenant knew full well the repercussions calling ATF would have with his partner. But O'Brien also knew he needed someone else to help him with this fatal scene and Miller was a guy he could count on to give him an experienced assist. Fire Alarm got back to him within minutes reporting that Miller would be on scene within thirty minutes.

O'Brien grabbed a cup of hot coffee from the assisting canteen truck. Then he made his way back up the stairs to shoot several rolls of film documenting the scene before it was disturbed any further. He knew something wasn't right about this fire, but he couldn't piece the puzzle parts together by himself.

As promised, Miller showed up thirty minutes later. When he walked up to the bedroom where O'Brien was still pondering the fire, Miller said, "Hi, Mike. Thanks for the invite."

Mike replied, "Damn, Mark, you look like hell. Some action last night?"

"Oh, I was busy, out late. Then, tossing and turning until your guys called. So, less than a couple hours' sleep." Changing the subject quickly, Mark remarked, "Jesus, buddy, what a gruesome one you have this time. Let me take a moment to consider her life and her last minutes." The unique stench of overcooked human remains overwhelmed his sense of smell. Mark believed this distinct and disgusting odor would continue to reek within his mind for a long time. And the repulsive sight of this former living, breathing human being will always stick in his mind's eye. He knew he could never unsee the scene that confronted him. But something else bothered him. The scene held a certain attraction to him. He felt connected to the fire in a puzzling, unknown way.

Just then, the Medical Examiner (ME) arrived in the room snapping Mark back to the job at hand. "Hi, guys. Let's not touch anything until I get a good look around."

Lt. O'Brien greeted the ME, "Hi, Doc. A grisly one this time. This is ATF Special Agent Mark Miller, one of their new Certified Fire Investigators. Since my partner wasn't available, I called Mark to assist me with this scene."

Dr. Denise Williams said, "Nice to meet you, Miller." Then she turned her attention to the deceased. "Well done, I'd say, crispy. A rather unusual position for a fire victim. She is completely splayed out, spread eagle. Normally, people end up somewhat in the fetal position with arms in particular in a pugilistic pose, fighter's position, as the muscles contract in the fire."

Miller stood for a few minutes, arms crossed, looking at the room from different angles. He loved the multi-dimensional puzzle that laid before him. "Do you mind if I look at her closer, Doc?"

"Sure, just don't disturb the body."

Edging toward the head of the bed, Miller bent over the outstretched deeply charred right arm and nub of what remained of her hand. His eyes peered at the exposed forearm muscles and bone, but something strange caught his gaze. He moved to her right ankle area to examine it more closely. Then he repeated his scrutiny of her left ankle and left wrist. "Look here guys. She was bound to the posts of the headboard and footboard with plastic zip ties. See here, under the remains of each limb. See the edges of the plastic up against her wrists and ankles where the exposed plastic burned away, but the plastic under her body parts was protected enough to preserve it?"

Lt. O'Brien took a closer look. "Yeah, you're right. She was trussed up."

The ME concurred, "Looks like we have a murder on our hands. Now, when I get my look at her, I'll be able to tell you whether she was alive at the time of the fire, or not. For her sake, I hope she was already dead or, at least, unconscious."

At that moment, Boston Fire Lt. Dick Scherner walked into the room with Boston Police Detective Artie Taylor. Without hesitation, Scherner squawked, "What the hell is he doing here? This is our fire, Boston Fire jurisdiction." He pointed at Agent Miller while glaring at his partner.

"Hi, to you, too, Dick. I asked him to assist me, knowing we had a fatality and you were busy," Lt. O'Brien responded somewhat defensively, but he stood firm, refusing to let petty grievances stand in the way of justice.

"Hi, LT. Remember, my badge says U.S. on it. I can go anywhere I want especially when I'm invited by an official from Boston Fire. Look, I'm not trying to take anything away from you guys. I just want to help. Let's do the job together and find out who murdered this young lady."

"Murdered? How do you know that already?" snapped Scherner.

The ME, who had stayed out of the brief fray, chimed in. She explained what they had discovered thus far.

Miller interjected when he observed a barely discernible fire pattern. "Guys, look at this. Is this a trail from the doorway to the corner of the bed here?" He followed a burned line on the carpet that was a little deeper than the surface char that covered much of the exposed carpet. It led to the corner of the bed's footboard.

Lt. Scherner was now onboard, forgetting for the moment his professional wariness. "You're right. This line extends from the door to the bed. It would allow a quick getaway for the arsonist. And look here under the edge of her body. Doc, do you have your photos? Can we roll her just a little to check under her body?"

"Sure, Dick, I'm all set. But let's all do it together to try to keep her intact." All four of them donned two sets of protective gloves, then lined up on the same side of the bed. Using all eight hands, the investigators rolled the body remains slightly to expose the material that had been protected by her body during the fire

"No apparent wounds here on her back," advised the ME.

"And look at the remains of crumpled newspaper under her upper thigh and butt," Mark pointed out, "And I can see yesterday's date on the paper. The way its crumpled, you can bet she wasn't reading the paper in bed. It's a protected section of the trailer."

The accelerant detection canine handler, Bob Awrey, stuck his head in the doorway, "Hi, guys, could you all clear out while I run my dog? It will give me room to work and fewer distractions for Mattie.

"Dick," said the ME, "Let's stop here a few minutes so we can get some more photos and collect these newspapers. Maybe we can get them checked for fingerprints and possibly for DNA analysis."

"Good idea. Mike, can you and Mark grab some cans and bags so we can save these items? I'll watch Bob work the scene." The two men and the ME stepped outside. "So how's it going, Bob?"

"I've been straight out busy. Between formal training, and daily training with Mattie, I've been called to fires all over New England since I've got the only accelerant sniffing dog around these parts. She's a great worker, alerting at quite a few scenes. And she's a good companion."

Bob turned his attention to work with Mattie. Since the apartment was so small, their job was done within minutes with no alerts. "Nothing here on our part, Dick. I checked that area of the line pattern on the floor, plus around the bed and the body. I'm out of here. See you next time."

All of the other investigators returned to the room of origin. In a moment of levity, Mark quipped, "Now, back to the dead. I wonder if she had ever wed. It looks like she lived alone. Lying here burned to the bone."

"Oh, brother," Dick turned to his partner, "Where'd you dig this guy up? Poetry school? Let's carefully collect all the evidence we can find and help get her remains down to the ME's van so we can try to figure out what the hell happened here."

✳   ✳   ✳   ✳   ✳

The newly formed fire investigation team worked well together despite Lt. Scherner's dislikes and suspicions toward ATF and especially Special Agent Mark Miller. They divided up assignments. Scherner and Taylor conducted interviews of the deceased woman's family and friends while O'Brien and Miller canvassed the neighborhood.

Her family could not supply any information about her relationships or where she worked because they had little contact with her. All they could say is that she was a rebel against what they referred to as society, and she disliked men in general.

The neighbors neither heard nor saw anything to help with the investigation. Two of the nearest neighbors said the woman was mostly a loner with only occasional visits from friends.

As they pondered the possible motives behind the senseless tragedy, the investigators were left scratching their heads, wondering who could have harbored such hatred toward the innocent victim to kill her in such a bizarre manner. It was a question that lingered in the air, a chilling reminder of the darkness that lurked in the hearts of men.

CHAPTER EIGHT

The three ATF Agents, friends for years, walked over to Doyles for an early evening libation. It had been months since they had a chance to hang out together with no other associates tagging along, providing them with a chance to catch up.

Although dreary, hot, and humid on the hectic city streets, the three amigos were playful like kids just let out for recess. Wojo asked, "Hey, Barney, how come you're not with your girl tonight?"

"Hey, boys' night out for a change. I miss not hanging out with my best buds. Besides, she's meeting some of her old college friends in Cambridge. You know, we do spend some time apart?"

"You could have fooled us," Carlo quipped. "We've seen neither hide nor hair of you ever since that party we had here at Doyles after the big bust." As he spoke, they walked through the door of their preferred watering hole.

Grabbing seats at the end of the worn mahogany brown bar, bartender Frank greeted them with his usual friendly banter, "Well, if it isn't my three favorite Feds. It's been a while since I've seen the three of you together. I guess crime must be down tonight, so you all have the night off. What will it be, boys?"

After looking with questioning eyes to the faces to his left and right, Mark held up three fingers, "Make it three Sam lager pints, Frank, thank you very much. And we'll have a second as soon as you see our glasses getting low and don't be slow."

"You got it. I won't let the well run dry."

"So, Wojo, how's your wife and the kids?" Mark inquired. He hadn't seen or heard much about them since the collapse of his own marriage. It seemed to Mark that his divorce turmoil got in the way of socializing with his friends' families.

"Oh, they're great, Barney. Heather's busy at her antique shop. And the kids are growing like weeds. They keep us straight out with tennis and soccer. We're always running around when work doesn't get in the way."

"That's sounds wonderful, Woj," Mark replied. "Maybe someday I'll get the chance to experience kids. I love watching and interacting with kids so much. My jaw ends up hurting from smiling and laughing when I get a rare opportunity to be around young ones."

"Be careful what you wish for, buddy. As great as they are, and I wouldn't give them up for anything, but I end up worrying about everything with my two growing up in this crazy world."

"And, Carlo," started Mark, "How have you been keeping busy outside the job? Still causing trouble, I presume?"

"Oh, I have a couple sexy things I'm trying to juggle, if that's what you're asking. One's got brains and beauty. The other is just drop-dead gorgeous, but lacking upstairs. I'll probably move on from her. I need a little something to challenge me," Carlo then flipped it over to question Mark.

"So, you've been working with Boston Fire on a new arson murder? How's that going?"

"Challenging in more ways than one. One guy, I think you met him, Dick Scherner, well, he can be a regular dickhead. Ever since that press conference screw-up, he's been giving me crap. Nothing I can't handle. I just dish it back out to him in my usual gentle way."

"Yeah, yeah," interjected Wojo, "I've been on the receiving end of 'your usual gentle way.' You tend to diffuse the situation by going to your rhyme time, you goof ball."

"Well, it works most of the time, you slime." They all chuckled. "Back to the fire. The scene was not that tough to figure out with a newspaper trailer and probably a liquid accelerant was used. But whoever did this is messed up. Most likely a guy must have been really pissed off at this woman. We don't even believe she had a man in her life, so it could be anyone. She was trussed out to the four corners of the bed. Worse yet, she was alive when the bastard set the fire."

"Whoa, what a way to go, that's one sick mother. If there is one thing I know, when you call a fire an arson, I believe you because you're so good at your job. Did you get a chance to check for similar fires, or a list of arsonist murderers? Any leads at all? Wojo asked. Carlo shook his head in agreement.

"None. No leads, right now it's a dead-end. And, by the way, thanks for the compliment. The Boston guys and I did a preliminary search but found nothing yet. But just because we didn't find someone with a matching criminal record, it may only mean this offender hasn't been caught. So, how about you guys, what are you working on? Did I hear something about an arson-for-profit fire in Cambridge?"

"Wojo and I are assisting the State Fire Marshal's Office and Cambridge FD with a restaurant fire. It looks like the owner set it up elaborately to burn it down completely, but a passerby noticed it before it got out of hand and the firefighters made quick work of the fire. We're getting great info on his motive. We'll be seeking an indictment soon.

Hey, did I hear about Internal Affairs coming up to interview you. What's that all about, Barney?"

"Yeah, Jack called me into his office to give me a heads-up. You know that female informant I have? That dancer, Monique, who used to work in the Combat Zone?"

"You mean that super sexy stripper we caught a couple years back?" Carlo whistled. "She was so hot, she could bring a dead man back to life. So, what's going on with her?"

"If you remember, she gave me great information that helped lead to the arrest of one of the arsonists, the cop that was dating her. Well, apparently, she called ATF saying that I was screwing her and coerced her to testify about something that allegedly never happened."

"Really, Mark, that sounds bad," said Tom, his leg nervously shaking. "You know that IA will rip you on that with the slightest whiff of impropriety. Did you ever have sex with her?"

"Never, not once, not even close. Having sex with an informant is a line even I wouldn't cross, I don't care how sexy she is. There are enough other women in the world. And I think that's what caused her to lie. She wanted to fuck me. She was coming on real strong, but when I blew her off, she wanted a thousand bucks from me. I told her to get lost. A couple weeks later she called the office."

"You know, it's just like IA to take her word against yours. They're always trying to put us in the trick bag. They will screw with us every chance they get," added Dennis. "So, what are you going to do?"

"We might not like what they do, it's just their job, Carlo. They have to investigate every allegation, no matter how bogus, to keep us civil servants in line the best they can. I'm not too happy about having them investigate me again. As a matter of fact, I'm shitting my pants a little. I could get fired over this or at least tarnish my reputation. Right now, it's my word against hers. It could be a problem, but I have some ideas how to handle it."

Tom said, "I remember when IA investigated you after one of your recorded interviews of an informant was on one of those national news programs. How did that end up, anyway?"

"They really had a weak argument on that one, so it died a quick death. That was the one where a local cop and I had our first interview with Diane, another female witness. We recorded her for four hours, asking about so many different crimes she was aware of. On TV, they only aired one question where she admitted lying to us about a bank robbery. That show was so skewed to make it look like paid informants were all liars, not to be trusted. Later, during our interview, she admitted she lied about that because she didn't know us enough to trust us, but everything else she told us was the truth. Those TV bastards didn't care about any of that.

And why would I release the recording? Those IA guys were so dumb. We gave the recording to the Assistant U.S. Attorney who had to hand it over to the defense. So, who do you think would want to make the witness appear to be lying?"

"As we were told as rookies," said Dennis, "When you're out there on the street doing the job, you'll most likely be investigated by IA at least once in your career."

"This is already the second go around for me. When are you guys going to do the job so you get investigated, too?" Mark liked to bust his friends' balls.

"Screw you, buddy," added Tom.

"Oh, no, not you too! I'm already getting screwed in more ways than one. So, listen, this is what I'm going to suggest to IA we do, and if they refuse, maybe I can get Jack to go along with my plan."

CHAPTER NINE

Brantley ventured out on a warm late spring afternoon to one of South Boston's staple food stops, Sullivan's at Castle Island. Since opening in 1951, Sullivans has been enjoyed by generations of Bostonians and visitors alike. Set on the grounds of an 1850s granite fort, it is a unique location on the edge of Boston Harbor. The food was always quite tasty and affordable with a family-friendly low-key vibe.

Brantley, as usual, was alone. As he approached the counter, a young redheaded woman, who looked shapely in her black skirt and white blouse buttoned tightly up to her deep cleavage cheerily greeted him. He ordered a raspberry lime rickey, a pint of white clam chowder in a red and white cardboard container and a fried fish sandwich where the fish overflowed the bun.

Expecting nobody else to dine with him, he chose a secluded spot on a green painted park bench under a leafy tree closest to the salty bay. He left the permanent tables for families or parties of more than one.

Brantley relished his solitude after a brutal workday. Earlier that day he had stopped by his dreaded Roslindale office to account for his monthly sales. Just thinking about it nearly wrecked his appetite. I despise selling medical supplies, or anything else; it makes me so uncomfortable. My personality will never be conducive to making a successful salesperson. I hate the job so much but it allows me to wander the city rather than be tied down to an office. That would have suffocated me. Luckily, my salary plus an occasional sales commission provides sufficient income for me to pay my bills.

A handful of salespeople were in the office. Except for a nod or a simple greeting, they all avoided Brantley as if he had the plague. In one sense that bothered him, but he really didn't care to fraternize with them either. He simply trudged to a corner desk to complete his task and get the hell out of there before his boss accosted him.

He loathed her, too. Ariel Garcia detested Brantley in return. Fortunately for him, she was busy with another employee in her office. In short order, he completed his monthly paperwork quickly and made his way toward the exit just as swiftly.

"Oh, Brantley," Ariel called out with a sing-song tone. "Leaving so soon without saying hello? Another lousy month I see." He waved his hand, gesturing goodbye without looking back. The last thing he heard her holler as he hurried through the door, "Keep it up. You'll be walking right out of a job real soon."

That was only his morning. Then, Brantley suffered through three sales calls downtown where so many doctors congregate in offices around numerous world-class hospitals. The new month started off similar to the Boston Red Sox at bat—one, two, three strikes, you're out.

He was almost through savoring his meal when a nasty, one-sided ruckus broke out to interrupt his peace and quiet. Brantley saw a boy of about five at a nearby table, tears threatening to spill from his eyes. His frightened but yet obstinate and stubborn countenance betrayed his struggle. His left cheek puffed out, presumably from a sizable wad of food stored there.

A large, round woman with gobs of make-up smeared on her face and way-too much jet-black hair hanging to her shoulders berated the kid mercilessly. "Now, you're going to sit there until you swallow that food and eat the rest. You never appreciate that I take you out for a good meal," she shrilled. Her pancaked face was screwed up into the most vile look she could possibly make. "I'm glad you're not my kid, you little bastard. Does your mother let you get away with this? Now eat. And swallow that food in your mouth!"

The woman wouldn't shut up. On and on she rebuked the little guy as he began to sob, withering in his chair. "Oh, don't you dare start crying or I'll give you something to cry about!" Her right arm went up about head high with her hand cocked and ready to strike. One of the kid's legs swung rapidly back and forth under his stiff metal chair. But he didn't look like he was going to give in.

* * * * *

Brantley's heart twisted with empathy as he witnessed this scene unfold. His seething anger at the injustice of it all ignited a fiery rage within him. The woman's harsh words echoed in the deepest recesses of his mind, triggering his earliest memories of his life, one dominated with pain and suffering. He couldn't bear to witness the same cruelty inflicted upon another innocent child.

When he was about the same age as that little boy, he and his "mother" lived in one of the two-story brick projects in Albany, New York, their first home after his father abandoned them. In his mind's eye, Brantley relived sitting on the ugly drab brown twelve-inch square tile floor laid over concrete. The floor was so cold, he trembled. He cowered against a bare wall next to his wood toy box, the kind with a hinged top embossed with a cowboy scene. There, he stared at the shrieking monster who kept screaming at him, trying to make him do things he did not want to do. His mouth, like the little boy before him, was chock full of food, stuffed into his cheeks like a chipmunk during a feast. Except this was no celebration. It was a dinner, or a lunch or breakfast he didn't want to eat.

"You sit there until you swallow all that food, you little bastard. And then you can get back in your chair to finish the rest of that food in that dish. Are you going to do that, or are you going to sit there all night?" His mother screamed at him a lot.

The cold floor nipped at my butt. Scared, but the more she yelled, the more adamant I became. I don't care if I sit here forever. I'm not going to give in. I don't like it, and I'm not going to eat it. Brantley withdrew into himself. He hated her for this. Seething, he clenched his fists close to his sides so she couldn't see. *What a witch, that's what she was!*

*   *   *   *   *

That's what this woman was too, a no-good witch. She scolded this helpless child so ruthlessly. Did she not realize how this might affect him for the rest of his life? Brantley easily imagined the emotional toll on the boy's psyche, breaking down his self-esteem possibly forever. He continued to stare at the drama.

"What are you looking at, buddy? Mind your own freakin' business!" The witch shrieked in his direction as Brantley continued to glare at her transgressions. He could only shake his head in disgust.

Brantley had learned to hate any person fighting, arguing or screaming, especially a woman. His mother screamed incessantly, always yelling, swearing, embarrassing him in front of his friends. *Stop screaming, you bitch.* A shiver traveled up his spine causing the little hairs on the back of his neck to quiver.

But it was more than that. That burning, seething sensation arose within Brantley, bile escaping up his esophagus. Like the acid caught up within his throat, intense red-hot fire consumed him inside and out. Trembling, but with fierce determination as he stood up from the bench, Brantley ignored the witch's menacing presence, instead offering the small boy a warm, encouraging smile that spoke volumes of support and bravery. The tot's eyes expressed an understanding that bolstered his resolve.

Brantley strode quickly to his Challenger, but he didn't leave the premises. He knew what he had to do to soothe his blistering pain while helping this kid move forward with his life devoid of the crushing effects from this so-called adult.

Sitting in his car for a short time, Brantley witnessed the ugly hag drag the boy by one arm from the restaurant to her car, a dented, grimy-looking beige, older compact sedan. He could still hear her haranguing the youngster, "If I said it once, I've told you a thousand times, stop crying or I'll really give you something to cry about." The woman flung the kid into the front passenger seat, before she tore out of the parking lot, annoyingly blasting her car horn as she nearly hit an oncoming car.

The predator discreetly pulled into traffic following two cars behind his quarry. His "go" bag sat in the passenger seat. It was time to teach this bitch a lesson that she won't get a chance to forget. Less than five minutes later, Brantley saw her park in front of a neatly kept small Garrison Colonial on West 8th Street, still in Southie. He pulled to the curb about a hundred feet short of the house.

The young boy leaped from the front passenger seat, running as fast as his little legs could carry him to the open front door where a good looking blonde, apparently the boy's mother, greeted him with a smile. Pausing only momentarily, the boy quickly continued into the house, not even looking back as he successfully escaped from that mean woman who had badgered him.

The boy's mother's smile instantly disappeared when Brantley saw the bitch step outside her car while pointing her finger in the mother's direction. Gesturing with contempt, she yelled something about the boy's lack of manners and how he didn't listen to adults. Brantley couldn't make out most of the words, but there was a loud, heated discussion between the two women. Abruptly, the bitch gave the other woman the finger, then she jumped back into her car and squealed into the street westward bound.

Brantley trailed closer to her car, not wanting to lose his quarry at a red light. She drove onto busy Southampton Street, over the Southeast Expressway and coincidentally past Boston Fire Department Headquarters. Unbeknownst to Brantley, the Fire Investigation Unit was housed there. But he laughed anyway and waved as he went by the building. "*Catch me if you can, boys!*"

The cars tracked through Roxbury, zigzagging through city neighborhood streets, avoiding cars, trucks, buses and pedestrians along the hectic streets. Finally, the target turned off Centre Street in the cosmopolitan Jamaica Plain section of the city where she pulled into a tiny parking lot behind an equally cozy Hispanic restaurant. Brantley watched the woman as she walked up an exterior rear wooden stairway that led to what appeared to be a small apartment. He pulled over to park. A blend of the rhythmic, heavy beat of Latin American music and the intense aroma of cumin and garlic from the restaurant drifted through his open car window.

Brantley's stomach rumbled. He realized he could eat again. And a couple Margheritas would ensure he was ready for his nocturnal fiesta. Darkness was over two hours away, so he had time to kill, so to speak.

As Brantley ate three tasty beef fajitas, with the fixings of refried beans and rice, he pondered the bullshit that parents and other adults put their kids through forcing them to eat. He, like many kids, didn't eat sometimes when he didn't feel like it, but parents cause so much mental anguish. And in his case, pain and hatred. After all, how many kids died of malnutrition when food was available to them?

These thoughts only fed his anger against the tormentor who made that kid so miserable, causing him to cry and obviously fear his caretaker. Brantley felt that familiar searing pain spread throughout his body. *Damn, even with my mother and stepmother dead, that pain they caused still tortures me.* He focused on the task at hand, taking care of that piece of rubbish so she could never abuse a kid again, to make him feel so afraid and worthless. *That is the only way to stop my fiery pain.*

Since Brantley was a planner, he already knew every facet of how his scheme would unfold, except for one aspect. What ruse would he use to get inside her door? Moments later, he knew exactly what he would do.

As he strode back to his car, Brantley saw the woman's car still parked where he last saw it. He glared at the woman's upstairs apartment. Her lights were on as dusk had settled in. Through her open blinds, he could see her possibly at the kitchen sink and then move into what looked like her bedroom where the walls were painted a lilac color.

Brantley sat, his thoughts streaming from the woman to his plan, to how the fire would progress, and finally to how his brother and the Boston team might investigate the fatal blaze. He imagined they would figure it all out without too much difficulty. After all, this time he was going to use a little gasoline on her body and bed. From his readings, he knew a safe way to use the volatile liquid and get away before the fire took off. And even though he devised additional changes to his scheme, he wondered if his super sleuth brother would tie this fire to the one he set in Southie. A smile spread from his lips to his cheeks and eyes as he envisioned Agent Miller scratching his head at the fire scenes.

Shortly after 9 o'clock, the restaurant closed. Employees threw trash in a small dumpster behind the restaurant where the woman had parked her car. They then hopped in their own vehicles and left the area. Street pedestrian and vehicular traffic had slowed to a trickle. Brantley noticed the lights turn off within the upstairs apartment. It was time to strike.

First, Brantley donned his kerchief, tying it so it would fit tightly over his nose and mouth, then slipping it down onto his neck. After his previous use of pepper spray on his victim, he added a pair of plastic safety-style glasses that wrapped around to the sides of his eyes. He needed this extra protection so that the irritant was less likely to affect him.

With go-bag in hand, he stepped from his car, softly closed the door, then padded toward her rear exterior stairs. Wearing dark jeans with a black hooded sweatshirt, he was nearly invisible on the dark street. Taking the stairs two at a time to minimize any creaking noises, Brantley perused all around him to see if he was alone and unseen. He took a deep breath to calm himself, slowing his heartbeat. He covered his nose and mouth with his kerchief before placing the glasses over his eyes. After he slipped on his pair of latex gloves, he loosened the light bulb from the exterior fixture next to the door.

All the lights were still off in her apartment. With one mighty swing of his bag, he smashed the glass to the upper half of the storm door. The deafening crash was only momentary, but it seemed even louder during the stillness of the night. Brantley checked his surroundings again for any neighbors alerted by the noise. He noticed nothing but the bedroom light coming back on and an utterance from within the room, "What the…?"

Brantley flattened himself against the outside wall next to the door. Holding the pepper spray canister at the ready, he waited for the woman to open the door. As soon as she did, Brantley sprung toward her spraying a substantial dose of the aerosol directly into her face through the upper storm door now void of its glass. She howled only for a moment until he roughly grabbed her head with one hand and shoved one of his cloth strips into her gaping mouth.

Rushing her back into the room while shutting the door, he knew he had the upper hand already. She was so shocked by his sudden attack that she couldn't muster any defense. However, Brantley was surprised when a light coffee-colored, scruffy haired terrier yapped at him from several feet away. Thinking quickly, he looked on the kitchen counter where he found a box of dog biscuits. He grabbed a handful of treats, opened the exterior door and enticed the dog to the outside landing where the woman's pet relished the unexpected crispy delights. The arsonist put several more biscuits in his pocket for later use.

Not wasting any more time to maintain control of his prey, he shoved her into her bedroom where he thrust her face down onto the bed and tightly tied a cloth strip around her face covering the cloth he had already stuffed in her foul mouth. He gave her a second shot of spray to keep her writhing in pain so he could get to work securing her.

Luckily, she had one of those brass bed frames that would facilitate his efforts. For this fire, Brantley grabbed a handful of cloth strips from his bag to restrain the woman to her bed. As he tied her first wrist to the headboard, the woman started flailing while she cried. One quick, hard punch to her jaw put a stop to her fighting the inevitable. Her eyes were still scrunched and watering from the pepper spray, so she couldn't make out her assailant's details. She started sobbing uncontrollably.

Brantley was efficient with his knots, getting one wrist, two ankles and the final wrist secured before she could thrash beyond his control again. Sweat dripped from his face. Between the adrenaline rush and the exertion of tying her up, he realized he was exhausted with perspiration under his sweatshirt. He stood back for a moment looking upon his work with satisfaction, while at the same time feeling revulsion toward his victim.

He relived the woman's crude behavior toward the little boy hours earlier. The thoughts made him livid as the burning pain inched up his backside again. *Why were you so mean to me? Always forcing me to eat, screaming at me and hitting me just because I didn't want to eat. Why didn't you love me?*

"Lady, do you know why I'm here?" She could only shake her head rapidly back and forth in terror. "Remember that little boy you took out to dinner earlier today? What is he, your nephew?" She nodded up and down, shivering and sobbing in fear and pain.

"Well, you're a disgusting witch of a woman," Brantley raised his voice to emphasize his point. "That little boy you verbally and physically abused was so scared. He was confused as to why someone would act the way you did. You made him whimper and suffer. For what? Just because he didn't want to eat something? Was he going to starve? Or were you just aggravated because you spent your precious money on him and he wasn't grateful enough to eat the damn food?"

"I see that you live alone. Were you ever married?" Her head shaking affirmed his thoughts. "And no kids of your own, right? That's because you are one nasty, mean bitch who no man in his right mind ever wanted. Now, enough talk. I want you to think about yourself, how cruel and monstrous you must have seemed to that little, defenseless boy. Maybe you'll learn a lesson. A life lesson that you won't have time to put into practice because you'll never change."

With that last remark, Brantley went about his business. From his bag he grabbed several newspapers again, crushing several sheets into little fuel packages that would help turn his initially small fire into a raging inferno. He piled the paper all around her body as she writhed and struggled against her bindings. As in his previous fire, he made an interconnected trail of old news from her bed along the carpeted floor to the outside door.

Next, he took two soda bottles from his bag along with a cigarette and book of matches. For a little ventilation, he opened a window a couple inches. He quickly sprinkled gasoline on the papers all around her, continuing along the entire trailer, splashing some onto the carpet. Smelling the distinct odor of gasoline, the woman grew even more frantic. Now, her eyes were wide open in terror. But her struggle was for naught; there was no escape from the evil about to envelop her.

After checking his work one last time, looking down and shaking his head at the backside of this despicable woman, Brantley stood outside the open exterior door with his bag, striking a match to light the cigarette. Interweaving the cigarette through the matchbook, he left the lit end of the cigarette a fraction of an inch away from the match heads. He then reached inside the door gently placing the simple device under the end of his trail of crumpled newspapers. With his handiwork complete, Brantley called to the woman, "Maybe I'll see you again on the other side, bitch, but I hope not."

He left the wood door slightly ajar, for additional ventilation to feed the gasoline-fed fire that was about to erupt, but he closed the broken storm door so the terrier didn't try to go inside the apartment. After throwing his glasses and gloves into the bag, the arsonist lowered his bandana. With the biscuits from his pocket, Brantley lured the terrier down the stairs to the neighboring yard. After all, he thought, this pet didn't deserve to die for the sins of its owner. He watched for a moment as the little dog intently devoured his dessert before the arsonist quickly, but nonchalantly, headed to his car. Not a person in sight.

While starting his car, he saw the glow of the initial fire. Then, a loud whoomph sound was followed by nearly instantaneous flames throughout the small apartment. As he pulled away from the curb, he heard breaking glass and witnessed fire extending from her bedroom window. Brantley turned onto Centre Street before pulling onto another side street to escape the area, knowing he had completed another job well done. *Another evil creature eliminated, another innocent soul saved from suffering. She never would have changed.*

CHAPTER TEN

The fire grew so rapidly that the second-floor apartment crashed down, collapsing into the first floor kitchen and dining room of the Mexican restaurant before the Boston Fire Department had a chance to put water on the flames. BFD Lieutenants Scherner and O'Brien stood across Centre Street watching as their fellow firefighters continued to wet down the hot charred mass of debris. White steam rose from the remains of the structure, which was now a total loss. The powerful odor of burned wood and other materials hung near street level.

The Incident Commander spotted the two arson investigators, so he walked across the street to fill them in on what he had learned so far. "Hi, guys. A tough one here. It had a big head start on us, which is a little unusual for this neighborhood shortly after nine at night. We already had collapse of the second floor with full involvement when we got here. It could be a lot of things. Maybe the restaurant cooking system caused it. But a witness said the entire second floor apartment suddenly lit up before anything happened on the first floor.

Another possibly more significant situation, though. There's a car parked in the rear parking lot. It's registered to the woman who rents the upstairs apartment. We have to assume she was home, but her remains will be somewhere deep in that steaming rubble. Sorry to say there won't be much left of her now."

"Thanks, Chief," responded Lt. Scherner. "As soon as your guys cool it down, we'll get in there, but we'll have to get an excavator to help us make it safe and methodically tear it apart. I'll make some calls. Mike, could you start with some photos all around the exterior?"

"Sure. Hey, Dick, what do you think about giving Mark Miller a call? That first-floor restaurant business most likely qualifies for him to work the fire. And with the way the witness described the entire fire nearly simultaneously lighting up the second floor, this could be an arson."

"Why the hell do you always want to call him? You know I don't particularly care for him or ATF working on our fires. He's a little too arrogant for me. And I'm still pissed about not being called for that press conference. He and ATF want to take all the credit when arrests are made."

"Well, think of it this way," O'Brien reasoned. You know he'll be an extra pair of hands and eyes, plus with our budget cuts, ATF has the money for the heavy equipment we need to do this job. The Commish will be pleased about not spending money we don't have. Oh, yeah, and remember how he spotted that good evidence when that girl was murdered in our last fatal fire? He's the one who pieced that puzzle together."

"Like a clairvoyant, yeah, I remember. Okay, okay, you make good, valid points. But I don't have to like him or have a beer with him when we're done, right?"

"Sure, Lieutenant, anything you say," smirked O'Brien. "Even if he's buying?"

"Enough, wise guy. Give him a call. I'm sure he'll like a 3 A.M. wake-up call."

✳   ✳   ✳   ✳   ✳

After Mark fumbled for the phone in the pre-dawn hours, he recognized Lt. O'Brien's voice. Mark, soaking wet with sweat, noticed he also had serious heartburn. He was still tired, working as hard in his dreams as he does during his workdays. For some unknown reason, one dream of desperation was worse than usual, but he couldn't recall any of the details.

"Hi, Mike, what's up?" O'Brien filled him in about the fire incident. "Hey, thanks for the call. Is Lt. Scherner out there with you? How does he feel about me coming out?"

"Oh, he griped about it at first. He's just a grumpy old man before his time. I think he got over it fast when I said you would buy the beer."

Mark laughed, "I'll be out there as soon as I call my supervisor. See you in a bit." After hanging up, Mark rolled over. He ran his fingers along the naked curves of Michelle's breast down her side and along her thigh. She was already half asleep, after initially jumping awake when the phone rang. He and she both sighed.

"I'm out of here," Mark whispered in her ear, "Heading to a big fire in J.P. Lock up when you leave. I'll see you when I see you." With that, he jumped out of bed to get dressed.

But Michelle wasn't satisfied with his dismissive tone. "Gee, I expected a little more than 'I'll see you when I see you.' Not even a kiss or anything? What's going on here? Are we a real couple or what?" she asked, more than annoyed.

"Look, you know I care about you. We just have to be cool about things because I'm not so sure how the office would feel about me fooling around with a rookie agent. And I really don't need this right now."

Michelle started crying, "I guess I'm a good lay for you, huh? Just another notch in your belt. You stay out late doing who knows what and have me come over at midnight." She popped up, covering herself with the sheet. "Well, I'm not just going to be your good time fuck any time you feel like it." Now, she grabbed her clothes, and stomped into another room to get dressed.

"Jesus, Michelle. I don't need this crap right now," Mark harshly raised his voice, exposing his aggressive side for the first time in Michelle's presence. "I've already gotten divorced once and had to deal with all that shit. I've got work to do. I don't need to explain to you or tell you about every little thing I do at night. And I don't need any more complications right now!"

"Well, you should have thought about that earlier, you bastard. I'm out of here and I don't know if I'll ever come back! With that, she slammed the door, running out only half dressed, but fully pissed.

Mark looked at himself in the bathroom mirror as he rinsed the sleep away. Shaking his head, all he could think of was what a way to start a day. *It's 3 A.M. and I've already screwed something up. I really don't need this. Another relationship that I can't hold together. My friggin' passive-aggressive behavior reared its ugly head again. Isn't that what that damn therapist called it?*

Mark notified his supervisor, Jack, about the fire call. "Yeah, Mark, definitely head to the fire. It's a good thing that Boston Fire is calling you, and this seems like a fire that's worth you looking at. Hey, but don't forget, you have that meeting with IA today in my office at three this afternoon. Don't be late. They're already headhunters, they don't need another excuse to go after you." With another problem hanging over his head in the wee hours of the morning, he trudged out the door.

✳   ✳   ✳   ✳   ✳

By dawn, the investigators had learned that the potentially missing or deceased woman was 38-year-old, Stephanie Myers. They learned from the landlord that she had rented that second floor apartment for the past five years. She was an okay tenant, but she wasn't the nicest of people said the landlord. She always paid her rent on time, but she was nasty to him and complained about everything. As far as he knew, she was single, lived alone and had no partner, either male or female.

The excavator was already setting up. It wouldn't be long before the fire investigators could get a much better look inside. They all had gotten a view from high above the scene by ascending a ladder truck's 80-foot stick. The initial look suggested the fire originated in the second-floor bedroom area and then collapsed into the restaurant. They caught a glimpse of a brass bed headboard, but not much else could be discerned in the twisted pile of rubble.

"The ME and Detective Artie Taylor from the D.A.'s office should be here shortly," Lt. O'Brien informed Mark. "Where should we start digging? Some firefighters managed to make entry through a rear bulkhead to get a look into the basement. They said that there was no fire down there and the first floor supports are all intact."

Mark suggested, "That's good news. Makes it easy to rule that area out. Why don't we set up on the side street and work our way in from the side of the building. Once we open up that wall and clear some of the collapsed debris, we should be able to get a good lay of the land for what was her bedroom and apartment. And we'll be able to secure her remains if she is, in fact, in there. Then we can search for any evidence that may help us determine how the fire started and why she didn't make it out."

The rising sun made taking photos difficult with shady spots and glare in other areas. Unusual warmth with summer-like humidity caused sweat, combined with black soot, to continuously run down the men's faces. They all toiled away to find the answers to their quest.

The heavy equipment operator worked under the guidance of the investigators. They wanted to carefully remove material to minimize any further disturbance to the scene and potential evidence. The operator moved his bucket with a thumb to pick at the debris with the dexterity of a classic piano virtuoso.

Suddenly Mark yelled out, "Stop!" He raised his right hand up high with a balled fist, an indication to the operator to stand fast. "Look, right over there. See part of the brass bed frame and the springs from the mattress. Let's crawl over there to get a better look."

After a large, well-developed fire that burns for a while, the only remains of a bed mattress are the coil springs and any other metal parts. The second-floor apartment had neatly pancaked down into the first floor restaurant when the roof came down adding more weight to the de-stabilized floor supports. This allowed Mark and the BFD investigators to walk on flooring remains toward the bed, although they still had to maneuver over and under structural components and furnishings.

"Mike, take some photos as we get closer. It would be good to capture as much as we can on film. Oh, God! Do you guys see what I see?"

Less than ten feet away, still partially covered by bedroom ceiling components, was a totally charred arm. It was outstretched from under the debris. The bony-looking wrist was still bound to the brass headboard with a blackened wrap that appeared to be made of cloth.

Mark asked, "Dick, could you go over there and just take that sheetrock off the bed so Mike can get some more photos before we do anything else. Then, I think we should head back outside to notify the ME and the D.A.'s office."

"Whatever you say, boss. I'm on it, boss." Scherner still didn't like the way Miller assumed the leadership role. But, he thought, he had to give him credit for doing the job right.

Once he removed the debris, the full picture was ghastly. There lay the grisly remains of a woman lying face down with the remnants of her arms and legs extended outward toward the four corners of the spring mattress. The fire had thoroughly consumed her flesh, leaving muscle and fat tissue, along with bones, visible. Only the one wrist was still secured to the bed frame, but her hand and finger bones were missing. The remnants of these bones may be found below the bed within the debris unless they morphed into ash. The other extremities appeared to have also been tied to the brass frame, but the restraints had been consumed. These limbs terminated in ghastly stumps. To most, this would be a sickening sight.

The men paused for a moment, each with his own thoughts. Mark wondered, who was this person? Why did she die this way? What were her final thoughts? He shook his head and sighed deeply when he ventured into her head near the end. The absolute fear she must have felt was palpable. A life cut short in one of the worst ways imaginable.

He forced himself to get his own head back into the right frame of mind. "Okay, guys, let's get out of here for now, take a break, get something to drink, and fill in the ME and D.A.'s office.

In Boston's Mobile Command Center, Lt. Scherner greeted the ME and Artie Taylor, now a detective working in the District Attorney's Office. The men cooled down while they told the others what they have found thus far.

Once the initial information was digested, Mark threw out something that had just popped into his head. "Do you think this fire is connected to the fatal last month in Southie?"

Lt. Scherner replied, "That's a thought. Two women, both restrained to their beds, but the method of restraining them was different. The other one was zip-tied; this one appears to have been tied to the bed using cloth strips. I don't think we have ever had a similar arson murder in all my years. To have two women killed this way within a few weeks is really strange. I think we have to at least consider the possibility."

"Maybe he, and I say "he" because if we have a serial arsonist burning women, it's most likely a male," Mark interjected. "So, maybe he is still trying to perfect his fire sets by using diffcrent restraints."

"I think you guys may be right," added Mike O'Brien. "Let's go back into the scene to see if we can find anything else likc a trailer like before, or some other evidence. Doc and Artie, why don't you come with us to pronounce her so we can remove her before she gets too ripe?"

"We'll get our gear on and join you shortly."

"Hey, guys, is your canine coming out?" Mark asked. "I think if he's carried into the area of her bed, maybe he can find whether the arsonist used an accelerant, especially considering how the first witness described how fast the second floor took off."

Scherner replied, "He should be here any minute." As he finished his sentence, in walked the canine handler, Bob Awrey. Looking at Mark, Scherner quipped, "Your wish is my command. Hey Bob, we were just talking about you. How's things?"

"Hi, Dick, guys. What's going on here?"

The team filled him in. They, then, all moved back out to the scene. The ME suggested, "Bob, why don't you run Mattie before I spend time around the body? Less chance we disturb any evidence and contaminate the scene that way. "

"Absolutely, good thinking." Bob retrieved Mattie, a young black Labrador Retriever, from his air-conditioned van. He carried her through the debris to the remains of the bedroom. Upon putting Mattie on the floor, he instructed her. "Seek, seek."

Mattie immediately went to work by putting her nose down to the flooring. Nearly instantly, Mattie alerted. She sat next to the spot where she hit, looked up at Bob, then repeated the process. Nose to the spot, sit, look up at Bob. "Good, girl." He handed her a few kibbles of dog food.

Bob placed a marker on the spot and moved forward with Mattie. "Seek, seek." She made several more alerts on the carpet remains, then she placed her front paws on the bed. Everyone but her handler suddenly got nervous, thinking the well-done body was about to be lunch for the canine. "Relax everybody. She's just doing her job." Sticking her nose under the edge of the body, Mattie alerted again where some cloth material remained where it had been protected under the woman's body. "That's a good dog."

"Okay, guys. I'm going to take samples from those spots. I'll get them to the lab this afternoon. Maybe we can have the results by tomorrow. Lts. Scherner and O'Brien assisted Awrey to collect the samples while Mark and the Doc watched the process. After placing the carpet remains in a clean metal can, Awrey placed the cover over the can for a few moments, then removed the cover to take a whiff of the contents. "Oh, the sweet nectar of gasoline! Here, check this out."

Mark and the others did a quick sniff. All of them confirmed that the odor wafting from the can was similar to gasoline as well as burned material. Awrey stated, "Gasoline is such a common component, it is a smell that most people can readily identify and even testify in court that it smelled like gasoline."

Through midday the investigators worked the scene. The demolition of the structure was meticulously done so that the total bedroom was exposed. The entire bedframe, and the mattress with the remains of Stephanie Myer's body was removed all together and carried into a refrigerated box truck for transport to the morgue. Her body would then be separated from the bedsprings so that nothing would be lost.

Of particular interest was the cloth that bound her to the bed. It would be examined closer to possibly identify where it came from. Then, it would be preserved because an investigator would never know its importance to a case. Other evidence might later be discovered that connects to the cloth binding.

Just as the arson investigators walked out of this fire scene, a major development relating to forensic investigations was progressing at the speed of light. Classes for investigators were beginning to discuss how DNA, the molecule that contains the genetic code, could be used to identify subjects involved in a criminal investigation and in other applications. Bodily fluids collected at a crime scene such as blood, saliva and semen can be analyzed and compared to a suspect's fluids.

The analysis would be similar to using a fingerprint to connect a person to a crime. Even hair and the dead skin that falls from humans daily can be used to identify someone who had been at the scene. DNA can positively link a sole person to the evidence to the near exclusion of any other person on earth. This exciting developing field caused the investigators of this fire to save every item that came to their attention. And with each step they took, they vowed to honor the memory of the person who had been lost, to seek the truth no matter the cost.

CHAPTER ELEVEN

Mark arrived at the ATF office with plenty of time to spare before his inquisition by Internal Affairs. He stopped in the men's room to clean up and change his clothes. As he entered his office, he still smelled the combination of the odor of smoke from his hair and the smell of death in his nostrils.

Carlo was sitting at his desk. He mouthed a barely audible, "Good luck," as he motioned with his head and pointed toward Jack's office indicating IA had arrived a few minutes early.

Jack stepped out to see if Mark had shown up yet. "Oh, good, you're here. Why don't you step in here? I'll keep you company to witness the proceedings."

Mark feigned confidence as he strode into the office where two ATF Agents, a male and a female, attired in business suits stood up to introduce themselves. The woman spoke, "Hi, Agent Miller. May I call you Mark? I am Special Agent Karen Petrocelli and this is SA Curtis Arcand. We need to speak with you today about a very serious allegation. Have a seat, please."

After Mark shook their hands, he sat in a hard plastic chair, cornered by two walls, on his left side and behind him. Jack sat next to him, also in a plastic chair, in the cramped office that normally holds only three chairs. Agent Petrocelli sat behind Jack's wooden desk in his high-backed leather chair while Arcand sat next to the desk in a cushioned, rolling chair.

With a stern look, Agent Petrocelli started. "Mark, we have information from a woman, an informant of yours, Monique. She's documented by you, right?

Mark was weary of her 'I'm your friend attitude.' "Yes, she testified in a large arson case recently."

"She alleges that you had sex with her and you intimidated her to testify. We interviewed her. Her story sounds credible, but we are in the information gathering stage, so we want to hear your story. At this point, we have not judged you one way or another. Just like any other allegation, we have to perform our due diligence. Could you tell us about your relationship with Monique?"

"Sure." Mark was understandably nervous, but he maintained his composure because he knew he had done nothing wrong. *But I'll be damned if I'm going to go down because of this woman's lies.* "About eighteen months ago, the Boston Police arrested Monique for possession of a handgun with the serial numbers obliterated. I tagged along on an interview of her and turned her into an informant. In exchange for a reduced sentence, she provided information about the Boston cop who was part of a large arson conspiracy that plagued Boston for almost two years.

Monique had previously slept with that cop before I met her. He told her about some places they burned plus names of one or two other conspirators. I verified her information. All of it was true. After conferring with the Assistant U.S. Attorney, he wanted her to testify before the Grand Jury seeking indictments on these guys. I personally handed her the subpoena twelve months ago. She was reluctant to testify. Who wouldn't be in that situation?"

The IA agents nodded their agreement. Agent Petrocelli asked, "So, how did you get her to testify?"

"For the Grand Jury, I persuaded her by reminding her of her agreement to assist the government in exchange for leniency in her case and told her that none of the bad guys would be present. I told her that the proceedings are closed to everyone except the prosecutor and the jurors, plus with any luck the eventual defendants would plead guilty.

But the cop chose to go to trial, so Monique really balked to testify. She was scared. I had to get creative. One day about a week before trial, I brought another witness in the case, a woman by the name of Kathy Whitaker, and the AUSA to visit her. Their presence seemed to relax her somewhat. And on the day of the trial, I picked her up and brought her to the courthouse. Maybe not the best judgment on my part, but nothing happened. That's about it.

Agent Arcand spoke, "That's about it? Is there something else?"

"Well, long before the Grand Jury, I met with her several times, once or twice with Agent Dennis Caggiano, and I met with her three or four times by myself, just gathering more details and getting her mentally ready for what was to come. Any time I met her, I did it at a public place, never alone with her. You can check my diary. I'm sure I made the appropriate entries."

From Petrocelli, "Did you ever have sex with her?"

"Never, not even close, even though I went through a divorce during that period. I never even kissed her."

"Did you pay her to testify?"

"No."

"Did you pressure her to testify?"

"Not any more than reminding her of her deal. I know where this is going and I'm going to try to short-circuit your investigation. Monique came onto me before the Grand Jury and then again before the trial. She even rubbed my leg under a restaurant table trying to reach for my groin area. In no uncertain terms, I rejected her advances. Then, she got pissed at me. She said she would refuse to testify if I didn't have sex with her. When I adamantly refused, she demanded a thousand dollars. Again, I refused. That's why I brought the AUSA and Kathy Whitaker with me. She was a woman scorned, that's why she called and lied about me."

"That's all well and good, but you still chose to meet with her alone and then you picked her up the day of her testimony. Extremely poor judgment on your part. Her story is quite a bit different."

"I imagine it would be. May I ask, where and when did she say any sex occurred? Did she provide a date, an hour, what week at least?"

"We can't tell you that," responded Agent Petrocelli.

Mark began feeling the crushing weight of this inquiry. His fear of any sort of failure caused him to act belligerent, "Is that because she didn't have specifics or is it because you never asked?"

"Mark, there's no need for anger here. We're only trying to find the truth. And we can't divulge anything she has given us thus far."

"Well, damn it, check my bank account. I didn't take any money out to give her, plus I never used government funds, check. Did you check hers? How about this, did you ask about any physical attributes of mine? I have a large birthmark, several inches across right here just below the right side of my stomach. Unless we had sex in total darkness or with my clothes on, it is clearly visible. I can tell you that anybody I have ever had sex with never missed it."

Without waiting for any rejoinder from them, Mark continued. "Let me suggest this. Wire me up. I'll meet with her. You'll hear for yourself that she lied. What do you think?"

Arcand, looking at his partner, shook his head from side to side. Petrocelli said, "I'm sorry, Mark, we don't do that and can't allow that."

Now Mark raised his voice in frustration. "For God's sake, this is my life and my career. It's the best way! The only way! Otherwise, how does anyone prove 'she said, he said'? There is no physical evidence such as a condom full of my seed? No video or recording either, because it never happened. Period, end of conversation."

Arcand stated, "Agent Miller, there's no need for vulgarity and we'll say when this interview is over."

Mark jumped up from his chair, "Well, screw you! You guys are in IA because you don't know your ass from your elbow."

Jack, who had been silent up to this point, also stood to keep his agent separated from any possible altercation. It was time to protect his man. "Okay, Mark, you did a good job. Get out of here. Karen, Curt, we're done here. Mark answered everything you had. If you need anything else, you can set up another meeting. Right now, I don't think you have any kind of case. Mark is a great agent. I've never had any trouble from him. He's a straight shooter." Jack escorted the IA agents to the office door.

CHAPTER TWELVE

Mark had a well-deserved day off but chose not to sit home all day roiling about the Internal Affairs investigation. *Just thinking about how much trouble I could be in because of that bitch is driving me crazy.*

Instead, he planned to make the day into two pleasurable events, a date with the bruising Boston Bruins, who were skating deep in the playoffs, and hoping for a date with his friend with benefits, Michelle. It would be a fun day if she was still talking to him considering how they left things off. Just being with Michelle so far has always been pleasurable except for their heated argument the night before last. But first he had to repair the damage he caused.

Having to apologize and make amends with Michelle would be difficult for Mark. Saying "I'm sorry" was always problematic for him. The stubborn streak instilled within him as a young boy usually prevented him from uttering those words. Just the words to him sounded hollow and devoid of genuine meaning.

Mark's mother constantly punished him for every minor infraction. It never seemed that he could do anything right in her eyes. 'Don't touch that. Why are you sniffing? What did you do now? Clean that. Why do you walk that way? That's so stupid.' She picked on him all the time. And she wanted him to apologize for every misdeed, but Mark didn't even know most of the time that he had done anything wrong.

And he was never taught why or how to apologize, because she, herself, would never say sorry or express regret for anything, big or small. It was not in her vocabulary or part of her nature. So naturally, as Mark became increasingly more obstinate, he struggled to express remorse, admit fault or find the words, "I'm sorry."

But he had to put his best effort into it this time because he knew Michelle was a special woman. He was excited to explore where this fledgling relationship could go.

With flowers in hand, Mark found Michelle at her apartment. Her initial look of dismay when she opened the door instantly softened as her eyes lit up with a smile of surprise when Mark revealed the flowers from behind his back. "Will you accept these flowers as an apology from a jackass who doesn't know how to treat a woman right?"

"I don't know about a jackass, but I can accept your apology. How can I stay angry at that face? And, that bouquet is gorgeous!"

"Look, Michelle," Mark gulped, swallowed hard. "I really am sorry. I'll work on being more responsive to you by saying and doing the right thing. I have some stuff to work on. It's been a while since I've spent real time with a woman. It's no excuse, but I'm dealing with issues that I should not allow to affect our relationship, especially how I treat you. That call for the fire threw me off, and I mishandled how I spoke to you."

"Thank you, Mark, for coming to me and explaining yourself. I couldn't stay angry with you for long. You can trust me with whatever is going on, no matter what it is. I want us to keep moving forward as a couple. I genuinely care about you." Michelle avoided the "L" word so as not to put additional pressure on Mark.

"I'd be happy to see where we can go as a couple. You're the light in my life. There are a few things both personal and job wise that I'm going to keep close to the vest in the short term. Please bear with me in the meantime. I'll let you in on these issues soon, okay?"

"Okay, babe. I trust in you, and I'll be patient, as long as you continue to show me how much you care about me."

"Well, in that case, would you like to take in a Bruins game with me today? I'll try not to be a jerk even though it's one of my quirks. It will be nice to watch this game on ice."

Michelle laughed, rolled her eyes and shook her head. "Let's go before I change my mind."

*   *   *   *   *

Walking hand-in-hand with Michelle into the bandbox of the Boston Garden, Mark could feel the history of the venerable stadium, over sixty years old now. Besides the Bruins, one of the original six teams in the NHL, the Garden housed the Boston Celtics, winners of sixteen NBA championships. Mark loved this place. He could smell and taste the energy of the past heroes. It was intimate and friendly, a place where he could just enjoy life, a place where he forgot who and what he was.

Michelle had never been to the Boston Garden before, nor had she ever seen a Bruins game. Her eyes were aglow, like a little kid on Christmas morning, taking in the vastness of the stadium and the hubbub of activity. Mark was happy to be there for her first time. He didn't want her to forget her firsts.

Before locating their loge level seats near center ice, they stopped at the concession stand to purchase two beers and a large popcorn. Michelle insisted on paying since Mark had purchased the tickets.

Only once did he ever badge his way into a game. Other guys had coaxed him into going to a Red Sox game where they all used their badge as currency. Mark didn't like the feeling. He knew he was a square shooter who could be the target of ridicule, but he also knew that underneath all the machismo, he was still respected. This is what his mother hammered into him; if it didn't belong to you, it was not yours. He firmly believed in paying his own way through life.

Once in their seats, Mark looked over at Michelle. That's one cute kid, he thought. She was smiling as she munched on a handful of popcorn and sipping her beer. She really enjoyed taking in the moment, the atmosphere. And he enjoyed that she did.

Michelle glanced toward Mark. Her hazel eyes glistened more than ever, accented by her light green wool blend jacket. "This is going to be a lot of fun! I'm really glad you asked me to come."

"And I couldn't be happier to have you here. You really are great to hang around with and you make my life so much more enjoyable." Michelle didn't say anything in response, but the look from her eyes radiated her warm feeling toward him. Her squeeze of his forearm confirmed her look.

"Hey, Cute-stuff, before the game starts I want to talk to you about something, but only for a minute because I don't want to spoil this fun day we're going to have. Did you hear that IA was here interviewing me?"

"Not really. Somebody in my group mentioned IA was in town, but there was no other information. What was that all about?"

Mark described the entire meeting to her. "Michelle, I hope you believe me. I would never fool around with an informant. It is a definite no-no for me, nothing but trouble. So, I'm in trouble anyway for not fooling around."

"Mark, honey, I have no reason not to believe you. You can act weird at times, but I'm pretty sure I can trust you. I certainly appreciate you telling me. You really didn't have to tell me considering how sensitive it is. What do you think you're going to do?"

"I'm glad I told you. Kind of get it off my mind for the day. I'm going to speak with Jack on Monday. We'll figure this out, but it's tearing my gut apart."

"I know you'll be fine; I can feel it. Now, the game is starting. I can't wait to see my first game, especially with my guy." Michelle interlaced her arm through his and held his hand.

The first period action was intense, fast-paced, up and down the ice, back-and-forth, with slap shots and incredible saves. Near the end of the period, the puck was flipped into the crowd almost directly opposite from where the couple sat. Mark noticed someone near where the puck landed. He stared. Then, he blinked and squinted his eyes trying to clearly see the man he focused on. That man looked just like him!

Really! How could he look just like me, my twin? A doppelganger! He could be me, or at least my brother. Am I seeing things?

Mark suddenly couldn't focus on anything else. The stranger's presence stirred a mix of curiosity and apprehension in Mark. The hockey battle continued. In a flash, the Bruins scored the first goal of the game. Mark struggled to notice. Michelle jumped to her feet along with the other 14,000 fans with pure jubilation. Belatedly, Mark stood, but his reactions were muted as he stared toward the man across the ice. He clapped, but he lacked the full enthusiasm that Michelle expected.

"What's wrong? Are you okay?"

"Oh, yeah. I just thought I saw some guy across the way who interests me."

"Where? Who is he?"

"Near mid-ice, about six rows up." I'm not sure who he is, but he looks familiar. He's probably nobody. Just a figment of my imagination." Michelle could see it was more than that, but she couldn't locate the guy who concerned Mark.

As the first period ended, Mark watched as the stranger left his seat. Mark leaped up, "It's my turn to buy. Plus, I need to use the men's room first. I'll be back in a few, give or take, with the size of the crowd at the concession."

"Okay, but don't get lost lover boy! I'll be waiting right here for you."

Mark raced into the bustling concourse, but he did not waste time buying any beer. Surveying every male face as he made his way around to the opposite side of the Garden, he searched each concession stand with no success. Spinning around, looking left and right, peering over the heads of the overflowing crowd, Mark finally spotted his double coming out of a men's room less than fifty feet away.

The eyes of Brantley met those of Mark. Surprise registered in both stares. Each man was seeing a mirror image of himself. Only their hairstyles were different, not drastically. Mark's hair was neatly trimmed, but not too short. Brantley wore his somewhat shaggy. But both men had the same hair color. All other features were identical.

Brantley quickly spun away from his counterpart, seeking the nearest exit. He moved as fast as the crowd allowed while elbowing disgruntled patrons along the way to facilitate his escape. Mark was equally aggressive, using his hands to part the sea of the intermission throng. He wanted to meet this man, to at least say hi, and learn something about him to discover how he came to look just like him.

Brantley's flight was more frantic. He didn't want to meet or get to know his twin like this. He had other plans for his brother that would come soon enough.

At the wide stairway, Brantley could see the exit. He looked behind him, searching for his pursuer, but he could only see members of the crowd being plowed through. Taking the stairs three at a time he reached the lower lobby in seconds. He shoved the glass door aside. The cool fresh air on noisy Causeway Street wacked him in the face. The Green line elevated train rumbled directly overhead with the ear-piercing screech of its steel wheels on the steel rails.

Turning to his left, Brantley ran under the elevated tracks, diagonally crossing Causeway. He took the first street to his right onto Canal Street, glancing again over his shoulder to check to see if he was still safe. Running hard past Doyles bar and restaurant, his chest heaving to suck air into his overworked lungs, Brantley aimed for an outdoor parking lot where he could escape from the area in his car.

Meanwhile, Mark also skipped down the stairs to the exit determined to match the stranger's elusive maneuvers. But the advantage was with the escapee who knew where he was heading whereas the pursuer had to weigh multiple options. Winded from his fight through the crowd, Mark looked left and right on his side of the street before scanning up and down the opposite side of Causeway Street. Nothing.

He gambled and scrambled across the bustling thoroughfare looking down streets and alleys perpendicular to Causeway, but he couldn't find his likeness. *My gut feeling says he went this way.* So as a last resort he sprinted down Canal Street, but the only thing Mark noticed was the taillights of a red Dodge Challenger swerving as it raced away from his position. Frustrated, he slowly made his way back to the Garden.

Once inside, Mark was stopped by security. "Hey, where do you think you're going?"

Searching his pockets, Mark produced his badge first, followed by his ticket stub. "I had to run outside, chasing some guy I had to ask some questions."

The guard quipped, "You had me at the badge. We don't normally let people back in. Enjoy the rest of the game." Mark waved thanks and rushed back to his seat as the second period was well underway.

With a quizzical stare, Michelle queried, "Where the heck have you been? I was thinking you took off on me, leaving me high and dry. Or maybe, there was a really long line at the men's room or beer line. As it is, you apparently left me dry. Where's the beer? Are you okay?"

"Oh, my bad. I saw that guy who was sitting across the ice. I tried catching up to him to ask him a couple questions, but he ran outside. I gave chase but I couldn't find him."

"Wow, you must have wanted him bad. What's with that? Who was he?"

"I don't really know who he is. He just looked so familiar, I needed to talk to him."

"Well, I know you're supposed to be a dedicated investigator. But I didn't know you were such a strange guy and a weird date."

"Ahh, I'm sorry about that. I'll make it up to you. I promise."

"I'll hold you to that promise," Michelle smirked with the cutest smile. That adorable look temporarily took Mark's mind off the enigma that eluded him. He resolved to focus on the present, cherishing the moments shared with Michelle amidst the electrifying energy of the Boston Garden.

CHAPTER THIRTEEN

Mark arrived at the office early. He had to get some obligatory paperwork done before heading over to the Boston Fire Investigation Unit. The open office had eight metal desks with fake wood laminate tops spaced four on each side of the room. The supervisor's office was located to the front left of the room with the secretary's desk immediately outside the boss's door. Windows lined the short wall behind her desk and the long wall across from Mark's seat.

Jack was already in his office. "Good morning, Jack, can we talk for a minute?"

"Sure, Mark, take a seat. What's on your mind?"

"That meeting with IA, that's what's been on my mind. Jack, let me meet Monique while wired. I'll get her to admit the truth. We can make up some ruse that will work. That can't be true, what IA said about it not being allowed. It's the only way I can clear myself. What do you say?"

"I checked the regs. There's nothing in there that says we can't do it. And I agree with you. This is the best way to resolve her bogus claims. Do you think she'll fall for it?"

"This is what I was thinking. Let's get Carlo and Wojo in here. I just heard them come in. I'm sure the four of us can come up with a workable scenario."

✳   ✳   ✳   ✳   ✳

Mark was pleased with how receptive Jack was to his idea. Taking this proactive approach to his problem alleviated some of his apprehension. *Once again, he has my back. I'm so glad he's my boss.*

Back at his desk, Mark pulled open the lower right file drawer of his desk to grab a folder. As he fingered through the folders, Mark found the manila folder marked "passport." It was always in his desk in the event the job required him to travel abroad on short notice. He hadn't looked in the folder for a while, so he pulled it out, opening it on his desktop revealing forgotten relics from his past.

Below his blue-covered passport book, Mark spotted a yellowed copy of his original birth certificate. An undefined inner drive caused Mark to pick up the paper. He quickly focused on his parent's names. Mother, Anna Miller, maiden name, Mueller. Father, William Miller.

Every once in a while thoughts crept into his head, wanting to know more about his father, maybe even meet him, if he was even still alive. He had no ill-will against Bill Miller even though he walked away from his son when he was only six-months old.

Mark was willing to give a person a chance rather than harshly criticize them. He always believed that one had to walk in someone's shoes before judging them. The meandering paths of one's life causes a person to act with reasons that are often unknown, not only to those who are affected by one's decisions, but possibly also not completely understood by the person themselves. There are always at least two sides to every life story. Mark knew this only too well. His life story always had missing pieces, a void resulting from an elusive father.

After contemplating this for a few moments, Mark, summoning his courage, made a major life move. He walked down the hall to the Teletype room, his footsteps echoing in the silence of the corridor. With trembling fingers, he entered Bill Miller's full name and date of birth into a nationwide motor vehicle license database. Mark had heard tidbits about his father before his mother died, including that when he retired from the U.S. Army, he was a civilian air traffic controller in Alabama. An active license match came up in Hoover, Alabama, a suburb of Birmingham. Right in front of his eyes was his father's address, providing a glimmer of hope his father was still alive.

In this momentous moment, Mark picked up the phone on his desk. Everyone in his group had gone downstairs for coffee, so the office was empty, giving him the privacy to make this call. He dialed 411 for information, asking for a number for William Miller at that Hoover address. With the receiver up to one ear, as his fingers nervously pushed the correct buttons on the phone, Mark connected to his past. His pulse quickened with each ring. He had to sit down, or he might collapse to the floor.

"Hello?" A male voice mumbled into the phone.

"Bill Miller? This is your son, Mark." An extended pregnant silence.

"Is this Mark? Really?!" Mark heard a crack in his father's voice, which spoke volumes, a testament to the weight of the years that had passed under the bridge.

Mark blurted his words out in the event his father hung up the phone. "Yeah. I just wanted to let you know I'm here. I have no expectations, but if you want to meet and talk, I'm here. I would like to get to know you and more about your life. But if you don't want to get together, no pressure."

"Mark, I'd love to meet you! I've been trying for years. I've sent multiple letters to your mother, but, I guess, they never got to you. You know, I've been married five times," he mumbled in a Southern accent. Mark sensed his father's voice faltering.

"Wow, I didn't know that! Or, for that matter, not much else about you or your life. It just so happens I'm going to be in Biloxi, Mississippi in two weeks for a conference. Any chance you could meet me there so we can talk and get to know one another?"

"Sure. I can make it. That would be great! I'm looking forward to it.

"Cool, me too. It would be really nice to meet you," Mark beamed. As he hung up, he knew this call unfolded like a dream. He had high hopes for a chance at reconciliation. It could not have gone any better. *I'm finally going to meet my father! How cool is that?*

✳   ✳   ✳   ✳   ✳

Two weeks later, Mark was seated at a patio bar at one of Biloxi's oceanfront hotels, his heart pounding with anticipation. On his head, he wore his ATF baseball cap with large lettering so his father could identify him. A pint of chilled lager sat on the table in front of him.

Mark scanned the crowd of strangers for any man who could be his father. A man of about sixty-five shuffled directly toward him. It looked like his feet or legs hurt. He was mostly bald and considerably overweight, but not in a grotesque way. Aside from those attributes, there were features within his eyes and smile that revealed he was family.

As Mark rose, he extended his hand. He hadn't considered how to greet his father for the first time. Dad? Bill? A hug or a handshake? So, nervously, he just said, "Hi, how are you? It's nice to finally meet you."

They shook hands as two men do, as two strangers do. A rush of emotions washed over Mark, finally a sense of connection. There was no hug or embrace, but Bill Miller smiled as he sat down. Mark could only begin to imagine how nervous he must have felt, meeting his son for the first time in thirty-two years since he was only six months old.

His father broke the ice, "I've dreamed of this day for a long time. I'm so happy you reached out." His voice was shaky, perhaps a reflection of years of longing and regret.

Mark explained, "I've been curious for a long time about you, but I guess I was too busy with my own life or maybe I never had the guts to explore finding you, thinking you may not care or were too involved with your life to have a relationship with me. As I mentioned on the phone, I want you to understand, I really have no expectations that we end up with a real connection. I just wanted you to know I'm here and available to talk. I'm not one to place blame on someone like you for leaving. It's my belief that everyone has a life story with twists and turns that cause someone to act the way they do."

"Well, you sound like you have a good outlook on life. So, tell me about yourself. Like, what do you do? Married? Hobbies?" There was so much to catch up on. Father and son took turns.

When Mark told his father about his work at ATF, he stated, "Mark, I'm so proud of you. You have accomplished so much. Hey, do you think I could get an ATF hat?"

Thus far, Mark couldn't have asked for a better outcome. Their conversation flowed like a rushing river, each word bridging the past with the present. Amazingly, after a couple hours, Bill asked, "How's your mom doing?"

"Oh, she died two years ago. She got so crippled from carrying heavy trays as a waitress. Lots of arthritis and operations took their toll. She was on Oxy drugs for years. It all wore her down."

"I'm really sorry to hear that. She was a beautiful woman. A really tough, but beautiful woman. She was too much for me to handle, so I started drinking a lot. Of course, that didn't help. We fought all the time. I just folded my cards. She hated me because I left.

Once she said she never wanted to see me again, I left completely. I shirked my fatherly duties, but there was no way she was going to share parenting. I'm so sorry I didn't help you grow up. Her yelling and screaming, I just couldn't take how mean and miserable she could be. Growing up during World War II in Austria under Nazi rule really hardened her, I think. It carried over throughout the rest of her life. It's a shame."

"Yeah, I know what you mean. I often thought of her as a drill sergeant. I'm surprised she didn't have me do close-order drills and march up and down the street. And through it all I still loved her because she was my mother, but I certainly recognize some of my own faults came directly from her. I have work to do on myself to become a better person."

"Don't we all?" Mark felt a strong connection to his father despite only speaking to him for a short time. It is a familial bond he had desired his entire life.

"We've been babbling on and on, I've forgotten to ask you about your twin brother, Brantley. What's become of him?"

Dumbfounded, stuttering, "Di-, did I hear you right? A brother named Brantley? How could this be? A twin brother, no less! I never heard of him! Really, are you kidding me? What the fuck!"

"Oh, of course I didn't know you didn't know. Your mother gave him to her sister to take care of after I left because she didn't think she could handle raising the two of you. I don't know anything more than that, sorry."

Mark was reeling. The news hit him to his core, a gut punch. "Wow, wow, wow! That's freakin' amazing. I meet my father for the very first time after thirty plus years and now I find out I have a brother and, I guess, an aunt. I need some time to absorb all this. And you don't know anything more about them?"

"No, because your mom's sister and I never got along, we never spoke. And just like I lost track of you, I knew nothing about him."

Disappointed, Mark said, "Oh, man, that's too bad. Maybe I can come up with something. After all, I am a trained investigator."

"Mark, I have faith in you. Hey, maybe I can help. You remember how I mentioned on the phone that I was sending letters to your mother? Well, your mother and her sister had been close to my aunt and cousins in the Albany area when we were married because they knew nobody else. That's who I sent the letters to so they would pass them along to your mother. I think they kept in touch for quite a while. I'll see what I can find out. Get back to me when you can."

"How about a woman in your life, Mark. Is there anyone special?"

"Oh, she's incredibly special, exceptional in all ways. Michelle is her name. She's an agent, too. Our relationship is still fairly new, but I can tell you this, I'm hooked. She's beautiful and smart, plus she doesn't take any crap from me. If I don't do something stupid to screw it up, she could be the one. But, I already did that once. I'm divorced because I just neglected my ex too much. My work consumed me. How about you?"

Bill laughed, "Oh, I'm married now. For my fifth time! But you and Brantley are my only kids. It's just too bad I never hung around to be there as you two grew up. I know it's easy to say that we can't go back, but perhaps we can go forward together."

The two spoke for another hour about their life experiences, but no more about the newly discovered sibling. Somehow, the familial bond provided Mark with an unexpected kinship with his father. The two men stood to leave. They shook hands again, but this time, they clasped each other with both hands, their bond having grown during their hours long conversation. "You asked me for a hat earlier, how about this one? It was brand new before I put it on today."

"Sure, I'd love it, thanks." Their departing smiles solidified their budding relationship.

When Mark left to get back to his conference, his brain flooded with thoughts of years missed with his brother. *Why did my mother never tell me? Why did she keep this secret? What is Brantley like? Where is he now?* Although the road ahead was full of uncertainty, Mark knew he would face it head-on armed with the knowledge he was no longer alone.

I'm going to make it my mission to find Brantley, my very own brother, meet up with him, maybe bond with him. His mind buzzed with so many possibilities, his heart brimming with newfound hope. In his soul, Mark knew this was the start of his journey to discover his missing family. This was just another puzzle in his life that needed solving. And he knew he was up to the task of completing that puzzle.

Meeting my father certainly had an earth-shattering outcome. Somehow, I feel that meeting my brother will be another momentous occasion.

CHAPTER FOURTEEN

The Warren Tavern opened its doors for the first time in the late 1700s. In the Charlestown neighborhood where the centuries old residential buildings were built shoulder to shoulder, the tavern still has original floors and rooms with low-slung ceilings. The dark, intimate bar is crowded most nights.

Brantley had been here before. He liked the darkness. On this Thursday night, he sat in the last seat at the small L-shaped bar with his back against the wall where he had the best seat for people watching. He was on the prowl, trying to find his next target, needing to keep the pressure on the Boston Fire investigators and more so, on his ATF brother, Mark. His goal was to set at least one fatal fire a month, always varying his days of the weeks and neighborhoods so as not to create a pattern. Brantley wanted to wreak as much havoc as possible without getting caught.

His plan was beginning to unfold as he expected. Who is the better and smarter brother? As he mulled it over, he envisioned the clip of his rising star brother soaking up all the accolades, shining brightly for the television cameras. One thing Brantley knew for sure, if I go down, he's going down with me.

His eyes were drawn to a middle-aged couple who took the last two seats at the bar furthest from him, but a mere twenty feet away. Their designer clothing plus the woman's glittering jewelry broadcast their well-off position in life. They both ordered a top-shelf Scotch. As soon as the bartender placed their drinks on the bar, Brantley watched as the woman downed hers straight away.

Although the chestnut-haired woman's visage was strikingly beautiful, the look on her face betrayed a sour disposition. He wondered what was wrong with women these days as he heard the nasty words spewing from her bright red painted lips. "You know, you're really not much of a man, letting that guy talk to you that way. He walked all over you and you just let him," the shrew shrilled at her husband.

"What did you want me to do? You know I don't like confrontation. It was just easier to go along with him. I've told you a million times, I prefer to pick the mountain to die on and that guy certainly wasn't worth it. What was it going to get me anyway?" he pleaded.

"It's respect, Norm! Standing up for yourself gets you respect. Sometimes, if it wasn't for your money, I don't know why I stay with you. You're such a mouse."

He downed his drink and noticed she had already finished hers. That's par for the course, he thought. Always the ugliness, then tomorrow she'll wake up acting all loving again. Norm also wondered why they stayed together. Although Brantley was intrigued by the drama, he found himself in the man's shoes questioning why he put up with her crap.

The woman's piercing tone alerted everyone within earshot of the bar that an ugly skirmish was brewing at the base of Bunker Hill. Her voice irritated Brantley as he felt that horrific burning spreading on his backside. Bile rose into his throat. Disgust showed on his face, but no one noticed. All eyes were glued on the feuding couple.

A slight slur to her words suggested that her Scotch was not the woman's first drink of the night. Her husband didn't bite after her jabs. "You really are a weak bastard of a man. You wouldn't even stand up for your wife when someone insults me. I can't even sleep with you anymore. Just the sight of you sickens me!"

The eyes of the onlookers all turned away in embarrassment with the spectacle. Some had smirks on their faces, others had a look of disdain.

"Listen, Arlene. I didn't take you here to be the object of your ridicule. I want to go home. You coming?"

"No, Norm. I'm going to have another drink and maybe find a real man. You go ahead with your tail between your legs. And take a cab. You're not driving my brand new Mercedes."

"Sure, even though I paid for that damn car. Okay, good luck with your search! I'm not sure who would have you when you get so damn nasty." With that, Norm threw a $50 bill on the counter to take care of the past and any future drinks. And out the door he went, never looking back.

After that last exchange, Brantley knew that he would be her "real man." He stared at Arlene's face, thinking she really was a beautiful-looking woman. It's too bad she is such a foul mouthed, revolting bitch. For just a moment, Brantley felt his manhood stir, but an image of his mother's scornful expression haunted him with that wicked voice piercing deep into him. He knew what he had to do to rid himself of the painful memories. That did not include sex with this woman. It would take fire to quell the burn within him.

Arlene's eyes caught Brantley's stare. Eye dialogue between the two lost souls commenced. It didn't take her long to find a man in whom she was interested. Arlene fell into Brantley's trap with her come hither look. With a slight nod of her head, she gestured to the empty seat recently vacated by her husband. Not wanting to play too hard to get, he sidled over to Arlene, brushing his hand across her back as he walked past her to the seat to her left. Then he placed his right hand over her left hand.

With her right hand she lifted her second Scotch with a welcoming clink against Brantley's Bourbon Old Fashion. "Hi, there, young man." He was about ten years her junior. "I'm Arlene, darling. And you, Mr. Sexy, are?"

"Randy," he lied, not wanting anyone to overhear his real name. "Glad to meet you." If she only knew how glad he was. "Why don't we finish these drinks and get out of here? Everybody is gawking at us after that little exchange with your husband. I don't want to waste any time."

"Yeah, fuck them, it's none of their business. But I like a guy who likes to get right down to business." Brantley appreciated how easy she was. He was thinking, formulating his plan on the fly as he paid for his own dinner and drinks with a hundred dollar bill.

Arlene slid off the barstool, landing unsteadily on the floor. "Here, let me help you," offered Brantley as he interlocked his right arm to her left arm.

"Stop looking at me!" Arlene shouted at those patrons who still stared in her direction. "Don't you have anything fucking better to do with your time than checking out what I'm doing?" Her vulgar yelling caused several more to turn to look at her. "You can all go to hell!"

Brantley realized she was so much like his mother, always yelling and swearing. It used to make him cringe with embarrassment in front of his friends. Now, Arlene repulsed him, much as his mother had. This woman's behavior solidified his resolve to rid the world of another contemptible person.

As they stepped outside, Brantley asked, "Where's your car parked? I live just over the other side of the hill. We can go to my place, then when you're ready, you can take your car to wherever you want to go, okay?" He was a good liar, a real charmer.

Trying to comprehend what he just proposed and remember where her car was parked took Arlene several seconds before she responded, "Oh, it's that black Mercedes right over there." She pointed across the street, about three cars down.

"I imagine you plan to take advantage of me tonight, if you're like most men who all want to get into my panties. You men are all alike, so predictable and then, so disappointing."

"Your wish is my command, lady. I plan to show you a hot time."

"Oooh," she giggled. "Take me away you nasty boy."

"Let me just grab something out of my car, it's right here." Brantley unlocked his passenger side door, reached in and pulled out his go bag.

Arlene asked, "What is that, your bag of tricks?"

"It certainly is. Just wait, you'll be so surprised what I have in store for you."

He tossed the bag in the back seat of her car. When they were both seated in the car, Brantley began to drive to a nearby spot where they could have some privacy. Arlene asked, "So, Randy, what's your story? That's an unusual name."

But before he could speak, she went on a tangent, digressing into a diatribe about her husband and their relationship. "That bastard husband of mine is so useless. All he can do is make money, but after that, nothing. He doesn't know how to take care of anything, especially me. He thinks everything is fine because he has money, but he never even gives me the time of day. When it comes to loving and sex, forget it. I think he's paying someone to get laid because he never has any energy for me."

She continued for another five minutes, yada, yada, yada. Her alcohol intake caused her volume to increase to a fevered pitch. Within that short time frame, Brantley already had her complaining up to his earlobes. Bitching like that always drove him mad. Again, thanks to his mom's constant griping and screaming, he needed to conquer his demons by striking out at this woman.

Brantley drove along Terminal Street to a deserted parking lot in the shadow of the Tobin Bridge. He figured nobody would bother him there while he did his deed, a.k.a. taking care of this loathsome lady.

"What do you think we're going to do here?" Arlene inquired, and then complained some more, "I'm not fooling around with you in my new Mercedes. I'm way past those days. Besides, I would like that new leather smell to linger, not have my car smell like sex. Where are you going?"

Brantley opened his door, "I've just got to get something out of my bag, maybe we'll have a little drink while we watch that full moon rising over there." Unzipping his bag, he slipped on his gloves, then pulled out two long zip ties, instantly connecting them so they would do the job he had planned.

Then, with a sudden movement, he reached toward Arlene. Zap! Brantley had switched to using a stun gun instead of the pepper spray he had used on his previous victims. This change prevented him from suffering from the effects of the spray, which allowed him to do away with the nuisance of covering his face and eyes for protection. His new weapon worked like a charm.

Arlene emitted a loud, "Aargh." She convulsed with painful muscle spasms. "Aah, aah, aah," she moaned over and over. Her lack of body control and obvious disorientation allowed Brantley to make his next move. He grabbed a mass of her chestnut hair to snap her head backward against the headrest. Wrapping the inner crux of his arm around her forehead, he managed to get the double length of zip ties around her neck where he then fastened the ties behind the headrest steel rails. Brantley tightened the ties enough to control the woman while still allowing her to breathe comfortably. Once she sufficiently recovered from the electrical charge, he wanted her to be aware of the circumstances leading to her demise.

Next, Brantley quickly moved to the front passenger door so he could easily access his prey. There, he secured both her hands with more zip ties to the shoulder restraint portion of her seat belt. As she began to realize her predicament, he managed to tie her ankles together with his cloth strips before she could kick him.

"Wha, what are you doing?" Arlene stammered. "Don't hurt me, you bastard," she cried. "Why are you doing this?"

"Lady, because you're a bitch, a nasty mean witch. Because it's you I disdain, I will inflict you with burning pain. You were at the wrong place at the wrong time, so you'll pay for your life's crime." Brantley smiled at his poetic skills. Then, he forcefully gagged her with another cloth strip so she could only grunt and snort without being able to talk. He had enough of the crap she had already spewed.

From his goody bag, he retrieved a large bag of potato chips and two 12-ounce soda bottles now filled with gasoline, as well as a disposable long stick lighter. Brantley ripped open the bag of chips, grabbed a few to chomp on, but he wasn't there for snacking. From his diligent research, he learned that when set afire, the greasy potato chips boil off the oil creating a semi-controlled flame that becomes a time-delay device. This delay would provide the time for Brantley to calmly, but swiftly walk away from the impending vehicle inferno. His Challenger was still parked across from the Warren Tavern, a short fifteen minute jaunt.

While his quarry squirmed in the front seat, watching his moves as best she could, her executioner cracked open the two gasoline bottles and placed them on the floor behind the two front seats. Brantley slid the chip bag under the driver's seat. He marveled at his exploits. *What an accomplished arsonist I've become!* Starting the Mercedes for a moment, he lowered the four windows slightly to provide adequate ventilation for the fire to take off. After grabbing his bag from the back seat, he flicked the lighter, bringing the flame to life. This very flame was about to extinguish a beastly human life.

As he lit the chips on fire, Brantley saw the frantic look in the woman's eyes while she fought and struggled against her restraints. The incipient flames ignited the underside of the car seat. With one last flourish, he flipped his middle finger prominently in front of the wretched hag.

Brantley never thought of his targets as real people, only objects of misery and internal agony. "Sayonara, bitch. In the moments left in your life, think about your vicious transgressions against the people you wronged." With that, he slammed the door. Thinking for a moment about any evidence he may have left behind that could divulge his identity, Brantley used one of his cloth strips to wipe the four door handles in case the exterior of the new, black Mercedes didn't burn sufficiently to destroy his fingerprints.

It was a pleasant late summer night for a stroll. From a short distance, Brantley looked back just as the vehicle burst into flames. *What a nice job I did with my first car fire! Let's see how my hot shot brother and his pals do with this one.* He noticed how good he felt.

That woman should be good and crispy by the time that fire is put out. She never would have changed anyway. The world is now a better place without her.

Just as Brantley was relishing his success, a Boston Police cruiser responding to the report of a nearby fire, raced down Chelsea Street toward the plume of heavy black smoke pushing into the night sky. As the female officer spotted a hooded man carrying a black bag walking in her direction, she immediately yanked her cruiser to a halt abreast of the man. She guessed a man walking away from a fire in this neighborhood at that time of night likely had some connection to the blaze.

Brantley immediately broke into a sprint crossing behind the cruiser, running onto the first street facing him. The officer jumped from her cruiser, pulling her pistol from her holster while screaming, "Freeze! Stop! Police!" She knew she had no authority to shoot the man just because he ran from her. Turning back toward her front seat, she reached for her radio mic to report the runaway stranger, her location, a description of the man and requested assistance with a neighborhood search.

Cutting through an alley, although he hated to do so, Brantley tossed his go-bag into a large dumpster to lighten his load. *I'm not going down this way. I have a lot more to prove before my task is complete. Damn, am I glad I threw that spare bag in my trunk.*

He zigzagged between houses, many built one or two centuries earlier, through backyards, up narrow sidewalks, over fences. The sweat poured down his face. Removing his hoodie, he stopped long enough to stuff it into a trash can that had been placed curbside ready for the next morning's pick-up.

Sirens wailed throughout lower Charlestown. Although he took a circuitous route, Brantley aimed toward his car parked across from the Warren Tavern. His soaked shirt stuck to his body. Almost safe, he laid flat on the ground behind a wood stockade fence as a cruiser with blue lights flashing, slowly drove down the street while shining a search light in his direction. *I'm smarter than these cops. No need to panic. They may be hunting me, but I have the advantage. There are hundreds of places to hide around here.*

Peering around the corner of a house onto Warren Street, and seeing no movement of cars or people, he now walked at a normal pace as he crossed the street finally reaching his car on Pleasant Street.

Brantley found a bright orange colored parking ticket tucked under the driver's side windshield wiper. He had parked his Challenger in a resident parking only zone. By the time he put his car into drive, he heard more sirens in the distance.

CHAPTER FIFTEEN

"Dick, why does it seem that the fatal fires always come during our shifts?" lamented Lt. Mike O'Brien as he wiped the sleep from his eyes.

His partner quipped, "That's because they know we're the best investigators around. That can be the only explanation, Mike."

"Yeah, yeah, let's get going and see what's up with this one. I'll go pull the car around to the door while you finish dressing." Both men had been in their bunks at the Boston FIU. The door opened onto Massachusetts Avenue near the intersection of three sections of the city—Roxbury, the South End and South Boston.

Within five minutes, the pair was standing near the burned-out hulk of a car. Steam was still rising from the steel frame. An engine company was standing by with a charged line in the unlikely event the fire should re-ignite. A Boston PD cruiser with its blue lights flashing plus an unmarked detective's vehicle and the Fire Chief's car were in the lot.

"Hi, Chief. Another early morning body, huh?" Scherner inquired.

"Hey, guys, thanks for rushing out here. The ME is on her way. Detective Artie Taylor is over there by the car taking photos. He did a wide 360 around the vehicle looking for anything useful, but with the asphalt pavement and our guys pouring water over this thing, he never found anything but charred junk. It was roaring when we got here. We didn't even know we had a body in the car until we knocked the fire down.

As our nozzle man walked up to the front passenger door to finish dousing the interior, he reported a body laying across the front seat. Whoever it was is so badly charred that we can't tell if it's a man or woman, what race or an approximate age. This will most likely be a dental identification I'm afraid."

"Thanks, Chief. We'll give it a good look over," said Lt. O'Brien. "What do you think, Dick, wake Miller up again?

"Hell no! I don't need him looking over my shoulder all the time."

"But, Dick, I was thinking with a dead woman and all, this fire might be connected to the other fires."

"This is a car fire, not a building. It doesn't affect interstate commerce. And we're not even sure it is a woman. We don't need him to help dig. With this car fire, there's nothing to dig like in a building. Plus, it could be an accidental fire for all we know. I don't like that hotshot. There's something off about him. I just can't put my finger on it yet. Let's do this ourselves. If we have anything to connect this fire to the other women, then we'll see."

"Okay, partner. We'll do this one your way until we see what we have here. He still would have been another pair of eyes. You know he always spots something. He's had a good eye for hard-to-find evidence."

"Are you done bellyaching, yet? He's not a car fire expert, you know. Let's get to work."

"Okay, okay. Let's figure this thing out so we can get some breakfast."

"Now that's the Mike O'Brien I know and love. Let's do this, brother."

Scherner yelled out, "Hey, Artie. Take enough photos yet? See anything good?"

"Hi LT, good morning, Mike. I'm finished with all of the exterior shots and as much of the interior as possible without moving anything. The victim is certainly well cooked. Definitely a woman, though. No male genitalia."

"It takes a cop to notice that right away." Lt. Scherner took his first look inside the remains of the vehicle. The woman's head, mostly a skull with little brain matter left, was actually detached from her body. Her body had been ravaged by the inferno.

"I have a couple immediate thoughts. Why was she in the passenger seat? Was there a driver who escaped before the fire? What is this Mercedes doing here in an empty parking lot in an industrial section of Charlestown? If it was an accidental fire, why didn't she bail out? Could it be a suicide? Or is it a murder?"

"Hey, Dick, I think there is a VIN stamped in the steel frame under the passenger seat," Mike interjected. "It will help identify the owner of the car, possibly even the victim."

"How the hell do you know that, Mike?" his partner asked quizzically.

"Remember that week-long car fire conference I went to last year? There was a lot of great information, and I paid attention. Plus, I regularly review the books they gave us."

Dick remarked, "Well, it's great to see the city's money is being well spent. I think I can pry open this door and look for the number without disturbing our vic." With that, he aimed a flat pry bar into the space behind the front door and, with considerable effort, Scherner popped the door open.

Grunting, Dick kneeled on both knees. He pushed aside some charred material with his gloved hands. The beam of his heavy box flashlight lit up the engraved identifier. "Son-of-a gun, you were right, here it is. Hey, Artie, can you get a picture of this? And Mike, can you write down the number that I dictate to you?

Well, I'll be damned! Look what the son-of-a-bitch used," exclaimed the investigator. O'Brien and Taylor moved closer, looking over the kneeling Scherner's shoulder while flashing the beams of their lights toward his cupped hands. "He freaking used ruffled potato chips to set the fire. There's a nice little pile of charred chips under the seat."

"Oh, my God. I've seen this done at seminars, but this is the first time I have ever seen this in the field. This guy changes things up again, if it is the same guy who burned the other women," remarked O'Brien. "I was surprised when we found them after we set a fire with them in that class. The instructor explained that once the oils burn off, the charred potato is a poor fuel that does not burn to completion so they can be found with a careful examination of the area. And ruffles are more easily identifiable than regular chips. Do you think this guy knew that just to see if we could find them?"

"I'll get you an evidence can," offered Detective Taylor.

As Taylor headed for the FIU vehicle to retrieve the can, Lt. O'Brien called out, "You had better bring a couple more and get back over here with your camera. I think I see something else we might want to collect." O'Brien flashlight illuminated the re-solidified remains of the melted plastic soda bottles on the floor behind the front seats. With the seat material consumed, leaving only the metal frames of the seats, the crumpled bottles were relatively easy to spot.

The police detective stood by the rear passenger side door with his camera. "Where do I shoot?" O'Brien aimed his beam to the nearest bottle. After the photos were taken, the bottle remains were carefully removed by cutting the stiffened and blackened floor carpet. "What do you think, are the bottles important, Mike?" The detective was not fire science savvy.

"Here, sniff," said O'Brien as he stuck the first bottle near his counterpart's nose.

"Whoa, that reeks of gasoline. How does that work like that?"

"Hey, buddy, that's for me to know and you to find out. That's why you have fire guys working with you. When there was gasoline in these bottles, the liquid kept the bottles cool, and the gas vapors burn off at the mouth of the bottle contributing to the fire. This continues as the plastic softens, opening pores so to speak, until the bottle melts down. As the fire is extinguished, the plastic re-solidifies capturing the gasoline vapors, molecules are trapped within the plastic. Great evidence of an arson, but we won't be able to get any other evidence, like fingerprints, off them."

"Well, now, that's pretty cool stuff to learn. And, I won't soon forget it," remarked Taylor.

After Dr. Denise Williams from the Office of the Medical Examiner did her thing, including pronouncing the woman as dead, a flatbed truck arrived to remove the car from the scene with the deceased still inside. In order to preserve the vehicle and not lose any additional critical evidence, the truck operator wrapped the vehicle in a blue tarp. Further, he towed the car onto the bed of his truck where another tarp was waiting to complete the secure enclosure around the parcel. The car was bound for the garage beneath the FIU office.

✳   ✳   ✳   ✳   ✳

Back at their office, the trio of Boston investigators learned the Mercedes had been registered only two months earlier to Arlene Thompson from an affluent section of Chestnut Hill near Boston College. A little further digging revealed her husband was Norman Thompson, a wealthy architect.

Since it was only 6 A.M., Detective Taylor teamed with Lt. O'Brien to head over to Chestnut Hill to notify Mr. Thompson of his wife's demise. They hoped to catch him before he went to work, or maybe wake him up to catch him off-guard, so they could interview him about his knowledge of the circumstances that led to his wife's death. Notifying a family of a sudden death was always one of the toughest parts of the job, even more so when the victim died in such a hideous way.

Teaming a police investigator with a fire investigator was a wise move. Those from the fire department are specialized in firefighting and the science of all aspects of fire, including reading the fire damage to determine where a fire originated and the cause of the fire. The police are trained interviewers and investigators. It is the best way to effectively work fires.

Ringing the doorbell at the front door of a gorgeous multi-million dollar brick house, the investigators waited several minutes before the homeowner answered. He was disheveled, with that just woken-up look, dressed in a bathrobe covering silk pajamas. "Mr. Thompson?" inquired Detective Taylor with his Boston Police shield displayed prominently in his left hand as his right hand stayed ready to grab his weapon should the need arise.

"You're here about my wife, aren't you?" he asked.

"Yes, we are. Why do you ask? Is she home?"

"No, she apparently never came home last night. What's happened to her?"

Showing Mr. Thompson a close-up photo of a woman's rings, "Do you recognize these rings?"

"Yes, those are my wife's engagement and wedding rings. I bought them for her." He started breaking down. Knowing something awful had ensued overnight to Arlene, despair showed all over his face. Wrinkles formed on his forehead, around his swollen dampening eyes and around his dry mouth.

Immediately after notifying him of his wife's demise, Taylor and Lt. Scherner reached out to support the husband from collapsing on his highly polished marble foyer floor. Everybody moved inside to the living room. Through gulps of tears and mucus dripping from his nose, Mr. Thompson reiterated the details of the previous night, leaving out none of the facts as he remembered them, including the good, the bad and the ugly even though some of them painted a poor picture of him. Providing a receipt from a Brookline deli where he had his cab driver stop on the way home revealed he was miles away from the fire scene at the time the fire was reported.

The investigators left Thompson to commiserate with himself over leaving his wife after an argument. He would never get to be the object of her castrating ridicule again.

They needed to check with the bartender at the Warren Tavern, but it would be several hours before anyone would be at the locale. Maybe he could give them a lead as to the last hour of Arlene Thompson's life. In the meantime, the three investigators grabbed some sandwiches and returned to the Fire Investigation Unit's office.

CHAPTER SIXTEEN

The Arson Task Force office was buzzing with activity by mid-morning. Mark was aware of the fatal fire in Charlestown, but he would have to deal with that a little later in the day. Audio/video tech Dave Watson was busy wiring a recorder to Mark's waistline and taping a microphone to his chest. "Hey, Dave, when are you going to start using that kind of tape that doesn't tear my skin off when we're done? Ripping off my chest hair is agonizing, so painful."

"I'm just making sure it sticks well to keep everything in place. You'll live big boy."

"When you tear my hair, it's the pain I disdain. If you try some tenderness, I will like you best."

"Guys, this knucklehead is rhyming again," announced Dave.

Jack and a couple other agents were there to assist with the undercover operation when Mark met his informant, Monique. Cautioning the team, Jack advised, "This is a low-key undertaking. There should be no danger but keep on your toes. Don't take anything for granted, she was arrested once with a gun and when Mark doesn't give her what she wants, who knows what might happen.

Mark, we have the phone hooked up to record your conversation. Are you ready to call her?"

"Absolutely. Let's do this. I'm ready to clear my name. You're not going to get any heat from the front office for this, are you?"

"No, I cleared it with them. For a change, they agreed it was the best and only way to fix this despite what IA said. Go ahead, ring her up."

"Hey, Monique, it's Mark. How are you?"

"To what do I owe this call?"

"You wanted some money. I have some money for you. Where can I meet you? It's burning a hole in my pocket because it belongs to you."

"It's about time you called. I've been thinking about you. How about noon at the club?"

"I have been thinking about you, too. See you then," Mark replied, with a thumbs up to his listeners. "That was easy enough, guys. I hope the meeting goes easy, too."

Less than two hours later, Mark was seated alone at a table in a darkened strip club, facing the door. The stink of stale beer assaulted his olfactory senses. He looked around at the few patrons who stared at a gyrating dancer on the stage while drinking their overpriced booze.

Only five minutes late, Monique sashayed through the door in a super short red dress that looked like it was glued to her skin. Mark had to admit, but only to himself, *damn, she looks sexy hot*. He stood to greet her with a quick hug. "You're still the hottest woman in this place. Always have been, always will be."

"I was hoping you liked what you saw. I dressed like this just for you." She sat opposite Mark, crossing her long legs, exposing most of her shapely thighs while dangling a shiny red high heel shoe from her right foot.

"Don't give me that, Monique. You dress like this every day. So, what have you been up to besides dancing?"

"Nothing much, except pining for you, babe. You know I miss our little get-togethers. I've always found you to be one of the sexiest men I have ever met."

"What? Only one of the sexiest, not the sexiest? I'm outraged," he kidded with her to assure she was comfortable with him.

"Mark, there's only one thing that keeps you from being numero uno." Monique slid her hand up the thigh of his navy blue suit pants.

Before she reached the peak of his inseam, he grasped her hand. "You mean if I sleep with you again, I could reach sexiest man in your life status?"

Falling for the trap, she responded, "Again? Was I there? You couldn't have been much in bed if I don't remember the occasion."

"Oh, I must have slept with you in my mind. I know I've thought about it."

"Babe, I've thought about you that way so often, I ache for you. I want you. Did you come here to give me money or finally give me your body?"

"You know, Monique, I care deeply about you, but as I've told you before, I can't and won't have sex with you. How many times have I told you that?"

"Way too many times I'm afraid." The listeners all looked at each other, grinning, flashing the thumbs up sign. She continued, "So, if we're not going to have sex, then how about that thousand dollars I asked for?"

"Monique, I never gave you any money before. Why would I do so now?" Her greed got the best of her.

She uncrossed her legs, leaned forward and surprised Mark by roughly grabbing his balls. "You shithead, you're not going to give me any fucking money? And I just bought this dress for you! I need some money to pay for it."

Until Mark squeezed a pressure point on her forearm, he couldn't speak, only grimace. But now, she was in pain, releasing her grip on Mark's private parts. "Listen, you got me in so much hot water with Internal Affairs. We always got along well, why did you do it to me?"

Now crying, Monique sobbed, "I fell for you, Mark. You are the only guy who always treated me like a lady, with respect. I loved that. You were always so sweet to me. I loved being with you and I wanted more, much more." Mark released his grip on her arm.

"I was so scared to testify, but I did it because I wanted to show you how much I cared for you. I got so pissed when I couldn't have you, at least I wanted some money. If you wouldn't give me any money, I just wanted to get back at you. I'm so sorry," she sobbed.

"Okay, okay, everything will be all right. We can still be friendly, but I can't have you as an informant anymore because you lied. I'll be fine although you caused me a lot of heartburn. If IA wants to speak to you again, just tell them the truth, just what you told me. Now, here's a couple hundred dollars toward your dress. Take care of yourself."

Mark walked out, elated. Cleared. Time to get back to real work.

✳   ✳   ✳   ✳   ✳

"Hey, guys, I called your secretary, Janice. She said you'd be here having lunch. I'm in a good mood, so I thought I'd pop in with some dessert from Mike's in the North End. I also heard about that fatal car fire in Charlestown with another dead woman. Is there any indication it is connected to the other fires? Any leads?" asked Mark as he strode through the FIU doorway with a delicious assortment of cannoli and Italian cookies. He hoped the goodies would soften his detractors' reactions caused by his uninvited appearance.

The usual good-natured Lt. O'Brien spoke first after he swallowed his last bite of a meatball sub. "What timing! Let's see what you have there." As he reached for the box, Mike wanted to short-circuit any surly remarks from his partner, Lt. Scherner, who still managed a long glare at Miller.

Boston Police Detective Artie Taylor didn't know about the animosity Dick held against Miller and ATF. "Hi, Mark. Pull up a seat. We'll give you all the gruesome details." Scherner only rolled his eyes undetected by neither Miller nor Taylor.

O'Brien and Taylor did all the talking. When they completed the update, Mark asked, "So, are you all feeling that the husband had nothing to do with her death?" For some gut feeling, Mark already knew the answer. He felt this killer was a ghost lurking within his head.

Dick chimed in, "It appears that he's only guilty of being a dickhead in the nighttime, leaving his wife in a bar because she was a repulsive witch. We're about to go over to the Warren Tavern where she was last seen alive. We need to speak to the bartender."

The phone on Lt. O'Brien's desk rang loudly. Mike scooted his chair over to his desk. "Fire investigation, Lt. O'Brien here. Yes, sir, we'll be there in fifteen minutes." He hung up. "Hey, Dick, we got a boyfriend who tossed a Molotov cocktail through the window of his girlfriend's house. There's a couple injuries, but none life threatening. The Chief would like us out there, pronto. What would you like to do?"

Contrary to his better judgment, Dick suggested, "Why don't Artie and I take it? That way we keep the fire and police team together. You go over to the tavern with Mark." He wished to keep an eye on Miller, so he didn't steal the investigation, but he really didn't want to work side by side with him either. So, he trusted Mike to handle Miller.

"Okay, Artie, let's roll. I'll probably see you here tomorrow, Mike. You can fill me in then on what you find out."

✳ ✳ ✳ ✳ ✳

Once outside in the parking lot, Mark suggested they take separate cars. "But Mark, the parking can be pretty miserable over there."

"Yeah, I know, but we won't be long. Then, I have something else I've got to do when we finish. Also, why don't you lead the interview. It will be good experience for you. I'll stand aside and add something if necessary."

"Okay, Mr. Interview Expert. Just watch the great information I get out of this guy. What do you have, a hot date?"

"No, not tonight. I need to check out something else. Okay, let's get going wise guy."

Walking into the tavern together, they saw the bartender with his back to them. He was busy stocking the coolers under the bar. Initially, he didn't look up from his task, but says, "My first customers of the evening. Grab a stool. Make yourself comfortable. I'll be right with you."

"Hey, Mike, I've got to hit the men's room. Those desserts aren't sitting right with me," as Mark slid his hand over his upset stomach. "I'll be a few minutes. Feel free to start without me." He walked slowly toward the restroom admiring some old-time photos lining the wall along his path. As he passed the bar, something drew his interest to a certain barstool. There was some quizzical pull toward the stool, but he continued into the men's room while pondering that strange magnetic attraction.

After Mark disappeared into the men's room, the bartender, with his mouth agape and his eyes wide, managed to whisper to Mike, "What's that guy doing here?"

Mike responded, "What are you talking about? That's ATF Special Agent Mark Miller and I'm Lieutenant Mike O'Brien from the Boston Fire Investigation Unit."

"I don't care who he is. He was in here last night and left with that woman who was killed in that car fire!" The bartender could barely contain his astonishment.

Now it was O'Brien's turn to be amazed, "What did you say? Are you sure? Maybe you remember him from TV. He's kind of famous."

"I'm telling you, man, he looks just like the guy in here last night. Only his hair seemed a little bushier last night. He was sitting right over there," pointing to the far corner of the bar. He was alone. I served him dinner and drinks.

Then the rich, loud-mouth woman was with her husband right here where you're sitting. They were arguing and as soon as the husband took off, that guy you're with moved onto the empty stool and started putting the moves on the woman. She was some looker, but what a bitch. He was pretty smooth. They had another drink, then they left together, all lovey-dovey."

Mike tried not to panic. Thinking on his feet, "Listen, real quick. When he comes out of the men's room, don't say a word about this. I'll come back to get some more info from you later after he leaves. By the way, did he pay with a credit card?"

"No, I distinctly remember cash because it was a $100 bill. Then he left a good tip. And the ladies' husband left money on the bar when he took off, which the woman used to pay their tab."

"Shhh! Here he comes. Try to act normal."

"So, Mike, you get anything?" Mark looked directly at the bartender, who stared, tight-lipped. Suddenly, he turned back to stocking beer bottles.

"Yeah, he did pretty good. I'll tell you about it outside. Then you can take off." To the bartender, he said, " Thanks, buddy for the info, if we think of anything else, we'll get back to you."

Standing outside on the narrow sidewalk in front of the tavern, Mike said, "Yeah, he remembered the guy and he knew the woman was killed in the car fire. The man paid cash. He was a white male, in his 30s, average height and build, with no remarkable features other than a mustache."

"Really? He remembered that much, huh? He looked at me kind of funny when I came out of the men's room. Did you ask him if he could describe the guy to a sketch artist?"

"I did, but he said the guy was just average. And he sees so many people on any given night that he didn't think he could do it justice. But I left him my card. He was really spooked to think that the woman died just down the street right after she left here, and she was killed in such an ugly way."

"He should be spooked. Just thinking he was one of the last people to see her alive and being a witness who could possibly identify her killer, I would think he should be worried that the guy might kill him next. Oh, well, not my problem. I'm going to head out. Thanks for doing this, good job."

"Sure thing, Mark. I think we'll get the guy soon. Bye for now." O'Brien waited a couple minutes, then returned inside the tavern to get a written statement from the bartender. Unable to contain himself, O'Brien radioed to his partner. "Where are you? I need to talk with you immediately, if not sooner! Wait until you hear what I just found out!"

✳   ✳   ✳   ✳   ✳

The morning after the car fire, Brantley turned on the morning news to check if there was information about the fire. He was surprised how much coverage there was.

There was video of the fire in progress moments before firefighters hit the blaze with water. Huge flames swirled high above the Mercedes mixed with copious plumes of black smoke. Soon after extinguishment of the fire, a reporter stood several feet from the vehicle while Fire Investigation Unit members made observations and took photos next to the car.

Completely blackened, stem to stern, the car was missing all its paint and tires. The banner along the bottom of the screen reported, "An Overnight Fatal Car Fire in Charlestown Under Investigation." Reporting live from the scene, the reporter said there was limited information at this time, but a badly charred body of an unidentified person had been located in the front passenger seat after the firefighters extinguished the fire.

Brantley knew the investigators would soon have more information but based on the damage he saw on the TV, it would be awhile before details would be released. He imagined the body of the woman was charred beyond recognition, merely a crispy critter. Most likely, her identification would have to be confirmed through dental records. That's what he had learned from reading those fire investigation books.

CHAPTER SEVENTEEN

Waking up alone in a cold sweat, Mark's chest was heaving, breathing heavily from the dream that caused him to awaken. He was chasing his brother through the Boston Garden but lost him outside. Mark had forgotten about his lookalike who he saw at the Garden months earlier. Now he realized that the man he chased that night most likely was his twin brother, Brantley.

Not able to fall back asleep, Mark went for an early morning jog. His mind was racing about his brother, so he thought he might as well burn some energy while he formulated a plan. The best place to start would be with his father. Over the past few weeks, they had spoken a couple times, but never about Brantley. Now it was time to delve into his mysterious sibling.

One thing Mark had learned about his father was that the man was an early riser. After a shower and a shave, Mark dialed his father while he sipped on a steaming cup of coffee. As soon as the phone was answered, Mark started, "Hi, Bill, it's Mark. Good morning."

"Good morning, Mark. But, please, if you can find it in your heart, call me Dad." Mark had not felt comfortable with that familial closeness yet. It was still difficult for him to embrace that level of intimacy. Having a father is one thing, but that is a far cry from having a dad.

"Okay, I'll try," he replied, "but it's still not an easy thing for me to comprehend."

"That's fine, Mark. I guess I can understand that. Believe me, I wish I could do it all over and have been a dad to you and your brother."

"Well, I called you because I want to learn more about Brantley. I was in such shock when you first told me about him that I never asked you for more details. You said you were going to check with your aunt or something, but I never even asked what my mother's sister's name is. You know, being the trained investigator I am, and all."

"I can understand your surprise. I would have thought you knew about them. Since we met, I wondered why your mother never told you about him. Maybe by the time you were old enough to understand, she was afraid to tell you. And as time went by, it was harder and harder to let you know. I've been curious myself about your brother, too. So I did some checking with my aunts and cousins who took care of your mother when she first arrived from Austria. Her relationship continued with them even after I took off. Did you even know that you had an aunt, who became Brantley's stepmother?"

"No, my mother was very tight-lipped about her life until just before she died. That's when she finally told me about you. Can you tell me anything more about her sister and Brantley? What was her name and where did they live?"

"Her name was Brigette Mueller. They didn't live that far from you in Rhode Island."

"You said Brigette Mueller? I know that name. Oh, my God!"

"What, you know that name?"

"Unbelievable! I recently investigated a fire in Rhode Island where a Brigette Mueller died. Her name was on a prescription bottle. She had terminal cancer. We found her cigarettes and remains of butts in the bathroom trash. Everything we looked at led us to believe the fire was accidental having been caused by improper handling, maybe careless disposal of her cigarettes in the trash container. She could have been somewhat out of it, being so sick and taking pain medicine and sleeping aids."

Bill sighed, "Oh, that's so awful. What an ugly way to die. I never heard about any of this from my relatives. Your mother never told them about this. Oh, that's right, she had already died before this happened. My bad."

"If it's any consolation, she at least died in her sleep. The evidence showed she never moved from her position in the bed. The smoke got to her before any heat did. And, you know, a neighbor told the Rhode Island guys that she may have had a son, but they couldn't find any record of a son. And the local investigator told me that no family attended the funeral, only a few friends. Now I know why they couldn't find any info on a son. I wonder where Brantley was?"

"What are you going to do next, Mark?"

"First, I think I'm going to check for license information on Brantley Mueller to find out where he lives and what he's driving. Then, I'll take it from there, maybe knock on his door, introduce myself. That would be a kick!"

"Okay, but again, just like reaching out to me, don't set yourself up with unrealistic expectations. You never know what he'll be like. It could be a shock to him, too."

"Hey, I just dreamed last night about when I was at a Boston Bruins hockey game recently, there was a guy sitting across the rink that looked just like me except for his haircut. It was quite a distance, so I couldn't be sure. But when I tried to locate him in the concourse, I saw him as he looked directly at me. Then, he took off running right out of the Garden. I tried to follow so I could meet this guy who looked like me, but I lost him out on the streets. I wonder if he already knew he had a twin brother and he didn't want to meet."

"Maybe," wondered Bill, "Just take it easy, be careful."

"I guess I just need to find out. Perhaps we'll end up having a great relationship. Brothers after all these years. I gotta go, thanks, Dad. I'll let you know what I find out."

Mark hung up before his father could respond. Bill caught the word he was waiting to hear. Dad.

✳   ✳   ✳   ✳   ✳

Brantley awoke in a foul mood since today he had to visit his office to complete his monthly sales reports. Normally, he would be on the road in eastern Massachusetts selling medical equipment. He wasn't particularly good at sales, barely making his monthly quota. Every month his boss would be on his case, hounding him to hustle more, seal the deal and make more sales.

What really riled up Brantley, was that his boss was a gorgeous woman. Long shapely legs always in heels, voluptuous ass and breasts, all topped by a stunning face framed by perfectly coiffed brunette hair. But the problem was that she was a bitchy, wicked woman who thought that her shit didn't stink. She wouldn't give him the time of day. *Better yet*, he thought, *she wouldn't tell me if my pants were on fire.* He giggled at his clever notion. *If she doesn't watch out, she's going to catch me on a bad day and she's going to be sorry.*

Walking into the company office, the first person he faced was his boss. "Morning, Ariel," was all Brantley managed to articulate. He was afraid if he said anything further, his loathing would get the better of him.

"Oh, look who honored us with his presence. What do we owe the privilege? Are you going to surprise us with a big sale today?" Her sarcasm oozed from her painted red lips.

"A 'hi' would have been nice, Ariel. You know I always check in once a month to complete my monthly paperwork," retorted Brantley. "What's going on here?"

"Everybody else is out selling their asses off. I'm the only one in the office today taking care of the monthly tabulations. Why don't you take a seat, Brantley? We need to talk."

Slowly, Brantley pulled a chair up close to Ariel's desk. He couldn't help but notice as she crossed her perfectly shaped legs. Her thighs became exposed as her short navy blue skirt inched up. Her lace bra was visible under a silky white blouse that allowed a view of ample cleavage. Brantley felt a sexual stirring. His eyes widened with the pleasurable view. And his nose flared as he breathed in deeply to inhale her sexual fragrance.

But this little tête-à-tête did not bode well for Brantley's psyche. "Okay, I want you to listen closely. I don't like you, Brantley. Besides being the worst salesperson I have ever encountered in my fifteen years in this business, your weird personality makes it difficult to warm up to you."

"You know, Ariel, if you bothered to try to get to know me, you might change your opinion. But you're too damn smug with a stick up your butt to learn that I might be this way for a reason." Brantley plainly stated his side in a soft matter-of-fact, but malicious, manner. His words only served to agitate Ariel.

"Listen to me, you pathetic, useless "little" man. There's no way on God's green earth that I would ever want to know anything about you! Apparently nobody does. You're so pitiful that you have no friends and not even a girlfriend." Her attacks were becoming more and more personal, more and more vicious.

Those words—pathetic, pitiful—pushed Brantley's buttons. Up rose the stinging fiery pain from his butt up his back to his neck and ears, both which were turning red as his body reacted to her disparaging remarks. This time Brantley relished his discomfort. He smiled at the vile woman sitting in front of him.

Ariel continued her onslaught of Brantley, "What the hell are you smiling at, you fuckin' sick little puppy? I'll bet you can't even satisfy a woman." Her voice rose higher and higher. More lewd and crass words flowed like an obscene river from that otherwise gorgeous mouth. "You're such an asshole. You loser! You're fired! Get the fuck out of my office now, and don't come back, ever!"

As Brantley rose from his chair, he continued to smile at Ariel because he knew what was to come soon. *You're gonna burn lady. I'll show you who the boss is. This one is going to be a fun job. It's even more personal this time than those other jobs. You, just like the others don't deserve to know the day or the hour of your death!*

"That's it, you little mutt. Go with that tail tucked between your legs." As Brantley exited the glass doorway, he didn't turn around as he waved goodbye with his middle finger.

But I'll see you real soon, bitch!

CHAPTER EIGHTEEN

As soon as Mark arrived at the office, he ran into his on again, off again girlfriend, Michelle. She looked as good as ever in hip-hugging black slacks and a black pinstripe blouse.

"Hi, kiddo. How's it going?" asked Mark.

"Good morning, sir."

"Oh, it's sir, huh? That type of day, is it?"

"Well, I'd like it to be dear or honey, but you keep me at arm's length all the time. I don't know if I'm coming or going. How do you expect me to feel? I really like you a lot, but I don't know if I can continue to play whatever game you're playing."

"Uh, yeah, about that. I'm sorry I don't give you what you want. I always seem to have a lot going on. How about this? I promise to try to do better in actions and in words. Why don't we grab something to eat tonight, and I'll fill you in on something that I'm working on right now?"

"That sounds like a good start," Michelle responded with an endearing smile. Talk to you about that later, okay? I've got a group meeting in a few minutes. See you later. You've brightened my day!"

"My day is pretty bright, too, after my little undercover operation cleared me of any wrongdoing. What a lift of impending doom off my shoulders! I'll fill you in when we get together."

"I would love to hear the details, I can't wait!" Michelle was beaming. She thought about how much work she had been putting into her own budding career. Like Mark, she wanted to excel on the job. She imagined falling in love, marrying a great guy and having kids. I would love being a mother. Kids are so great. Hopefully, someday in the not-to-distant future. And Mark could be the right guy, but there are some weird red flags that I have to think through. He has so many of the qualities that I want in a guy, but we need to figure some things out first.

Following his talk with Michelle, Mark went straight to the Teletype where he checked the Registry of Motor Vehicles data base. With Brantley's date of birth obviously the same as his and now knowing his last name, it was simply a matter of entering the data into the RMV's system. Brantley's info instantly popped up on the screen.

The records indicated Brantley lived in Apartment 4 on Lagrange Street in West Roxbury. A couple more clicks revealed he owned a 1971 red Dodge Challenger. Instantly, Mark connected the red Challenger he had seen that day near the Boston Garden with Brantley. *So, that was him at the game! I wonder why he ran from me.* He thought how funny it was that his brother also drove a muscle car, like himself. The only obvious difference was that Mark preferred his blue Chevy SuperSport over any Dodge product.

Also of interest to Mark was a slew of parking tickets listed for Brantley's car. He jotted down the date, time and location for each of them.

It took only a moment for Mark to decide to take a ride to West Roxbury to check out the address and maybe meet his brother. He yelled to the group secretary that he had to run to check out a lead. He shoved his notes on Brantley in a folder he stashed in the bottom right drawer of his desk.

Running and leaping down several stairs at a time in the stairwell that led to the basement of the new Tip O'Neill Federal Building, Mark's excitement energized him. There were so many questions and emotions swirling within his head. *Heck with work for now. This is another major piece of my life.*

Maneuvering his G-car in and around slow-moving cars westbound on the two-lane Storrow Drive along the Charles River, Mark exited onto congested Back Bay streets. He had to contend with one traffic light after another. As he sat at one red light, exasperation took over his body. Mark drummed his fingers along the top of the steering wheel while he blew out an audible deep breath.

I wonder what he's like. Will he like some of the same things I like? If he was at the Bruins' game alone, then he must like hockey. But he has no wife or girlfriend? What was his upbringing like? Was his stepmom more loving than our real mom was to me? She never once said, "I love you." She never once gave me a hug. Just like our father described her, 'She was a tough woman.'

Mark's mind raced from topic to topic. Between her Germanic upbringing and the lack of love between my father and her, then being a single mother scraping together enough money for us to live, that's the only way she knew how to love me. She was so cold, virtually no loving emotion. Just always demanding, commanding, pushing, pushing, pushing. She pushed me and any friends away because she was incapable of being close to anyone. I guess that's why I have such a hard time keeping a female relationship.

Mark absentmindedly turned left onto Lagrange Street from the VFW Parkway because a few years earlier one man involved in Mark's big M16 case lived a block down the street. Within seconds he saw the house numbers heading in the wrong direction plus these were all single family homes or two-family structures. He pulled a U-turn at his first opportunity.

Back at a stop light at the intersection with the VFW Parkway, Mark eyed a three-level brick apartment building right on the corner of the Parkway and Lagrange. He intuitively knew that was the right place. Once he reached the building, he parked in the small parking lot. The Dodge Challenger was not there, so he decided to wait a while to see if Brantley showed up.

After a short time, Mark imagined Brantley could be at work somewhere since it was nearly midday. He walked up to the main entrance to check the mailboxes in the small lobby. As he got to the door, a thirty-something woman exited the building. "Good morning, could you help me, please?" He pulled his badge out of his jacket pocket even though he was not there on official business. The badge made it easier to get information. "I'm looking for Brantley Mueller. Do you know him?"

"If that's the name of the guy that looks like you, I've run into him in the hallway a few times, but I didn't really know him. For a second, I thought you were him. Just your hair differs from his. But I think he moved out recently. I haven't seen him or his car lately. Here, look at his mailbox, Apartment 4. The name now is Rodriguez."

"Oh, wow, I just missed him. That's too bad," Mark was dejected. "Could you tell me anything about him?"

"Well," the woman paused, "he seemed nice enough, but a little standoffish, like he didn't want to be friendly."

"Any idea where he moved to or where he works? How about a girlfriend or something?"

"No idea what he did for work, he came and went at different hours of the day. I heard him come in sometimes in the middle of the night. I never saw him with anyone, no friends, no girls. And I heard from the mail carrier that he moved nearby, but I don't know where. Sorry I couldn't be more helpful."

After Mark thanked her, he headed to the local post office, which he knew from earlier travels was a mile away on Centre Street. Once there, he badged the postmaster seeking a forwarding address for Brantley. "Here it is," said the postmaster as he flicked through a stack of papers. "Yeah, he didn't go too far, just around the corner on Corey Street. A single family house, I believe."

Taking a right onto Corey, Mark found the two-story Colonial within a minute. No car was in the driveway, but he pulled in anyway. He rang the doorbell at the side door, but after no answer, he scouted the area. Luckily, there was a side street across from his house and another one ran next to his yard. These were perfect to view the driveway because there was no good place to park on the busy Corey Street.

He had come this far. His nervousness parched his throat. Mark knew he didn't want to leave. He was this close. Suddenly, he realized he had a date with Michelle that night. Deciding to bite the bullet, Mark drove to a shopping center on Centre Street where he used a pay phone to call Michelle's group. The group secretary, Donna, answered. "Hi, Donna, it's Mark Miller. Is Michelle around?

"Yes, she's at her desk. As a matter of fact, we were just talking about you. Hold on."

Upon answering, Michelle said, "Hey, there, mystery man. How's it going?"

"That's what I'm calling about. I've come up with something that I want to see through. I can't tell you about it now. But I might be tied up, so I need to break our date for tonight."

"Oh, really! Where are you? What's going on? Does Jack even know what you're up to?"

"Look, Michelle, I can't tell you anything, except I'm in Boston. It's kind of personal and work combined. Please don't ask anything else. I'll tell you when I know more. Nobody knows where I am or what I'm working on, but it's important to me."

"Well, if our relationship is going to grow, you're going to have to trust me instead of shutting me out. I'm not happy about this, but good luck and stay safe." End of conversation.

Mark stared at the receiver, shook his head. *Man oh man, I'm going to screw up a good thing.*

✳   ✳   ✳   ✳   ✳

Michelle frowned. With a huff, she stomped to the break room to grab a coffee. There, she ran into Carlo and Wojo. She didn't know them well, but they had kidded her about hanging out with Mark. When Carlo saw the unusual scowl on her face, he asked, "Hey, Michelle, what's going on? You don't look too happy. Did you have a lover's quarrel?"

"Well, at the moment, I'm a little miffed. Mark just broke a dinner date we had planned for tonight. He's being so weird and mysterious. You guys know what he's up to these days?"

Wojo responded, "We have no idea. We thought he was working on that serial arson case where women are getting torched. But now that you mention it, he has been acting a little strange lately with us, too. And I called him around eleven the other night and he didn't answer the phone. Was he at your house by any chance?"

"No, he hasn't been available for "me" time lately. I really like him a lot, but he's difficult to read. And when he gets in strange moods, he pushes me away. I'm starting to feel like a yo-yo. Our relationship has been a lot of ups and downs, like my emotions."

"I'm sorry to hear that," said Wojo. I spent many hours with him when he went through his divorce. It was rough on him. Did you hear that I even took his gun from him for a few days because I was afraid he might do something stupid?"

"Yeah, he told me how you guys stood by him and were so helpful. He seemed so grateful. And he owes you both so much."

"And did he tell you about his peculiar relationship with his mother, who was somewhat of a tyrant? She was not a loving mother, but rather, she was a bully. She intimidated and tormented him all the time. And his father left when he was a baby, so he never had a man in his life or the normal nurturing from parents. Somehow, he is a self-made man. It's a wonder that he has gotten to where he is today."

"He has barely talked to me about his mother. I could tell they weren't close. He seems secretive about something. I wish I could be there for him, get close enough so he would fully trust me to share everything."

"Well," started Carlo, "Hang in there. Give him time. I think you'll be good for him. We're rooting for you two."

"Thanks, guys. You really are good guys. I'll give it a good chance."

✳   ✳   ✳   ✳   ✳

On the quiet side street across from Brantley's house, Mark had an unobstructed view of the house front and the driveway. He settled in with his favorite, a giant Italian sub with all the fixings, a bag of ruffled chips and a Diet Coke to wash it all down.

Hmmm, he thought.

I'm going to stay here until he gets home. There's so much I want to know. This could be great. Or it could be a disaster. Will he embrace me as a brother? Does he know anything about me? Probably not, or else he would have reached out to me.

Mark's mind was swirling with so much of the unknown.

Is this obsession with meeting my brother going to destroy my promising connection with Michelle? I think she's great, cute, beautiful, sexy, fun, and really smart. She's so motivated. There's nothing I don't like about her. But, man, I'm starting to piss her off. I hope I don't push her away too much while I see this through. I know she's getting frustrated, but I don't want to tell her what I'm doing yet. Damn secrets.

As night fell, the darkness surrounded Mark. With his mind occupied with so many different subjects, he hardly noticed losing daylight. Still no Brantley.

Damn secrets have shaped my life. Now, I'm doing the same thing my mother did to me. No wonder she kept my aunt, and especially my brother from me. She was probably ashamed or embarrassed because she couldn't care for the two of us. Giving him away was probably torture.

Hell, she couldn't really care for me either! I can understand a parent has to be strict for the good and safety of the child, but she was always like a Nazi drill sergeant, just like the way she was brought up. Not once did she ever show love. She never even hugged me, never said, "I'm proud of you, son."

And then I always wondered if every time she looked at me, she saw the image of my father who left her in the lurch with two baby boys. She punished me at every turn, always yelling, scolding and being negative. I'll never forget when she slapped me across the face or the time she hurled a dry cell battery, hitting me square in the face. You would think she would have apologized for something like that. No, it was more like, "Look what you made me do. You deserved it." I've gone over this so many times in my head. Enough already, I need to get rid of these thoughts, start a new chapter.

She always said, "If you want to become anybody in this world, don't count on me for help. I don't care what you do. You'll just have to do it yourself."

And that's just what I did. Between working my ass off, student loans and scholarships, I put myself through school. And I always managed to be near the top of my class all the way through college. I guess I have her to thank for my stubborn drive. And that stubbornness can be a blessing and a curse. I don't quit or ever give up, but I know I can be hard to live with. With me, my way was always the right way, exactly like my mother always shoved down my throat. Nothing I did was ever done correctly. My obsessive traits, my passive-aggressive behavior, stems from how I was raised, no doubt. Now, at least I know my faults. I heard it all from my ex-wife and my psychiatrist.

Down days, hell, I had plenty of those going through the divorce, a lot of time to contemplate how my personality affected other people. I'm trying to be a kinder, gentler person who thinks and acts on emotions instead of bottling everything inside, then blowing up. I'm getting there, but I've got a ways to go.

Nine o'clock now. No Brantley. Mark wondered about where Brantley could be and how long he would wait. What was he up to? I'm feeling it's not something good. It was time to focus on something else. Surveillances, especially when I'm alone, always provide a lot of time for thinking, for introspection. More time for thinking, but a different tract now.

What are we going to do next about this guy cooking women? What do we have so far, three, four? The woman in Southie bound to her bed, no accelerant detected except crumpled newspaper. The one in JP, a liquid accelerant, also bound to her bed posts, but with cloth ties. The car fire in Charlestown. Potato chips and gasoline according to the Boston guys but too much damage to determine if and how she was restrained. The fires have been all over the city, so geographical profiling probably won't help pinpoint the perp.

Why does Scherner dislike me so much? O'Brien told me how his partner didn't want to call me for that car fire. Well, to hell with him. I'm going to keep pushing on these fires until we solve this case and any other that comes across my bow.

It certainly didn't help that my office and I did most of the work to crack that enormous case involving a Boston firefighter. And then the bosses really screwed up by having the press conference without BFD being present. It seems I'm always riding against the wind, sometimes a gale force wind.

We have to get a profile together on this guy. How does this arsonist pick his victims? They apparently don't have anything in common. How does he subdue these ladies? It seems like he's experimenting with his restraints and his method of setting the fires. What is his motivation?

With the brutal viciousness of his murders, there could be a deep-seated hatred for some real or perceived wrong. At least, that's how they explained it in the profiling class I took. Could have been some sort of abuse involved, often from a domineering mother.

As if I didn't know one of those. And so, it comes around again. Some people can handle the crap dished out to them, some can't. And there's always degrees of abuse and other related factors to consider. Yeah, like I didn't have a father around to help me grow up to be a man. The stubbornness that my mother drummed into me caused me to push myself to succeed. I know I still have issues to work on, but who doesn't.

Enough about me. Back to the bad guy. More profiling. The timing of his fires is always after dark, but before midnight. What does that suggest? Does he stalk his targets? How much planning does he do before he attacks? And so far the fires have been set on three different days of the week, so there is no pattern there to help us catch him. This could be a tough one to solve. It probably will come down to some fluke that gets him caught.

Mark fell asleep, drifting into a dream.

CHAPTER NINETEEN

As Mark sat across from his brother's house, Brantley was only a mile away checking his freshly stocked go-bag to be sure he had everything he needed to quell his burning desires. There was one new addition to his bag that he expected would play a significant role in his scheme. He was not going to waste the beauty and seething sexuality that radiated from his former boss.

As the sun started to dip in the western sky, Brantley cruised in his Challenger with the music blaring from his CD player. He was rocking out to Aerosmith's *Dream On, Walk This Way* and *Devil's Got a New Disguise*. But he particularly loved when he heard one song from the album, *The Crazy World of Arthur Brown* as the singer ripped these words, "I am the god of hell fire and I bring you, Fire." It gets him juiced up for the deliciously vicious deed he would soon commit.

Brantley pulled into the small parking lot out of view of the company's windows. There was only a handful of vehicles in the lot.

Ariel would be working late as she always did to complete her monthly review. Hopping out of his car with his go-bag, he pulled the hood of his black hoodie up to mostly hide his face from any people still working in the area. Brantley couldn't help himself from whistling the tune from *Fire*. He was in a joyous mood as he walked through the glass door into his old office.

As he flipped his hoodie back, Ariel spotted him striding toward her with a confident look that she had never seen before. "What the hell are you doing here? I told you to never come back."

Brantley dropped his bag at her office door, then used a ruse similar to the one he used against his first victim. "I know, I know, but my lawyer told me to hand this to you." Without further explanation, he quickly closed the gap with the envelope in his outstretched left hand.

Ariel's eyes were focused on the envelope. Brantley's right hand embraced his stun gun hidden in his hoodie pocket. He yanked it from his pocket, instantaneously brandishing it, then hitting her neck with a burst from the gun before she knew what was happening. *Zap!!*

Ow!! Ariel buckled to her knees, writhing, shaking with spasms, then collapsing into a fetal position as she howled with the stinging pain. Confused and disoriented, Ariel remained on the floor as Brantley swiftly grabbed his bag before he grasped her right leg. Dragging her a couple feet to her desk, he knocked her shiny four-inch heels off her feet, then tightly zip-tied her ankle to the desk leg, leaving her other limbs free so he could have some fun.

After pulling on his latex gloves, Brantley closed all the window blinds as Ariel started futilely flailing at him, but he leaped just beyond her reach. "You rotten sleazebag, son-of-a-bitch! You're not going to get away with whatever you're planning."

"That's for me to worry about. And I don't worry about it because I may be a terrible salesman, but I'm a very good criminal. Now, listen very carefully. We can do this the easy way or the hard way."

"Fuck you, Brantley. I don't take orders from you."

"You're not really in a position of power to not do as I say." He approached Ariel, putting himself within her reach. With surprising strength, she lunged at him, kicking with her one free leg and thrashing at him with all her might. She figured all she could do was fight to try to gain control of her attacker. She connected several times, gouging his face with her painted fingernails and ripping at his hands and arms.

"Whoa, bitch, take this." He zapped her a second time with the stun gun. Ariel howled a second time as she crumpled to the floor again. Brantley plucked her off the floor, throwing her dazed body into her high-backed black leather chair. "I guess I have to do this my way. That's okay by me."

Brantley ripped open her filmy, delicate blouse and yanked her bra down below her breasts. He marveled at the contrast of the summer bikini tan lines she had with the round, creamy flesh, topped with perky reddish brown nipples standing at attention. Cupping her boobs in each hand, they were a perfect fit, so soft, pliable, yet firm. He awkwardly manipulated her breasts, lightly squeezing them until he realized there was more he wanted.

Ariel's face was still flopped to one side, positioned toward her chest and shoulder. Her eyes were closed, but her red-lipped mouth hung slightly open as she drew in gasps of air. Brantley pushed her tousled hair aside, making it look much neater.

Next, he forcefully jerked down her skirt, leaving it hanging on her restrained right ankle. A pale blue thong covered a small patch of pubic hair. Brantley moved back to his bag where he retrieved his old Polaroid camera. He didn't want to risk having this sexy photo of Ariel developed in a store.

Standing back a few feet from his trophy, Brantley admired the stunning beauty that Ariel displayed. *Every inch of her body is perfectly perfect, so beautiful and, damn, she is so sexy.* He took two photos of her, capturing her beauty for perpetuity. He had a plan for one of these.

Again, although his prurient interest in Ariel caused his loins to twitch, he remained limp. *You filthy man. What a disgusting pig you are! Are you going to make a mess again. Can't you control yourself?* His mother's voice echoed in his head.

Anger took over. *Go away, you witch. Can't you leave me the fuck alone?* Suddenly, the searing pain enveloped him, overwhelming his entire being. His body throbbed more than ever. *Please go away. I can't take this anymore.* Brantley began to sob.

"Oh, what's the matter, the little boy can't take advantage of the nearly naked woman in front of him?" Ariel had regained consciousness. She oriented herself to her circumstances. "Do you find me sexy, Brantley?

Do you want to fuck me?" She pulled her panties aside to expose herself completely to him. She laughed at him. "I guess you really are a pathetic excuse for a man. You really can't get it up, can you?"

Brantley felt his manhood stir, start to harden as he stared at Ariel's sexy body. "*Stop looking at that, you dirty, disgusting boy.*" His mother's voice again reverberated in his mind. Get out of my head. Leave me alone! The agony, both physically and emotionally. Life's derision ate him up. Everyone mocks me. I've had enough. Time to take control and show her and everyone else that I am a man. And I'll be a revered murderer.

"Okay, you witch. Even now, when you are losing, you can't even bring yourself to pretend to be a nice person."

"Why should I? Would that fool you to change your mind about whatever you're going to do with me? A loser will always be a loser."

With that, Brantley pounced on her, firing his stun gun again, this time directly on her left breast. Nothing happened. He squeezed the trigger again. Nothing. *Damn batteries must be dead.*

"Nothing happened, loser. Just like you, your little gun couldn't get it up either." Ariel fought Brantley off the best she could considering the two bursts from the stun gun she had already received.

But Brantley had had enough. "Shut your fucking pie-hole, bitch!" With that he hurled a horrific right upper cut to her jaw, shattering some teeth. He nearly knocked her senseless again. Gathering his own senses, he rapidly secured her free ankle to the same desk leg. He cinched both wrists together behind her back with multiple wire ties.

After crumpling newspapers all around Ariel, and leading papers from the desk out toward the door, Brantley recklessly splashed gasoline all over her and the papers. Emotions rushed his actions. As he stood by the doorway, he began to sing out loud, "Fire, I'll take you to burn. You're gonna burn, burn, burn." Ha, ha, ha, ha! His fiendish laughs were rip-roaringly loud.

Interlacing a cigarette within a matchbook, Brantley struck a match head against the abrasive striking surface of the matchbook. *FLASH!*

WOOMPH! His sloppiness caused an instantaneous flash fire of the accumulated gasoline vapors. The entire office area became a giant fireball that danced with a rapid ebb and flow of oxygen consumption. The office windows fractured catastrophically sending glass dozens of feet from the building.

The force generated by the fuel-air deflagration forcefully propelled Brantley right through the swinging office door into the main lobby of the building. Landing on his back with a thud, the intensity of the fall knocked the wind out of him. Once he got his breath and realized what had occurred, he picked himself up, steadied his wobbly legs with the help of the wall, retrieved his bag, then hurried to the parking lot. As he moved, he pulled off his latex gloves, shoving them into a pocket of his hoodie. He then flipped his hood up again to obscure his face. He was afraid the little conflagration he caused would attract immediate attention, so he dashed to his car and peeled out of the parking lot.

A mile from the fire Brantley pulled into a well-lit supermarket lot. He sat back for a moment sucking in a couple deep breaths to slow his heart rate. With the aid of his interior lights, he checked his face in the rearview mirror. There were red blotches with skin blisters all over his face. The injuries burned like hell. Even his eyebrows and the front of his hairline were singed and crinkled. He hardly noticed the scratch marks near his left ear and on two fingers of his left hand. *Man oh man, I kinda screwed that one up. I let my emotions get the best of me. My head must have been up my ass.*

Finally, thoughts of Ariel came to mind. *That fucking, bitch. I hope she suffered. This would never have happened if she hadn't fought me. It's too bad that a woman's physical beauty doesn't translate to an equally lovely inner persona. What a waste! I don't understand people. Why do they have to be so mean and treat people like crap. Even if someone is weird or different, that's no reason to be nasty toward them. I wonder if she died from the fire.*

For the first time in his fire-setting career, Brantley decided to go back to the scene. But he knew he had to park some distance from the building and be careful so nobody sees him. He learned from his research that investigators often photograph the crowd so that a possible arsonist could be identified.

Parking his car in the nearest office park, Brantley tracked through the woods to a vantage point where he could see the gaping office windows of his former place of employment. From his location he watched a chaotic assembly of fire vehicles, police cruisers and ambulances with first responders scurrying around to perform various duties. Red and blue lights were flashing brightly, bouncing off every facing surface. The diesel engine roar from the fire apparatus blocked out most other sounds. Pungent odors of charred wood, plastics and other burned materials permeated the air.

No flames were visible, only various shades of gray smoke plus clouds of whitish steam generated by the cold water from the firefighters' hoses on the initial flames and hot surfaces within the office. Ladder trucks poured water onto collapsed sections of the roof while firefighters on the ground manned hoses aiming their water through the openings where the windows had blown out.

Brantley tentatively watched the action. This is the first active fire scene he has ever witnessed from the 'spectator seats'. The open burns on his face continued to sting and throb. But his obstinacy refused to let the pain interfere with his curiosity. It was merely a nuisance.

Suddenly, there was a new flurry of activity, a rushed, almost frantic commotion. EMTs and paramedics sprinted into the building carrying a stretcher and rolling a gurney. Brantley waited anxiously for them to exit with a patient or a body.

Within minutes, the gurney rolled out the front door surrounded by firefighters, one holding an IV bottle high above the sheet covered human. Brantley could only imagine the person lying on that rolling cart must still be alive. Otherwise, a body would be carried out by the ME's office. And no IV would be necessary. When the crowd moved momentarily away from the gurney, he was shocked to see an oxygen mask on the face of a woman with thick brunette hair hanging off the side of the cart. *Ariel! She's alive!*

✳ ✳ ✳ ✳ ✳

Another dream unnerved Mark as he slept in his car while he waited for his brother to come home. Michelle and Brantley were dancing at a club as he watched from a distance. He had to get something out of his car. Once outside the venue, on a darkened city street, Mark couldn't remember where his car was parked. *It must be this way.* Turning this way at the corner and the other way at the next corner, he realized he had no idea where it was. He anxiously continued on, turn after turn, street after street, until he finally found it.

Mark took his gun out of his trunk, holstering it on his right hip. Time to get back before that brother of mine steals my girl. Everything looked alike. Sidewalks, parked cars, pitch-black storefronts. *Now, which way do I go to get back? I'm lost. Again.*

Finally, he sees the club down the street, but something else alerts him. Brantley is pushing Michelle into a car. *"No, no, don't go with him!"* Mark tried to scream, but no sound came out. Brantley turned toward Mark with the most malicious smile on his face.

Suddenly, Mark awoke to the sound of a slamming car door. He was a little fuzzy after the cat nap. Looking at his watch, it was 11:30. Then he looked up. Brantley had pulled into his driveway. Mark slouched as low in his seat as possible while still being able to see across the street. The mature maple tree he was parked under shaded his car from direct street lighting. Using a pair of binoculars he always keeps handy, Mark spied on his brother.

As luck would have it, the illumination from the streetlights on the corner shone on Brantley at the trunk of his Dodge Challenger. He furtively looked around as he gathered a black bag before scurrying around his car toward the side door of his house. His eyes looked directly toward Mark's position, but there was no look of recognition or curiosity. As he moved, Mark saw Brantley's face through the binoculars. He had fresh red blotches of sores on his face. A look of apprehension was highlighted by what appeared to be crinkly, freshly burned hair. Then Brantley disappeared into his house.

"What the hell?" Puzzled by what he saw, or at least thought he saw, Mark decided this might not be a good time to meet his brother. Waiting a few minutes so as not to alert Brantley that someone may have seen him, Mark sat still, confused and disappointed. Then he started his car and headed home. Fog was moving in, both outside his vehicle and within his head.

CHAPTER TWENTY

Lt. Mike O'Brien dialed Agent Miller's home number. He had just received notice from the District Chief in Roslindale that there was another dead woman at an office fire. Miller's phone rang a dozen times, but nobody answered. "Where is he at this time of night?" O'Brien wondered aloud. He then left a message on Miller's answering machine.

"He's not home again?" quizzed Scherner. "Seems like every time you call him at night, he's never around. That's fine by me. I still don't like him. His egotistical nature irks me. I also hate that he is so controlling, always telling us what to do at a fire, like he's our boss or something. And I'm telling you, there's something about him that's going to come back to bite us right in the ass. As I've said before, I can't put my finger on it, but he doesn't make it easy to like him. Not only is he standoffish, but he could be an arsonist."

"Dick, I don't think you give him a chance. You're going to have to fake it, or at least put up with him until we figure this out. He can tell you don't like him, or ATF for that matter, so that probably affects his personality around you. I think he just gave me his new pager number. Yeah, here it is. I'll give this a try."

Fifteen minutes after the pager alerted, Mark dialed the number back. "Fire Investigation Unit, may I help you?"

"Hi, this is ATF Special Agent Mark Miller. Someone just called me from this number. Maybe it was Lt. O'Brien."

"Oh, Mark, Mike left a message for you. He went to a fatal fire in Roslindale. He thought you might want to go. Here's the address."

Mark had just arrived home from his long day and night trying to locate and meet his brother. He was dog tired, but he knew he should join the others at the fire scene. He washed his face to freshen up, pulled on some suitable clothing to wear, then hopped back in his car.

✳   ✳   ✳   ✳   ✳

During his thirty-minute trip to the scene, Mark got to thinking. He didn't blue light it to the fire because he needed time to ponder what he saw at Brantley's house and his own anxiety that was eating at him.

Where was he before he got home? What's with the sores on his face and the singed hair? It looks like he suffered some burns. Could he have something to do with this fire tonight?

But he's my brother for Christ's sake! I don't even know him yet. Just when I began to think I found another missing piece in my life, a brother who could be my buddy, my family, I might lose him. How could I think that he could be setting fires? There must be some explanation.

I wonder what happened at this fire. I don't even know if there was a fatality. But, since Mike called me in the middle of the night, it might be another one that killed a woman. Damn! Is there any possibility that Brantley, my brother, the brother of a fire investigator is setting these fires?

God, oh God. Now I'm in the middle of this shit. I have to do everything I can to figure this out before anybody else does. What should I do? I'm going to get myself in trouble here if I don't tell someone. But tell them what? That my brother, who I have never even met, is murdering women by fire? Where's my proof? I have no evidence. They'll think I'm nuts, going off the deep end.

Should I just go up to Brantley and introduce myself? Hey, I'm your brother, what have you been up to? Or maybe he'll just shoot me dead. That's a little overly dramatic. But just to get to meet him, I'm going to have to surveil his house again because I don't have any other way to contact him. I could be screwing things up with Michelle, my buddies, with the Boston Fire guys, and even with my freaking career.

Okay, slow down, Mark. You're getting way ahead of yourself. Let's see what they have tonight, and I'll go from there.

Mark pulled into the parking lot of the fire building, where he had to badge his way past a police detail at the head of the driveway.

✳   ✳   ✳   ✳   ✳

BFD Lieutenants Scherner and O'Brien, along with BPD Detective Artie Taylor had been working the fire scene for over an hour. "Well, your buddy is late, figures. Doesn't ATF stand for After the Fact? We do all of the hard work, then pretty boy shows up to take the glory. That guy hardly ever gets dirty," griped Scherner.

"All you do is complain about Miller. He's a busy guy you know," replied O'Brien.

"Oh, yeah, he doesn't let me forget that his badge says U.S. So, I guess the hotshot could be anyplace in the old U S of A."

"Dick, if you weren't bellyaching all the time, maybe we could have solved this case by now."

"I'm working on it, Mike. When Miller finally gets here, pay particular attention to his attitude, what he does and what he says. We have to keep him as our primary suspect until proven otherwise based on what that bartender told us. As they say, 'Keep your friends close and your enemies closer'."

"So, Miller is on your enemies list? Won't you be surprised when he proves you wrong?"

Dick was on his knees using a handheld garden cultivator with metal prongs as a small rake to carefully sift through the smaller pieces of fire debris. "Oh, guys, look what I just found." He was working on the floor at the base of Ariel's desk. Using his trowel, Dick pointed to a small cream-colored object.

Not being able to figure out what Dick was pointing toward from his standing position, Mike bent closer, but still couldn't determine the identity of the item. "What is it, Dick?"

"Oh, it's only something that can break the case wide open. It's a fingertip piece of a latex glove, most likely from the arsonist. She must have bravely tried to fight back."

Detective Taylor stated, "We can try to get a fingerprint or maybe DNA from that. Let me get some photos of it. While I do that, why don't you put on double latex gloves yourself, Dick? That way, the outer pair is not contaminated by you touching it directly with your bare hand. And use this."

A minute later, Dick plucked the evidence off the floor with a pair of tweezers. Holding the piece in his palm, the three men stared at it. "Do you see that dark brownish stain on the inside edge of the latex?"

Artie said, "That could likely be dried blood. What a great find, Dick. Keen eye."

Dick placed the sample in a small brown paper bag. He then stored that in a special case where he held any evidence until he could deliver it to the appropriate forensic lab for detailed scientific analysis. "Now, listen Mike and Artie. Listen real close. Miller's going to walk in any minute. We cannot, under any circumstances, tell him about this. This piece could prove or disprove whether he is the arsonist. Remember, Artie, we told you about him being identified as walking out with that woman from the car fire? Are you on board?"

"I'm not comfortable with this, Dick, but I can understand. It won't hurt either way except if we identify somebody else as the torch and he gets pissed because we hid the evidence on him. Will we at least tell the other ATF guys, Tom and Dennis, maybe enlist their help or get their advice?"

"I guess we could. If we do I.D. someone else, yeah, he'll probably get angry, but we can explain everything to him. It's up to him to either accept what we did or be pissed off. I'm willing to take that risk. And I don't give a shit about his feelings. What do you guys think?"

Mike and Artie looked at each other, shrugged their shoulders and nodded their agreement.

*   *   *   *   *

As predicted, Mark walked through the door wearing his blue BDUs with the large 'ATF' lettering across the back of his shirt. He saw Dick and Mike with their heads down, focused on their task of clearing the floor with full sized rakes while Artie stood behind them with a square blade shovel to scrape the discarded debris into a pile.

"Gentlemen, sorry I'm late."

"Again," Dick responded. "We don't need to hear any excuses. We give you a courtesy call, but you're never around and show up after a lot of the work is done. I think that's to be expected from you Feds."

"Okay, okay, you're right. I deserved that. Now, that we got the admonishments over, can you fill me in on what you know so far?"

"Sure, Mark," offered Mike while nodding at Dick. "Here, have a water. We were just about to take a break. Mark, where's your helmet? You won't want to be in here without one."

"Oh, I left it in our response truck the other day."

Hey, Artie, can you run out and grab one of ours, but wipe it out real good with some alcohol so Mark doesn't have to deal with one of our dirty, sweaty helmets." Dick was thinking on his feet about the potential for DNA evidence.

"Okay, Mark, the fire came in at 7:22 this evening. Automatic alarm from the building. A police officer got here first. He said flames were blowing out all these windows," as he pointed toward the empty window frames. "But he said the flames died down fairly quickly when a section of roof collapsed into the office.

The Chief told us when his people made entry to knock down the remainder of the fire, they flipped over some fallen ceiling tiles where they discovered a woman. Both her ankles were zip-tied to the leg of this desk here," indicating a corner of the desk nearest to the outer wall. Also, her wrists were zip-tied together behind her back."

Mark interrupted, "Where is she? Dead, I presume."

"Not this time," Dick answered. "What must have happened was there was a gasoline fuel-air explosion that caused a raging flash fire. The windows blew out. The tiles from the suspended ceiling dropped to cover and protect most everything under them, including the woman."

"Ohhh, wow." The three local investigators noted the drawn out phrase and the scrunched facial expression on Mark's face. "Was she able to say anything about what happened? What condition was she in?"

Taylor answered this time. "She was in poor shape. She was nearly naked when the fire happened, but her panties were still on. She was in and out of consciousness. The flash fire may have seared her throat. If it swells, she might not make it. The Chief said she probably had at least fifty percent of her body covered with second degree burns. And something else, he said a bunch of her teeth were busted. We found a couple broken pieces behind the desk here."

"Oh, that's too bad. Sounds like she might not make it. And sounds like our guy escalated to a new level. Or maybe this was a copycat fire," offered Mark.

"I don't think so hotshot," Dick sneered. "Too many similarities we never publicized. The zip ties. We found newspapers protected under the fallen ceiling tiles. They were used as a trailer with gasoline splashed on them."

"But stripping the woman first and then attacking her are different. Maybe he thought about raping her, but in a fit of anger, he ended up knocking her teeth out. And this fire is in an office which differs from the bedroom fires and the car fire."

"Well, nobody said the arsonist knocked her teeth out, Mark," said Mike.

"Uh, you're right. I just assumed that's what happened. Trying to think like the profiler."

Dick tried baiting Mark. "And maybe he's an opportunist, like picking up that woman in the Warren Tavern. He could have stalked this woman and watched her here to target her when she was alone."

"Yeah, I think he probably stalked every one of these women, like an animal stalking his prey."

"Are you trying to get inside his head, Mark? Sounds like you have insight into his psyche?" Dick added, "Is that what you've been doing with your nights and spare time, brushing up on serial criminals?"

"You know, I certainly find the specialty of researching serial offenders, especially serial arsonists extremely interesting. A serial offender lives in all of us. Life, more than genes, is what makes one commit crazy obsessive compulsive deeds like these offenders do."

"Okay, Dr. Miller, the crazed serial investigator!" Mike laughed heartily. His partner just frowned at Mike's attempt at wit.

✳   ✳   ✳   ✳   ✳

After completely clearing the debris from the office floor and performing their due diligence to examine other potential ignition sources, the investigators concluded this fire was intentionally set by the same arsonist who previously killed several other women. Evidence samples were collected and placed in appropriate containers.

The three local investigators all remained mum about the one potentially crucial item of evidence they found earlier, the fragment of a latex glove.

✳   ✳   ✳   ✳   ✳

As they exited the same glass office doors where Brantley was abruptly discharged a few hours earlier, Mark asked, "What is this business anyway, MedRX?" Any employees?

Detective Taylor answered, "It's a medical equipment sales business. The sales people only come in and out once a month according to the building management company. We recovered the woman's handbag from her desk drawer. Her name is Ariel Garcia."

"We'll have to check to find out the sales people's names. Then, interview them all," stated Mark. "Should someone head over to the hospital in case she can talk?"

Dick immediately offered, "I'll run over with Artie. She's probably not going to be alive, much less conscious. But we'll maintain the police/fire team anyway." He didn't want Mark anywhere near Ariel if she could talk. He had a plan that might pay off.

"Okay, then. If we're all set here, I'll head to my office to see if I can locate a parent company for MedRX, or maybe their main office. Hopefully, I can get a list of employees. Oh, here's your helmet, thanks. Bye for now Mike, Dick, Artie. And thanks for the call. Next time I'll be on the ball. I'll work on being more accessible to you all next time. And I'll try not to be late for our next fire date." Mark laughed.

Nobody else did. "Yeah, Mark, see what you can do about that. *Catch* you at the next one," Mike replied. He inwardly smiled at his clever double meaning.

CHAPTER TWENTY-ONE

"So, how many do we have now?" asked Chief Jack Brown, who headed the Boston Fire Department's newly renamed Fire Investigation Unit, formerly known as the Arson Squad.

Lt. Scherner spoke up, "Counting the office fire two days ago, we have four fatal fires with solo female victims, plus we have at least two others that we are working on that we think are linked to the same arsonist."

The chief opened the first meeting of the Serial Arson Task Force being held at the ATF office only because their large comfortable conference room could hold this crowd of investigators. Besides Chief Brown and Lt. Scherner, BFD was represented by Lt. Mike O'Brien. BPD Detective Taylor represented the Boston Police.

Mark was the ATF case agent, but ATF assigned two other experienced arson investigators, Tom "Wojo" Walkowski and Dennis "Carlo" Caggiano. Jack, the Arson Group Supervisor, also selected Michelle to work on the task force for two reasons. She had studied psychology courses such as deviant behavior and serial criminals as part of her criminal justice curriculum, plus she had accomplished outstanding work since she came on board.

Other members included Dr. Denise Williams from the ME's office and ATF Special Agent Daryl Hawkins from the Arson Branch in D.C. where he specialized in criminal profiling. Prosecutor Marty Regan represented the Suffolk County D.A.'s Office.

This investigation was unlike any other these members had ever worked on except for profiler Hawkins who had worked on dozens of serial arson cases. Everyone introduced themselves to the group before getting down to the serious business of trying to solve this investigation before this murderous arsonist killed another victim. Chief Brown started things off, "Since all of us who are local have pondered these fires as they occurred, Agent Hawkins could you fill us in on your analysis of the fires and the arsonist?"

"Sure, Chief," responded Hawkins. I have discussed the case with Agent Miller, your Lieutenants Scherner and O'Brien, plus Dr. Williams. I think she has some more news for you all, too. I'll give her the floor after I tell you what I think. I have also reviewed all reports that have been generated to date, and I have visited each crime scene, viewed all photos and looked at the physical evidence. In addition, either you or I personally have interviewed family members and any people close to the victims. So far, you have all done everything that could be done except for this profile and any DNA analysis.

First, I think we all can agree that our perp is a male. Most serial arsonists are men, but with this level of malice against women, it is definitely a male. Most likely a white male because, again, the stats show most serial arsonists are white. Here, with all of the targets being white women, previous analyses have learned that a white male is committing these crimes.

So far, there is no evidence to suggest how he chooses his targets. The only commonalities in the women, besides being white, are that they are all between twenty-five and thirty-five years old, unmarried and they live alone. None of them knew each other, went to school together or worked together. They all came from different neighborhoods and did not frequent the same locations for groceries or socializing.

His age is most likely in the same category as the women, which puts them in the same locale where he targeted them. He is educated and may even have training in police or fire background because his fire sets have progressed with trailers such as newspapers and liquid accelerant.

We're not sure how he subdues his targets, but after he does he restrains each one so they can't fight back or escape. Again, it appears that he is evolving on his use of the types of restraints he uses. For some reason he has changed back and forth using cloth strips and/or zip ties. The perp does not care that the fires are rather easily determined to be intentionally set. He is organized, planning his every move and taking everything he needs with him.

All we can figure is that he lives, and possibly works, in Boston because all of his victims have been here, but there is no pattern yet to give us a clue as to where he lives. The temporal patterns indicate that his fires are set in the evening, usually after dark, but not too late, before midnight. There is nothing we can hang our hat on about the day of the week he sets his fires. So far, we have sets on all week days. None have been set on Saturday or Sunday, so it's possible he does something different or goes away on weekends.

The guy is probably a loner with no well-established friends or female relationships. He has not raped, sexually assaulted or had sex with any of the women."

Carlo interrupted, "So what does that say about this animal?"

"Good question," replied Agent Hawkins. "Glad to see you're all paying attention. The lack of sex means he may be inadequate in that department. Perhaps he can't perform or is insecure in his masculinity. Something is keeping his sex drive under control.

Something like this often indicates mommy issues. Possibly mental, physical and/or sexual abuse from a domineering mother. And probably no father figure in his life, someone who he could look up to or learn from. He likes to exert control over women, not sexually, to show them who the boss is. It makes him powerful. That power over them is probably payback for some actual or perceived wrong by his prey. He objectifies them, only sees them as objects, not people with souls. He has both sociopathic and psychotic tendencies.

The perp exhibits antisocial personality disorder with a lack of empathy for the women. He does not feel guilty for what he does to these women and he most likely separates his acts from the rest of his daily activities. He is impulsive with a passive-aggressive disorder meaning he lets things go that bother him until he explodes by burning his prey. This most likely relates back to his relationship with his mother where he let her actions slide because he loved his mother as a son. Deep down he hated what she did, but he never did anything about it until it was too late. He hates the women he chooses to kill.

The id portion of his brain is dominating his actions. His dark aggressions against women are impulsive, possibly trying to avoid some internal pain. But at the same time, he is seeking pleasure with the instant gratification provided by his deadly fires.

The psychopathic traits are exhibited by similar tendencies to his sociopathic behavior but add narcissism and his violent criminal behavior. He may even show some of these women his charming side, but it is only a superficial façade. These men make excellent liars. His killings serve to inflate his self-worth because he has low self-esteem.

And, oh yeah, he probably drives a hot rod of a car that he keeps in tip-top shape. This serves two purposes. He likes to live on the edge in the fast lane and the vehicle is his way to safely get away from his crime scenes."

"That's a lot a great information, but how does it help us catch this murderous bastard?" asked Wojo.

"You're Tom, right?" Wojo nodded affirmatively. "You are all going to have to work even harder. Conduct more interviews. Make sure every neighbor is contacted around the crime scene. Trace every movement of the victims on the day they died. And pray he makes a mistake. These perpetrators are often caught only by a combination of hard work plied with a large serving of luck.

One thing is for sure, he will not stop on his own. These are probably not his first fires, but maybe there was some recent traumatizing life event that pushed him to start killing women in this fashion. We don't have a good handle on his timing of fires, but he may well escalate if these fires tend to satisfy some demon within him."

Up to this point, Mark had been unusually quiet. The description he just heard disturbed him. Could Brantley be the serial arsonist/murderer?

He checks off so many traits. A white male, in the right age category, lives in Boston, check. Lives alone, check. A well-kept muscle car, check. An unusual early life with no father, probably a domineering stepmother since she grew up with my mother, check. A possible traumatic event wherein his mother, or his stepmother if he even knew that fact, dies in a fire, check. Was that really accidental, or could he have set it? Coming home late at night with apparent heat and fire damage to his face and hair after another woman was burned in a fire. Check, check, check! Mark knew he needed to learn much more about his brother before he jumped to too many conclusions. Besides, this profile could fit a thousand, or even more, men. It proves nothing.

Michelle had been quiet, too, but that was mainly because she was the rookie among all the experienced investigators. And when she looked over at Mark, she could see his mind was elsewhere. His brow was furrowed with a serious inward gaze.

I already know he is a good investigator, but I'm concerned about what else is going on with him. Why is he so distant sometimes? What is gnawing at him? I know there is some sort of secret he is keeping from me, but what the heck is it. What is so big that he feels he can't confide in me? This keeps me awake at night, tossing and turning. I wish I knew what's going on so maybe I could help him.

"Okay, Doctor, it's your turn to let us know what you found. The floor is yours," said Chief Brown.

"Thank you, Chief. First, as Agent Hawkins alluded to earlier, there was no evidence to indicate any of these women were raped or had sex shortly before they were killed. None of them had any illicit drugs in their system. Mrs. Arlene Thompson's toxicology showed she was intoxicated since her blood alcohol level was about twice the legal limit at .15 percent.

None of the women had any signs of pre-fire trauma except for the broken teeth of our last victim, but no gun-shot wounds, stabbings or blunt force trauma. On our South Boston victim, I could discern the restraint marks at her ankles and wrists caused by the tight plastic zip ties. You already know that the Jamaica Plain woman had cloth strips used as restraints which left no injury indicators but left those areas somewhat protected from the fire, leaving telltale patterns.

The zip ties are commonly sold at hardware stores and every big box home improvement store so tracing them would be extremely difficult. The cloth strips were common cotton t-shirts, age and brand unknown.

Finally, the best part, or the worst part, depending on your point of view, the manner and cause of death. Each of the women was alive when the effects of fire killed them. They all suffered, and being restrained, they, in effect, were tortured. They all had soot in the esophagus, so they were breathing when the flames and heat attacked their bodies and killed them. Each of these deaths were murder. Now, it is your job to identify the monster who slaughtered these women. Sorry, but I have to run. I'll grab a burger, rare, before my next autopsy."

"Wow, Doc, thanks so much. That was descriptive, informative and powerful. Now, on that note, let's take a break for lunch," informed Chief Brown. "Sandwiches have just arrived. I hope they didn't burn the bread," he quipped. Everyone else moaned.

✳   ✳   ✳   ✳   ✳

Between bites of his Italian sub, Carlo asked, "So, folks, where do we go from here? Really, how are we going to catch this son of a bitch?"

"Yeah," added Wojo, chomping on his kielbasa with pickled onions, plus yellow mustard on a fresh bulkie roll. His right leg was bouncing up and down in his characteristic nervous twitch. "This guy has the entire country to set his fires, or at least the entire city, so where do we start looking?"

Michelle spoke up for the first time since she devoured a vegetarian wrap that included roasted red peppers, avocado and a creamy herbed

Boursin cheese spread. "Guys, I understand everything Daryl and the good Doctor said, but they didn't mention one important thing. Our torch may be organized, but I think he is strictly impulsive when it comes to picking his targets. Since there is no direct commonality, there must be some trait common to them that triggers him to action. I don't know what that trigger is, but that impulsive behavior means he will take risks that could be his downfall. He could get careless and make mistakes. When he does, we have to pounce on them to catch him."

"Very perceptive, Michelle. What do you all think about this?" asked Lt. O'Brien as he gulped down the last bite of his hot pastrami and Swiss covered with spicy mustard. "What if we hold a press conference, tell them that there is a serial arsonist/murderer on the loose in Boston? We can advise all women to be careful, be aware of their surroundings more than they ever have before. And we can have a tip line to report suspicious activity."

"Yeah, maybe we'll get a tip from a friend or family member that will help break the case," added Lt. Scherner. He wiped the ketchup off his lips after his double cheeseburger dripped on him. Or maybe the perp will reach out to us to taunt us or let us know his motive like those guys did in *your* big arson conspiracy. What do you think, Mark?" Scherner wanted to put Mark on the spot.

Miller still had not uttered a solitary word throughout the meeting or lunch except to place his order for a turkey with mayo on wheat. He barely heard the suggestion. His mind continued to churn with a possible messy conundrum that he needed to figure out. "Uh, yeah. It could work. Probably worth a shot," was all he could manage to say.

Everyone around the table could only stare at Mark. Each one knew he was not himself. His silence and inattentiveness were uncommon behaviors. Michelle and Mark's friends were especially dumbfounded. They all had their own thoughts as to what was going on in his head. Not one of them had the right answer.

Boston Police Detective Taylor interrupted the pregnant pause. His fried fish sandwich with a side pile of fries was half eaten. "It's a good thought, Mike. However, I fear panic in the city. Then, the press will haunt us daily for updates. And the number of tips will require an army to handle them. Plus, the crackpots will come out of the woodwork. Possibly even a copycat will surface. This guy could also flee the jurisdiction, start setting his fires elsewhere. We have a lot to consider."

Profiler Daryl Hawkins had long ago finished his blueberry yogurt. He knew he was a guest at the table, but he also knew he had to share his experiences. "You all make good points, and any of the possibilities you mention could very well occur. This series of murders may go on forever if you don't do this. The downsides are worth the risk.

You need to go all out by putting as many people as possible on this investigation. A fully staffed task force will handle those phone calls, including every screwball that will call in. While you're at it, offer a reward. Every arson carries a $5,000 reward. How many arsons do you have, four, five? So that's $20,000 or $25,000?

Another thing, don't worry about the press. Give that to a Public Information Officer or let the bosses handle that. Don't let the media run your lives. Yes, the public has a right to know, but on your time, not theirs.

Remember the Unabomber case. Kaczynski's brother read Ted's manifesto, that the Washington Post published. He recognized the writing as that of his brother. Because he notified the authorities, the ghost was arrested. This could happen in your case. Use the media for your benefit. Make them work for you.

Put enough information out there to tempt him. Studies of serial killers show they have an ego that can be stroked. Make it known that you don't have any leads yet as to who is setting these fires, and you don't know why he is setting them. There's a good chance that he won't be able to resist reaching out to the media or even one of your offices. But he won't be careless when he does it. He's cunning and smart. You just need to bait the hook to get him to react. Because you folks are smarter than he is, you will get him.

Best of luck to you. Keep me in the loop. I have a plane back to DC that I have to catch. Mark, can you give me a lift to the airport?"

✳   ✳   ✳   ✳   ✳

Before leaving, Mark asked Michelle, "What do you think about meeting me at Doyles? Five o'clock sound good to you? We can discuss some of what we talked about today, okay?"

"Sure, Mark, I'd like that if you actually show up. Are you going to leave me high and dry again? I'm still a little miffed about the last time."

"I totally understand, really, my bad. But I'm here in the office the rest of the day. I'm not going anywhere so I'll be there for sure."

On another note, are you all right? I was looking over at you and you seemed upset, and you even acted like your mind was elsewhere."

"Yeah, I was thinking about some details Daryl was giving us. We can talk more. See you at the bar. Hey, Carlo, Wojo, catch up to you guys soon."

Wojo responded, "Yeah, yeah, Barney, whatever you say, buddy." He was perplexed by how his long-time friend was acting. He seemed so strange and distant.

Carlo said, "Hey, Woj, I'll be back in a few. I have to take a leak."

In the men's room, Carlo ran into O'Brien and Scherner. "So guys, what do you think? We certainly have a mystery on our hands."

The two Boston fire investigators looked at each other and nodded.

CHAPTER TWENTY-TWO

Dick Scherner started the conversation with trepidation. "Dennis, both the doctor and your profiler gave us a lot to think about. But Mike and I need to talk with you and Tom about something. It's really important and, aah, very delicate."

"What's up, Dick?"

"It's about your friend, Mark. Can we get Tom and talk somewhere privately? We don't want to have to explain ourselves twice."

"Sure, it sounds serious. Follow me." Dennis led his counterparts back into the office and sent them into a small interview room. "Nobody will bother us in here or hear us. I'll get Tom."

Within two minutes, all four men were seated. The door was closed. Tom started, "So, guys, what's bothering you?"

Mike said, "Tom, Den, I think you know I like Mark a lot and working with him is a big plus for me. And I don't know whether you know that Dick here is not a fan of Mark or of ATF for that matter because of the way you guys shut us out of the press conference after the arrests in that big arson case."

"Yeah, we're still pissed about that ourselves," interjected Tom. "Our own bosses screwed us big time on that one. And we have to live with the mess with guys like you. Believe me, we street guys are really sorry that happened."

"Well," Scherner said, "we appreciate you saying that. I think Mark is a strange duck. There's something not quite right about him. But I'm not sure what it is. But now, Mike and I have something that potentially could be a blockbuster."

"Come on guys. Let it out."

"We're a little leery because you guys are such good friends and you all work together. But we know that we can't do this by ourselves. So, we have to trust you guys will do the right thing," stated Mike. "Here goes.

After the car fire in Charlestown, Mark and I went to interview the bartender where the woman was last seen alive. When Mark had to go to the men's room, the bartender, who was acting a little strange, whispered to me that the man who left with the woman the night before looked just like Mark. He couldn't believe his eyes when Mark walked through the door behind me. The bartender added that the hair seemed slightly different, but he insisted Mark was the guy, or, at least, a dead-ringer for the man from the previous night."

"Whoa, whoa, whoa," Tom rapidly shook his head side-to-side in bewilderment, his leg bouncing faster than ever. "Mark has always had our backs and we have his. What are you implying?"

"The thing is," Dick asserted, "we're not implying anything yet. We can't believe what we learned, but we can't ignore or explain it either. We need your help with this. And there's a couple other things, too, that really have us scratching our heads. Go ahead, Mike, you tell them."

"So I called him at home around midnight after that fatal fire in Rozzie the other night. There was no answer. And when we had those other fires in Southie and JP fire, he looked like hell, exhausted. When I asked him about it, he was vague saying he was out late, but not in a fun way, if you get my drift."

"Yeah, so? There could be a lot of reasons he was out. We work a lot of late hours you know. Plus, he has something going with our rookie agent, Michelle, that he might like to keep under wraps," argued Dennis.

"You're reaching, guys. There has to be some explanation for everything you're saying. We've known him a long time. He's a straight arrow, a great guy. I have a hard time thinking that he could be an arsonist, a murdering arsonist," added Tom.

Mike continued, "I hear what you're saying, Tom, and I agree with you. We wanted to bring this up to you to enlist your help to figure this out. Maybe we can easily prove he is not the arsonist. And I hope that is the case."

"But remember that famous arson investigator on the west coast?" interjected Dick. "Then one investigator discovered some circumstantial evidence that linked the guy to some fires. He was a pariah, just for suggesting the guy was an arsonist. Nobody wanted to believe it.

Oh, another tidbit from that case was the arsonist/investigator always remarkably found the origin and cause of the fires when nobody else could. It's like he was a super sleuth, a psychic or the arsonist. Miller has found things at these scenes that others never saw, like he knew where to look and what to look for. But in that California case, once they looked closer, they nailed him with no doubt. Let's do the same here. Our work could prove or disprove this one way or another."

"Wellll," Dennis drew out the word as he was thinking aloud. "You know, Tom, when we were talking to Michelle last week how she said Mark was acting strange. He had been withdrawn and out late at night with no explanation. And you and I know how he's been rather off with us." His hands bobbed and weaved as the words spewed from his mouth. "Plus, we know that he has no other active investigation that would be keeping him out late at night. Especially with no one else working with him or knowing anything about it. Even our boss has no knowledge of him working nights on any case. That is weird to say the least."

"Now that you say that," Tom responded, "did you all see how Mark was spaced out during our meeting this morning? That is definitely not like him. He would have been all over that discussion. He normally eats that stuff up. It's what he lives for.

Okay, I'm going to tell you two some insider personal information about Mark that I want you to consider, but you have to promise not to tell anyone else what I'm about to tell you. Mike? Dick?" Both men solemnly nodded affirmatively.

"Let me go about it this way. Let's follow the profile analysis. Besides being a white male in the right age category, Mark is a very bright guy who drives a perfectly maintained muscle car. He is single because he failed miserably at his first marriage. His ex-wife told me he could be verbally, and even once or twice, physically abusive. He often seemed aloof with her.

During his divorce, he went through a period of deep depression. I even feared he would do something stupid, like kill her or himself, so I took his gun from him for a while. For me to even think he could do something like that could indicate it is perceivable he could be involved with something like this.

His childhood was not a Hallmark one. His father left when he was a baby, and his mother never remarried. She was an extremely strict and non-loving mother. Her background was rough, growing up in the Hitler youth during the World War II era when the Nazis took over Austria. She raised Mark as if he were a soldier in the German army. So, this covers the domineering mother and no father figure. And since she died recently, that could be the precipitating event that triggered him.

Oh, another thing. Even as a young kid, his violent tendency showed its ugly head when he broke a broomstick handle over a purported friend's head because he spit a cherry seed at his cousin. And he even shot a U.S. Mailman with mud stuck in the end of an air rifle he had received for Christmas. These rash, impulsive acts of juvenile violent behavior, along with what he did with his wife, show he might have deep-seated problems and may be capable of other criminal acts.

Also, Mark can be very charming. Sometimes I think he is not being genuine. It's all a façade because he can't allow himself to be close to anyone. And he is driven to be the best at all costs."

Dennis jumped in, "Yet, Mark has been our friend for years. Somehow, despite his flaws, we still like him. But just listening to your description starts to make me begin to believe that he could be the arsonist."

"Damn, Tom, we had no idea about any of his background," Mike said. "That is an unbelievably in-depth view of Mark. Wow, some of that is baffling when you think of his incredible achievements thus far in his early career. What do you think we should do next?"

"First," answered Tom, "is keep this amongst us. Let's not go off half-cocked. If we can exonerate him-a big word huh-then we tell no one. But if he is the torch, then we'll get the evidence to prove it beyond a reasonable doubt. What we all need to do is go out and catch the real arsonist, that son-of-a-bitch!" Tom's voice rose an octave, and his volume increased as he completed his sentence, driving his foot into the floor to force his bouncing leg to stop.

"Hey, Wojo, we're not going to approach Mark on this, right? It's too early for that, don't you think? That could screw a lot of things up. He could be forever pissed at us. He could go into a cocoon and isolate himself from everyone. Or if he is doing this, he could suddenly stop or do the opposite and escalate his activities, but be more careful knowing we think it's him."

"No, Carlo. We won't talk to him about this. If he is the guy, I wouldn't expect him to confess to us. Maybe I'll talk to Michelle about how he is acting strange, but not let on about this arsonist thing. I'll pick her brain about his nocturnal pursuits outside the bedroom, but I'll tell her I'm concerned about him. She'll help, I'm sure.

Okay, guys, let's keep our eyes and ears open. We'll review the fires we already had to see what new information we can gather on them. Let's make sure we get our bosses and/or public information people to call a press conference. We should make sure one of you BFD investigators stands behind the bosses with Mark. That could shake up something, either Mark or the real arsonist," explained Tom."

"Mike and I will do everything within our power to help you out. Either we are going to crack a big arson/murder case, or we're going to crack the biggest arson/murder case involving an ATF agent who is considered a rising star. Just because I don't like Mark, I'm not sure how I'm going to feel if he turns out to be the arsonist. Mike, let's head over to the Squad and tell Chief Brown to get ready for a press conference on this investigation."

As Mike and Dick waited in the hallway for the elevator, Dick turned to his partner, "I told you there was something odd about that guy. There really is something I don't like about him. Did you hear all that about his upbringing? He certainly fits the profile. Looks like he wants to be a hero or he's making up for some deep-seated issues. Now I'm going to do everything within my power to prove he is that murderous bastard!"

CHAPTER TWENTY-THREE

After all the guests left the ATF office, Carlo and Tom went downstairs to the cafeteria to grab a coffee. "Woj, let's sit down here for a few minutes. My head is spinning. I need to consider this stuff about Mark. Could our good buddy possibly be involved with setting fires that kill women? It's too hard to fathom. We have always had each other's backs."

"Yeah, Carlo. It's certainly tough to swallow. During all our time together, I find this next to impossible to believe. But we have to at least consider it so we don't get caught with our pants down. That eyewitness who said Mark left with that woman who died in the car fire is disturbing."

"Absolutely, but we know all too well how wrong eyewitnesses can be," stated Carlo.

"Sure, but the bartender was standing less than five feet away and served him drinks. It's really hard to get that wrong. Then, we know about his upbringing. Mark fits so many of the profiling traits. And with his divorce and signs of depression sometimes, plus his mother dying, it all could have put him over the edge. We know too many stories like that California investigator. People can certainly fool others, especially when they already have a great reputation like that Cali guy or like Mark has."

"So, how should we handle this?" Carlo suggested, "Do you think we should talk to the boss? And what do you think those Boston Fire guys are going to do?"

"This is what I think. First, definitely not tell the boss. Then he'll be stuck in the middle. He'll be forced to go to the front office with something potentially this big and sensitive. Let's wait until we get something definitive."

"I can go with that, but we have to move when we get the slightest inkling of evidence. This really could get us in some deep doodoo if this goes sideways, you know."

"For now, it's a chance we'll have to take. As far as the Boston guys, I don't trust Scherner as far as you can throw him, but Mike's a good guy. They might do something stupid like try to surveil Mark, but that's another chance we have to deal with."

"Maybe we can control them a bit by keeping them in our loop. And, by the way, I resent that comment. I could throw Dick much farther than you."

"Probably. What do you think, Carlo, about letting Michelle in on this? They have gotten real close, sort of hot and heavy, but Mark's been screwing up their relationship because he's been aloof and acting weird."

"That's a tough call. We don't know how she'll react. If she's head-over-heels about Barney, she'll be shocked, but she could be a great asset. Right now, she is closer to him than any person on earth. However, if they are on the outs, and she has her doubts about his feelings for her, then it could be touchy with her. She could be stuck in the middle, too. Telling her might make her feel she has to go forward with this. Being a youngster on the job, she won't have the benefit of our long term work reputations.

Damn it, Wojo! This is the most complicated problem I've ever dealt with in my whole life. I'd say we should feel her out, and I didn't say up."

"Okay, I know your long history with women," laughed Wojo. "Who else in the world could walk along a beach, ask ten women if they would like to get married for a day, and end up going home with one of them?" Carlo laughed uncontrollably watching himself in his mind's eye. "Let's go back upstairs and get her into an interview room. Follow my lead."

✳   ✳   ✳   ✳   ✳

Tom opened the conversation. "Michelle, we need to ask you a few questions about Mark. You probably know him pretty well by now."

"What's up guys? This sounds serious. Should I be nervous?"

"You saw and heard him in that meeting. He was on some other planet. I've never seen him pass up the lead on an investigation, especially something like this one. Investigations this big usually attract him like a magnet.

You told us a while ago that he's been out late, being secretive and mysterious. Has anything changed? Have you found out anything new?"

"No, and no. Mark has been so distant, and doing that yo-yo thing that keeps me guessing about his feelings for me, and if he is right for me. But I want him to be the one. I have really, really powerful feelings for him, so I want this to work with him. So, as I said earlier, what's up?"

"That sounds like the 'L' word to me, right, Tom?"

"Okay, what we're about to tell you, kid, is very serious. We need your help. And we don't know how you're going to react. But if we all work together, we can figure this out, most likely to benefit all of us."

"Now, you are really scaring me. Tell me what this is all about, please." Michelle's eyes welled up. Her body shivered.

"You know that woman who died in that car fire last week?"

"Yeah, of course I do. It's part of this serial arsonist's trail of terror. What does that have to do with Mark?"

"When Mark went with Mike O'Brien to interview the bartender at the Warren Tavern, Mark went to the restroom while Mike started interviewing the guy. The bartender was shocked to see Mark because he positively identified Mark as the guy who left the bar with that woman less than an hour before she died. And at the interview, Mark kind of ducked into the men's room and let Mike ask all the questions. Since when does he do something like that?"

"Tom, what the hell are you saying? Mark couldn't have been there. There's no way he was picking up a married woman in a bar. If he did, I really don't know him at all. And he couldn't have had anything to do with that fire."

Dennis said, "We feel the same way, Michelle. He's been our friend for years. But, so far, we can't explain what the bartender is saying. Was Mark with you that night? Can you recall?"

"No, he wasn't. I specifically remember we spoke about going out and then staying at my place, but he begged off because he had something to do that was going to keep him out late."

"Here's the thing. When Dennis and I were speaking with the Boston guys after our meeting, we couldn't help but compare Mark, his personality and his life including how he was brought up, with the profiler's analysis. And we're sorry to say that he fits a ton of the characteristics that the serial arsonist might portray. Besides, you already told us that he's been distant and secretive, keeping something from you."

"Yeah, but he's a rock star with ATF. He works so hard and makes all the right moves. And when he wants to be, he can be so charming. How could he be the same guy murdering these women?"

"Remember," added Tom, "his divorce and his domineering mother dying could have been the precipitating factors that pushed him over the edge. I hate to tell you this, but that sweet charismatic side could be a total front, sort of like a Dr. Jekyll and Mr. Hyde transformation. One more thing, the Boston investigators have become suspicious about Mark at fire scenes. He seems to find somewhat obscure evidence way too easily before anybody else locates the items."

"Well, isn't that what makes him one of the best arson investigators? His mind is always going, analyzing things, and his sense of observation is over the top. I just can't wrap my head around what you guys are suggesting. Dennis, how could you even suspect your friend of this?"

"Oh, Michelle. Tom and I feel the same way, but we are trying to be objective and follow the clues and the evidence. We understand it is all weak at this point, but circumstantially, it is starting to form the building blocks toward establishing a criminal case against Mark. And that is so fucking insane to comprehend!"

"For sure, the evidence is really weak," Michelle asserted. "No physical evidence or direct evidence to connect him to the fires. You're going to need a lot more before I can begin to think of my Mark as an arsonist and murderer. This entire theory is such an unimaginable paradox. Where do we go from here, boys?"

"This is what Den and I were thinking. We, including you, keep our eyes and ears open to try to figure out if there is any connection between Mark and any new fires. We keep track of where he goes to the best of our ability. And maybe we can work more closely with him so that he won't be out at night alone.

But Michelle, we can't stress enough, we need your help. You cannot talk to him about this, and we can't confront him yet because of how little we have. There are too many possibilities if we tell him about this. If he's involved, he could run. Or he could kill himself. Or escalate."

"If he's not involved, he could laugh in our faces or be so pissed off that he'll never speak to us again. At this stage of our suspicion, he would have a difficult time understanding how we could imagine that he could do this," explained Dennis. "And I think we're all on board with that same sentiment." The other two nodded in agreement. "Now Michelle, you're in the most unique position with Mark. I don't know how you're going to deal with him and still act normal at the same time."

She thought about that for a moment. How can I sleep with him, but not talk to him about this? What an awful position to be put in! "Oh, how can I deceive him like this?"

Tom answered, "You're not really deceiving him. You just have to be more aware of what he does and at the most try to find out what he's been so secretive about. If he's up to something, and maybe not setting fires, he's the one who may be holding out on you. We know it will be one of the toughest things you have ever done."

"Yeah, Michelle, this will be an undercover assignment like no other. Just talk to him like any couple should. Without pushing or alienating him, merely ask him if there is anything he wants to tell you about what he's been up to. Didn't you say he told you to just hang in there, he'll tell you soon?"

"Den, he did, but he has kept stalling. He keeps blowing it off. It's going to be so hard to look him in the face, never mind going to bed with him. Please don't let this go on too long. I'm not sure how much I can take." Michelle felt lower than she ever has. If the worry lines on her face remained much longer, they would either betray her undercover assignment or become permanent furrows. Her increased heart rate surely would have caused her to flunk a polygraph exam.

"Michelle, we have faith in you. It won't be easy, but you can pull this off. We'll work as hard as we can to find the answers we need to clear Mark from any suspicion. This won't take long. I think we can assure you of that. Just know that you can come to us any time of day or night with any problems or concerns. We still want to be the same guys who always had Mark's back."

"Thanks, Tom, Dennis. So far, I've been thinking of my own feelings. But this has to be so hard on you two. Now, get to work and figure this out so we all can put this behind us. Let's go out there and catch the real murderer."

CHAPTER TWENTY-FOUR

That evening, after work wound down for the day, Michelle slowly walked down Causeway Street, turned right onto Canal to meet Mark at Doyles wondering how her night was going to unfold. *I feel like I'm a character in a dream. No, more like a nightmare.* What a whirlwind of a workday it had been. The meeting of the different agencies and professions had been enlightening. But the private meeting afterwards with Mark's closest friends, Tom and Dennis, could only be described as a crushing avalanche.

While listening to the profile of the arsonist, Michelle thought how detailed the analysis was and how there was a maniacal murderer stalking the streets of Boston who fulfilled most of the traits of that assessment. When she looked over at Mark, he was off in Neverland, seemingly daydreaming during such a crucial discussion of the suspect in his investigation.

I had never seen him like that. Then, to hear two trained investigators who also are Mark's best buddies tell me there is evidence pointing toward Mark being that killer made my day especially rough. And now I'm part of the plot to smoke him out. That made my day exceptionally brutal.

Stopping for a few moments to lean against a brick wall outside Doyles, Michelle sucked in a deep breath.

I think I love this guy. That night we walked hand in hand along the Charles River, the way he squeezed my hand, I felt his kindness, his heart, his love. Then, when he pulled me against his body with his arms wrapped around me, I swooned. His kisses solidified my feelings for him.

I want to live my life with him as husband and wife, both of us as agents working for the betterment of our country. I'm loving this job, everything about it, and the people are so great, but why did something so absurd have to come up? My life has been so easy up to this point. Yeah, I've worked hard to get here, but this is the first time I have been challenged with such a mind-blowing, difficult mess to work through.

How the hell will I manage facing my love and doing my job at the same time? I'm so conflicted right now, I have no idea how I'm going to get through this. And I'm never going to believe Mark is committing these despicable acts until he gets caught red-handed or he confesses to my face. I've only begun to see the beautiful person he has hiding inside. And I want to see all of him.

'Act natural,' they said. They must be freakin' kidding me. As soon as I see my lover's face in the next minute, I'll be lucky if I don't faint or pee my pants. So far, my only undercover experience beyond training practicals at the academy, was a five-minute stint with an experienced agent. I was only there to be eye candy to distract the bad guy. My sole line was, 'Hi, nice to meet you.' Well, here I go.

Blowing out another deep breath, Michelle walked through the door.

✳   ✳   ✳   ✳   ✳

"Hi there, beautiful." Mark was on his third pint while on an empty stomach. His smile still warmed her heart. Michelle's own stomach just dropped to its lowest point.

"Hi, yourself, stranger. I've missed you." She leaned in close for a kiss. Mark grabbed her, pulled her in tight and returned her kiss with a deeper one.

How could this great kisser be a bad guy? He's such a charmer. What do I do next? What do I say next?

"I missed you too, kid. What would you like to drink? And let's order some dinner before I get too drunk." Following a quick look at the menu, Mark called out, "Hey, Frank, my lady will have a white wine, pinot grigio, to go with fish and chips. I'll have your Shepherd's Pie and another IPA, sir. Thank you very much."

"Welcome, Michelle, it's nice to see you again," Frank said as he placed her drink on the bar before her. Smiling, he teased her. "Are you hanging out with this degenerate? I'd be careful if I were you."

Michelle replied, "Frank, I was just thinking the same thing, the being careful part that is." Turning back to Mark, she said, "I'm hoping we can get back on track with this dinner. Maybe make this an all-nighter." She cringed inside. *How could I have sex with a man who burns women in bed?*

"Let's talk about today's meeting. What's your thoughts on all that happy horse shit profiling stuff? Where did it get us? It doesn't get us any closer to identifying a suspect?"

"Mark, that seems like a strange response from someone so progressive like you. Don't you think it's another tool that will eventually help when we do ID someone?"

"Yeah, when we find one man out of ten, twenty or maybe fifty thousand men in the city. We can't even pick which part of the city yet. Or why he does it. Or how he picks his targets. He's really good at what he does. Maybe he should be envied."

"Now, that's really a weird thing to say. What, just because he has gotten away with his murder spree without getting caught yet? In that peculiar context, I guess there are very few men that could succeed like he has. Maybe he has special knowledge or something."

"Good, I'm proud of you. You could well be on the right track. But let's talk about something different now."

So far, Michelle had played her part well. "Okay, I would like us to grow as a couple, so I need something from you. Why do you keep ducking me? And what have you been doing at night?" She hoped she wasn't pushing too hard.

"Oh, come on, babe. I told you I would tell you when I could. I've got something personal that may involve work, too. It's too tough for me to discuss the details with you. Please be patient with me. This will come to some sort of ending soon, good or bad."

"I've been trying so hard, Mark, to be patient with you. But I'm worried about you." Michelle started crying. "Can't you just let me know something?" she pleaded.

Mark reached out gently using a couple fingers to push Michelle's hair away from her face. With his fingertips, he wiped her tears away. She knew at that moment that Mark really cared.

"Oh, baby, please don't cry. I want to be your guy. Once I get over this hurdle, we can be a fantastic couple. Listen, I'll tell you just one little detail. I'm dealing with a family thing."

"What?! You told me that you don't have any family." A fragile Michelle spoke much louder than usual as the stress of the situation got to her. "What the hell are you trying to pull?" Are you telling me the truth or are you making something up to shut me up?"

"Michelle, I'm not bullshitting you. Something new came up, something very private. Right now, it's a delicate situation, so I don't want to tell you any more about it at this time. I need to follow up on this stuff on my own. Nobody can help me with this. There are nights when I'm going to be out and about. Now, I'm sorry, but it has to be this way. So, try to trust me and deal with it."

His words were less than consoling for Michelle. "You fucking confuse me so much." She was yelling now. "On the one hand, you act like you love me, you want to be a couple. Then you keep me at arm's length and tell me to *deal* with it. Couples share everything. They don't keep secrets. Secrets can cause problems that can tear couples apart. When you're ready, let me know. In the meantime, good luck with your life. I'm out of here!"

"Michelle! Michelle!" She made a move to leave, turning away from Mark. He impulsively reached out to prevent her escape, roughly grabbing her arm.

Michelle glared at him with a combined look of hurt and anger, tears flowing down her cheeks. "Ow, you're hurting me."

Once he let loose, she spun out of her barstool and raced for the door. After Mark slapped himself on his forehead, he sat deflated.

Frank delivered their two meals, placing them on the bar in front of Mark and the empty barstool. "I just saw Michelle leave in a huff. By the look on your face, I would say young love just took a turn for the worse. Sorry buddy. Maybe this food will fill some of the void."

Mark's look soured further. Sulking, he picked at his food. Damn it. I never could say the right thing to a woman. I hate myself for hurting Michelle. She's the best thing in my life, and such a sweetheart, and I'm screwing it up.

I know I have to deal with Brantley soon before I lose everything for good, my job and any chance with Michelle. I just can't tell anyone yet. Besides being embarrassing, I have virtually no evidence, just my hunches about what my brother may be involved in. Why get everyone on his track if he's not the arsonist? We could all be spinning our wheels. I just need a little more time to find out more about him.

✳   ✳   ✳   ✳   ✳

From a dark corner of the restaurant, an inconspicuous Brantley, huddled under a baseball cap with his hoodie pulled up tightly around his neck and ears, watched the entire production at the far side of the bar. He knew precisely how to get the couple together again. A devious smile spread across his face. His hunt for his next victim was over.

CHAPTER TWENTY-FIVE

Two days after the joint press conference, The Boston Globe had a banner headline across the top of the front page.

MURDERING SERIAL ARSONIST RESPONDS TO FIRE INVESTIGATORS

In a stunning turn of events, the person responsible for at least four Boston arson murders of local women responded today to the joint press conference on Tuesday held by the Boston Fire Department, the Boston Police Department and the Boston office of the Federal Bureau of Alcohol, Tobacco, and Firearms. In this letter sent directly to The Globe's main office, a person who claims to be responsible for these fires, the arsonist self-anointed himself as "The Burning Man."

Printed below, in its entirety, is a response allegedly written by the arsonist. At this time, there is no way to corroborate the authenticity of the writing, but the authorities say there are clues in the poem that indicate it is from the perpetrator. At the press conference, they also said that they have no suspects or possible motive for these fires at this time. This self-proclaimed 'Burning Man' goes on to taunt the investigators in the poem.

The authorities can't stress enough for all women to remain vigilant. If anybody has any information that leads to the arrest of the person responsible for these arson/murders, there is a $25,000 reward. The agencies also urge the person responsible for these fires to turn himself in before any other person is killed. It would seem obvious that the letter writer reads our paper since it was sent exclusively to The Boston Globe.

To the Boston Fire, the Boston Police and ATF

I've heard that you're the best.
Better than all the rest.
Who's next for me to burn?
What woman will next have her turn?
So you don't know my motive,
Here's a tip I want to give.
If she's a witch or a bitch,
She deserves fire to make her twitch.
I will tie or bind them
But I won't touch above their hem.
How dare you call me a reprobate
A new fire already has a date.
After you read this letter,
You will discover that I am better.
From this poem, my identity you will not learn.
Good luck because I will continue to burn.
Who will be my next Mark?
Just wait until it gets dark.
So try to catch me if you can.
You can call me "The Burning Man".

✳   ✳   ✳   ✳   ✳

As Brantley picked up a copy of The Globe at a local convenience store, an evil laugh escaped his lips.

I'm sure they'll have some fun with this. Keep them all guessing, especially Mark. I wonder what they are going to think with my play on words using his name. I gave them just enough information so they know I'm the real deal. Nobody but the investigators and I know I restrained these whores, but I never sexually assaulted them. I wouldn't stoop that low.

With a scowl on his face, another thought flashed through his head. Who is that idiot who called me a reprobate during the press conference? I am not a morally depraved degenerate. I have a real purposeful goal for my fires to rid this world of wicked women who certainly fit that description.

And I really love the press. They are going to refer to me as "The Burning Man" forever. Everybody will be talking about "The Burning Man." All I have to do now is make a plan for my next target. A hunting we will go.

✳   ✳   ✳   ✳   ✳

Meanwhile, across town at the Boston FIU office, Mike O'Brien high-fived his partner's hand. "Wow, can you imagine the arrogance of this guy, Dick?"

"Knowing how conceited and odd Miller is, yes, I can imagine it! That was a great idea to put out the information to the media, Mike. It worked like a charm. He just couldn't resist responding. The press conference sucked him right in. He sure has some balls, but they're going to get caught in the wringer."

"Oh, it's so funny how he rhymes all the time, and he even used his own name in his poem," added Mike. "How do you think we should proceed? It's going to be hard to face him and continue to work with him on this investigation knowing what we know."

"Yeah, it will be difficult, but we'll come up with something. I think we have half-convinced Tom and Dennis, but we need to invite them over here and show them the new information we have. That should prove to them that their buddy, Mark, has been fooling them for a long time. What a freaking, amazing case this is going to make. Locking up their star investigator will be the highlight of my career. Plus, I'll be rid of him forever. Yes! For life!"

"Okay, quit celebrating until we wrap it up, Dick. Let's call Tom to get those guys over here."

✻   ✻   ✻   ✻   ✻

At the ATF office, Michelle and Mark, with his two old friends, Wojo and Carlo, had also finished reading The Boston Globe article. Mark had a Cheshire cat smirk on his face. Michelle and the others were thrilled by the arsonist's response but pondered over every line of his poem. However, Wojo and Carlo kept eyeing their close associate who they have fondly called Barney for years. They were looking for any telltale clue that their friend had gone down a twisted path to the dark side.

"Wow, this really worked, eh, Barney. That profile business can be right on the money," baited Wojo.

"Yeah, Barn, do you think The Burning Man will strike after dark tonight? Is that what he means by that line, 'Just wait until it gets dark'? And why do you think he capitalized the 'M' in Mark?"

"It could be tonight, Carlo. We'll just have to wait and see. But he is pretty clever isn't he? Could he have seen my name somewhere and he's goading me? I think he wants to be famous. That's what he wants to be." Mark was now nearly convinced Brantley was responsible for this nasty string of fires. He decided that he, and only he alone, was going to catch his brother. For Mark, it was a matter of understanding Brantley and why he was a murdering arsonist.

"Let's fax a copy of this article with the poem to Daryl Hawkins and have him call us as soon as he analyzes it. Maybe he will have some additional insights on this guy," suggested Michelle.

Within fifteen minutes, Hawkins called the task force office. On a speaker phone, he said, "By sending that poem, your arsonist is absolutely taunting you. He has opened a dialogue with you that you may use to your advantage. He's a megalomaniac. His view of himself as self-important is evident by giving himself a moniker. He's going to love the media referring to him by his self-appointed name.

By letting you know his motive, it doesn't help to narrow down a person as your suspect, but it gives further insight to his mental state. He has what is called dissociative disorder where he does not have access to some deep-seated trauma.

He lives within two states of consciousness. His normal state is when he goes about his daily life fooling everyone around him. But his trauma stage is when he acts out. This guy harbors rage, anger, and resentment most likely from his mother's routine beatings and torture, which was a normal state of affairs during his upbringing. The humiliation wrought on him by his mother now results in his desire for revenge by choosing women who spark-uh, terrible choice of words-trigger him. He sees these women who lack nurturing qualities because his mother never kissed him with love in her heart. This void is deep-seated within his being."

Tom asked, "Did we tell you that the latest victim had several teeth broken? They were shattered."

"Oh, that's something new and different," replied Hawkins. "This is the first time that we know of where he got violent with his victim before torching her. I don't want to say it's an escalation for him. Perhaps this woman was talking. Whatever she said pissed off your unsub, so he popped her in the mouth to shut her up. But this was another sign of his passive-aggressive personality."

"Daryl, what did you say, unsub?"

"Hi, Michelle. Yeah, I got that lingo from working with the FBI profilers. It means unidentified subject. The perpetrator in your investigation is still not known, so he is referred to as an unsub."

Carlo sighed aloud, "Wow, this guy is one sick puppy. Will he ever go to prison, or will they put him in a mental hospital?"

Hawkins answered, "Remember this, he obviously knows the difference between right and wrong. And that is the deciding factor. It really doesn't matter if he has all this deep-rooted damage, except maybe in his sentencing. With the murder of these women and how he committed such atrocious acts upon them, it will either be life in prison or death. That's about all I have for you.

Oh, I forgot, I checked for any other similar crimes like this anywhere in the country. Nothing. You guys win the trophy. Your guy is unique. Good luck. Keep me apprised of anything new." With that, he hung up.

Michelle asked, "So, what are we going to do next? We can't just let him go on killing women, can we?" Listening to this latest dialogue began to drive her mad. Wild mixed thoughts raced through her head about the absolutely insane possibility of Mark's involvement in this puzzling mystery.

Tom suggested that the task force members go out in teams of two, sort of a roving surveillance. "We'll wait in the neighborhoods the arsonist had already hit, South Boston, Charlestown, with one team patrolling the Jamaica Plain and Roslindale areas. It's a long shot, but if any fire comes in, the closest team should race to it, get some preliminary information, and, if it fits the pattern, we'll call in reinforcements to saturate the scene and area. How does that sound?"

Everyone, including Mark, concurred. "Okay, we're going to have a fed ride with a local since they know the roads better. How about Tom, you team with Dick Scherner? Michelle ride with Mike O'Brien. Carlo, jump in with Artie Taylor. Artie said he would have another detective on the streets tonight. I'll go with him. I think his name is Slim, or maybe it was Jim. Tim? Let's meet at the FIU at 6 pm. Tom, could you give them a call to let them know the game plan? I've got to run to the US Attorney's Office on another case."

CHAPTER TWENTY-SIX

"Fire Investigation Unit, Lt. Scherner, may I help you?"

"Hi, Dick, it's Tom. Can we meet at your place at six to team up for tonight's surveillance?"

"Sure, I imagine Miller set this all up. How is he doing?"

"He mostly set the teams up, but he's been playing coy. I'm still on the fence about him, but you've got to know how tough this is for Carlo and me. We've been together since the academy. Just imagine how you would feel if it was Mike."

"Well, Tom, I guess I can visualize that, but I'm going to blow your mind with what we have here. Can you, Carlo and Michelle come over early, say 5 o'clock?"

✳   ✳   ✳   ✳   ✳

"Hi there, my ATF friends," Dick greeted the three agents in the most jovial mood few have ever experienced. "Take a seat. You're going to need it." They all grabbed a chair at the empty desks in the ancient office.

Not wanting to waste any time, Dick immediately divulged the newly acquired evidence. "A week after the Roslindale office fire, we received a call from the office park management. They discovered this surveillance video from an office across the parking lot and gave us this copy yesterday. Watch this, then let us know what you think."

Scherner hit the remote for the VHS video cassette player on the stand below a boxy TV. Immediately, a grainy black and white recording revealed the exterior of the MedRX office. The lights were on within the office, but barely visible. Within a moment, violent flames erupted from the office windows shooting twenty to thirty feet outward from the building. The investigators all knew in their mind's eye that the flames were undulating in hues of reds, oranges and yellows.

As they stared in awe, a hooded figure stumbled out the front door. He carried a black canvas-looking bag. Transfixed on the character, they squinted to ascertain features of the person. Dick rewound the tape a few seconds. He stopped the tape with the best facial view of the individual. Although most people would have a tough time with the poor quality of the video, others who knew the man under the hoodie best could make an identification. An audible gasp escaped from Michelle's lips before her right hand clasped over her mouth.

"That's right, Michelle. As best as we can tell, it is your boyfriend, otherwise known as ATF Special Agent Mark Miller. We were shocked, too," Dick gloated in the moment.

"Fuck!" Carlo exclaimed. Refusing to accept what he just witnessed, he pleaded, "There's got to be an explanation, right, Tom?" Walkowski sat still in stunned silence.

"What else do you guys need?" Scherner let the tape run. The profile view showing the nose, mustache, lips and chin confirmed the onlookers' opinions. The camera view lost sight of the man's movements. "If this doesn't convince you that the man on the video is Mark, we have more."

"Listen," explained O'Brien who, to this point, sat quietly at his desk, "Dick and I were asked to check on Ariel Garcia at the hospital. We stopped by there every day. Initially, the doctors kept her in an induced coma. But since they didn't think she was going to make it, they let her wake up so we could try to interview her.

When we got there yesterday, she couldn't speak because edema or something like that swelled her throat to the point she couldn't talk. She couldn't even breathe without the tracheostomy performed in her neck with a tube allowing her to breathe. What we did was show her this photo array."

O'Brien handed Dennis a thin manilla folder with six cut-out windows. Each opening bore a color photo of an adult white male. Each man wore a mustache. Mark Miller's photo sat at the bottom left of the folder in the position labeled #4.

"We asked Ariel if any of the men portrayed on the folder did this to her. She looked it over carefully, but it only took her three seconds to point her finger to Photo #4, Mark. We videotaped this little session. There's no doubt she was medicated heavily, but she didn't hesitate when she identified Mark. It's really a good thing we recorded this. Ariel didn't make it. She died this morning."

The mouths of the three agents hung open. They had no words. They were beyond stunned; they were paralyzed.

"So, what do you think now about your star agent?" Dick delighted in their shock. "We're thinking of going to the District Attorney's office to get a warrant for Mark's arrest for arson and murder. We probably have enough probable cause already. I say we should do it soon before he kills some other innocent woman. What's your thoughts? Tom? Dennis, anything?"

Swallowing hard to wet his cotton mouth, Tom spoke first. "I'm flabbergasted, absolutely dumbfounded. I see the evidence, but I can't wrap my head around it." Dennis and Michelle gurgled agreement. "Can I ask this favor? Let's not be rash about this."

Scherner interrupted, "What the hell do you mean, let's not be rash? Are you fucking kidding? If it was anybody else in the world, you would be snapping the handcuffs on him right now. You wouldn't wait one more minute." He was apoplectic. If he had not said a word, his ruddy face disclosed his feelings.

"No, no, that's not what I meant. Let me say it differently. Let's figure the best way to make this stick. We can't go off half-cocked. We are all in shock, so we need to gather ourselves and come up with a rational plan.

You know how you virtually have to catch the arsonist with the match in someone's hand to get a conviction. Think how hard it would be to convict a nearly famous arson investigator." Tom pleaded his case further. "Should we take this to federal court or state court?"

Dennis answered, "Tom, the only fires that we could bring to federal court would be the JP restaurant fire and this office fire because they were businesses. The car fire and the house fire don't qualify. If we split the cases, would it provide the best chance for a conviction? Sort of taking two bites of the apple. If we put all of our eggs in one basket, it would have to go to state court. In that instance, all of the evidence so far could make the case stronger than if the case was split.

So far, there's the bartender saying Mark left with the woman who was killed in the car fire. In the office fire, we have Ariel Garcia identifying Mark as her assailant, but that evidence is a little weaker because she was so drugged, and she died so she can't testify. But that video is damning, albeit grainy enough so that only those who know Mark can ID him."

"What a mess," moaned Mike. Michelle started whimpering. "Oh, kid, I'm sorry you're involved in this with him."

She sobbed, "I know I'm crying for myself, for Mark, the entire situation, and for the murdered women plus their families. It's even horrible for ATF and all other fire investigators. This would only be worse if I was married to him." With that, the waterfall of tears let loose.

"This sucks royally," lamented Tom, "but we need to figure out something else quickly before Mark gets here. We know that he won't be able to set a fire tonight because he'll be with us. So that gives us a free day to still work this out. What do we do about telling our bosses?"

Dick said, "He'll be here any minute. Okay, we'll hold off on arresting him for tonight. How about we do this? Did you say Michelle and Mike were supposed to ride together? You two get out of here. Plus, Dennis and Artie, get going too.

Tom and I will talk further while we're out there. We'll work on the boss issue. We'll probably not have a fire since Mark is out with us. So, we're just going through the motions.

Mark will be with Detective Jim Murphy who only knows we're doing a stake-out relative to an arsonist who targets women. We haven't told him any details about the investigation. Mark can fill him in on whatever he wants to tell him.

Tom, why don't you and I wait downstairs in the car until Mark and Jim get here? We'll just say hi, introduce them, then head out to our areas."

"Sounds good, let's roll everyone. Keep your chins up and eyes open. Mike, take good care of Michelle. It's going to be a rough night for us all."

✳   ✳   ✳   ✳   ✳

"Hi, Mark," said Scherner. "This is Detective Jim Murphy. Jump in with him. He knows the city like the back of his hand, but he knows nothing about the investigation, so fill him in. Everybody else already headed out to their area. Let's see what we get tonight."

Heading to Jamaica Plain in a blue Mustang seized from a drug dealer who had an automatic rifle with him for protection, Tom and Dick had an opportunity to further discuss the evidence building against Mark. Neither man particularly liked nor trusted the other. But both men were similar in nature. They were good, tough investigators who pulled no punches when it came time to speak their minds.

"Dick, if Mark is really this serial arsonist who so crudely burns these women, it's going to kill me. I know you're not a fan of his or of ATF, for that matter. But he is still a human being, a man, a friend and a damn good investigator. I still need some sort of physical evidence that directly points to him before I'm fully on board."

"You're right about my feelings about him. I often find him condescending. He can be so arrogant because he thinks he's so good at what he does. Now, for some reason, he may be taking his ego to a new level of trying to be the best arson murderer. As far as some direct physical evidence, Tom, we may have it."

"What are you talking about?"

"I'm going to tell you, but we wanted to wait until we got test results back. Mike, Artie and I were working the office fire scene. I was on my knees using hand tools under the woman's desk when I found a piece of latex glove. It was a finger section torn or ripped presumably from the arsonist's glove. We photographed its location, documented it, and, when I collected it, we saw a reddish brown stain on it that may be dried blood."

"Whoa! That could be huge! I imagine you sent it out for fingerprint exam and definitely for DNA. They might be able to check the blood, or sweat, or I think I heard they maybe even be able to check for skin cells. When do you expect the results? This could confirm or clear Mark of being the arsonist. He worked with you at that scene, didn't he? Does he know about this evidence? What is the sample DNA going to be compared to? How are you going to get Mark's DNA?"

"Let me take those questions one at a time. He did come to the scene, but he showed up late after we had done a lot of the work. When we found it, we all agreed not to tell him for obvious reasons. We weren't trying to hide this from you guys. We just wanted to wait for the results.

The Boston PD ID section did a quick look, but they couldn't see any latent prints. They also didn't want to play with it for fear of destroying any success of testing for DNA.

As far as Mark's DNA is concerned, I did some really fast thinking. We gave Mark a fresh bottle of water. When he finished it, I collected it and placed it in a new evidence can. It's possible that his saliva around the bottle neck will be enough to analyze. If that doesn't work, we lent Mark one of our helmets, but we cleaned it with alcohol just before giving it to him. It has one of those canvas cloth liners that captured some of his hair. The lab told us some hairs included roots, plus maybe some sweat and skin cells. Hopefully, one of these will work. Do you think a DNA match to Mark would get you on board that your buddy is a diabolical murderer?"

"I'm afraid I would have no choice. That would be a significant change that clinches the case. Carlo and I will be right in there with you to arrest him. He would have betrayed us and the badge. If the DNA is a match for Mark, then we are going to have to get the bosses and the prosecutors involved. They are going to explode because we kept it a secret for so long and, even more so, because one of ours could do something like this."

"Tom, I think we can explain the reasons we held it close to the vest. Getting too many people involved before we had any concrete evidence could have fouled up our investigation. You know, loose lips sink ships. And we tried to keep him close, sort of kept him reined in."

"But they are going to scream, 'What if he kills somebody else while we play around with this?'"

"I think we can handle that, too. We only had suspicions, no proof, no direct or physical evidence. Until now, maybe."

"Yeah, Dick. No matter what we tell them, they're going to ream us up one side and down the other. Most likely we'll weather the storm with a slap on the wrist. We're the ones out here trying to solve this thing, nobody else."

For most of the remainder of the uneventful night, the pair rode in silence, engaged in their own thoughts about these most recent inconceivable revelations.

CHAPTER TWENTY-SEVEN

It had been over a week since the last fire. Everyone was on edge, holding their breath, waiting for the next call. Sitting at his desk, Mark spoke his thoughts aloud, "Hey, Wojo, I can't help thinking there is a murderer out there and we're all anxiously waiting for him to pick his next victim."

"Barney, I don't know about you, but I feel the weight of the world hanging on my shoulders because of this guy."

"Yeah, I think we all do. Everybody is looking to us to solve this case—the people of Boston, the press, the Mayor, all the bosses, even headquarters and Congress. I can't help but wonder if he has completed his gruesome, murderous mission. What do you think?"

Wojo answered, "I doubt he's done unless he's dead or been arrested for something else." Tom still tried to read his friend and test him at the same time. "Where is he going to strike next? Who will his next target be?"

"I've been thinking about that myself. I bet it's someone who will make the biggest splash yet with the media. That's what he wants, the exposure. Let's get back to work. There's lots to do. Remember the job isn't done until the paperwork is finished."

The brief respite brought temporary relief to those tirelessly working to apprehend the merciless arsonist. For now, everyone involved with this serial criminal investigation breathed a sigh of relief, knowing another fire could change everything for the worse. A gnawing apprehension hovered over the team.

While not actively at a fire scene, each investigator on the Serial Arson Task Force diligently pursued their assigned duties. As in any investigation, some tasks are far more crucial than others. In a case like this, everyone knew that the smallest detail could unravel the mystery before them.

Investigators chased down peripheral witnesses such as family members, co-workers and friends of the deceased women. Michelle was tasked with the laborious process of tracing records at the Suffolk County Registry of Deeds. Here, Dennis Caggiano tutored Michelle in the tedious research necessary to gather the paper proof of ownership for each burned building.

Frustrated, Michelle toiled through the process of hand reviewing files and by viewing microfilm on a microfiche reader. She was a woman of action, but she had a hard time concentrating while performing this monotonous task. *I've always been able to trust my instincts, but all this crap is totally against all I know in my gut to be true. All that evidence pointing toward Mark is breaking my heart and causing my head to spin out of control.*

This boring job gave Dennis an opportunity to question Michelle about her tumultuous interactions with Mark since she learned about his suspected nocturnal activities. "So, how did it go with Mark?"

Michelle sighed, her expression a mix of conflicting emotions. "All I can say is fuck. That pretty well answers all your questions. The man I know is just not capable of the things all you guys are accusing him of.

Honestly, Dennis, I am so confused! The evening started off so sweet with him. I was falling hard for him at that moment. I thought I knew right then and there that it was impossible for him to be capable of committing such heinous atrocities.

Then, after refusing to tell me what has been going on with him, he spun a bullshit story about it being a family thing. But, as you may know, he has no family. And he was so callous when he told me to deal with it. He suddenly flipped a switch and became so coldhearted. It's like I didn't even know him anymore. When I was trying to leave, he grabbed my arm so tightly he hurt me. It was then I got scared. Could he be a demon dressed in sheep's clothing? I don't know what to do next. The ball is in his court now. He knows how I feel because I simply laid it out for him. Could he really be the monster we're hunting?"

Dennis listened attentively, his heart heavy with empathy for his young colleague. "I'm sorry you have to go through this, Michelle. You're too sweet for this bitter pill. You've got to stick in there for now. Despite the mounting evidence that seems to point to Mark, I'm still not so sure about that. I feel there's more to this story. I promise, we'll get to the truth, one way or another."

"I hope so, Den. I can't bear much more of this. If something doesn't change soon, I'm afraid I'll go crazy and give up on Mark for good."

"Well, for now, let's finish up this work," Dennis suggested, mustering a reassuring smile. "Then, let's treat ourselves to some lunch. Subs from the best Italian deli in the North End sound good?"

"Now, that is something that will work just fine. Actually, that's perfect. I'm famished! A little indulgence might do me good to get my mind off this nightmare."

✳   ✳   ✳   ✳   ✳

Meanwhile, Mark was hunkered down at his desk grappling with his assigned duties relating to this increasingly critical investigation. He was in a horrible mood. His plate was overflowing with problems. The tangled web of Michelle, Brantley, crackpots and the front office, and the case itself all threatened to suffocate him.

Oh, Michelle, what the hell? I don't want to lose you. What should I do to keep you? Boy, did I screw up the other night. Drinking on top of everything else didn't help. I should have told her something more when I had the chance. That's what I'll do. As an act of good faith, I'll explain to her about how I found my father. But I'll stop there. Maybe she can begin to trust me again.

What the hell am I going to do about my brother? This is not going to turn out well. So far, everything about him is starting to smell. I hope I'm wrong, but I need to keep pushing to find out whether he is the terror of Boston. Maybe I should get more aggressive and just confront him, head on.

Oh, yeah, that friggin' letter to The Globe, just like we thought, it sparked pure chaos. It generated so many false leads and confessions from all sorts of cranks who are just looking for notoriety. Our phones runneth over. Between Boston Fire, Boston Police and ATF, we could be busy for a year following up on every tip called in.

I'm so damn exhausted. The stress of this conundrum is wearing me down as well as the lack of sleep because of all the extra late hours spent following up on one dead end lead after another. We are all working our asses off with nothing to show for it. My mind can't get any rest constantly wondering where the hell my brother is and what he's planning next. Except for a few fitful hours of sleep at night, Mark had no time for Michelle or anything else for that matter.

Mark got up from his desk. He walked to the row of file drawers across from Jack's office. He needed to locate a file from a previous arson investigation. Just as he pulled the drawer open, Mark paused when he heard Jack in a heated discussion apparently with the SAC.

"But sir, we're doing everything we can at the moment to catch this guy. Miller and the rest of the group are putting in a ton of hours. We're working with Boston every day. We're doing surveillances, conducting interviews, and so much more. They're getting close, but good, hard work usually results in a break to make the case, just like on Miller's big conspiracy case.....yes, sir. Yes, sir, I'll tell them and keep you in the loop."

When his boss hung up, Mark poked his head through the open door. "My God, Jack, I overheard your conversation. I'm so sorry all of this is landing in your lap. Thanks for having our backs, keeping the wolves at bay."

"Yeah, the ASAC and SAC are screaming for results on this investigation. Headquarters is all over these murders, with women being burned to death in Boston. And they're hearing it from the Mayor and Governor. You know how it is, shit rolls downhill."

Mark interrupted, "I know. And I'm at the bottom of the hill. We'll get this done soon, Jack. I can feel it in my bones. Trust me."

With that, Mark headed back to his desk, completely forgetting about the file he was looking for. Thank God for Jack. He's such a great supervisor. If it wasn't for him saving my ass when I was a rookie I never would have made it six months on this job. He worked magic with the bosses when I screwed up by leaving my portable radio in my G-ride one night and the car got stolen. When the car was recovered, the radio was missing. That alone was grounds for the bosses to fire me, but somehow, he made it right.

Now, I need to solve this before more women die. Should I tell Jack about Brantley now? But I don't have anything yet that's worthwhile, just a gut feeling. I have to make something happen, and soon. Maybe I should just meet my brother and get a feel for him. That could possibly resolve this whole thing.

Following through on that track, Mark opened the bottom right drawer of his desk, remembering a folder that could prove helpful. Fingering through his files, he found the one with no heading. Inside, he found the printout of Brantley's car registration information and the notes relating to his parking tickets. He had gotten nine tickets in all. Mark perused the list. Several from downtown. No surprise there. Parking is horrible on the city streets. But one ticket caught his attention. Charlestown. Let's see, that was a weeknight, 11:00 P.M., Pleasant Street. That's the same night the woman was killed in that car fire.

Mark pondered something for several minutes. If Brantley set that fire, let me mentally rewind the tape to figure out how the night unfolded. I think Mike O'Brien is holding out on me. Must be Scherner rubbing off on him.

No, no. Mike learned something he couldn't tell me. I sensed he and that bartender were acting weird when I walked out of the men's room. The bartender saw Brantley leave with that woman, and then he saw me the next day. He identified me thinking I was Brantley! Now, I understand why everyone is acting so strange around me. They think that I, a freaking ATF arson investigator, is the serial arsonist murderer! Could that really be possible, could the people I have worked with for years really believe that?

As Mark grappled with the tangled threads of his troubles, a sudden revelation struck him with chilling clarity. *Brantley, you son-of-a-bitch! You really are the murderous bastard. Now, I am going to be the one to get you and put an end to this. My brother the arsonist is taunting me.* The pieces of the puzzle are finally falling into place.

CHAPTER TWENTY-EIGHT

Over at the Boston Fire Department's FIU Office, Lt. Dick Scherner and Lt. Mike O'Brien strategized their next moves hoping they would result in a criminal case against the deadliest serial arsonist in Boston history. They felt nearly certain that the arsonist was in fact ATF Special Agent Mark Miller. But they needed one hundred percent certainty, because this could be the most sensational case in Boston Fire history.

"Think about this, Mike. We are on the verge of arresting the most celebrated federal arson investigator in New England if not in the country. After all, Miller did much of the work that culminated in the prosecution of nine men who set over two hundred buildings on fire. He was the man who broke what was termed the largest arson case in the history of the country."

"It is amazing, Dick, how hard the mighty can fall. Do you think he knows we're on to him?"

"I doubt it. He still thinks he's the smartest investigator in town. He'll slip up soon, especially when we put pressure on him."

Mike nodded solemnly, turning to peer at the phone ringing shrilly on his partner's desk. Dick picked up the phone. As soon as he answered, he frantically waved at Mike to pick up his phone. Dick silently mouthed, "It's the lab." Mike pushed the button for the extension Dick was on.

The head technician of the private laboratory that tested the DNA samples was speaking. "Lieutenant, we ran the tests twice to confirm the results. The blood in the glove matches the analysis of the known samples you sent us of the hair retrieved from the helmet and what we took from the water bottle. It is absolutely confirmed that all the samples come from the same person."

"You're really sure? We can't afford to make a mistake," Dick appealed to the tech.

"It's a definite confirmation. A match like that is in the order of maybe one in a billion." He confirmed their suspicions with a certainty that would send shockwaves throughout their community.

Both Dick and Mike thanked the tech for the information, exchanging a triumphant glance. Then they jumped up and down, high fiving each other repeatedly while laughing and hollering, "We got him. We fucking got him!" This was a pivotal moment that not only would define their careers but devastate the lives of several of their colleagues.

✳　✳　✳　✳　✳

Settling down after their euphoric high, Dick stated, "Mike, we're going to the Chief right now. We need to cover our asses. With the evidence we now have, if we don't divulge it to the bosses, we could be in deep shit if something else happens. As it is now, we could already get in trouble, but I think we can explain away everything to this point as conjecture. But the DNA is direct physical evidence that sinks Miller."

"And us, too, if we don't go to the brass immediately," agreed Mike. "Let's head over to the Chief's office and lay it out for him. He might want to get the Commissioner over to hear what we have. Besides being pissed at us for waiting this long, they may be excited to get this feather in their cap. I certainly could use a break from checking out all these leads that every nut in Boston has called in."

At Chief Brown's office, the two investigators sat in well-worn wood chairs with ripped leather cushions. The layout of the office was equally underwhelming. The Chief sat behind a twenty-year-old metal desk. Mike O'Brien perused the drab beige walls behind the Chief's desk, lined with four-drawer metal file cabinets that contained files of every Boston fire over the past thirty years. The floors had dark brown linoleum tiles whereas the water-stained white suspended ceiling tiles housed four florescent light fixtures. Mike thought, for a chief's office, this was all rather shabby compared to the nice new digs the Feds had in their ATF office.

Dick, being the senior lieutenant, laid out the investigation findings to his immediate boss. The Chief had a full head of white hair over an already ruddy complexion. As he listened, his stern face transformed to a furious shade of crimson. "What the hell were you guys thinking? I've been nursing a decent relationship with their Arson Group supervisor for the past two years. After that debacle of a press conference where they screwed us from being present, they're going to think we are just out for revenge. I've got to get the Commissioner on the phone right away so you can explain this mess to him."

Within twenty minutes, the four men were hashing over the pros and cons of the biggest arson murder case in modern Boston history. The Commissioner was not happy on the one hand, but on the other he was elated. "If we bring this case home, it will get the mayor off my back for good. "Listen," he said with his right index finger pointed squarely at his two lieutenants, "I think you guys screwed up, but it's not a fatal screw up. I can somewhat understand waiting because you didn't have definitive proof, but with that DNA match as you explained it to me, since I don't have a clue about that, you immediately informed the Chief. So, in my eyes, you guys are good.

Now, where do we go from here? Do we tell the ATF bosses right now or do we finish this investigation ourselves?" the Commissioner asked, his face now a mask of official determination.

Again, after glancing at his Chief who nodded to him, Dick spoke. "Sir, since I have the most investigative experience, I spoke with our BPD counterpart, Detective Taylor, who has worked many homicide cases over the past two decades. Taylor is also an attorney assigned to the District Attorney's office. He suggested that we seek a warrant charging Mark Miller with arson and murder for that office fire because we have the video of him at the scene, and that's where we got the DNA confirmation."

"Okay, go for it," the Commissioner replied as he checked his watch. "But it's after five already. Isn't that the way it always happens? And Monday is a holiday, so I guess we can't do anything until Tuesday." In the meantime, what do we do about Miller and about ATF?" The Commissioner aimed his question toward Chief Brown.

"Well, first, with your blessing and the okay for some overtime money, we'll get a full team out there every night to surveil him. In the event he sets another fire, we'll nab him in the act. I'll have Mike and Dick give him a call with a ruse so we know where he is, whether in the office, his house, or at his girlfriend's place. His girlfriend is a young ATF Agent who knows everything we have on this investigation except for the DNA and she has been cooperative thus far trying to get information for us.

And then, sir, I think we should keep this to ourselves. I can't help but not trust how they would handle this if we tell them before we make the arrest. They don't have or even know about the DNA evidence. Only we do because Dick and Mike, who already suspected Miller, kept the evidence from him at the fire scene. But ATF might confront him seeking a confession. Then they could arrest him without us. Or they might try to protect him, whitewash the case in some way. I don't particularly care how they feel about us arresting him without their knowledge. And it will be good for the city to calm the fears that he has thrust on everybody. Miller is one depraved son-of-a-bitch who needs to be taken down as soon as possible."

The Commissioner nodded his head in the affirmative, "You have a green light from me. We have a responsibility to the city, and to the truth. Let's ensure that justice is served. Go get him and stay safe out there."

CHAPTER TWENTY-NINE

It was late afternoon when Michelle and Dennis strolled into the office with the folder containing the building ownership information. Mark, still seated at his desk, shifted his gaze upward from his paperwork as they approached.

"Hey, Carlo, are you enjoying working with the best looking and smartest young ATF agent in the country? Is she keeping you on your toes like she does to me?" Mark's voice carried a hint of playful banter, a feeble attempt to mask his inner turmoil.

"Actually Barney, she is quite easy going and really fun to work with. And, boy, can she eat. She polished off a large chicken parm sub this afternoon. You had better watch out. If you're not nice to her, she won't share her secrets with you," laughed Carlo.

Michelle forced one of her trademark smiles that told Mark her heart was still open for a relationship. He returned her smile as he stood up and approached her. "I have been seriously thinking about what you said the other day. I owe you an explanation, finally let you in on what's been going on with me. And I'm terribly sorry I hurt your arm. You okay?"

Michelle nodded, a mischievous glint in her eyes. "Yes, I'm fine. But, buster, you better not let it happen again. Remember, I told you that I finished numero uno at the academy in the boxing and in the physical training. I'll kick your ass."

"Okay, okay," Mark responded as he playfully extended both arms with hands up in a defensive mode in case she struck out at him. "How about we talk this over at Doyles? And I'll be there with hat in hand.

It's just about five now. I'm wrapping up. I'll meet you there, okay? Plus, I'm buying." Their exchange indicated a mutual desire to bridge the chasm that had formed between them.

"I'll be there shortly. But please, I need you to let me in, Mark, so we can move forward. We can't keep dancing around this forever. I appreciate your apology, but I need your honesty and trust. That's what I want more than anything."

"I promise I'll do the best I can. I'll see you there." Mark knew he still had to hold back part of the truth. He hoped to appease her for the moment, with more to come when he solved the case against Brantley.

✳   ✳   ✳   ✳   ✳

Michelle was getting ready to meet Mark when the group secretary called to her. "Hey, Michelle, this fax just came in for Mark. He told me to let him know as soon as I saw it. It's from MedRX, the list of sales people for the company. You're going to meet him, right?"

"Yes, how did you know?"

"My eyes and ears are always open, Michelle. Good luck, sweetie. Here's the five-page list plus all of the employees' information."

Michelle knew the fax could yield a breakthrough in the case. With a sense of urgency, she scanned the list. On page three, a name popped off the page as if printed in bold. She never forgets a name like this one.

✳   ✳   ✳   ✳   ✳

Being a Friday of a holiday weekend, the vibe of Doyles was lively, a familiar friendly backdrop to their early shared history. "Hi, babe, I saved your favorite seat. Frank, could you pour that wine for my beautiful guest here? That okay with you, miss?" Mark's gesture of reserving her favorite seat spoke volumes, an unspoken appeal for forgiveness.

"Perfect. I love the mood I'm seeing. That's the man I fell for."

"And I hope to be a better man. It's time to let you inside my walls. What do you have there?" Mark pointed toward the folder of papers in her hand.

"Oh, this. It's nothing except maybe a colossal lead on your arson murder investigation. Thank you very much."

"That sounds good to me. Don't keep me in suspense. What is it? I'm hanging on with bated breath."

"Here, look right here, page three." Michelle pointed at a line halfway down the page. That's Brantley Mueller. Isn't that the same last name of that woman Brigette who was killed in that Rhode Island fire? It's pretty interesting that he worked at MedRX where another woman was brutally beaten and killed in an arson fire. You don't believe in coincidences like this, do you? That's big isn't it? Really big, right?"

Mark stared at the name. He gulped, then took a deep breath. "Michelle, you are amazing. That's an incredible find. And likely a connection that will break this case wide open. May I give you a big wet kiss?"

"What took you so long, lover boy?" Immediately, Mark gently took Michelle's face in both hands. He moved in, stared into her liquid hazel eyes, then he planted a long kiss. Their tongues intertwined, flicked back and forth. As they separated, Mark nibbled and sucked her lower lip.

After their lips separated, Michelle felt awful not divulging how the Boston Fire guys and his close friends suspected Mark of being the arsonist. At this moment, she could not reconcile all that she knew including the eyewitness bartender, the video, and the nocturnal ramblings of Mark with this sweet, sexy man. *Does this Brantley have anything to do with these fires? But even the profile and Mark's life confound me. I've got to figure out what to do with all this. I feel like I'm cheating on him.*

Mark snapped her back to reality. "Let me check this guy out, pronto. Maybe we should hit him up, see what he has to say." That's all Mark was willing to tell her about Brantley at the moment, feeling guilty about still holding back on Michelle. Changing the subject, he said, "Now, I want to tell you about that something that's come between us."

"I'm all ears. Keeping things from me can't keep happening. I've been waiting for this for a while."

"Remember when I mentioned I'm dealing with a family thing? Well, I went and did something really big. I looked up my father and then I met him."

"Oh, my God, Mark! That's wonderful, that's so amazing! At least I guess it is. Tell me, how did it go?"

"Michelle, meeting him could not have gone any better. I called him on the phone and told him I had no expectations. I just wanted him to know I was alive and curious. When I went to that fire conference in Mississippi, we met. We spent hours talking about his and my life. He's married right now to a woman who has an adult son. We're going to make plans to all get together."

As Mark spoke of his encounter with his father, Michelle's heart swelled with joy for him. With his vulnerability spilling forth, she felt their flourishing bond. She said, "You've got to be kidding me. That's sounds incredible."

"And, and, you know"…Mark paused, still holding back about his brother. He hated himself for lying, but he didn't despise himself enough to tell her the truth.

"Mark, what's up? Come on, you can tell me."

"Oh, nothing babe. I forgot where I was going with that. I was just thinking about how life seems to reveal its secrets over time. You've heard me talk about my mother and my tough upbringing. This IA investigation also had me on edge. And you know about my divorce, plus you have seen my erratic behavior, so you already know, I'm sorry to say, I'm damaged goods with a fair amount of baggage. Sometimes I wonder if I'm worth your effort or worth any woman's time."

"Yeah, but it's only a carry-on bag," she laughed, as did Mark. "Nothing I can't handle, and we can't manage together. Besides some of the strange crap I've seen from you, I have also seen so much beauty from you, your integrity, your caring side, your passion. And I've seen you trying to work so hard on your shortcomings. You're a good man, Mark. Maybe with a little more work, you'll be a great man. A man I would like to be part of my life." After she sent a left jab against his shoulder, they giggled, hugged and laughed some more.

For the next hour, he filled her in about his initial meeting with his father, including his explanation of how and why he left his marriage and son behind. He also told her of his follow-up call to learn more about his mother's relationships with his father's relatives, again leaving out any mention of Brantley. Secrets continued to lurk in the shadows. Mark played a fragile, teetering game beneath his semblance of revelation.

"Mark, I'm so glad for you. That's such life-changing news. I'm also so proud of you because that was a courageous act. And your emotional handling of that call and meeting are to be admired. But may I ask you something?"

"Sure, babe. Thanks for your support. Go ahead."

"Why couldn't you, or why didn't you tell me? If we are to be a couple, I am part of you, and I will stand with you. I don't understand why you had to keep this a secret that was crushing our relationship."

"Michelle, I'm so sorry. I don't have a great answer for you. Between this serial murder investigation and meeting my father for the first time, I just felt so stressed out, overwhelmed. Imagine what it's like to meet your father who left you when you're six months old. Does he want any part of you now? I never had a father figure, a man to look up to. I'm not sure how I would have handled his rejection. I wanted to see how my relationship with him progressed before I got you involved."

"Oh, sweetheart, I can only begin to imagine your swirl of emotions."

"Then try to understand the pressure that's building to solve this investigation soon. Boston women are becoming petrified. Headquarters is feeling the heat from our local members of Congress. This all eventually falls on me. And with my previous successes, I feel like I'm the golden boy who can no longer produce that golden case. I have to put this case to bed. I can hardly sleep, so I wander around at night for inspiration or something. I don't know what that something is. But, just, maybe, I'll find that clarity or resolution to this puzzle."

"So, that's what you've been up to at night. I've been curious about that. And you know the saying, there's no 'I' in team. We have a great team of investigators. You certainly don't have to do this alone."

"Yeah, look where that team has gotten us so far. I still don't trust how Boston Fire is handling this. I think they want to solve this on their own to get back at us for that botched press conference or professional jealousy."

This statement stung Michelle, her own inner angst mirrored the uncertainty that plagued their relationship. She couldn't help but think how fragile trust can be. *How can I do this to him? I am not so sure I'm a good person. Can I just let this all shake out on its own? Somehow, my gut says this will turn out okay. If Mark and I are meant to be, it will happen.*

"Mark, just keep going. If you continue to work with the team, I know this will work out just fine. I have a feeling, right here." Michelle pointed to her young, hard body midsection.

Her lover nearly swooned. He reached his hand toward her belly. "I would love to touch that feeling right there." Mark slid his hand around her stomach, then inched lower.

"Maybe you'll get to touch this body a little later. But, before play time, just one more thing. What are *we*, and I did emphasize 'we' going to do about this mysterious Brantley? I think it's a really exciting lead."

"I do too. I will do everything I can to find all there is to know about the life and times of Brantley. Then, maybe we will put a full court press on him if he is worthy. How does that sound to you?'

"Okay Special Agent Miller. Let's get out of here so I can discover what's so special about a special agent, one in particular."

"Michelle, I have a great idea! Why don't we make this a special three-day weekend? Let's head to your place to grab some clothes. I have a bag with me as I always do in the event I get called out on a multi-day job. Then, how about heading up to Portsmouth, New Hampshire? I checked an inn there. They have a great room left. Can we take your car, so we don't have to go all the way to my house?"

"That sounds great! What are we waiting for?" This time, they slid off their bar stools together.

Frank, the bartender, took away their empty glasses and called out to the pair, "Now that's what I like to see. A young couple enjoying themselves. Have a great weekend kids, see you soon."

As they walked hand in hand out the door, Michelle thought this feeling is exactly what she had been waiting for. Both lovers departed with a tender sense of anticipation within their hearts. At the same time, their minds were preoccupied by deception. Michelle and Mark's bond would soon be tested, their resolve challenged by the trials awaiting them. But for now, their embrace established a beacon of hope amidst the madness that encircled them.

As soon as the door closed behind the couple, a large 'BREAKING NEWS' banner flashed across the screen of the TV above the bar, casting a stark reminder of the dangers that awaited. The evening news reported that The Boston Globe received a photograph from The Burning Man of the woman killed last week in the Roslindale office fire. She was bound to her office chair and desk. They showed a blurred image of the woman with the surrounding office space still intact, just before the fire wreaked its havoc. Brantley didn't want anyone to forget his name. He craved the attention.

CHAPTER THIRTY

Despite the ghastly demise of Brantley's boss, the company, MedRX, still functioned. He still had a job even if he did that job poorly. His professional ineptitude hadn't caught up to him yet.

On a lovely early fall day in the Hyde Park section of Boston, during one of his many breaks, Brantley found himself ensnared with thoughts of his brother's girlfriend. He had pulled to the side of the road next to an elementary school playground. His front car windows were fully open so he could bask in the sun's warmth before the days became as cold as his victims. Brantley yearned for some ultimate act that would test the fortitude of Mark, as well as horrify the city. It had to be an act so despicable that he would go down in the annals of Boston crime history.

Brantley smiled with delight while watching the simple joy of dozens of youngsters out for recess running and jumping while squealing with innocent glee. He hoped their lives would be so different from his, free from the scourge of a tyrannical parent. May they be blessed with the love and understanding of a caring adult, in stark contrast to his own tainted upbringing.

His reverie was short lived. A schoolteacher, her features etched with weariness, stood on recess duty next to the doorway of the decades old brick building, well within earshot of Brantley. Through pursed lips, this middle-aged woman drew on a cigarette. Her scowl focused on one nearby adolescent boy who was rough housing with a group of other kids, typical playground commotion.

"Hey, you, Patrick, get over here right now!" she commanded. The boy either did not hear her demand, or he simply defiantly chose to ignore this ogre. With a huff, she took one more puff. Then she threw the butt on the ground where she forcefully ground it into the macadam surface with her black boot.

Brantley's gut churned as he witnessed her tirade. His focus seemed to turn inward as memories of his mother's verbal abuse rocketed through him.

The woman stomped the fifteen feet to close the gap between her and the boy. Grabbing Patrick by the scruff of his jacket collar, "I told you to get over here!" As she yanked him toward the doorway, she continued, "When I say something, you had better listen to me, Mister. You are the biggest troublemaker. You never listen, you stupid little boy." She wagged her finger in his face, "I'm taking you to the principal's office and let him deal with you. You're never going to amount to anything, ever! Now, let's go," she bellowed as she dragged him inside the building.

A surge of indignation welled within him. Brantley slowly shook his head, disgusted with what he just witnessed. *Maybe he will amount to something. Maybe he'll be just like me.* He felt despair for the child and revulsion for the adult. Brantley mused bitterly. I can't even call her a teacher. I fear for our youth if she represents our educators. She should be instructing them how to live a life, not be sucking the life out of their youthful spirit. Who the hell do you think you are, you oaf, to talk to that kid or any kid like that? Don't you know you look like a monster to those kids?

That stupid little boy comment riled Brantley to action. *Well, I guess I have to do something about her to protect an entire generation of kids from her oppression. My brother's girl can wait another few days for her demise.*

Brantley pulled his Challenger to an advantageous position so he could view the school's front door when the school day ended. His wait lasted only two hours. After watching all the students either hop on a school bus or walk toward home, his target shuffled to a small adjacent parking lot with another cigarette hanging from her lips. Starting her nearly decade old VW Golf, dark gray smoke belched from the diesel vehicle.

The hunter fell in behind the hunted. Unaware of the predator lurking in her wake, Brantley trailed her through the labyrinth of streets and traffic from Hyde Park to lower Mattapan, where the woman pulled into the driveway of a single-family house.

He waited for the woman to get inside the house before he drove past her car to settle in a spot on River Street where he could watch her location. He thought of himself as a first-class stalker.

Knowing he had plenty of time before nightfall, the torch grabbed a couple burgers, fries and a soda from a nearby hole-in-the-wall grill. He ate in the front seat of his car while listening to selections of his favorite music. Then, at the top of the hour, he switched his radio on to the local Boston news station. The first news story was about his alter ego, The Burning Man. He chortled when he heard his nom de plume mentioned several times.

Brantley knew this fire was going to rattle the city further. He enjoyed causing terror in the city. No woman was safe even in her own home. And he loved how the growing pressure resulting from his crime spree would further humiliate the authorities, and his superstar brother.

Once done eating, he double checked his go-bag, each item a silent accomplice to his infernal designs. His stun gun had been fitted with new batteries-check. Zip ties-check. Newspapers-check. Cloth strips-check. Gasoline-check. Matches, cigarettes, two bottles of alcohol-check, check, check.

Church bells chimed in the distance, eight o'clock. With anticipation and calculation, his thoughts danced with the thrill of impending madness. It's plenty dark and quiet now for the predator to strike. He only comes out at night, attacking under the cover of darkness. With his hoodie in place, his bag in hand, and his stun gun in his right hoodie pocket, Brantley crossed River Street. He paused in front of his prey's lair, his pulse quickening with each passing moment.

The torch thought for a few moments about how to set this fire. I can't allow myself to be as careless as I was during my last fire set. This time I'll ensure only my target will burn, not me.

The murderer also pondered what ploy he would employ to approach his unwitting victim. Why not try a variation of what succeeded for him during previous assaults? Brantley walked around the house to recon the premises. Interior lights were illuminated in the front living room and in a back corner bedroom. He saw no activity through lace curtains in the bedroom. Returning to the living room area, the woman was visible sitting on a sofa. She was eating and smoking at the same time. A television program was playing loud enough that he could plainly hear it.

Brantley checked the mailbox next to the front door. He was in luck. There were several envelopes. By the dim light shining through the picture window, he could see all of the items were addressed to Evelyn Baxter. I'm not surprised to learn that she appeared to live alone. Who could stand someone as miserable as this bitch?

Peering through the window as he rang the doorbell, Brantley could see Evelyn glance up with a quizzical look that instantly changed to annoyance. With some effort, she pushed herself up from the couch. She turned on the exterior light next to the door and in rapid succession, she asked, "Who is it? What do you want? Just leave me alone, will you?"

Brantley answered, "Sorry to bother you, Ms. Baxter. I'm Randy Johnson. I live a couple houses up across the street. Some of your mail was mistakenly delivered to my house." He held his breath awaiting her response.

"Oh, damn it, I forgot to bring my mail in, too." As she made a fatal error by opening the front door, she said, "You didn't have to bother me, you could have just put it in my mailbox."

"Then, I wouldn't have had a chance to meet a neighbor," he lied effortlessly as he held out the envelopes.

Evelyn's eyes focused on the mail. "In five years here, I never met any neighbors." She was frumpy looking in her tattered bathrobe.

Like the flick of a frog's tongue to snare a fly, the stun gun in Brantley's right hand struck its target with a crackle of electricity, emitting the pungent scent of burning flesh from Evelyn's doughy neck. "It figures," he replied sarcastically to her last remark as she swooned backward into the room, bellowing in pain, collapsing onto the floor.

Stepping through the doorway as he glanced over his shoulder to see if anyone might have observed the action. He closed the door behind him. In an instant, he zip-tied her wrists, then her ankles together.

Brantley had no intention of wasting time with this repulsive wench. But he couldn't help himself. "Do you have any idea who I am and why you're in this nasty predicament? I'm known as The Burning Man."

With her realization of his identity, Evelyn writhed and thrashed against her restraints with every fiber of her being, flopping around like a limb-less seal. All to no avail. "You are my next victim because you are not a human being. How can they let you be a teacher when you're really a tyrant who hates her job and abuses the very children you're supposed to be nurturing and caring for? I'm here to protect hundreds of innocent kids from your horrible behavior. Think about that for the next five minutes because that's all you have left." Evelyn rolled on her side, hiding her crying eyes under the edge of the bed comforter. She had given up.

✳   ✳   ✳   ✳   ✳

After completing his deed, Brantley sat in his car back on River Street until the fiery action erupted. He watched with proud satisfaction as the flames licked the night sky. His black soul burned as his legacy grew within the blaze of defiance against the world that had long ago forsaken him. His name would forever be whispered in the future with fear and awe.

CHAPTER THIRTY-ONE

Just after 9:30 P.M., Boston Fire Alarm radioed the BFD Fire Investigation Unit vehicle. Lt. O'Brien's voice was terse as he answered, "All right, got it. We're enroute. Thanks, bye. Let's roll, Dick. Mattapan this time. That's a new neighborhood. A woman toasted in her bedroom."

"Tracking Miller is like playing Whac-A-Mole. He's a ghost! We're sitting on his house. His personal car is here, but he's not. We called his house, no answer. We paged him earlier, but he never responded. Artie is sitting on Michelle's apartment building. He reported that her G-car was in the parking lot at her apartment building, but not her personal car, a Toyota Camry. He called her house, no answer.

Miller could have set this fire, and we missed him. What a friggin' nightmare! This could cause enormous problems for us," Scherner growled, his voice rough with anger and frustration.

"Oh, man," said Mike. "We did all we could, Dick, once we got the confirming evidence. After we notified the bosses, we formed a plan and implemented it immediately. It would have taken an army to follow him. Miller slipped through the cracks, and now we're left picking up the pieces.

The only other step we could have taken was to work with ATF on this. They most likely could have kept tabs on him."

Dick was not in favor of sharing the glory that this case would garner. "But they could also screw up the entire case in so many ways. There's no way we could trust them with handling one of their own or this sensitive investigation. We will probably take some hits if the entire story gets out, but our eventual success will be celebrated by everyone in this city.

And we're not going to call him to work with us at this fire. No freaking way. There's no way I could be in his presence knowing for sure he set these fires. I would probably end up punching him in the face."

✳   ✳   ✳   ✳   ✳

O'Brien's hands tightened on the wheel as they pulled up in front of the charred remains of the house. "We need to focus," he said sternly as he gazed at the smoldering property. "We can't let our emotions regarding Miller cloud our judgment while we're working this scene. We need to figure this one out and get as much evidence as possible to nail this bastard."

At the scene, the two investigators saw common fire patterns outside the small single-story ranch-style house. When the fire self-vented from the rear corner bedroom windows, char patterns formed at the side and rear windows of the room. Along the eaves near the rain gutters, there were soot deposits caused when the smoke within the building pushed through the cockloft.

Detective Taylor met Scherner and O'Brien inside the house. "Hi, guys, I saw nothing worthwhile at Michelle's place. Her car was already there before I arrived. The lights went on in her apartment as soon as it got dark and remained on, but I never saw movement by the windows. It's possible her lights are on a timer. Let's get to work documenting this place. What do you know about the vic?"

Mike filled him in. "Neighbors told us they knew nothing about her except she was a teacher here in Boston. They didn't even know her name. She was not friendly enough for anyone to want to know her name. But we found her mail on the floor near the front door. Every piece of mail had Evelyn Baxter on it. All indications she lived alone."

"Oh, my God," uttered Artie, "Evelyn Baxter. She was my son's fifth grade teacher in Hyde Park. He didn't like her because she was mean and always yelling at the kids, particularly the boys. And he's not the type to complain about someone. He has liked every one of his other teachers except her."

"Interesting, Dick mused. "According to Miller's twisted manifesto he sent to the papers, he said something about if the woman is a witch or a bitch she becomes his target. Your little tidbit about your son, Artie, would seem to affirm that.

I wonder where Miller ran into her. Then he probably followed her home. Somehow, he got into her house and subdued her. We know he's a clever fellow. Plus, with his charming mannerisms, Miller could talk his way into a lot of unusual situations. Let's see what that murderous jerk did to an innocent woman this time."

Over the next several hours, while the investigators documented the scene, they found chilling similarities to the previous fires. What they discovered was the signature of the arsonist.

The torch used newspapers as a trailer from an exterior door to the victim in her bedroom. A time delay device was used as the filter of the cigarette and the remains of the matchbook were found at the beginning of the trailer. Gasoline was detected all around the deceased. And the woman was trussed at her hands and ankles, then tethered to the bed legs. A partially burned cloth gag was still in her mouth. There was one variation in this fire. The woman was found on the floor, not on the bed.

Dr. Denise Williams of the ME's Office made the grim official pronouncement that the former teacher, Evelyn Baxter, was dead. "I can already tell she was alive when the fire got to her. She didn't stand a chance. Your firefighters put the fire out pretty quickly because the thermal damage to her didn't extend to full thickness except in a few areas."

"They sure did a good job knocking this fire down as you can tell by how much of the contents and walls are still intact. Another thing about the torch's actions this time is that he didn't pose her like he did at the office fire, but all she had on was a bathrobe," said Dick. See the material sticking out here under her body." He pointed toward the thickest part of her torso.

Mike O'Brien shook his head, partially in disgust at how the woman died, and partly because the arsonist was still out there. "We have to catch this guy, and sooner rather than later. We can't let him get away with this."

"I spoke with Marty Regan at the D.A's Office this morning. He, along with most of his office and all the judges, headed to Myrtle Beach for a huge conference this morning. They'll be out-of-pocket until Tuesday morning. We'll apply for our warrant then. We'll have Miller in our pocket by nightfall."

✳   ✳   ✳   ✳   ✳

In the aftermath of the Friday night fire, the spotlight of scrutiny crashed upon the authorities. Saturday's morning newspapers lambasted the Boston Police and Fire Departments, as well as the federal investigators from ATF, for failing to solve this murderous arson spree. Local TV and radio news joined in the attack on the authorities.

All of the bosses were furious. From the mayor to the Fire Commissioner down to the Chief of the Fire Investigation Unit, this investigation was backfiring in their collective faces. They called their task force members into an emergency meeting. Only the mayor wouldn't attend. He delegated the trashing session to his commissioner.

At Fire Headquarters, the mood was somber as they gathered for the meeting. Everyone was tense as the Commissioner entered the FIU office. His flushed face betrayed his temper. He fired the first salvo. "This is one colossal fuck-up, guys! I thought we were going to watch Miller and arrest him setting a fire. What the hell happened?"

Chief Brown, remaining calm while under fire, answered for his men. "Trying to find his location and keep tabs on him is far more challenging than we figured, sir. We would need at least a dozen vehicles out there. He was never spotted. His personal car stayed at his house and we never found his G-car. This is outside our normal job description. We never conduct surveillances without working with other agencies."

"Well, damn it," thundered the Commissioner, "I guess we expanded the job description when you and your guys jumped at the chance to catch Miller on your own. Now, we are taking a beating from the press plus ATF is going to crucify us for not letting them know what we have and for not working with them to catch their man. So, what do you suggest today? We're going to need something good to cover our asses. Right now, they are just hanging out there in the breeze. How are you going to fix this disaster?"

"We agree with you on everything, sir. It's quite the fiasco. My men and I were discussing this before you arrived. I think we can take care of any situation with ATF. The other day Lt. Scherner told one of their agents on the task force that we had samples from a fire scene that were being tested for DNA, along with samples that we surreptitiously took from Miller. They discussed that if the results came back with a match, then the ATF Agents would tell their bosses and they would come up with a plan to have him arrested."

"You secretly took samples from Miller? Is that even legal? I don't want to screw up this entire investigation because of some technicality on the evidence."

"Oh, no need to worry about that, Commissioner," piped in Scherner. "We checked and double-checked with the District Attorney's Office. We collected the samples in two ways. After he finished drinking from a plastic water bottle, he left it behind, and we were the ones who gave it to him. They told us that as long as he discarded the bottle when he was done with it, we had the legal authority to take it.

Miller also wore one of our helmets when we investigated that office fire because he forgot his. After he gave it back to us, we collected some hair samples left behind on the canvas in the helmet. That also was legal. And both DNA profiles from the hair and the bottle match the blood on a piece of latex glove we found under the woman killed at the scene. So, we are on solid ground there, sir."

"That sounds fantastic, Lieutenant. Great work on that part. So, how do we proceed with ATF now, Chief, to finally put this murderer to rest?"

"Sir, we are going to reach out to the two agents we have confided in and let them know the DNA results confirmed that Miller is the arsonist. Since it is a holiday weekend, we don't know if we will reach them, but Lt. O'Brien has the pager number for one of them. We will offer to work with them, but we will also let them handle their bosses as they see fit. This way they won't know we learned about the DNA a day ago and we did our own surveillance."

"Okay, Chief, that sounds pretty good. That strategy should turn out okay. I'll still get you more people to join with you on surveillances, but if you team up with ATF, you should make out fine with their people and their expertise. Good luck. Let's do this. We still need to end this to calm the city down, get justice for these women, and might I add, get the mayor off my back."

✳   ✳   ✳   ✳   ✳

With a renewed sense of urgency, Scherner and O'Brien paged their ATF counterpart. "Hi, Tom, thanks for calling me back on a Saturday. I've got the phone on speaker. Mike is on this call, too."

"Hi, Dick. My wife and I are in New York City for the weekend. We just finished breakfast, so I had a chance to call you. "What's up? Something important, I assume."

"Yeah, I'm afraid so. First, we had another fatal arson last night. This one was in Mattapan. Everything fits. Woman lived alone, supposedly not a nice person, she was bound with zip ties in her bedroom, plus newspapers and gasoline was used."

"That's not good. The DNA come back?"

"It did, late yesterday afternoon. Bad news for your guy. Both the sample from the bottle and the hair came back as matches to Mark. Sorry, buddy. I know you were hoping for the best."

"Fuck, fuck, fuck! And I know you were hoping for the worst. Well, you got your wish." Tom's rage stuck in his throat.

Ignoring the rebuke, Dick replied, "We spoke with the Commissioner. He said to work with you guys. Whatever you need from us, we're here."

Sorrow and disbelief crept into Tom's heart. "Dick, as you can imagine, I'm in shock. It's just too hard to believe my friend could be doing this. I'm going to hate telling Dennis, and then the bosses. This will kill them."

"We need to come up with a plan immediately," Mike added grimly, his voice filled with determination. "Together, we can bring him to justice, but we can't let him slip through our fingers again. Any ideas? Do you know where Mark is this weekend?"

"We spoke yesterday. He was hoping to spend the entire weekend with Michelle, if they could patch things up, but I don't know if they were going anywhere or staying in Boston. You realize, don't you, that if he did stay with her last night, he could not have been the one to set this fire?"

"I would need to have confirmation from her that he was with her the entire night before I could believe he didn't set this one. It looked just like the others. It came in just after dark and a cigarette with matchbook was used for a time delay, but that would have only given him a few minutes. Mike has Michelle's pager number. He's going to give her a buzz. Okay with you?"

"Sure thing. She likes Mike. Let me know if you need anything. And after we speak with the bosses, I'm sure they will contact the U.S. Attorney's Office. They have a 24-hour number with someone always on call. They might seek a warrant right away. Then we'll have to pick him up as soon as possible, but only for the office fire. You guys can charge him with all the other fires. Will that fly with your bosses?"

"They might not be happy, but it sounds fair as long as we get to go on the arrest. The Chief would be really pissed if we get shut out on his apprehension. The most important thing is we get him off the street immediately, if not sooner. And all of our attorneys and judges are out of state at a conference. So, let's do it." Despite plans being hatched and alliances forged, the weight of the task before them hung heavy in the air.

CHAPTER THIRTY-TWO

As the golden sunlight of Saturday morning filtered through the curtains, Michelle and Mark awoke, wrapped like human pretzels within each other's arms in the warmth of their shared intimacy. Mark unknotted himself from Michelle's arms. He walked over to the fireplace where he arranged sheets of crumpled newspapers, before adding wood kindling, all topped with three split oak logs. After lighting the fire, he hopped back into bed, pulling Michelle close. She laid her head on his chest. The fire took off with blazing flames warming the room.

"Now, let me explain the science of that fire to you. The crumpled newspaper has lots of area versus volume. It readily ignites with a match. The burning paper heats the kindling, volatizing the readily combustibles of the wood. Now, I'm going to blow your mind with this—wood doesn't burn. It's the wood gases that burn."

Michelle interrupted Mark's lecture. "Whoa, lover boy. Let's save the lesson for another time. Please don't take the romance totally out of that beautiful fire in this lovely moment."

"You're right, babe, I get carried away. You know how I get excited by fire science and fire investigation. Sort of like how I get aroused by you."

"And I love how I excite you, but shush for now," she said as she put two fingers to his lips, then brought her lips to his.

Mark's heart brimmed with ever-growing affection for Michelle. After another playful romp in bed, Mark jumped in the shower. He planned to take Michelle to a waterfront restaurant for breakfast.

Mark was in such a great mood, with his feelings for Michelle soaring he started singing blissfully in the shower.

Michelle, buoyed by the affectionate mood, was giddy with emotion. Hearing Mark's joyous tunes echoing through the room, she began laughing. But her joy was swiftly tempered as the insistent buzz of her pager sounded. With apprehension, she checked the number. It was Mike O'Brien with the addition of 911 after his number. Her heart dropped. Not now, she thought, I don't want anything to interfere with our private time. But I better call him to see what's so urgent. Duty overcame her momentary reluctance.

She snatched the phone on the nightstand next to the king-size bed. Her mood transformed into a tense, stomach-churning nightmare. Her fingers trembled as she dialed O'Brien's number. "Mike, hi, what's up?"

"Hi Michelle, sorry to bother you. We had another fatal fire last night that fit the pattern. Where are you? Do you know where Mark is?"

Michelle instantly knew what Mike's words meant. Mark was with her, so he could not have set the fire. This also means he probably didn't set any of them. But she knew Boston Fire planned to go after Mark.

Michelle mustered a pretense of composure. She had to have Mark's back. Her first duty was to her fellow agent who also happens to be her lover. And she needed to speak with him before she divulged any information to an outside agency, even if it is a friend on the line.

With only a moment's hesitation, she concocted a plausible lie, "I'm visiting my mother for the weekend. She's been deathly sick lately." Masking her anguish, she expounded upon her alibi, "Mark and I haven't been able to work things out lately, so I needed to get away. I have no idea what he's up to this weekend."

Mike replied, "Oh, that's not good. We need to get eyes on him. There's something else I need to tell you, more evidence that directly points to him. We just learned that blood found on a glove at the office fire matches Mark's DNA. I'm sorry to tell you, but Mark is the arsonist.

We spoke with Tom who said they will probably get a warrant for his arrest. If you hear anything, please let us know right away, okay? We're counting on you, kid. And we know how hard this is for you." O'Brien wilted. Giving this devastating news to Michelle deflated him, similar to providing a death notification to a family, but in this particular case, it was more personal to him because he had come to like this young agent.

Stunned by what she just heard, Michelle heard the shower turn off. "Oh my God, Mike. This is so awful. I'll call you as soon as I find out where he is. Gotta go, my mom's waiting. We're heading out to the ER to get her checked out. Talk to you soon." She hung up.

Hating the guilt of her deception to a friend and colleague, Michelle felt horrible being in the middle of this bizarre position. The damning revelation of the DNA was a body shot to her gut, leaving her breathless. And the gravity of a looming arrest warrant for Mark sent her reeling, falling to the mat. But she was not down and out. *I need time to figure this out with Mark. Right now!*

This was about to be their judgment day. Mark walked out of the bathroom with one of the inn's bathrobes wrapped around him. Oblivious to the brewing turmoil, his carefree demeanor was about to be shattered.

Michelle knew their delightful morning had taken an unexpected twist. She couldn't delay the inevitable, unable to keep the truth hidden any longer. This was far too important to let it slide for a moment more even though it could destroy the fabulous start to this day. With a serious expression on her face, she patted the bed next to her. "Take a seat here, Mark. I need to tell you something." Her voice shuddered as she prepared to lay bare the damning accusations threatening to tear them apart.

Mark noticed her intense look and firm instruction. "What's going on, babe? Why so serious? We were having such a great time."

Seated on the edge of the bed, Mark sensed the gravity of Michelle's solemn demeanor. "Mark, last night and this morning have been wonderful. And we're going to continue with this, but I need to be honest with you about something that's killing me."

"Go ahead, babe. Let's clear the air."

"Okay, here goes. It's going to be tough, but just remember, you're my guy and I'm on your side. I'll get straight to the point, then fill in the background. Dick Scherner and Mike O'Brien think you are the murdering arsonist." She paused to read Mark's response.

"I know."

"You know?" Flabbergasted, Michelle's mouth hung open, her eyebrows arched upward. "How do you know?"

"I've got to tell you something big, but I really would like to hear that back story first. So, shoot."

"This won't be easy, but here goes. Try not to interrupt me, so I don't lose it before I get it all out." Mark nodded. "Dick, who I'm sure you know, doesn't like you, started getting some weak circumstantial evidence that made him feel you could be the arsonist. Stupid stuff like you were never home when they tried to reach you by phone at home. He also felt you found very obscure evidence at the fire scenes like you knew ahead of time what to look for. I guess they just never realized how good you really are at your job." Mark smiled while listening intently.

"Then, after the car fire, the bartender at the Warren Tavern saw you when you went there with Mike O'Brien. He told Mike you were the man who left with the woman who died in the fire. To Scherner, that was pretty damning."

"Yeah, I know all about that."

"You do? How?"

"Sorry, I interrupted you. Finish before I tell you."

"Okay. After our Task Force meeting, Scherner and O'Brien told Tom and Dennis about their suspicions. They didn't believe it, but a seed had been planted. That's when they told me.

You know I couldn't believe it either. But things got strange with you. You were out somewhere the night of the car fire. You were being very secretive with me. And, in that meeting you were so spaced out, which is not like you. You started confusing the hell out of me, but, on the other hand, every time you were so sweet with me, I fluffed off the negative stuff." Mark still listened attentively. Michelle's narration piqued his interest.

"The kicker for Scherner occurred when a video surfaced from outside the office fire that showed a grainy view of a man in a hoodie. That man looked just like you. When they showed me the video, I said there had to be some explanation." This revelation caused Mark's eyebrows to raise, his forehead to furrow.

"That, coupled with the bartender's identification, is seriously incriminating, but still all circumstantial evidence. Until now. Mike O'Brien just paged me when you were in the shower. There was another fatal fire last night that fit the series of fires. But he told me two shocking revelations that absolutely terrifies me." Michelle began to sob as she tried to finish.

"They had a glove with blood on it and the analysis of the blood's DNA came back as a match to you." Mark's forehead creased even more, but then a faint smile spread across his face. "And when they told Tom, he said they are getting a warrant for your arrest. Oh, Mark, I don't understand, but I know you can't be the murderer because you were with me last night. So, it's impossible no matter what they have! What are we going to do? Michelle crumbled in despair.

"Okay, everything's going to be just fine, honey." Mark reached over, lifted her chin and wiped her tears away. "Listen, I'll start to explain with two words, Brantley Mueller."

"Wha-, what about him, Mark? Did you check him out?"

"He's my identical twin brother." Mark paused and stood, pacing next to the bed. Michelle swooned, nearly fainting from the implications of his words. Her mind struggled to comprehend the enormity of what he had just revealed.

Speechless while she absorbed Mark's surprise disclosure, she pondered what he said, slowly nodding her head up and down. Mark waited for Michelle to say something. "Now, I get it. So that's why everything pointed to you." The truth had finally come to light. As Mark unraveled the twisted web of deceit that had entangled them, the weight on both of their collective shoulders commenced to melt.

Screaming with joy, Michelle leaped into Mark's arms, locking her legs around his midsection. She smothered his face and neck with kiss after kiss.

"As much as I love your loving, let me tell you my story, babe, and find our way through this mess. I'm glad I can finally feel I can be honest with you. I'm sorry I still held things back from you, and even lied to you. When I explain everything, I hope you can forgive me. I wanted to figure this out by myself. Well, first I just wanted to find him, then meet him before I told you about him.

After my mother had the two of us, she couldn't handle it, so she gave Brantley to her sister, Brigette Mueller. You know that name."

"Of course, the woman killed in the Rhode Island fire."

"Right. That's where he grew up, less than fifty miles from me. Once I got his name from my father, I checked his license and vehicle information. He lives in West Roxbury. The day I skipped out on you, that's where I was, trying to meet him. He wasn't home, so I waited until he got home, but he didn't show until nearly midnight. I decided it was too late to meet him, but I wanted to get a good look at him. With my binoculars, I saw what looked like burn marks on his face, and his eyebrows and hair looked singed. That was the night of the Rozzie office fire.

Then, when I got his RMV info, I also grabbed a copy of his parking tickets. One of them was directly across the street from the Warren Tavern. It was then that I knew Mike O'Brien was holding out on me because he and that bartender were acting squirrely. When that list of employees came in for MedRX with Brantley's name on it, it confirmed for me that he is the arson murderer."

As Mark recounted his clandestine quest to uncover the truth, Michelle marveled at his unwavering determination to clear his name. "Oh, Mark, this is great. You're completely exonerated. Oh, but it's not great that your brother is the one doing all this.

From my little knowledge of DNA, I'm quite sure I heard that identical twins share the same DNA. He looks like you and, in a weird way, he is you as far as the Boston guys and, I'm afraid Tom and Dennis think so too. But you have to believe me they didn't want to believe any of this until the DNA profile was a match for you.

Mark, we've got to call them to explain all this. Let's start with Tom and Dennis, then the bosses. They can explain it to Boston Fire and Police."

"No, no, no, Michelle." Mark was adamant. "That won't work. I need to bring Brantley in because the Boston people will think we're whitewashing this, making up something to get me out of this to avoid embarrassment for ATF. Even the bosses won't fall for this until I can show them the flesh and blood. It has to be me, Michelle. Can't you see that I'm the one who has to clear my name? Besides, can you imagine how embarrassing this will be for me, having my long-lost brother being this killer? I have to do this to minimize the blow-back on me and my family name."

"Mark, I hear you, but I can't agree with you. It's too risky and dangerous. Tom and Dennis will back you up. They have always been there for you."

"Oh, babe, they have, but they're in too deep right now thinking I'm the bad guy. For God's sake, my best buddy is getting an arrest warrant for me! I could probably call him and explain everything, but I don't want them to put the cuffs on me. And the media will crucify me and then try to retract it all. That never works too well. Some people will always think it was me who did all this and scream that there was a cover-up. Even if I'm let go in a day or two, it just won't work."

"Okay, it sounds like I'm not going to change your mind. I've heard about your stubborn streak and now I'm seeing it. Not that it's a bad thing. Sometimes. So, do you have a plan?' Mark's decision to confront his brother filled her with apprehension. His choice was fraught with risk, yet she knew that standing by his side was her only course of action.

"First, I would like you to be my back-up. Instead of Tom and Dennis, you know the story and believe me, so will you be my partner?"

"Always. I will be honored to work with you on this. That's what I dreamed about from that night I first met you." Together, they forged a plan, their resolve unwavering in the face of adversity.

"We have to make ourselves scarce until we find him. I can tell they are ready to pick me up because nobody has called me about last night's fire and neither Dennis nor Tom called to speak with me about this.

Let's stay right here for the remainder of the weekend. Nobody knows where we are. You go to work on Tuesday. Just tell anybody who asks that you haven't heard from me at all. Even tell them I never returned your pages. You already played the most difficult undercover role with me. I'm sure you can deflect anything they throw at you."

Michelle nodded her agreement. "You're right. I've got this. What about you?"

"I'm going AWOL. I'll worry about the heat I'm going to take later, maybe even suspension. But that's minor compared to the alternative. I'm going to stay at a hotel until I get Brantley, but I plan to end this by Tuesday night. I'll use a rental car, too, so I don't use the G-car or have to go to my house to get my car, just in case they are sitting on my house.

I'll run by Brantley's place in West Roxbury. Then I'll page you when I spot him. You head over to your apartment. They won't be sitting on your place because they figure you're on their side and I have deserted you. After I get Brantley parked, I'll pick you up and we'll surveil him together. How's that sound?"

"Workable, except if he moves while you're picking me up. I'm glad you're including me like this."

"It's a chance I'll take. If he moves, we'll go back to sit on his house. And I can't think of a better partner, in more ways than one."

"And, Mark, I want you to know if you haven't already figured this out, I love you. And I'll have your back no matter what. The hardships during these past few weeks have to be the most trying time any couple has had to face. We made it through to the other side of this trial by fire, if I may use that term, as a stronger couple."

Mark reached out to pull Michelle close to his body. With his arms wrapped tightly around her in a bear hug, he whispered, "I love you, too, very much. Thank you for being there for me. I know I failed you and made it hard for you."

Michelle pulled back slightly, putting her hand over his lips, "Shh, it's over now. I'm here. Now kiss me you fool." She knew their journey was far from over, but no matter what difficulties awaited them, they would face them together as partners in love and in life.

The couple fell onto the bed locked in a deep kiss. Forget breakfast, maybe they will make a late brunch, or perhaps lunch.

CHAPTER THIRTY-THREE

On a holiday Monday, those gathered around the ATF conference room table were none too happy. The usual banter and frivolity was overshadowed by the seriousness of the situation at hand. But most of these players knew that 'you do what you gotta do' to get the job done. That often calls for unusually late and long hours, plus weekend and holiday work. There was a tacit understanding that extraordinary measures were necessary to tackle the case before them.

Special Agent Tom Walkowski, assuming a grave demeanor, led off the formal meeting after everybody arrived and introductions were exchanged. No one joked around. Everyone was in a quiet mood for this extremely sensitive case.

For the first time, Lieutenants Scherner and O'Brien from Boston Fire and Boston Police Detective Taylor met the ATF Special Agent in Charge (SAC), the Assistant Special Agent in Charge (ASAC), the Arson Group Supervisor Jack Dunn as well as the Assistant United States Attorney (AUSA).

Dr. Denise Williams was present to provide detailed information of the cause and manner of death for each of the five women. Just the day before, she had completed the autopsy on Evelyn Baxter, the victim from Friday night's fire.

"We're all here this morning to finalize affidavits for an arrest warrant and multiple search warrants regarding this God-awful case against ATF Special Agent Mark Miller. Every one of us has worked with him and have known him as a friend, a colleague and a damn great investigator. But now, with the evidence developed particularly by our Boston counterparts, I'm sorry to say we will know Mark as an arrested arsonist and murderer of several women.

A federal magistrate is on standby to review and sign the warrants. AUSA Scott will hand carry the affidavits to be signed later today. What we want to do now is ensure we have all the information in the affidavits that will make them bullet proof. Because of the sensitivity and the explosiveness of this investigation, we want to be absolutely sure it's done right so the case sticks. As awful and embarrassing this will be to reveal to the world, it will even be worse if we screw it up.

Tomorrow, Suffolk County Prosecutor Marty Regan, who could not be here today, will also seek an arrest warrant for Mark to include the other fires and corresponding murders, where the buildings did not affect interstate commerce. ATF is concerned with the Roslindale office building and the Jamaica Plain restaurant with the apartment on the second floor.

Now, Dick and Mike, would you guys lay out the facts of each fire and give us all the information you received from witnesses, your own observations and about the DNA results. Then, we'll call our profiler, Daryl Hawkins, who will detail the profiling analysis that corresponds to Mark so that a motive can be established for the affidavits. He is waiting for our call."

Once the others completed their evidence, Dr. Williams described the chilling details about how Evelyn Baxter was trussed at her ankles and wrists to the bed legs. She also related the gruesome specifics that the evidence revealed Evelyn was burned alive, since she had indications of both smoke inhalation and searing deep within her trachea.

Outwardly, the SAC sat patiently listening to the reiteration of the investigation. However, inwardly he stewed as his face reddened. He spoke for the first time during a brief pause in the action. "Tom and Dennis, when did you become aware that Mark was setting these fires? How did it get this far without me knowing about this?"

Dennis glanced toward Tom, deferring to him to answer. Walkowski explained their cautious approach, their initial skepticism, and their gradual understanding of mounting criminal evidence. "Sir, the Boston guys first told us that a bartender stated the man who left with the lady who died in a fire that night looked like Mark. That would have been after the third fire a few weeks ago. But, since it was so outrageous to believe Mark could be an arsonist, we were skeptical about the identification since eyewitnesses are often unreliable.

Then, a few days after the Roslindale office fire, Dick and Mike showed us the security camera footage that depicted a man in a hoodie that looks strikingly like Mark. However, the footage was poor, very grainy. It piqued our interest, but it still was not direct evidence. Also, the woman who was burned in that fire, and subsequently died, picked Mark out as the person who set the fire, but she was so heavily medicated, that her identification could have been open to scrutiny. So, Dennis and I enlisted Michelle Monihan to assist us by keeping track of his whereabouts at night."

The SAC held up a hand to stop Tom, "You mean that rookie agent? Why would you have her help you senior guys?"

"For those of you who don't know, Michelle is Mark's on again, off again girlfriend. Thus far, she has exhibited great skills to be an outstanding agent and she is assigned to the Serial Arson Task Force, so she was a natural for us to confide in her."

"Okay, Tom," the SAC said, still under control. "What else did you know, and when did you know it?"

"I think you know the rest, sir. Lt. Scherner called me Saturday with the DNA match from the office fire evidence to Mark's DNA. They had just received the completed analysis late Friday. We couldn't deny the confirmation of direct physical evidence, which left no doubt. Dennis and I confirmed that Mark was not with Michelle on Friday night when the latest fatal fire occurred. Sir, we did our best to follow the evidence without flying off the handle based on unverified information."

"It sounds pretty good, but I think we'll have to revisit this in private. I'll have to confer with the Director and feel him out about his thoughts. This is not the forum to address this further. Let's continue preparing for Miller's arrest."

During the next three hours, the information was relayed from the investigators to the prosecutor who hammered out the affidavits. No detail was too small to include in these documents. As the day progressed, the stern looks on the faces of all involved grew more intense underscoring the magnitude of the situation.

After wrapping up this portion of their work, Special Agent Dennis Caggiano detailed the plans for the executions of the search and arrest warrants. "Right now, we don't know the whereabouts of Mark. He has sort of disappeared off our radar. He has no family to our knowledge. Our best guess, and this is only a guess, is that he took off for the weekend after he set the fire Friday night. A surveillance tried to spot him at his house on Friday and at his girlfriend's place in Dorchester, both without success.

She couldn't make this meeting today because she had to attend to her sick mother. We have been in touch with her and she told us she has had no contact with Mark since last week. She has been a key asset trying to get information from him and ascertain his movements.

We have a team sitting on his house now. His personal car has been there all weekend and his G-car is still parked in our basement garage. We have someone on that car, twenty-four hours a day."

Scherner interrupted, "Oh, we were wondering if you guys knew where that car was." He didn't let on that his crew had been trying to locate Mark before the Friday night fire.

Dennis continued, "He'll probably be back here to work tomorrow. Obviously, we called this meeting without his knowledge. And he does not know about the bartender eyewitness, or the security video footage and the DNA which directly tie him to the office fire.

If and when he comes in tomorrow, we plan to arrest him on the spot, carefully and safely considering he carries a firearm, and we don't know how he'll react. Knowing him all these years, I would think he would surrender peacefully, but, in light of his recent criminal activities, there is no telling what he might do. We have to guard against him trying to take us out or even shooting himself. What we'll do to prevent this is surround him while talking about our weekend, then one of us will put a hand on his gun, which he always wears on his right hip.

Once we take him into custody, we will process him here before transporting him to the U.S. Marshal's Office. They too will process him, then bring him before a Magistrate for his initial appearance."

The SAC added, "Lieutenants and Detective Taylor, in the morning once Mark is in custody, I'll call your bosses to invite them to a press conference, probably for noon time because this will be huge news that can be on the midday news programs. And I promise not to screw it up with your bosses like I did before on Miller's big arson case. Marty Regan will cover for the District Attorney's Office." The Boston Fire Lieutenants nodded their affirmation without smiling. As meticulous preparations unfolded, the palpable tension in the room mirrored the severity of the impending confrontation.

Tom continued, "After Mark makes his initial appearance, we will have a team of eight investigators conduct the search warrants on both his government car and his personal car, as well as at his house. We will be looking for items that were used during the five fires including zip ties, cloth strips, liquid accelerants, latex gloves, news articles of the fires, and anything else that may connect him to the fires like trophies he may have taken from his victims. We would really like to find that photo he took of that woman, Ariel Garcia, the one he sent to the press. Does anybody else have anything to add or have any questions?"

"When will Miller be taken over to the Suffolk County Courthouse?" asked Dick Scherner. "I can't wait for my chance to place him under arrest. His homicidal fires are the most despicable crimes any of us can remember ever occurring in Boston. What he did is far worse than those guys who set all those fires. At least nobody died during their spree. His actions were pure evil."

Tom responded, "Dick, I understand your feelings. We all feel betrayed, and in our case, we have been close friends and he is an ATF agent, so we are super pissed at him too. But to answer your question, he'll be transported by the Marshals to the courthouse, most likely between one and two in the afternoon. Okay?"

Dick nodded with a wink and clenched fists.

CHAPTER THIRTY-FOUR

Tuesday morning arrived. A full contingency of ATF agents was on hand earlier than many of them usually appear at the office. The anxiety level of all those present intensified with each passing minute. Tom and his team, acutely aware of the risks, found themselves at the center of this high-stakes manhunt.

Each agent spent the waiting time in their own way. Some spoke nonstop. Others paced the floor wearing a path in the carpet. Still others sat at their desk with their heads down, drumming their fingers on their desk. All the hearts in the office throbbed wildly.

The round clock high on the office wall kept ticking louder than the bell at the end of a round of boxing. The sweep of the second hand crept with far less speed than when one awaited lunch hour or the end of the workday.

For Tom and Dennis, their frustration mounted as Mark remained elusive. Mark's friends were far more anxious than the others. Along with Group Supervisor Jack Dunn, they shuffled to the SAC's office at his behest. "Gentlemen, it's now," pausing as he made an exaggerated glance at this watch, "10:15. Where is Miller? I don't give a good God damn who he is, but golden boy needs to abide by the rules of this office. Has he checked in? Do any of you know where the hell he is?" The boss was seething. Nobody had ever seen him so enraged.

Again, Tom took the lead. "We have no idea where he is, sir. He has not answered our pages. There has been no sighting of him at his house. His car is still downstairs in the garage. Michelle is at her desk. I talked to her, but she still has not heard from Mark since last week."

The SAC commanded, "Go get her. I want to speak to her myself. Damn it, I want answers and I want them now!"

Dennis hurried to her desk. "Michelle, come with me. The SAC wants to speak with you. I must warn you, he's furious that Mark is AWOL. Just be cool, answer his questions, but don't guess or volunteer anything. You're not in trouble."

"Are you sure? Meeting with the SAC right now makes me wicked nervous considering my status and my relationship with Mark." Michelle nearly crumpled to the floor as she arose from her desk. *What have I gotten myself into?*

"Just relax, kid, you'll be fine. Stay strong." The two quickly marched to the SAC's office.

"Good morning, sir. You wanted to see me."

Yes, Agent Monihan, I know being called into my office in a situation like this can be extremely stressful, but I need to sort this out. I just want to ask you a few questions about Mark Miller. I heard you two have been dating. Tell me about that."

Michelle was shaking, her nerves evident as she navigated the interrogation. "We started seeing each other outside the office a few months ago. But our relationship has been uneven, erratic at times because he was acting strange." Thinking fast, Michelle added, "He recently told me he just met his father who left Mark and his mother when he was only six months old. That had caused him a lot of mental anguish resulting in his weird behavior with me."

"What kind of weird behavior, Michelle?"

"Like canceling dates at the last minute. Or he disappears at night, that type of thing."

"Do you know what he's been doing on those nights?"

"No, sir. He mentioned he just rides around hoping to come up with something to catch the serial arsonist."

"Did you have any inkling that he was setting these fires?"

"No, sir, beyond what our guys and the Boston guys have related to me, including on Saturday Lt. O'Brien told me about the DNA match."

"Do you believe Mark has been setting these fires?"

"Sir, I know Mark almost as much as any person does. I find it really difficult to believe he could do this, but I know the evidence seems strong. Somehow, I still know there's some other explanation."

"Michelle, one more question. Do you know where he is right now?"

Torn between loyalties and the weight of the incriminating evidence, Michelle treaded carefully. Hedging her bets that semantics will protect her ass, "No idea, sir."

"Thank you for your help. Be careful out there and with your heart. If you hear from him, let us know immediately. Guys, can we put an APB out on Miller?"

The ASAC spoke for the first time. "Sir, an all-points bulletin on what? We have no clue what he's driving. So, we can't do it."

The SAC's frustration simmered throughout the room as he audibly exhaled a long breath of air. "Well, damn it, somebody do something to find him! Where the hell can he be? He's not a ghost."

✳   ✳   ✳   ✳   ✳

Carlo and Wojo, Mark "Barney" Miller's two best friends since the ATF basic academy several years before, took a shift sitting on Mark's house south of Boston. It was now noon on Tuesday. The whereabouts of Agent Miller were still unknown. The strain was taking its toll on everybody involved with this investigation.

As they maintained surveillance on his house, the two agents grappled with their own conflicting feelings. Having dual roles as friends and as law enforcement officers created a complex web of emotions. Their apprehension was palpable as they contemplated the improbable possibilities of their friend's darkest impulses.

Carlo spoke first of the insanity surrounding the situation. "Woj, can you believe where we are at this moment in our lives?"

"Not in a million years, Carlo, not in my lifetime. I really can't comprehend this. It is so surreal. Despite what Mark may have done, when it goes down, we still have to do what we can to have his back.

Where the hell is he? I hope he didn't do something foolish and off himself. I know how fragile he can be, like after his divorce when I took his gun away for a few days. I was afraid then that he would eat his gun."

Carlo said, "I wonder what he's driving? He likes great vintage cars like that beautiful Super Sport over there. You know, maybe we should try his doors and peek in the windows to make sure he's not in there, dead or alive." The agents popped out of their car to look around the property.

They peered through the garage windows and through every first-floor window of the main two-story house. Their perusal found nothing amiss and no clue as to their friend's whereabouts. They also checked the locked sports car but saw nothing of note. Returning to their vehicle, Carlo thought aloud, the stress apparent in his voice, "We'll have the warrant soon. I sure hope we don't find him upstairs."

"Me, too, Carlo. Me, too," Wojo said with a slow sullen tone. "Despite what the evidence says, I still feel that there is some other explanation. We all go through tough times in our lives, but we don't become serial murderers. I find it so hard to believe Mark could do anything like this."

Back inside their car, they continued to ponder this bizarre situation. Their sense of unease was exaggerated with each passing second. The men braced themselves for whatever grim truth awaited discovery. A sense of foreboding lingered in the air as they contemplated Mark's whereabouts.

CHAPTER THIRTY-FIVE

Once again Mark awoke in a cold sweat following another disturbing nocturnal conflict. His dreams, or nightmares, were increasing in both their numbers and their vividness. This time, the dream wove a familiar thread with Mark in relentless pursuit of Brantley again, but not in the Boston Garden. It was a scene of impending dread. Mark was about to confront his elusive brother as he was ready to set a fire. In the recesses of his subconscious, every detail was so clear. The location, the flames, the conversation.

The adversaries locked eyes, but there was only silence between the estranged siblings, a chasm between their disparate lives. As Brantley was poised to murder yet another woman, Mark aimed his 9mm SIG Sauer pistol. He had to shoot Brantley now, before he kills her.

Here lies the problem. Mark's finger hovered against the trigger. Poised on the precipice of an irrevocable act, Mark pulls on the trigger, but paralyzed by fear and indecision, he can't squeeze it enough to fire the gun. No matter how hard he tries, he cannot fire his weapon.

He's shaking. He's scared. Desperation claws at his chest. The gun is quivering in his outstretched hand. It's Brantley or the life of an innocent woman, or even his own!

Mark bolts upright, awake now. The dream is left on the sheets. But the feelings gripped him throughout the day. But this was not the first time he had been plagued by this dream. This was a recurring nightmare. What if, if and when, the time ever comes, he really can't pull the trigger? This thought petrified Mark to his core.

✳   ✳   ✳   ✳   ✳

Special Agent Mark Miller had gone completely rogue. He recklessly ventured into uncharted territory in an obsessive pursuit of his brother. While driving toward Brantley's house in West Roxbury in his rented gray Jeep Cherokee, Mark pondered his future. As he did, he couldn't help but also contemplate how his past brought him to the present. Memories, both bitter and sweet, flooded his consciousness, each one a jagged piece of the puzzle that shaped his life.

This could turn out horribly. Someone else could die, maybe even Brantley or me. I'm probably going to be suspended, or possibly fired. I've violated only God knows how many rules and nobody knows exactly where I am or what I'm doing.

At least I didn't know for a fact Brantley was an arson murderer until Saturday, although I had strong suspicions days before that. Now, it's up to me to bring him in, resolve this scourge that has been wrought upon our city. Not Boston Fire or Police, not other ATF personnel. It must be me.

Am I somehow responsible for Brantley's actions? If I had sought my father years ago, maybe I could have met Brantley under different circumstances. We could have been real brothers, friends instead of combatants. And maybe he wouldn't have become this monstrous murderer. What twisted path led him to become a demon? Was there still a shred of humanity buried beneath his dark soul? I wonder what my aunt was like, how she treated Brantley, what their relationship was like. I think I know the answers based on what he's been up to.

I have a brother who is not my brother. He's my brother by blood only, but I really have to place blame on my mother for that. It shouldn't have been all that difficult for her to tell me about my twin. What held her back? I'll never know. Damn secrets.

Because of her hatred of my father, and her own upbringing, she took out her life failings on me. She must have seen an image of him every time she looked at me. For every little thing, she criticized me. Her humiliations were nearly unbearable. Sometimes I just wanted to crawl into a hole.

With no male role model to grow up with and my domineering mother, it's a wonder how I made it this far. I have to give myself a lot of credit for turning lemons into lemonade. Everything that happened to me just propelled me to prove that I could be the best. I pushed myself no matter what obstacles stood in my way to succeed at any task thrown at me.

And some of that has also been my downfall. I pushed all that pain into a closet, but every once in a while it breaks out and attempts to sink me. That's apparently why I strike out when I'm stressed or feeling cornered. And my stubborn drive to be the best cost me my marriage and multiple chances at love. This same arrogance and pigheadedness might even cost me my job or life, too, considering the track I'm on right now. But I'm not going to stop. What will be, will be.

Mark thought further about how he viewed himself and how others might see him. And because I have become an expert at my job, I do come off to others as a conceited jerk alienating those around him. I try not to, but my impatience shows when I see what I perceive as incompetence. And that leads me to another one of my problems. I only see what's directly in front of me, rather than the bigger, deeper picture. The reality of my shortcomings always with a laser focus on the present at the expense of broader perspectives of life, more than hints at my self-important nature that borders on pure arrogance.

I don't know if I'll ever get all my shit together. After this, maybe I should take some time for myself for intense self-examination.

*   *   *   *   *

Mark turned onto Brantley's street. As he approached his brother's house, Mark saw his Challenger back out of his driveway turning so that his car faced Mark's Jeep. The brothers looked into each other's eyes as they passed, this time a real-life silent exchange passed between them. A fleeting moment of recognition registered on Brantley's face.

Mark pulled into the same side street where he had previously conducted his surveillance of Brantley the night Ariel Garcia was torched in her office. With a surge of adrenaline coursing through his veins, Mark reversed his vehicle back into the street. A car's horn blared in anger. Mark slammed on his brakes to avoid a collision as the speeding car swerved around his rear bumper.

That car separated Mark from the Challenger, whose speed increased far beyond the speed limit on the residential roadway. Brantley raced up to the traffic light at the busy, congested Centre Street. After only a moment's hesitation, he spun his sports car left through the red light onto Centre to the sound of squealing tires and piercing horns.

Mark attempted to maneuver around the car in front of him and turn onto Centre, but oncoming cars blocked his path. Without the benefit of emergency lights and siren, Mark was stymied. The light turned green in Mark's favor, but when he turned onto Centre Street, luck was against him. He was thwarted by a MBTA commuter bus that ambled along the thoroughfare directly in front of him.

Leaning his Jeep toward the center line, Mark could see the fire red Challenger on a curve several vehicles ahead. Brantley was breaking every motor vehicle moving violation as he zig-zagged in and around traffic. In this cat-and-mouse game, Mark hoped he could gain on his brother. But after another five minutes elapsed, he no longer had an eyeball on the Challenger. Mark scoured the area, then pulled over to a payphone.

Mark cursed himself, frustrated for losing his prey. *Damn, I'm a seasoned investigator. I can't even conduct a proper surveillance. If I* only had my G-ride, I would have used my lights and siren to pull him over. I bet he still would have evaded me instead of pulling over.

If only I wasn't so headstrong! I could have called for back-up if I simply played by the rules. I could even have Boston PD help. But 'no', I need to do this by myself. I'm only Superman in my own mind.

From a pay phone, he dialed Michelle's pager number with a pre-planned code and the phone number from which he was calling. Within seconds, the phone rang. "Hi, Michelle? Can you talk? I lost Brantley about thirty minutes ago."

"Hi, Joe. What can I do for you today?" Michelle used a phony name in case anybody could hear her conversation. Their coded exchange spoke volumes of the strength of the bonds they forged in their relationship.

"Why don't you head to your place? I'll be over as soon as I can. I'm positive he recognized me when he pulled out of his driveway. I'm going to search this area further to see if I can find him. I'll call you at home when I'm close. I'll come up because I need to hit the bathroom before we head out again. Okay?

Then, we'll go sit on his house even though he is now aware that I know where he lives. But he may need to retrieve something there. It's one of those things where it's so obvious that it's not obvious, if you know what I mean."

"I don't have a clue, but I'll see you soon. I'll let the boss know I have to head out. Thanks for calling." She had no intention of telling the truth to the boss. Michelle realized she was putting her career on the line for Mark, but he needed her. As they prepared to confront Brantley, the path of their clandestine collaboration was laden with peril. However, the couple remained determined, united by a shared purpose and an unyielding resolve to see justice served, no matter the cost.

CHAPTER THIRTY-SIX

Prior to speaking with Mark on the phone, she had received a troubling call. The group secretary answered the call. "Good morning, ATF, may I help you?"

"Is this the Arson Task Force group?" a voice inquired.

"Yes, it is, what can I do for you?" the secretary responded.

"A female agent interviewed me last week, but I can't remember her name. I have some information for her. Is she there?"

"Sure, that would be Michelle Monihan. Hold on a minute." She then relayed the call to Michelle.

"Special Agent Michelle Monihan, may I help you?" Nobody responded. Over the phone she only heard a truck's air horn in the background. Then, a voice responded.

"Yes, Michelle, you may help me, but not in the way you might think. We'll meet sometime soon. And maybe I'll meet your boyfriend, too. Bye for now."

"Hold it, who is this?" Michelle asked, but the line went dead.

Michelle shrugged her shoulders, looked at the receiver, and listened again before finally hanging up the phone. With a flash of panic, *that was Brantley!* Chills ran down her spine. He was taunting her, and by extension, he was also provoking his brother. The tone of his voice sounded menacing.

Oh, my god! What was Brantley planning now? He tracked me down. How the hell did he even know about me?

Feigning sickness so she could make a hasty exit, Michelle first reassured her supervisor she would call the office if she heard from

Mark. It wasn't a stretch to appear sick. She was trembling so hard with a newfound apprehension as her skin turned completely colorless.

Fear was getting to her. In the hallway, she punched impatiently at the elevator button. Her knees buckled with unexpected weakness. She nervously looked at her watch for the umpteenth time. It was now 12:30 P.M. Racing through the garage below the federal building to her car, Michelle drove out of the building via the overhead doorway. She never noticed the red Dodge Challenger tucked in at the loading dock next to the ramp leading from the garage.

A couple turns later, Michelle took the highway southbound toward her large apartment building next to the Southeast Expressway. Since it was midday, the ride would take less than fifteen minutes. Her thoughts focused on the potential events that could present themselves over the next twenty-four hours.

I need to get home, and I really need to tell Mark about Brantley's call. Will Mark and I confront and arrest Brantley? Or will Mark get arrested? Or could something worse happen? Will Brantley come after me, or us?

While waiting for Brantley to show at his house, Mark and I need to discuss how to explain our actions over the past three days. This could be one colossal screw up or it could end with a huge arrest of Mark's demon brother. Most likely the ultimate outcome will settle someplace in the middle.

Michelle wondered how Brantley's arrest and prosecution would affect Mark. He's already faced emotional issues that have put his psyche at risk. I would love to be there for him, to support him if he'll let me. Will we make it through this ordeal unscathed as a couple?

✳   ✳   ✳   ✳   ✳

Brantley reveled in his sinister scheme. From his phone call to Michelle's office to verify she was there, to actually speaking with her, to stashing his car near the garage entrance, and now to deftly following her without blowing his cover, he felt a twisted sense of accomplishment. He even thought, *"Geez, I could have been a skilled investigator, maybe even a very special agent. But I surely am one nasty, devious bastard. I probably scared the hell out of her. Good!"*

Today is going to be momentous. He outwardly smiled. A chuckle escaped his lips. His thoughts drifted from his self-loving to his target. Her voice sounded sweet. Not like the other trolls I torched. This will be different. I have nothing against her except she is my brother's girlfriend. She would most likely break his heart anyway. They always do. But, for now, I'll be the one who breaks his heart.

So, Mr. Investigator found out where I live. I have to give him kudos. He's good. Just not good enough. And too late for him. Right after I take care of his girlfriend, he'll know the pain like I felt growing up.

Following three vehicles behind Michelle so he wouldn't be detected, Brantley came well prepared for his ambush. Besides the usual tools of his craft, he had packed another glass bottle of gasoline. Not caring about a time-delay device to provide time for his escape, he wanted this fire to take off faster than any other, so it produced immediate results with the biggest splash. Actually, it would make the greatest flash.

Michelle took an exit to the Neponset River section of Boston. Trailing her, Brantley also steered onto the exit, keeping a safe distance from her with cars in front of him while still keeping an eye on her every move. She turned right onto a small street, then drove into the parking lot of a large apartment building. He continued past the lot entrance and pulled into a dead-end parking area before making his way into her parking lot just in time to catch a glimpse of Michelle entering the structure through a door centered on the long side of the building.

While giving her enough time to get into her apartment, Brantley coolly checked his go bag, even though he knew it was ready for action. Pulling a Red Sox cap down tightly on his head and zipping up his black hoodie tightly around his neck, he made for the door Michelle had gone through. He even had his hair trimmed a couple days earlier, so now he really looked identical to his brother. It was time for M-day, Michelle and Mark Day!

✳   ✳   ✳   ✳   ✳

Boston Fire Lieutenants O'Brien and Scherner were cruising around Boston popping into various locations where Mark Miller was known to frequent. "Where the hell is this bastard?" Scherner grumbled. His frustration from the lack of progress was palpable as they failed to locate their target. With each passing moment, the weight of the task at hand grew heavier on his shoulders. Not knowing Mark's whereabouts only fueled Scherner's annoyance. "Mike, do you realize how big this is?"

"Yeah, this is all I think about, Dick. Not only will we be helping to solve the worst serial arson murder case this century in Boston, but we'll be arresting a federal agent for those murders. I never, in my wildest dreams, ever thought I would be thrust into something so monumental."

"Absolutely epic, Mike. Here we are, standing on the precipice of history, a once in a career case. And it's not just about solving such a mysterious case. This is about confronting the darkest depths of evil within a person. But I feel like we're spinning our wheels out here, doing nothing but sight-seeing. Let's check out Michelle's place. They called us on the radio to let us know she went home sick. It's only a few minutes away. We'll give her a call when we get there to see how she's doing."

"Good idea. She's such a good kid. Too bad she's so tight with Mark. I think he would feel comfortable going to her place especially since he doesn't know the world is about to come down on his head. The teams just let us know there's no action with his cars at his house or at the office. So what the hell is he driving?"

Turning off the Southeast Expressway in view of Michelle's apartment building, Dick wondered if this case would culminate within those walls. He asked, "If we see the son-of-a-bitch, do you think we should arrest him on the spot?"

"I don't believe that's a good idea, Dick. We're supposed to be working as a team. Everyone will be pissed forever if we do that. How about this?

If we see him arrive, we radio the other teams right away, then sit on his car in case he tries to leave. We'll box his car in depending on how he parked and we'll approach him as if we were at the building for another reason."

"Yeah, we can do that," Dick responded grudgingly, "but if he tries to leave before the other guys get here, or if he becomes combative, we take him at gunpoint. You hear me, no more Mr. Nice Guy."

Once in the parking lot, Mike asked, "Where should we park? This is a big place. We want to position ourselves so we can see him when he comes in, but it could be bad if he sees us." The brick and concrete four-story edifice stretched a hundred yards long. There was a front center entrance main door with additional doors at each end.

"Let's go in the back row. We should be able to spot him, then we'll move up to his car once he goes inside." They parked strategically facing out, tucked between two other cars ready to spring into action. "This should do it. I hope we don't have to sit here all day. We firefighters weren't built to sit on surveillance."

No sooner had they backed into their parking spot, through a tree-lined grassy island that separated the front from the rear parking areas, both investigators noticed a man rummaging in the passenger side of his vintage red Dodge Challenger. His black hoodie was snuggled up tight against his ears. A Red Sox cap topped his head. When the man pulled a black cloth bag out of his car, he glanced around checking his surroundings.

"Well, I'll be… It's him. In that classic car in the front row. That's the son-of-a-bitch, Mark. And we didn't have to wait at all!" exclaimed Scherner. "Mike, get on that radio right now. Call for Tom and Dennis. Tell them to get here ASAP."

"Boston Fire calling ATF Car One."

Moments later, "Go ahead, Boston Fire." Agent Tom Walkowski responded.

"Tom, the eagle has landed. Agent Monihan's apartment. We need you here as fast as possible. If you can call anybody else, we'll stand by. Please advise, if the eagle prepares to take flight, can we cage him?" Mike used a code he remembered from some book he had read years ago.

"Okay, Mike, try to keep him there, whatever you have to do. But don't go inside. Give us fifteen to twenty. We'll blue light it. Hit us up if there is any change in status."

CHAPTER THIRTY-SEVEN

Brantley couldn't help but smile when a teenaged boy came out the door as he approached. As the boy held the door open for Brantley, he flashed a smile, "Hi, there, young fellow. Thanks. Everybody should have manners like you. Have a good one."

He easily found Michelle's last name listed on the row of mailboxes. Her apartment was on the third floor. Rather than take the elevator, Brantley hiked up the two flights of stairs to pump himself up for what was to come. He nervously pulled his hoodie even tighter around his neck and ears. Midway along the long hallway, he stood outside Michelle's door. Putting his right hand on the stun gun in his hoodie pocket, Brantley took an extra deep breath, blowing out slowly, hoping his deception would work for easy access into her apartment.

He playfully knocked a nonthreatening tune on her door, *Shave and a Haircut*, pause, *two bits*.

Brantley heard Michelle approach the door from the inside. He could tell she paused at the peep hole, "Wow, you got here fast." As she opened the door, Michelle cheerfully said, "I love the attempt at a disguise." *Zap!*

Michelle slumped to the floor, twitching, with her eyes rolled back in her head. A quick howl escaped her lips, then only moaning and whimpering as the electric impulses from his Taser did its job once again.

Brantley tossed his bag further into the room, then closed the door behind him. Reaching under Michelle's arms, he quickly dragged her into her bedroom and tossed her onto the bed. She had already changed from her business attire. Now she wore a light blue nylon t-shirt and a pair of navy-blue form fitting work-out pants.

Working efficiently while his victim was still listless, Brantley looped multiple double zip ties in order to secure her to the wood posts on the four corners of her queen size bed. He took a few moments to look Michelle over, thinking she is such a cute, good-looking young lady. *I can certainly see why my brother found her attractive.* Brantley compared Michelle to the nasty faces of his previous targets.

Michelle opened her eyes wide in recognition as Brantley was about to wrap a cloth strip to gag her from shouting out loud. He put his finger to his lips to silence her. "Can I trust you not to scream?"

"Yes, Brantley," she spoke softly. "I would love to talk with you. It's remarkable how you look exactly like Mark." Although restrained and fearing she was in a potentially deadly predicament, Michelle mustered her courage to maintain her composure. In a strange way, she found this opportunity to converse with Brantley to be fascinating.

"So, you know who I am. Pretty and smart, too."

"I'm not the only one who knows who you are. Of course, your brother knows who you are, too. And, there's others who think you are Mark."

"What do you mean by that?"

"I don't think there's any harm in telling you a little story. There are witnesses who can connect you with the car fire murder in Charlestown. Then, there's video of you outside the office fire where you murdered your boss. And, here's the biggie that will put you away for life. Do you know what DNA is?"

"Yeah, it's like a unique fingerprint of a person based on their genetic make-up, right?"

"That's a good, succinct way of putting it. Mark said you are smart."

"Oh, he did, did he?"

"Yeah, we can talk about him and you in a minute, but I need to finish about you and the fires first. So, do you remember a bloody scratch on your finger where you lost part of your latex glove at that office fire?"

"No, not really."

"Analysis of that blood matched your DNA profile."

"Really, how did they match it to me?"

"Because it matches your twin brother. And now, everybody thinks he set those fires except for me."

Falling back into a bedside chair, Brantley roared with uncontrollable laughter. Tears rolled down his cheeks. Still laughing, he chortled, "Oh, that is so funny! It went even better than I ever could have imagined."

"I'm glad you find that so amusing. You planned to hurt your brother by setting the fires?"

"I aimed to challenge him to see if he was actually the best while at the same time ridding the world of some useless women who were little more than cockroaches. And I hate bugs.

When I learned from my fake mother that I had a brother who was becoming a famous arson investigator, I took it upon myself to see if he really was good at his job."

"Brigette Mueller was your aunt, right? Who raised you."

"She was the fucking bitch who tortured me my entire life! Not once did she ever show an ounce of love for me. I am who I am because of her physical and emotional abuse every day. And she kept the secret about my mother and brother until her dying day. But I'm over that. I have found my path and I've become pretty good at it.

Plus, I hate my mother for giving me away and keeping Mark. I hate her for never trying to meet me. On top of that my father never existed in my life either. To top it all off, I hate Mark because he succeeded while I've struggled for everything."

"So that's why you set the fire that killed your aunt? Because you hated everything about her?"

"I sure as hell did. But, in a weird way, I did it for her. She asked me to put her out of her misery because the cancer was slowly killing her."

"Oh, so your motive was altruistic. How noble of you!"

"You're God damn right! It's the least I could have done for her, or for any of the women I set on fire. It's the least I could have done for the world. None of them would have ever changed to contribute to society. Instead, every one of them sucked the life out of anyone they came in contact with.

And I'll tell you this. Except for you, my victims stemmed from some chance occasion, like a woman forcing a kid to eat. Unlike other serial killers, I didn't scout out these women. And I never wanted to kill them any other way except by fire. Like strangling them would have been too up close and personal for me. Plus, I found that the only way to relieve my own burning pain was to burn the woman. Nothing else would suffice, I'm sure.

What I did to those women was not a game for me. It was just life…and death. But taunting Mark and the other fire investigators was a fun game. Sending stuff to the newspapers wasn't so much for publicity than it was to screw with Mark and the others."

"Well, thank you for telling me all this. What did you mean when you said the fires relieve your burning pain?" Michelle found these admissions intriguing, first-hand confessions of a serial murderer. *And I hope by keeping this dialogue going, I can buy some more time for Mark, or someone else to save me. Or possibly, she thought, if I connect with Brantley, I can get him to give up his quest and surrender.*

"I tried counseling for a short time where I learned a lot of hocus pocus, but I think some of the crap is real. Because my aunt repeatedly whipped me with the buckle end of the belt, I always felt the stinging, burning pain on my backside. Every time one of these women pushed a button in me, their disgusting action reignites that same horrific pain. It consumes me, makes me crazy. The only thing that makes the pain go away was burning those bitches."

"I'm so sorry, Brantley, that you had to live with all that. It sounds so horrible. Can I tell you about Mark?" Michelle was skillfully using her education and training to develop a rapport with her captor.

"You might as well. I'm in no rush. I have time to kill, so to speak. Tell me a little about the golden boy."

"Here goes. His life wasn't a bowl of cherries either. Your mother was also a tyrant who didn't know how to show affection. She berated Mark often, always yelling, swearing and humiliating him. Maybe he didn't get physically abused like you, but emotionally he is scarred. He has a difficult time with women, like I bet you do, too. After all, we know you never sexually assaulted those women you killed.

The big difference between you and Mark is that his stubborn side propels him forward. He never gives up at anything. One of his worse traits is that he always strives to be the best. Since Mark often thinks he is the best, he has to be the only person to get something done because it has to be done right. It's an obsession for him.

He really is a good person, and he would have made a terrific brother to you. He grew up without a father, too. Only recently he met your father who asked about you. It's not too late to get to know your father and Mark. Even knowing what you've done, he has never said a bad word about you.

But, unlike Mark, you wallow in your little world, surrounding yourself in misery. It's time to stop what you're doing and help yourself climb out of the rabbit hole that you've dug for yourself. What do you say?"

Despite her efforts to reason with Brantley, he remained steadfast on his destructive path. "Michelle, thanks for telling me this stuff, it's such a touching tale," Brantley sarcastically replied. "But it's too late for me. I don't want to get to know them. Nobody is like me. To quote a song, 'I am a rock. I am an island. I touch no one and no one touches me.' There is nothing left for me but to continue on my road to hell. As you can tell, fire and I go well together."

Michelle found herself amidst a whirlwind of confusing and conflicting feelings as she listened to Brantley. She experienced sympathy for this lost man-boy, but she also felt fear and loathing for his warped way of thinking. "Brantley, maybe you can find some good in life even though you'll be in prison. Don't let your life have a pathetic ending."

There's that word again, pathetic. The bile rose in Brantley's throat. His backside began to burn with that familiar searing, blistering agony. Welts from fresh whippings scarred his psyche further.

"I've heard that damn word all my life. I am not pathetic and I'm going to prove it right now. I'm afraid you are going to have a pathetic ending, and I'm going to crush Mark, so he ends up with a miserable life, too. I hope I push him right over the edge. Sorry, kid. It's time to set my most magnificent fire yet."

With that, he tried forcing cloth strips into Michelle's mouth, but she fought fiercely, twisting, biting, and writhing to thwart his attempts. Brantley powerfully jumped on top of his hostage with his knees landing on her mid-section causing the air to rush from her lungs. He gave her a mighty slug to her jaw with his right elbow. His actions incapacitated Michelle. She fought no further. Now, finally, only terror flashed from her widened eyes.

The phone on her nightstand rang loudly, shattering the quiet moments after Brantley subdued her. It rang and rang. "Your lover boy is probably wondering why you're not answering. I'd better get to work." But he felt that strange feeling of being followed. Also, something was strangling him again.

Michelle's pager also alerted, but it went unheard because it was in her linen jacket on the living room sofa where she tossed it when she got home. Her weapon was also there.

✳   ✳   ✳   ✳   ✳

As announced, Brantley began arranging his fire set. He explained his methodology to the terrified Michelle as he went about his business. "First, I like to use crumpled newspapers, lots of them around my prey's body, sort of a nest. I spread the papers in a nice path from the bed to the outer door. That's called a trailer as I recall from my studies about setting fires and fire investigation.

I take some alcohol and sprinkle a little alcohol here and a little alcohol there," danced Brantley as he splashed alcohol on and around Michelle, then followed along the newspaper trailer. "I learned to be a little more careful about using gasoline after using too much at the office fire, *woomph!*"

Pulling the glass bottle of gasoline out of his bag of tricks, Brantley proudly announced, "And now, for something new. You, my dear, will be the first to experience how fast a fire spreads when I toss this Molotov cocktail from your doorway into my little trailer." He unscrewed the bottle cap and inserted some cloth strips in and around the neck of the bottle. "There, see. This should be fun."

Michelle took in every word, every description, every one of Brantley's actions. In the event she survives, Michelle intended to describe in vivid detail should this monster ever stand trial.

The urgency of the situation crashed down on the young agent. *Where are you, Mark? I don't want to go out this way. I'm counting on you. You're my man. And I want to be your woman.*

CHAPTER THIRTY-EIGHT

Mark quizzically gazed at the silent pay phone at the supermarket on Gallivan Boulevard, a three minute drive from Michelle's apartment. He had let it ring a dozen times with no answer. Then, he even tried paging her using his badge number, but she didn't respond with the pre-arranged response of 10-4.

Mark was alarmed. He was concerned that something had gone wrong with Michelle. His brain began working overtime again as he jumped into his Jeep. *Is she okay? Is somebody else in her apartment? The good guys? No, she would have found a way to get me the message. Plus, they would have wanted her to answer the phone since they're looking for me. Or could it possibly be Brantley? I doubt it, but that's the scariest scenario of all. But that must be it. He's one smart bastard who is definitely devious enough to go after her to get at me.*

Mark sped to Michelle's place, merely four turns over a mile away. He slowed as he entered her complex to avoid drawing attention to himself. To his left, tucked away in a row of cars, Mark instantaneously spotted the BFD van. *So, they are sitting on her place just waiting for me to screw up.* He turned his face away from their direction, hoping against hope they didn't recognize him in his rental vehicle. Because he was so concerned with being spotted, when he turned his head away from the Boston guys, he also turned his head from where Brantley had parked, missing the red Challenger.

Mark parked discreetly at the furthest end of the lot away from the surveillance team. He swiftly moved toward the doorway at the farthest end of the building. Once he passed the corner, he stopped to glimpse back around the corner to check if there was any movement of the van or its occupants. Nothing. *I've made it this far.*

At the exterior door Mark used the key Michelle had given to him as a symbol of their relationship. She had said to him, "This key will bring you to me anytime and always. Mi casa es su casa."

After fidgeting and stabbing the elevator button multiple times with his index finger, Mark's impatience won out. He sprinted up the hall stairs to Michelle's floor, his heart racing faster than his legs, but not his thoughts. *My God, what am I getting into? My brother, my girl, our lives!*

Halfway down the long hallway he moved. The dim lighting only served to close the distance, narrowing Mark's focus, almost as if in a dream. At Michelle's door, he stopped. He sucked in a deep breath. He listened. A muted male voice chanted a little ditty. She was not alone!

*   *   *   *   *

Lt. Scherner drove the BFD van to park directly behind the Dodge Challenger, nearly touching its rear bumper so there was no room to put the car in reverse. The car had been parked nose in against another vehicle.

Meanwhile, the ATF guys, Tom and Dennis, flew into the parking lot. Their emergency blue bubble light was flashing on their dashboard. They pulled directly up to the front of the van, nose to nose.

All four men leaped from the two vehicles. Tom spoke, "Okay, this is it. We're going to take Mark down, hopefully without incident. Let's all be careful in there. We don't know how desperate he may be.

We'll go in the front door. I'll badge the person at the desk to determine the location of Michelle's apartment, then when we head up, be prepared with your weapons ready. Everybody got your vest on?"

Inside the main door, Tom learned Michelle's unit was on the third floor centered in the hallway. "Dick and Mike, you two go up the stairway at that end of the building," pointing to the left, "and we'll go up on this end," he said as he pointed toward the right.

As they scattered, the four men from the two teams stressed with the unknown they were about to face. There were so many variables. Each man understood this was a fluid situation that could turn volatile within a moment's notice. Their thoughts fluctuated in the time it took to ascend the two flights of stairs. *Here we are, about to come face to face with an arsonist, a sick murderer, a brother, a fellow agent, a friend, a fiend. And we have an innocent woman in the mix!*

Both teams reached the third-floor landing, cautiously stepping into the carpeted hallway. All four men saw Special Agent Mark Miller nearly fifty yards away standing at the entrance to Michelle's apartment, as he raised his semi-automatic handgun toward a target, not visible to them. Wojo hesitated, "Carlo, what the hell is he doing? Who is he aiming at?"

✳   ✳   ✳   ✳   ✳

Seconds before, Mark silently slipped his key into the lockset, turned it, then gently pushed the door wide open, hoping to surprise Brantley without upsetting him. He took the standard strong two-legged stance with his arms outstretched holding his pistol in a two-handed clasp.

What Mark saw horrified him. In the living room directly in front of him was Brantley facing Michelle's bedroom with a Molotov cocktail held high above his right shoulder and an unlit cigarette lighter in his left hand. Beyond him, Mark spied Michelle's bed with her splayed out on her back, her extremities restrained at the bed corners.

Brantley's body blocked her view from spotting Mark. He knew he had to react quickly. His thoughts instantly considered the safest approach he should take. *I can't shoot him in the back, but if he lights that firebomb, it could be all over for Michelle. My best move is to de-escalate the situation, talk him down.*

"We shouldn't be meeting like this, brother," Mark started, speaking softly so as to not startle his brother.

Brantley spun around; his incendiary weapon still held high. "Well, if it isn't golden boy. Nice to meet you, Mark. But don't come any closer or we'll all have one hell of a hot time." With a quick flick of his thumb, Brantley spun the metal wheel igniting a small flame of his lighter. His action dramatically raised the stakes. If he smashes or even if the bottle drops it could result in an explosive flash fire throughout the room.

"Brantley, my brother…"

"Don't call me brother."

"Well, we are brothers. We couldn't help what our parents did to us. I only found out about you months ago. Since then, I have been trying to meet you. I wanted you as my brother. Hey, were you at the Bruins game last spring?" Mark was trying his best to diffuse the situation. He could now see Michelle looking straight at him, wide-eyed in fear, but nodding to him as if saying, "Keep it up. You're doing good."

"Yeah, I was at the game. A little piece of enjoyment in my life. I saw you trying to catch up to me. I guess I'm faster."

"You certainly were that day, but we'll have to try a real race sometime. Could you do me favor and put the lighter down?"

"I don't think so, bro. I have some business to finish."

"Really? Come on," Mark pleaded. "I'm here now. Let's get to know one another. You've done enough damage. I think I can only begin to imagine what's behind all this."

Suddenly, Mark spotted movement to his right. With a quick glance so as not to take his eyes off Brantley, he eyed Wojo and Carlo at the end of the long hallway, both with the weapons aimed directly at him. *Shit! This just went from really serious to really, really terrifying.*

"Hey, Barney," called out Wojo, "it's over buddy. We don't want to hurt you. We just want to figure out what's going on. And you can't run, you're surrounded. Look to your left." Mark glimpsed left. Dick Scherner and Mike O'Brien also had Mark in their sights.

Mark addressed the four of his pursuers. "Listen guys, you have this all wrong. I have the arsonist right in front of me. Just give me a few minutes and I'll prove it to you."

Scherner yelled, "Mark, put your gun down, *now!* We don't want to shoot you, but we will if you don't put your weapon down. We're here to arrest you for the murders you so savagely committed."

"Dick, I'm sorry. I can't do that at the moment."

Meanwhile, Brantley still had his tools of destruction at the ready, but he was amused by what he perceived was happening in the hallway. "Hey, Mark. Why don't you just give up? Your compatriots are here to arrest you for the fires, right? Oh, brother, your girlfriend told me about them thinking you set the fires. That is so fucking funny. If I wasn't holding on to this stuff, I think I would pee my pants laughing."

"Yeah, yeah, it's a hoot. Why don't you come over here and show yourself to them so we can all get a good chuckle? Look, can you leave Michelle out of this? She never did you any harm and she's really a nice person, not one of those witches you wrote about in that poem to the newspapers."

Brantley was tiring of the banter. "Listen, just by talking to her for the past few minutes, I think you're right. She seems nice enough, but eventually she could turn on you. Besides, I only want to toast her to break your spirit. You have had life so easy. I want to show you how painful life really is."

"Hey, Mark," yelled Wojo. "What's it going to be, old friend? We're coming to get you, all right? You're not going to shoot us, are you?"

"Wojo, please, give me a couple minutes. I've got the situation under control. If you come over here, I don't know what might happen."

"Miller, this is your last chance," warned Scherner. "Put your fucking gun down now! I would like nothing more than to shoot you. Don't give me more of a reason than I already have."

"Dick, I'm telling you to stand down," Mark commanded. "You're interfering with a Federal investigation. You do anything and you'll either be arrested yourself or charged with murder."

Scherner and O'Brien looked quizzically at each other. "Who the hell does this guy think he is?" Scherner wanted a piece of Miller in the worst way.

Brantley joined in, "We have a regular four ring circus going here. And Michelle is playing the part of the audience. A captive audience you could say."

"You're a funny guy, Brantley. So you think I had an easy life. Our mother was a vicious, non-loving woman who never gave me anything. I had to work for everything, pulling myself up to make something out of myself. On top of that I got divorced. But I've managed to do okay for myself." Mark continued to reason with Brantley, appealing to their shared dysfunctional upbringings, but Brantley remained obstinate.

"Well, good for you. It doesn't sound like a piece of cake, but mine was more like a piece of shit. Your mother's sister was worse. She loved to whip me with the buckle end of the belt on my bare ass that left welts that still hurt to this day. She humiliated me daily, even when it came to sex. Because of her, I could never have a normal relationship with a woman. I never wanted to be like this. She made me grow up like this. I've been alone my entire life. So, I decided to go after women like her. Witches, all of them, God damn bitches.

Neither our so-called mother nor our father ever cared to reach out to me. They never cared. She kept you but gave me away. You were obviously her favorite from the beginning. When I found out about you, I figured fires would be a great way to take care of them and get back at you at the same time."

As he spoke, the weight of the years of his internal emotional turmoil came crashing in on Brantley. The intense scorching pain spread from his backside. This time the blistering plague crept down his legs, up his back, out the length of his arms and up his neck. His ears turned red as did his eyes. He was on fire from within, spontaneous human combustion.

Mark saw he was losing his brother, the situation becoming futile as the tensions escalated. For the first time in his life, Mark felt the familial bond of having a twin brother. He became conscious of an inner burning sense within the fibers of his own body. Overcome with this peculiar feeling, Mark lowered his gun. Something had always been missing. Now it was right in front of him.

"Brantley, we can work this out. I understand you faced unspeakable evil, the beatings, the screaming, the humiliations. I can't believe you're devoid of any conscience. To your way of thinking, you make order out of disorder by setting the fires. It's time to drop your mask of insanity.

You're my brother. I want to help you with the remainder of your life. There's no reason to feel alone, like a loser in life."

Mark made a poor choice using that word. "I'm not a loser!" Brantley screamed back, "And I'll show you I'm not." Knowing his brother was suffering a volatile crisis, Mark raised his weapon again, taking aim at the center of mass of the body across the room.

With the renewed outburst heard by the arresting teams, the two crews both slowly advanced on Mark from both ends of the hallway, inching along, ducking into each recessed apartment doorway for the minimal protection it provided, closing the nearly fifty yard gap.

Knowing he had every right to shoot Brantley, both legally and ethically, Mark started squeezing his trigger finger. He felt pressure from his finger against the steel of the trigger, the beginning of the firing sequence. *Shoot or don't shoot. It's my brother. But he's a murderer who may strike again any second. I need to protect Michelle.*

Mark's heart pounded in his ears as he applied more pressure to the trigger. His finger trembled slightly. Each millimeter of movement felt like an eternity, reminiscent of the nightmares that haunted his sleep. With each incremental pull, the mechanisms within the gun slowly shifted, inching closer to the critical point where he would unleash its deadly blast.

Mark held his breath as time nearly stopped. Every sound magnified in the silence of the moment. He now plainly heard the padding footsteps of his fellow investigators inching closer to him.

A chaotic whirlwind of fear and determination pressed down on him, threatening to suffocate him. But despite the hesitation and the fear, Mark knew he needed to act. He couldn't afford to falter now, not when so much was at stake. This was not a dream. This was real life.

With a final surge of willpower, he pushed past his doubts, committing to the action he knew he had to take. But Brantley interrupted Mark's stream of consciousness.

"Mark, it's been great finally meeting you. But you and I both know the only way we are ever going to learn more about each other is during prison visitations. I chose a path of destruction. I enjoyed my path in a fucked-up sense that few could ever understand. I might as well go out in a blaze of glory."

With that, before Mark had any further chance to speak, Brantley unexpectedly lit the gasoline soaked wick on the firebomb, crashing it to the floor at his feet. With a thunderous woomph, fire instantaneously flashed. The blaze furiously erupted from floor to ceiling, engulfing Brantley with bright red, orange and yellow dancing flames while consuming the oxygen within the room, creating enormous plumes of black smoke.

A wall of intense heat smashed Mark in the face. "Noooo!" he bellowed. Simultaneously, with the suddenness of the crash, Mark completed the trigger pull. The gunshot echoed through the air, adding a new sound to the tumultuous firestorm. The explosive deflagration rocked Mark enough to cause a wild shot.

At the same moment Mark fired, another blast reverberated in the hallway. His right shoulder stung like he had been stabbed by a doctor's needle. He had been shot. Overcoming the dual shock of the fire and the wound, Mark ran toward the fire. Already, as rapidly as the ferociousness of the flames erupted, they subsided as the gasoline vapors were consumed. But other combustibles within the room ignited, with growing flames.

In the chaos amidst the flames and gunfire, Mark's courage shone bright against the darkness, proof of the power of loyalty and love. "Michelle," he called out. "I'm coming, babe!" Although wounded, Mark was determined to rescue Michelle. He grabbed two blankets from a side chair outside the fire zone. Throwing one atop the flaming, moaning Brantley, Mark couldn't waste any further effort on his brother. He tossed the other blanket over his head and body in a quick protective wrap as he raced past flames hopscotching his way into the bedroom.

✳　✳　✳　✳　✳

Four men peered into the apartment doorway, all with a look of abject disbelief, totally perplexed by the scene that confronted them. Mike O'Brien pointed with amazement to the splatter of blood on the floor and doorjamb where they stood. "Yeah, I shot him," Tom explained.

"You shot him?" Mike couldn't believe it. "You shot your friend?"

"I didn't mean it. My finger was at the ready on the trigger. When the fire erupted and Mark fired, I flinched. Luckily, it looks like I only winged him."

Carlo yelled, "Mark, don't," but he said no more as Mark disappeared into the bedroom. "Dick, Mike, hurry. Get the fire extinguishers near the exit doors. And call 911." The two men sprinted in opposite directions. Upon their return, they rushed into the living room, concentrating spray on and around Brantley who lay motionless on the center of the floor. They all pondered who the hell that person on the floor was, and what had just transpired.

Dick Scherner demanded, "We have to get in there and arrest that son-of-a-bitch. Let's go get him before he does something to Michelle."

"No way," countered Tom, "We don't have any idea what the fuck is going on here. He's not going to hurt her, he loves her. The only thing we're going to do is help get them out of here. If you're not in, you can leave."

✳   ✳   ✳   ✳   ✳

The bedroom was cloudy with dark smoke that had banked down from the ceiling to four feet above the floor. Michelle, atop the bed, was in the relatively clean air zone. Still, her eyes stung, and she coughed through her cloth muzzle. But as Mark spider crawled into the room to survive below the choking hot smoke layer, the expression in Michelle's reddened eyes transformed from fright to relief and gratitude.

Mark yanked the cloth restraint from her mouth, pulling it below her chin. He then planted a wet, sloppy kiss on her swollen, plump lips. The kiss took her already affected breath away. She couldn't talk at the moment, but her eyes lightened with her love.

From his pants pocket, Mark pulled out his knife. He always kept a razor's edge on the knife. Making quick work of the zip ties at the four corners of the queen size bed, he attempted to lift Michelle off the bed, but his right arm went limp from the gunshot wound. Blood started gushing through Mark's jacket, creating a wet scarlet stream flowing from his shoulder to his wrist.

Dick and Carlo ran to his aid helping both him and Michelle. Wojo and Mike had already quelled the advance of the fire with the extinguishers. When their partners struggled into the living room with their injured colleagues, Mike and Wojo jumped to assist with the wounded. As they did, Mark collapsed onto the floor, passed out from loss of blood, shock and the adrenaline drain. "We got you brother," Wojo comforted, adding, "Michelle, you're safe now."

As the smoke cleared, the combatants emerged from the harrowing ordeal battered but unbowed, their spirits united by triumph over the fire of adversity. Their bond would be forever strengthened by this shared experience.

Brantley didn't make it. Taking pleasure from the searing heat, he laughed as fire overwhelmed him, thinking he had triumphed in his life war. But he suffocated from the flames he ingested as he chuckled. Brantley's disfigurements transformed him into a new man. A dead man.

CHAPTER THIRTY-NINE

In the dimly lit hospital room, Mark drifted in and out of fitful sleep. The pain medications induced surreal dreams far more bizarre than he normally had. He and Brantley were discussing sports while eating wiener schnitzel, an Austrian meal of fried breaded veal cutlets. The mouth-watering aroma of this meal was their absolute favorite. When they were kids, their Mom always prepared this dinner for them with such perfection.

However, the tranquility of the scene quickly shattered. Their father unexpectedly walked into the room, taking a seat at the dining table with his adult sons. When their mother saw him, she fumed, "What the hell are you doing here? This is my house. These are my boys. You have no right to be here so get the fuck out."

"Now, now, calm down. I just want to share a meal with my sons."

Their mother physically attacked him, throwing punches and dishes at him. The ugliness caused the bile to rise within the throats of both young men. The peace and enjoyment of the meal were destroyed. Both men got up and began screaming at their parents.

This is when Michelle gently touched Mark's uninjured arm, rousing him from his troubled slumber. "Mark, wake up, honey. You're having a nightmare." His eyes fluttered open. He was happy the florescent lights in the pale green painted room were not illuminated. Only natural gray light filtered into the small room.

Mark struggled to clear the fog from the medication. Turning toward the chair to his left, he saw the face of a smiling angel at his bedside. Michelle's presence brought him comfort in the wake of his ordeal. He patted the narrow hospital bed next to his raised position for her to sit with him.

Then he motioned for Michelle to hand him the water container on the movable tray. After sipping some water to loosen his parched mouth, he managed to speak, "You're a sight for my sore eyes. How long have I been out? You look tired."

"Since they brought you in yesterday. I stayed here all night. You look rather funny yourself. Here, look in this mirror." Mark saw that his eyebrows were missing, the hair on his head was crinkled from the heat of the fire, and a greasy salve covered his red blotched facial skin. He chuckled at his disheveled appearance, a stark contrast to his usual well-groomed self.

"Oh, I look so handsome. Just like diaper rash on a baby's bum."

Michelle could only shake her head and roll her eyes. "Well, I can see that your injuries and the drugs didn't dampen your rhyming humor."

But amidst the levity, the reality of his injuries and recent events brought Mark back to a somber world. As his head began to clear, he asked, "And where is Brantley? Did I shoot him?"

Michelle offered guidance to piece the events together. "In a strange way, I guess I'm sorry to have to tell you, but he didn't make it, Mark. No, you missed, but he died because of the fire he set, rather ironic. A fairly fast but extremely painful way to go. Just like those women he killed."

Mark closed his eyes, contemplating the events of yesterday, saddened by the fatal results. *I wish it all could have turned out differently.*

"Oh, Michelle, I truly felt a connection with Brantley. We could have had a brotherly relationship. You know how I told you I enjoy finding the right pieces to complete a puzzle? Well, when I saw Brantley, I felt that I finally found that piece that's been missing from my puzzle. And now I feel an empty pit in my stomach. My twin eliminated himself, leaving a hole forever. I'm hurting emotionally, but what happened that's hurting my arm so much?"

"You, my dear, were shot in the upper biceps area of your right arm. The bullet hit the bone. Doctors had to operate to remove the bullet and some bone fragments, but they said you'll be fine in a few weeks. You lost a lot of blood."

With a puzzled look, "I got shot? Who shot me? When?" That's when he noticed blood stains on the side of her blue t-shirt and a puffy bruise on her otherwise perfect jaw line. "Michelle, are you okay? Did you get hurt?"

"I'm fine, except for some smoke inhalation plus sore wrists and ankles from trying to struggle my way out of the zip ties Brantley used on me. And my jaw is a little sore from him giving me a pop when I tried fighting him. This is your blood from when you tried to pick me up. You didn't even realize you had been shot. Your arm was useless, it just drooped. Dick Scherner and Dennis managed to get into my room to help us out. My apartment is gone for now. And I'll need a whole new wardrobe."

"Maybe when I get better, we can shop for your clothes together. We can start at Victoria's Secret."

"Sounds like you're getting better already," she laughed.

"Hey, why don't you stay at my place?"

"Well, I guess I could until I find a new apartment."

"No, no, I meant for good. I have plenty of room, and I would be delighted to have my sidekick stay with me while I recuperate."

"You mean that, Mark? For good? For real? It's not just the drugs talking?"

"Michelle, honey. I mean it from the bottom of my heart. We made it through a lot these past few weeks. I'm truly sorry for everything I put you through. Let's explore a brand-new chapter. We already have a solid foundation."

"I think I would love to discover what the two of us can make together as a couple. Where's my house key?" She leaned over to gently kiss his lips, letting her tongue slip into his mouth to tickle his tongue. Mark let out a moan. Michelle leaned in a little closer.

"Ow, my arm. Who shot me anyway?

"I did." Wojo strutted into the room with Carlo, his supervisor Jack Dunn, and the two rescuers from Boston Fire, Mike and Dick. "And I'd do it again."

"Oh, you would, would you? I knew you always had my back, but this might have gone a little too far." Mark laughed at his buddy. Each of the men took a turn, clasping Mark's left hand with a greeting and a word of encouragement.

Wojo added, "I would probably do it again to you or somebody else if I keep mishandling my gun. I think the bosses are going to send me back to the academy for remedial firearms training. I'm sorry, buddy, but I had my finger on the trigger ready to shoot when the fire exploded, and your gun fired. My finger twitched, and pow, here you are. My bad. Forgive me?"

Mark couldn't help but laugh at a memory. "Well, it's a rookie mistake. I did the same thing at New Agent Training. I fired my gun when there was a loud noise because I had my finger on the trigger. But I'll forgive you since you're not a very good shot anyway." The entire room erupted in laughter.

Dick Sherner broke the mood. "Mark, I want to apologize for the way I treated you and even more so for what I thought about you. I still think you are a cocky hotshot, but when Michelle told me the backstory on Brantley, I almost understand what you were facing. Who would have thought that you had an identical twin? And that DNA of twins can be a positive match? Hollywood couldn't have dreamed that one up!

I hope we can work closer together when you get back to work. Mike has been on my case since the beginning to work with you, but I was so pissed about you guys having that press conference without us, and just my petty inter-agency jealousy blinded me from working with a guy who clearly has a lot to offer." With that being said, he reached out his hand as a sign of respect and reconciliation. Mark shook Dick's hand the best he could from his left side.

Mike O'Brien walked over to Mark's bedside. He leaned close to Mark's ear. "Brother, if there is anything I can ever do for you, call me.

I'm looking forward to some good times with you. You take care of yourself. I'll see you soon." With a tap on Mark's uninjured shoulder, Mike departed with his partner leaving the room full of ATF Agents.

Jack stood over Mark with his hand on Mark's good shoulder. "I'm glad to see you're doing okay, Mark. The SAC and ASAC stopped by earlier, but you were still out of it. They wanted to share their condolences, congratulations and best wishes for a speedy recovery.

You are the most confusing, controversial and incorrigible agent I have ever come across, all rolled into one highly successful investigator. I'm happy to have you on my team any day."

"Thanks again, Jack, for always being there for me and for having my back. I'm really privileged to have such a great boss."

"We'll see how pleased you are when this mess gets hashed out at headquarters. I could only say so many good things to protect you, but this fiasco was something out of the wild, wild west. I'll talk to you soon. I have to get back to the office. If you need anything that your groupies can't take of, give me a call. Take care of yourself. It looks like it's going to be some time before you're able to work again."

"Jack, I'm prepared to handle any punishment that HQ doles out to me. I'm sure you did your best, as always. I'll talk to you soon."

After Jack left, Carlo chimed in. "Hey, buddy, I'm sorry about how this all went down. It's horrible that you had to face your brother this way. But I'm glad you pieced it all together. It could have only been you. You're the man."

The four of them talked about how the fires and the evidence all came together from each other's perspectives. All of them mused how bizarre the puzzle pieces of evidence clearly pointed toward Mark as the arsonist.

Carlo said, "As despicable as Brantley's actions were, it's hard to comprehend how he could have been more like you Mark. He seemed fairly smart. What went so wrong with him?"

"I've come to understand, Carlo, that we all handle our upbringing differently. I might have been stronger, more willful than Brantley.

He was not strong enough to pull up his bootstraps to overcome his prior life. Being brought up by a sadistic, domineering, physically and emotionally abusive woman crushed his spirit. Her actions caused him to become a socially isolated man-boy who loathed anything that reminded him of the fear and pain that was inflicted upon him."

"And Mark is right," Michelle added, "When Brantley was talking to me while he had me captive, the way she humiliated him about sex caused him sexual dysfunction forever. Not only did this mental trauma prevent him from any real relationship with a woman, he was a man who would have at least wanted to experience sex, but his inferiority complex made him unable to find sexual partners. He even blamed and hated women for their successes. This inadequacy further destroyed his persona."

"Also Carlo," Mark continued, "Brantley was really bright in a cunning way. He exulted in his superiority over the common person. Just like his aunt, he became a master manipulator. Most of that criminal profile that we listened to was darn accurate. He had no remorse for his victims. He was cold-hearted, only thinking of them as objects, not as living, breathing, feeling people. You know, one thing I find amazing is that he never thought about the way those women might have been raised, resulting in their undesirable behavior. But Brantley was a cool, self-possessed charmer who was an expert at hiding his homicidal mania that helped him commit cold-blooded premeditated murder of at least six women, including his surrogate mother."

"Mark, I want you to know," Wojo said, "the way this investigation unfolded was so strange. The more Carlo and I fought our feelings, the more the evidence started piling up against you. We had no choice but to follow the evidence. You wouldn't believe how long we kept this a secret between ourselves. It was beyond our belief and comprehension that you could be this monstrous murderer. We even thought about confronting you, but there were just too many variables. Finally, after the DNA match, we had to tell the SAC who just about blew his stack."

As they reflected on the case, Mark couldn't help but marvel at the twists of fate that brought them together at the most critical time. Through their collective efforts, justice prevailed, albeit at a heavy cost. He still had to face the music for his maverick actions. "Oh, that's another issue that Michelle and I have to deal with. You guys have any insight on what the bosses are thinking?"

"It's almost out of the SAC's hands," Tom explained. "Headquarters might end up making the call. But it could go either way. You didn't do anything wrong until the end when you went AWOL and pursued capturing Brantley on your own.

But you were the one to make and break this case. It's as big or bigger than anything this district has ever accomplished. That's another huge feather in your cap after the machine gun case you made and after you broke that large arson conspiracy. It's hard to fire a hero. At worst, I think you'll get suspended without pay."

"What do you think will happen to this sweet girl?" Mark tapped the thigh of Michelle as she sat next to him on the bed.

"Being a rookie, she can be fired for no reason at all. But that's not about to happen. In one sense she was under your tutelage and influence, so you are responsible for most of her actions. She might get a week off, but the way she had your back proves she has what it takes to be a great agent. After all, she was selected to be on the task force as a rookie."

Michelle blushed. "Thank you guys for your support and confidence in me. If I get to stay on the job, I swear I'll be the best agent ever."

"You can't be the best, kid, because that status is for me and hopefully, I have a few good years left. So stand in line. But I'll let you have my back because I think you know I'll always have yours. There will be plenty of arsons to work in our future; there will always be more to investigate together. "

"There's something I have neglected to say to you all. Thank you for everything, for being there for Mark and me. Plus," Michelle had to catch her breath with tears starting to well in her eyes, "I love you all for saving my life. Without your dedication and heroism, I wouldn't be here today. And I want to save my special love for this guy. Mark, you're the best part of my life.

There's one more thing, Mark. I have a surprise for you. Give me a moment." With that, Michelle walked out of the room into the hallway. She returned almost immediately, but Carlo stood in the way, blocking Mark's view of the opening door.

"Hi, son. How are you making it?"

"Dad? Oh, wow, how did you know?"

"Well, you're not the only one who knows how to locate someone," kidded Michelle.

"Hey, Carlo, Wojo, meet my long lost Dad. After thirty plus years, we finally connected. He actually helped me find Brantley by reaching out to distant relatives for information on my brother." Everybody shook hands. Then Bill Miller gave his son an affectionate hug, being careful not to contribute to Mark's pain.

Embracing his father with tears forming in his eyes, Mark felt a sense of closure on the one hand, but newfound hope for the future on the other hand. He hid his face in the pillow, shaking as tears now flowed freely. As the pieces of his fractured life fell into place, Mark realized that in all the chaos and uncertainty, he had found something priceless—the love and support of those who stood by him through it all.

Carlo said, "Why don't you three catch up. Wojo and I will check on you tomorrow if you're still here. Get some rest, take care of yourself."

"Michelle, thanks, honey for getting my father here. Let's all get to know each other. We have a lot of catching up to do. I finally feel that the pieces of a new puzzle are all falling into place. Dad, I think you'll love Michelle."

"Mark, I'm so proud of you son. I think it will be easy to love both of you."

At that moment, Mark knew that with Michelle at his side, together they could navigate whatever trials by fire lay ahead, one step at a time, one puzzle piece at a time.

CHAPTER FORTY

The following year, Mark was hanging out on the rear deck of a rented beach house enjoying a gin and tonic while staring at the breaking ocean waves a couple hundred yards away. A majestic stone bath house built during the 1930s depression through the Works Progress Administration still greeted throngs to Scarborough Beach in Narragansett, Rhode Island. It was a perfect summer day, in the 80s, low humidity, with the water glistening under the sunny crystal blue skies.

Mark had mostly recuperated from his injuries although demanding physical therapy sessions continued for his damaged right arm. Just by picking up my drink, I can feel a twinge where Wojo shot me. Friggin' friendly fire, no less. At least this time off would give my arm more time to heal. I'm going to need a doctor's okay to fully return to the job because if I can't shoot, I'll be relegated to the bench until I can. I hate that I'm assigned to desk duty until I'm totally ready.

He pondered his month-long suspension for his indiscretions during the serial arson case involving Brantley. Because of the extended sick leave due to his months' long recovery from the shooting injury, he could not be suspended until he was able to return to the job. This time off is just what I needed, he thought, providing me with much needed quiet time to reflect on the past year and assess my future. Damn, what an amazing year! I realize how lucky I am to only get the suspension, but I also knew that it would have been hard to fire me after the major cases I've made thus far in my career.

Sitting there in the sun, Mark sorted through that day one more time, when the final act played out. I keep replaying that scene over and over in my head, Michelle tied to the bed with Brantley threatening to torch her. Could I, should I have done it differently? If it wasn't for my ego, I probably should have done it more by the book by telling everyone, including Michelle, about my suspicions concerning Brantley. Maybe we could have caught him earlier and prevented a death. But, it was so fucking hard to believe my brother was the arsonist, especially based on so little information.

Other than this forced time off without pay, I love this job. I always find it challenging. Each and every investigation provides a new puzzle dumped fresh out of the box leaving it to us to place all the pieces in the right places. There are always new people to meet, new places to visit, and more delicious food to discover. I truly am a foodie, maybe I should have been a chef, or maybe I'll write a book on the best places to eat for investigators.

Just the freedom to be out and about while working cases is so pleasing. Of course, there is always the bureaucratic crap to contend with, as well as the mountains of paperwork to complete, but these two drawbacks are minor compared to the rewards I get from doing the job.

My relationships, both professional and personal, are exceptional at the moment. The issues with the Boston Fire guys are now nonexistent. It's funny how after this last case, I have attained a rather unusual celebrity status within the police and fire communities. Everyone wants to hear about my story and so many organizations are asking for me to speak at training seminars all over the country.

My friends and I are tighter than ever before. Carlo and Wojo, thank God for those two, they continued to have my back throughout my months long recuperation. They are the best friends a person could ever have.

And my connection with my father is outstanding. Our bond has continued to grow over the past several months. I enjoy our phone conversations all the time and our monthly visits just bring us closer each and every time. This is how a father and son relationship should be, sharing our everyday life experiences. We have learned so much about each other.

But the most fantastic part of my life is Michelle. She has made my life worth living for sure. Every time I think of her, I feel my heart beat faster. To think, I came so close to losing her. I don't even want to imagine what that would have done to me.

Since the dismantling of the Brantley saga, our relationship has done more than blossom. I can hardly believe we're now a live-in couple, totally in love with loose plans to form a more perfect union. We no longer have any secrets between us. Everything has been going great. We get to share daily work experiences, and we love enjoying all that New England has to offer during our spare time.

Michelle managed to escape any major punishment for her part in the most unusual of cases. There was a lot of discussion between the SAC and ATF Headquarters about her, but they decided that she was under the control and tutelage of a senior agent. The bosses also agreed Michelle helped resolve this monstrous case and demonstrated she is the type of agent who stood tall in the face of adversity and who would always have the backs of her fellow agents. Mark was so proud of her. With hard work and some luck, he knew she would be a star one day.

Yes, my life is really going good, Mark thought. I'm so excited to see how my future unfolds. But for now, I'm just going to savor this drink, this gorgeous day and this beautiful view until Michelle comes here after work. This is exactly what I needed, pure relaxation.

From his perch on a hill, Mark continued to gaze over the low-slung building in front of him. Two small trees with dark fern-like leaves bracketed his view of the beach, the parking lot and the main drag that led to the ocean front properties. On this midweek afternoon, he saw traffic was light. Most people were already in place on the beaches. There were only a few cars per minute traveling along the roadway, with an occasional Rhode Island Public Transportation Authority (RIPTA) bus driving by. As his mind no longer reflected on the past or looked toward the future, he sat only in the present.

Mark wasn't focused on anything in particular until he heard, then saw a dark sedan squealing away from the beach parking lot, racing northbound. *Why do people drive like such idiots around a crowded beach?* Within seconds after the car grabbed his attention, the serenity of the day for many people changed dramatically, actually catastrophically.

Ka-boom! Mark froze. A detonation of a RIPTA bus sent a shock wave in all directions. The deafening thunderclap of the blast shook the ground supporting the deck where Mark sat. He stared as a colossal fireball consumed the bus, shooting a hundred feet into the sky with orange and red flames. A mushroom cloud of black smoke obscured his view of the beach.

Mark felt the diminished force of the shock wave against his body from his position but watched in horror as dozens of beachgoers writhed on the hot tar parking lot surface having been knocked flat by the explosion. He saw hundreds of car and building windows shattered and heard innumerable car horns sounding as the shock caused vehicle security systems to alert. Screams filled the entire area, stretching from the beach to the rental houses. He jumped to his feet disbelieving the incredible scene that erupted before him. Immediately, his first thought – this had to be a bomb blast. There normally would be nothing on that bus or on the street to erupt in a detonation like that.

So much for my suspension. These circumstances overrule everything else. Duty calls. Time to get back to work. He ran through the house, grabbing his bag with his uniform, helmet, boots, camera and notebooks, plus some towels that may be needed for first aid.

A million thoughts raced through his head. *There's no time to call the office. I'm sure the beach lifeguards have already called the local police and fire departments. The State Fire Marshals, our people* from the Providence office and the FBI will all be swarming the scene, too. There're so many things to think of and take care of all at the same time, but I'll start working along with the lifeguards and the local responders to triage the victims. And we need to secure at least several hundred yards in all directions at the same time to safeguard the evidence. This is going to be a monumental undertaking! But we will do it and do it right. And we'll figure out what happened to seek justice for all of the injured and the dead.

ACKNOWLEDGMENTS

I am forever indebted to my mentor and editor, C. Susan Nunn, who tirelessly puts up with tons of push-back from me over word choices and her suggested edits. But with her skillful guidance, she helped me to bring more depth and life to my characters and story.

To Angie Alaya@pro_ebookcovers, what a fabulous cover! It's what I dreamed about, thank you.

My sincerest thanks to Forensic Anthropologists, Dr. Elayne Pope, Fatal Fire Forensics, LLC of Tennessee and Michigan's Hanna Friedlander for pointers and explanations of how bodies burn and the aftermath of a fire death.

For members of the Boston Police and Fire Departments who worked and shared with me over the years, I am grateful.

Thanks to ATF for expending tremendous amounts of time and energy training us Certified Fire Investigators in all aspects of fire investigation, which I put to good use in this story.

Amit Dey, many thanks for his usual great job formatting. Look him up: about.me/amitdey Email:dey_amit35@yahoo.com

For the many people who furnished helpful suggestions and comments including my online classmates Scott Fishman, Heather McBogg, and Pam Verner.

Research from reading of books like *OBSESSION*: The FBI's Legendary Profiler Probes the Psyches of Killers, Rapists, and Stalkers and Their Victims and Tells How to Fight Back by retired FBI profiler John Douglas and Mark Olshaker, *CONFESSIONS OF A SERIAL KILLER*-The Untold Story of Dennis Rader, the *BTK Killer* by Katherine Ramsland, PhD and *AMERICAN PREDATOR*-The Hunt for the Most Meticulous Serial Killer of the 21st Century by Maureen Callahan provided invaluable insights into the mind of serial killers.

For those who reviewed my book, any success my book attains comes from your unselfish contributions. My friend, Bob Luckett (author of <u>SOLVING FOR X: Tracking the DC Serial Arsonist</u>) wrote the first blurb for this book. It was amazing, thank you, sir.

To my wife, Joyce, my love and heartfelt thanks for being my sounding board for so many words and sayings when I couldn't come up with the right jargon and for living with the hundreds of hours I dedicated to this book while mostly ignoring her.

To the readers who have enjoyed my true crime books and have encouraged this jump to a crime thriller, thanks for your loyalty.

ABOUT THE AUTHOR

Puzzles. Our lives are puzzles wherein we either seek the pieces to complete our journey. I have embraced the search for my pieces in both my personal and professional lives. This was especially true during my 25 years as a Special Agent criminal investigator with the Bureau of Alcohol, Tobacco and Firearms working undercover investigations or, as a Certified Fire Investigator solving complex, high profile arson and explosion cases. Finding the right witness, clue or evidence challenged me daily. The search for truth continued while employed for 17 years in private industry as a Fire/Explosion Analyst. And today, as an author of both true crime books and a novel, the complexity of writing is another enigma that tests my skills to put the right words in the correct places in order to complete a compelling story. In August 2019, I published my first book, **Burn Boston Burn** followed in 2021 by **Bang Boom Burn**, both award winners.

I reside in Massachusetts with my beautiful wife. Together, we enjoy our three children and six grandchildren. See burnbostonburn.com for more information or scan the QR Code.

If you enjoyed this book, please leave a review on Amazon and/or Goodreads. Reviews are essential for an indie author. I would appreciate it immensely.